RITUAL CRIME UNIT

Also in this Series

Spirit Animals

RITUAL
CRIME
UNIT

E. E. RICHARDSON

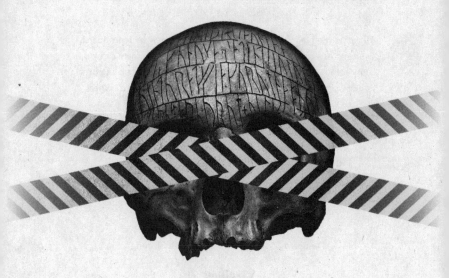

SOLARIS

This edition published 2022 by Solaris
an imprint of Rebellion Publishing Ltd,
Riverside House, Osney Mead,
Oxford, OX2 0ES, UK

Part One first published 2013 by Abaddon Books as
Under the Skin and copyright © Rebellion 2013

Parts Two and Three first published 2015 by Abaddon Books as
Disturbed Earth and copyright © Rebellion 2015

www.solarisbooks.com

ISBN: 978 1 78618 748 2

This is a work of fiction. All the characters and events portrayed
in this book are fictional, and any resemblance to real people or
incidents is purely coincidental.

10 9 8 7 6 5 4 3 2 1

A CIP catalogue record for this book is available from
the British Library.

Designed & typeset by Rebellion Publishing

Printed in Denmark

In memory of Lesley Richardson,
my mother and my biggest fan.

PART ONE

CHAPTER ONE

THE POLICE VAN jolted over the potholes of the rough farm roads at speed. DCI Claire Pierce gripped her paper cup tighter before the coffee could spill over and slop down the front of her tac vest.

Might have been the best place for it. "Christ, what the hell am I drinking? Did you run it through a goat before you gave it to me?" She chugged down the rest of the coffee without waiting for an answer. Any method of caffeine delivery was better than none.

Sergeant Mistry gave her a brief grin from the other side of the van. "Not my fault, Guv," he said. "North Yorkshire Police supplied the coffee."

"Yeah? Well, next time we call for a raid remind me to pencil it in on the budget." Pierce grimaced as she reached the bottom of the cup. It was all right for Deepan. He was barely closing in on thirty, still looking only half that with his chubby cheeks and artfully gelled hair. At fifty-four, she was considerably less bright and breezy. She wasn't keen to be out as late as this, but they didn't have much choice. The full moon was their best opportunity to catch the skinbinder they were after in the act.

There had to be one operating illegally in the area. They'd been chasing reports of unlicensed shapeshifters across Yorkshire for six months. This many enchanted pelts couldn't all be heirloom pieces dragged down from the attic, and the maker's rune on the one bearskin they'd seized didn't belong to any of the country's six authorised skin shops. Weeks of painstaking police work had finally led the Ritual Crime Unit to a farmhouse that the neighbours claimed had seen exotic animals delivered.

Pierce gripped the side wall of the van as the young driver swung them off the main road and through the farm gate. She didn't know his name. This team was only half hers, the numbers made up by North Yorkshire Police. Necessary with the RCU's limited manpower, but still not a happy thought. If there were shapeshifters on site, a group of untrained uniforms in hi-visibility vests were about as much use to contain them as a strip of POLICE DO NOT CROSS tape.

She could see the dark shape of the farmhouse coming up on their left, the stones lit by the headlights of the Armed Response Vehicle ahead. Beyond was a brick-built barn with a white van parked outside. The owners of the property were supposed to be in Spain.

Pierce reached for the radio on her vest.

"Leo. Your people ready?"

"*Just give us the word.*" The familiar gruff voice was cool and steady. Leo Grey she'd worked with before, the local Firearms Support Unit's specialist in supernatural threats. At least he'd be packing silver bullets in his Glock, but the ammo was rare and expensive, and the rest of his team were only supplied with Tasers. Theory said they should work just fine on shifters.

Pierce wasn't a great fan of trusting to theory.

"I want you with me in the barn," she said. "If the skinbinder's at work, that's where he'll be." Skinning was a messy business. The animals had to be freshly slaughtered for the skinbinding ritual to be performed.

"*I hear you. Henderson, you're with us,*" he told one of his team. "*Baker will lead the rest of the team on the house clearance.*"

Dividing their forces made her edgy, but with a site this big they couldn't afford to risk their suspects escaping in the dark. "Constable Keane and I will be coming in behind you." Pierce exchanged a glance of acknowledgement with Sally Keane, the RCU's resident expert in shapeshifting pelts. A plump, easy-going woman with blonde hair and red-framed glasses, she looked out of place stuffed into a tac vest, but Pierce knew she could handle herself in a crisis. It wasn't her own people that concerned her.

As she climbed out of the van, Pierce checked her belt for her silver cuffs and incapacitant spray. Limited use against a shifter that wasn't already subdued, but that was why they had Firearms along.

"All right, you know your orders," she said as the team assembled on the grass. "No heroics. You see a shifter coming at you, you get out of the way and call for Firearms Support." She looked over at Leo, and he gave her a terse nod. "Okay, everybody get into position. We're going in."

Leo took the lead as they advanced on the old barn at a jog. He must have been past forty, but he kept himself in shape, a lean, craggy-faced man with the kind of sandy blond hair that didn't show the grey. As she followed him across the grass, Pierce tried to tug her own ill-fitting tac vest into a more comfortable position, vowing yet again to give up living on microwave meals. Slim chance of that.

Her stomach tensed as Leo and Henderson adopted positions to either side of the barn's wooden door. Leo had his Glock held out before him in a two-handed grip, the barrel pointed down at the grass between them. Henderson had his hand on his Taser. They exchanged sober nods.

Henderson threw the door open and Leo charged in ahead of him. "Police! Get down on the ground!" he shouted. "Everybody stop what you're doing and get down on the ground!" Pierce followed right on their heels, Sally and a swarm of North Yorkshire's finest close behind her.

The barn was unconverted, a high-roofed open space with wooden beams and a dirt floor. Crates and vaguer shapes covered by tarpaulins were shoved against the walls to clear the centre. A square window in the rear wall allowed the full moon's light to spill inside.

The pool of moonlight and the glow of their police torches lit up a gruesome scene. The bloody corpse of a grey wolf was strung up, dangling from a beam, the half-skinned pelt peeled down over the muscle like a fur glove pulled inside out. The dead-eyed face reminded Pierce of her neighbour's pet husky.

No time to get sentimental. They'd caught the skinbinder in the act.

Focused on his craft, the young man didn't even turn, swaying and crooning to himself as he moved around the hanging carcass. In the shadows he looked hunched, misshapen, until she realised that bound to his back were a great set of eagle's wings, incongruous against a dark T-shirt and frayed jeans. His bare arms were covered with tattooed runes, and in one hand he held a curved silver knife with a hooked end.

"Drop the knife!" Leo demanded, moving closer but not yet ready to raise the pistol. Henderson followed a few paces behind, pivoting to look into the shadows as he passed. Sally moved after him and bent to lift one of the tarpaulins, pulling her torch from the clip on her vest and peering underneath.

Pierce kept her eyes on the skinbinder, not willing to trust he was as absorbed as he seemed. He was still humming, maintaining his focus as he made ritual incisions in the carcass. She was damn glad Leo and his people were professionals, not trigger-happy hotheads looking for a chance to fire. This could still end without tears, if they were careful.

"Holy *shit*." The curse from Sally drew her eyes away from the standoff. Pierce saw the young constable drop the raised tarp and jerk back. "Guv, we've got skins here," she said, swallowing as she looked up. "But I think they're—"

In the moment of distraction, the skinbinder made his move.

A flash of silver motion at the corner of her eye. Pierce spun just in time to see Henderson reel backwards, clutching his arm where the skinning knife had gashed it.

"Drop the knife!" Leo shouted again, raising his gun, but before he could fire a dark shape dropped from the roof beams, slamming into him and sending him staggering into the hanging carcass. As the thing bounded forward, launching from his shoulders, Pierce glimpsed gold feline eyes and a flash of yellow fangs.

A black panther.

Not a real one. "Shapeshifter!" she bellowed.

"Fuck!" Henderson scrambled backward, fumbling for the Taser at his side, but it was a clumsy move, reaching across himself with his uninjured arm. Before he could draw the weapon, the shapeshifter was on him, its jaws crunching down on his shoulder. It shook him like a toy and tossed him aside to slam against the wall. Pierce heard the crack of breaking bone.

"Officer down!" she shouted into her radio. "We need backup in the barn! Shapeshifter in the building!" Leo shoved the swinging wolf carcass aside to get a clear shot, but with everyone's torches moving at once the barn was a blur of shifting shadows.

"I've got Henderson, Guv!" Sally said, darting across the barn toward the injured man. But the shifter spun about as fast as any real cat, claws flashing out to rake across her throat. Her cry of shock strangled into a gurgle as she staggered back, a spray of blood spattering the dirt floor.

"Shit!" Pierce saw the shifter's head swinging towards her, and she grabbed for her spray. Wouldn't stop the damn thing, but it might drive it out, save the casualties from any further harm...

The deafening blast of a close-quarters gunshot echoed in her ears. It plunged her into instant ringing, muffled deafness, like the world heard from the bottom of a pool. Even that didn't soften the retort of the next shot.

The big cat jerked back as the bullet ripped into its shoulder—and, like an optical illusion, it was no longer a panther, but a man crouched on all fours with the pelt draped across his back. Taking no chances, Pierce lunged forward and slapped her silver cuffs on his tattooed arms, yanking his wrists together with no time to be careful of his shoulder. The man snapped his teeth towards her, still half lost in the mind of the beast.

But neutralised for now. If the silver bullet hadn't ruined the magic of the pelt, the cuffs would definitely stop him using it. Pierce straightened up—and spotted the skinbinder she'd half forgotten running towards the back of the barn. "Freeze!" she yelled, her own voice dulled in her ears to the point where she could hardly tell how loud she was shouting. "There's no way out!"

The skinbinder ignored her and took a running leap towards the window. It was an impossible jump... but as he left the ground, his body collapsed in on itself, bones folding away at impossible angles like a closing umbrella. The heavy wings on his back moulded into his outflung arms; his bent legs sunk inwards and curved into talons; his moonlit face elongated, stretching out into a hooked beak.

The great shape of the eagle soared away out of the window, disappearing into the dark night. Leo swore and ran forward to aim after it, but too late to take the shot.

"Eagle shifter coming out of the back of the barn!" Pierce shouted it into her radio, but she knew that no one outside would have a chance to stop him.

She turned to move towards the injured officers. It was clear that neither one would be getting up without help. Didn't look much like they would get up at all.

Jesus Christ. What a clusterfuck.

CHAPTER TWO

It took longer than Pierce liked to get the injured off the scene and the prisoner on his way to the station. She sent Deepan back to accompany him; she didn't trust jittery uniforms with a shapeshifter. The bullet should have rendered the pelt's enchantment inert, but that was still no reason to take chances. The panther's wound hadn't transferred to the man; small injuries were repaired in the flux of shifting bodies. It took major organ damage to kill a shapeshifter in animal form.

Police officers weren't so lucky.

Pierce would have liked to send one of their own off in the ambulance with Sally, but they were stretched far too thin as it was with a crime scene this size. In a perfect world, she'd have had two prisoners in custody right now, and Sally here to check the barn over for magical traps. Instead they had a loose skinbinder to watch out for, and she was stuck here waiting for Tim Cable to show up.

Tim wouldn't have been her first choice to bring on a bust like this. Three months in the Unit and still earnest as a puppy, he was textbook perfect on all the procedures—which might do him some good if they ever actually drew a textbook case. The books weren't even written to cover RCU work; when Pierce had first joined up, the only reference to consult was George, the cranky old sergeant who'd been around longer than God's mother-in-law. What she hadn't learned from him, she'd picked up through trial-and-error, and things that hadn't killed her yet.

Tonight was a grim reminder there could always be a first time.

She chewed the lip of another cardboard cup of coffee as the forensics van pulled up. The crime scene photographer who got out was half familiar, a weary-looking blonde woman with her tripod in hand. "Why is it you lot from Ritual always call us out to scenes in the middle of the night and the middle of nowhere?" she asked.

"Ritual magic. Brings out your average criminal's flair for amateur dramatics." Pierce turned her torch toward the open barn door. "Through there."

The photographer assessed the scene with a practised eye. "Just the barn?"

Slim chance they'd get much of value from the rest of the scene, with the number of feet that had been trampling over it. "Just the barn," she echoed with a curt nod. "Bloodstains on the left and most of the footprints are from the attack on our people. We need pictures of the rear window and the rafters—one of our suspects went out the back, and the other one came from above. Make sure you get that knife there on the ground."

The skinbinder had dropped the ritual blade in his escape—the silver would have stopped him from transforming. With any luck, they'd be able to lift some prints from it. In the shadowy dark of the barn she hadn't seen if he wore gloves, but she doubted he'd have risked it. Complex magic took precision, and the smallest bit of clumsiness could compromise a ritual.

"The dead wolf is relevant too, I'm guessing?" the photographer said. She wrinkled her mouth at the gruesome sight. "Poor puppy." She snapped off a few establishing shots.

"Guv?"

Pierce turned to see Tim hurrying towards her from the collection of cars. A lanky boy with short spiked hair and glasses, he wasn't quite as young and gormless as he looked, but sometimes it was easy to forget that.

"Sally was injured?" he asked, his eyes wide.

"They've taken her to hospital. You can call them for news later, but right now I need you to assess the scene. We need to know there are no magical surprises around the place before forensics start disturbing things." Self-destructing evidence was her least favourite kind.

Tim nodded solemnly. "Right, Guv." But he hovered for a moment, clearly at a loss for where to start. "Um... I should... check outside the thresholds for trigger runes?" He looked to her for approval, still caught up in the habit of treating every case like an assessment.

She'd have to shake that out of him before she sent him off on his own to butt heads with local forces who thought rank outweighed specialist expertise. She flicked a hand to send him off to do as he thought best.

A cultured voice interrupted from behind them. "That won't be necessary, thank you, Constable."

Apparently being a DCI didn't spare her from butting heads either. Pierce turned to face the new arrival.

He was a tall man in his late thirties, with thick dark hair and the kind of blandly handsome looks that were a nightmare of anyone trying to take down a useful description. He wore a black cashmere coat, the shirt collar and dark tie beneath as crisp as if he'd come straight from the ironing board.

Never trust a police detective who didn't look like he lived in his clothes. Assuming this man *was* with the police; if he wasn't and he'd still got through the cordon, heads would be rolling very soon. Pierce fixed him with a hard stare. "Sorry, you would be?"

He strode forward to meet her, unsmiling. "Jason Maitland, Counter Terror Action Team." That was a new one on her, but then they changed the names on these things more often than she changed her sheets, and the ID that he flashed at her looked real enough. "I'm afraid my people are going to need to take over this site."

And if that didn't smell rancid, she didn't know what did. She narrowed her eyes. "There's no reason for Counter Terrorism to take an interest in this case." A rogue skinbinder was a threat on several levels, but none of them involved national security.

"We have our reasons. I'm afraid I can't discuss them." Stock phrases, no apology behind them.

Dark suited figures were already moving across the site, herding the uniformed officers away. They even had their own forensics people, pouring out of an unmarked black van in coveralls. Terrorism was a buzzword with plenty of political clout—but Pierce had her own field of authority.

"This is an RCU case," she said, standing firm. "We can't allow anyone to start handling the evidence until it's been cleared as safe by our experts."

By her side she sensed Tim shifting, uncomfortable at being caught in a power struggle, but she wasn't about to concede ground by breaking eye contact with Maitland.

If he was ruffled by the challenge, he didn't show it. "We have our own specialists in ritual magic," he said.

"Specialists? From where?" She raised a sceptical eyebrow. True experts were thin on the ground, and ones with police training even more so. She could count the members of the RCU's northern branch without resorting to toes, and its southern counterpart wasn't much bigger. Either Maitland was overestimating the knowledge of his specialists, or someone was playing silly buggers with the allocation of police resources. The RCU was struggling to put together a useful crime database as it was without some shadowy subdepartment out there duplicating their efforts.

"All fully PRMC certified," Maitland said. The same qualification the Unit required—and stuck with a wet-behind-the-ears rookie as she was right now, Pierce couldn't even claim to have greater field experience on her side. She stepped back out of his way with a scowl.

"Two good officers were injured making this bust," she reminded him. "This suspect has been top of the RCU's most wanted list for months."

"I assure you, we're not going to let him go free." Maitland's flash of teeth was more predatory than reassuring. "He's been top of *our* most wanted list for even longer."

"But you can't tell me why."

His smile broadened into an even less likeable expression. "I'm sure you understand the realities of these things." He straightened up, already dismissing her from his attention. "Now, if you could please have your people clear the scene as fast as possible. The longer we delay here, the greater our suspect's lead on us becomes."

Our suspect. Her lips curved in bitter acknowledgement. They weren't going to win any concessions here. "Of course," she said, and held his gaze for a few seconds longer before turning to stalk away across the long grass. "Come on, Tim. Let's go."

The young constable chased after her like a bewildered puppy. "Are we just leaving, then?" he said, looking back over his shoulder.

"I'm going back to the station," she said. "He might have taken over our crime scene, but we've still got a prisoner to interview."

SHE GOT TIM to drive her back to the station. The journey passed mostly in silence, barring the lingering tinnitus from the gunshots. The headache only shortened her temper as she stewed in her own irritation.

There'd been no hint of a terrorist connection to the case before this. They still hadn't uncovered the skinbinder's identity—so what the hell did Maitland and his team know that they didn't? If Counter Terrorism had been watching the farm for reasons of their own, they should have been coordinating with the local police so both sides knew before the raid went down. The way things had shaken out, it felt uncomfortably like her team had been used to do someone else's dirty work, then kicked out.

"Do you need me here, Guv?" Tim asked as he stopped the car outside the station.

Pierce flapped a hand at him. "No. Go home." Somebody was going to need to be fresh tomorrow morning, and it clearly wasn't going to be her. She snagged another no doubt ill-advised cup of coffee before heading down to the cells.

Arthur Jakes, the Custody Sergeant, was there to let her in through the barred gate. A stout, broad-faced man with salt-and-pepper hair leaning towards the salt side, he'd been part of the scenery here for as long as she'd been at the station.

"Did Deepan bring our shifter in?" she asked him as the gate clanged shut behind her.

Jakes nodded. "Yep. We had a fun time with that one. Took a bite out of Constable Carter while they were stripping him out of his skin."

"Did you get a name?" She wasn't optimistic.

"Ha, yes. One Mr 'Grrr.'"

She gave that a wry smile that she doubted it deserved. "Did you put him in the special cell?"

With the RCU's limited budget, they only had one cell built to handle supernatural strength. A shifter removed from his pelt should be no more danger than a normal human, but Pierce wasn't prepared to bet the farm on it. Those who wore their animal forms too long or too often didn't always turn all the way back. Ritual magic was never as safe and controlled as its practitioners might like to believe.

"We did, but he's in interview right now," he said. Pierce turned to stare at him.

"Deepan took him in for questioning without me?" She would have thought he'd have realised she'd want to be in on this one.

Jakes shook his head. "No, these weren't your lot. Counter Terror Action Men, or some such bollocks. Had the proper authorisation so I let them in." He peered over his glasses at her scowl. "Problem?"

Pierce grimaced, but shook her head. "Mine, not yours," she said. If Maitland's people had authorisation from Superintendent Palmer, there was nothing she or Jakes could do about it. "They were throwing their weight around at the crime scene, too. Waited for us to make the bust, then kicked us all out as soon as the fur had stopped flying."

"I did hear it flew." Jakes pursed his lips in sympathy. "How's Sally?"

"Still no word," she said, and gave a tired sigh. If she'd known they were going to be turfed off the crime scene without the chance to collect evidence, she would have sent someone along in the ambulance.

She stared at the wall of the interview room, wishing she had a good excuse to storm in and take over. Tempting though it might be, squabbling in front of the suspect could only harm their chances of getting anything out of him.

She turned to Sergeant Jakes. "Do we have audio on the interview room CCTV?"

He snorted. "And waste his lordship's precious pennies when the interviews are all taped anyway? You jest, my lady. It's video only." He turned one of the charge desk monitors around so she could see it.

Not that it showed anything she couldn't have pictured for herself. The interviewers were both nondescript men in grey suits; the shifter that sat across from them lounged casually in his chair, still something subtly feline about his posture. Not a huge man, but solidly muscular, with a broad jaw and shaved head. The camera angle showed part of an intricate tattoo on his neck, no doubt a match for the corresponding maker's rune inside the panther pelt. She doubted that she'd get a chance to check, with Maitland intent on seizing all her evidence. She scowled.

It was impossible to tell what the interviewers were asking, but the responses came through loud and clear on camera. Studied indifference, the occasional curve of a cynical smirk; no protestations of innocence here, just the relaxed arrogance of a man who either expected to walk free or didn't care that he wouldn't.

She needed to be in there, asking her own questions and watching for the tell-tale twitches that an audio recording wouldn't show. Assuming she would even be allowed to listen to it; the national security umbrella could be used to cover all sorts of things.

"I don't suppose you can lip-read?" she asked the desk sergeant.

"And find out what the prisoners are saying about me?" He raised a hand to his heart. "I prefer to imagine they all think I'm lovely."

"Everyone thinks you're lovely, Arthur," she said absently. A flicker of something on the monitor caught her eye. Just a brief flash of darkness in between the shifter's lips seen as he sneered, maybe no more than a shadow on the footage.

Maybe not. She held up a hand to stop Jakes as he began to speak.

"Did those idiots let Deepan check the suspect over before they took charge?" she asked, her eyes still focused on the screen.

A faint motion in her peripheral vision as the sergeant shook his head. "Insisted on doing it all by themselves. Something up?" He rounded the desk to watch the monitor with her.

"I'm not sure." *Come on, you bastard...* Pierce tried to will the shifter into opening his mouth.

And there it was. A split second glimpse inside his mouth as he made another soundless jeer, and this time she saw it for sure: the shapeshifter's tongue was turning black.

"Shit!" She turned and sprinted for the interview room.

Jakes ran with her without questioning why, the keys jangling at his belt. As she threw the door open the two interviewers jumped up from their seats, and the nearest tried to crowd them back outside. "Chief Inspector! You shouldn't be in here. This interview concerns potentially sensitive information—"

"You idiots," she shouted. "He's got a suicide rune in his mouth! We need to get him to—"

But it was far too late. Sprawling back in his chair, glassy-eyed, the shifter still managed to offer her a mocking grin. His gums were black, the teeth loose in their sockets, and decay wafted out on his panting breaths like halitosis.

"Get medical!" she shouted at Jakes, though there was nothing they could do. The man was rotting from the inside out.

Dark spots began to blossom on his skin, spreading quickly into open sores. His eyeballs blackened and burst like crushed grapes, thick tarry goo oozing down sunken cheeks. By now what skin remained was bruise-black, thin as paper, like fragile fabric stretched over a frame. One of Maitland's men grabbed his arm, trying to pull him up, but the rotting flesh just tore with a wet squelch.

Within seconds, the decaying form was barely even human anymore; just a hollowed, shrivelled, blackened *thing* collapsing in on itself.

Outside in the hallway the alarms wailed, summoning help that was already too late. The shapeshifter was dead—and any secrets that he might have revealed had died with him.

CHAPTER THREE

BY THE TIME the medical team arrived, there was little to be done with the prisoner except scrape his oozing remains off the furniture. The stench of decay and death lingered on her clothes and in her throat even after several sprays of deodorant and yet another mug of coffee. She'd given up on getting to bed tonight.

If Pierce was resigned to being stuck at work until the early hours, Superintendent Palmer was bloody furious about it.

"This has been a complete cock-up from start to finish!" he said, hands clasped behind his back as he paced his office. He was a finicky little man, shorter than her and probably a few years younger, though you wouldn't know it from the receding hairline. Under normal circumstances he would have been happy to sleep through their after-dark raid and hear about the results in the morning, but Maitland's interference and the news of a death in police custody had dragged him out of bed and back to work.

And Pierce was the one who got called onto the carpet to account for it. If Maitland's two men were getting a bollocking for their part in this fiasco, it was taking place in private, with no opportunity for her to stick her oar in.

Which was a pity, because she had plenty to say. "Sir, the team from Counter Terrorism came waltzing in throwing their weight about and overrode all our procedures," she said. "My people would have checked the prisoner for ritual markings if they'd only been allowed to do their jobs. We're lucky it was just a suicide rune and not something worse. He *could* have taken half the station down."

"Lucky," he echoed, with a bitter twist to the word. He whirled about to face her. "Yes, Claire, I feel exceptionally *lucky* that the resource-intensive, high-profile raid *you* persuaded me to authorise has resulted in two injured officers, one suspect escaped, and another one dead in our custody!"

Now was not the time to argue. "Sir." She acknowledged the words with a carefully neutral expression, staring past him at the crime statistics posted up on the wall. The RCU lagging behind, as usual.

Palmer spent several more moments pacing himself out before he stopped and heaved a defeated sigh. He fixed her with a cool gaze. "A suicide rune," he said.

"Yes, sir." She nodded. "It would have been tattooed on the inside of his mouth. He only needed to hold his tongue against it for a set length of time to trigger the rune." She'd seen it before, though it had been over a decade ago; some ridiculous apocalypse cult or other with a vow to take their secrets to the grave.

He ran a hand back through his thinning hair. "Then it couldn't have been prevented?"

"It might have, if they'd allowed a team with the proper expertise to take charge," she said. "Sir, I don't know who these people are, or what their interest is in this skinbinder, but there's no way they're half as qualified as the RCU to handle supernatural crime. This should be *our* case."

Palmer pressed his lips together and gave another sigh, pulling the chair out from under his desk to sit down. "That's as may be, but it's not your decision to make—or mine," he said, shaking his head as he leaned back. "This is coming from above my head, Claire. The Counter Terror Action Team have full autonomy to do as they see fit, and we are to give them our cooperation."

"No questions asked, of course." Pierce scowled.

He gave her a stern look. "You understand perfectly well how important information security can be. Loose lips sink ships, and all that."

"On the other hand, maybe if we'd loosened some, we might have found the suicide runes hidden behind them."

He threw up his hands. "I can see that you're not going to drop this, but there's only so far even *you* can get running on stubbornness." He checked the time on his fancy silver watch and gave a grimace. "Go home, get some sleep, and consider this case off your desk and best forgotten. It's the Counter Terror Action Team's problem now."

* * *

PIERCE HAD LEARNED to sleep like the dead no matter how grim a day she'd come home from, but that alone didn't make three hours substitute for a night's rest. She dragged herself reluctantly out of bed, skipping the minimal time she had to make breakfast in favour of a phone call to Sally's husband.

He sounded more exhausted than she was, but he told her that Sally was stable after the doctors had given her a tracheostomy. She tried to call Leo, but he didn't pick up; she left a message on his phone asking after Sergeant Henderson.

The grim reminder of the raid's ugly results undid any work the rest might have done towards cooling her temper. The queue at the bakery where she grabbed breakfast made her late, and she arrived at the RCU with a cooling cup of coffee, a bacon sandwich, and a headache.

The detective branch of the Ritual Crime Unit worked out of an open plan office on the second floor. As she pushed through the double doors, heads popped up from behind the computers like startled prairie dogs. No Sally today, of course, but Tim had made it in on time, though he looked dreadful. So much for the resilience of youth. He followed Deepan's cheerful, "Morning, Guv!" with a vague mumble of his own, sinking back down low behind his monitor.

With the caseload they had, there ought to be more than the four of them, but the budget was tight and not many people stuck it out in the RCU for long. It was an equally bad career choice for both the ambitious and the lazy, dangerous work that rarely came to the sort of tidy conclusion that looked good on a CV.

Deepan crossed the room to greet her as she set her makeshift breakfast down on her desk. "Heard our suspect self-destructed after I left," he said, with an apologetic grimace. "Sorry, Guv. I should have insisted they let me check him over."

She shook her head. "Not your fault. They had Palmer's authorisation to take over—and from what he said, this is coming from over his head. We're officially off the case, kids."

A gloomy silence settled. Sally was usually the one to provide a note of cheer on days when the job was going badly, and without her the office seemed even grimmer.

"Did you get my handcuffs back?" she asked Deepan, to break the silence. The silver cuffs were special issue, and an arse-ache to replace.

"Oh, yeah, Guv." He moved to his desk and opened a drawer. "Got them right here." He held the cuffs out to her by one of the loops. "Good job I remembered. Those blokes were trying to confiscate anything that wasn't nailed down."

"Thieving bastards," Pierce muttered, crumpling her sandwich wrapper to toss at the bin. "*Six months* we've been after this skinbinder." Had Counter Terrorism known where he was operating all along? Or had they been riding along on the RCU's coattails, letting them do all the work before sweeping in to take over?

She spun the handcuffs around her finger as she pondered, the harsh artificial light reflecting off the battered silver.

And also off something else. Pierce raised the cuffs to take a closer look.

A single strand of thick black hair was caught in the hinge. Definitely not hers. She glanced across at Deepan. "Have you been rubbing these cuffs on your head, my son?" she asked him.

"Er... not recently, Guv," he said, giving her a sideways look.

She spun the handcuffs around to show him the strand of hair—or rather, fur. "Then we might still have some evidence from our panther friend after all."

THERE WAS NO point taking the panther hair down to forensics. It would take them weeks to get around to testing it, with their backlog—assuming they would even agree to process it at all, when it hadn't come through proper channels. Besides, she already had a good idea what kind of hair it was and where it had come from.

No, what she needed now was a different kind of analysis. She bagged the strand of hair and took it down to Sympathetic Magic.

Magical analysis was a hodgepodge field, still in its infancy—and utterly useless for securing a conviction. Ritual magic was tough to safely replicate, difficult to record, and harder still to explain to a jury. Sympathetic magic drew the shortest straw of all, since no lawyer on Earth could fail to clear a client charged with harming a victim from miles away with a few fingernails and some hair.

Hence, the station's Sympathetic Magic department was pretty small. About five foot one, in fact, and commonly known by the name of Jenny.

"Jen!" Pierce leaned in through the door of the small office, made still more cramped by stacks of books and file folders. "Got an analysis job for you." She held up the evidence bag.

"Fantastic." Jennifer Hayes peered out at her through a gap between cardboard boxes, a view that showed little more than a glimpse of her silver-framed glasses and wavy black hair. She gestured vaguely towards the left side of the room. "Put it with the other fifty-seven. I'm sure that I'll get caught up sometime in the next few decades."

"This one's a priority," Pierce said, stepping into the room and closing the door behind her. She squeezed her way past a box of ring binders to reach the desk.

"Aren't they all?" she said with a wry purse of her lips, but she shoved a stack of books aside to free up some desk space. "All right. What miracles are you expecting me to work for you this time?"

Pierce set the evidence bag down in front of her. "I need everything you can tell me about this."

She peered at the bag, for a moment more intrigued by the lack of labelling than the dark hair within. "Ooh, unmarked evidence." She looked up with a slight smirk. "What am I doing, hunting down your ex?"

"I don't know when you think I had the time for one of those," she said. If police work ate into your private life, then working for the RCU swallowed it whole and crunched up the bones. They were writing the book as they went along; so much about magic was still undocumented and poorly understood.

"You're telling me field investigation isn't the glamorous rock star lifestyle that I've been dreaming of so long?" Jenny grinned, then bit her lip. "Sorry, I suppose that was poor taste," she said, clearly thinking of the events of the night before. "Any word on how Sally's doing?"

"She's stable." A term that ought to be reassuring, but only served as a dark reminder of how close it had come. "Still waiting to hear from Leo Grey about the Firearms Officer who was hurt."

"Nasty business all round," she said soberly. She studied the hair in its evidence packet. "This is from that?"

"Hair from the shapeshifter's pelt," Pierce told her. "All that we've got left. Some goons claiming to be the 'Counter Terror Action Team' took over our case, seized all the evidence, and managed to give the suspect that we had in custody a chance to off himself while they were at it. Officially, it's no longer our business."

"Officially," Jenny echoed, and gave her a knowing look. She took a deep breath and pushed her chair back to stand. "Well," she said, regarding the unmarked bag. "Obviously, the chain of evidence has been compromised here, so there's no point passing this on to the officers handling the case."

"None at all," she agreed.

"*So*, since it doesn't need to be retained, I could always use it to test a new divination process I've been trying to refine." She slid a sidelong look towards Pierce. "Of course, I'd need somebody from the department to follow up on the results and verify the findings are correct..."

"Well, if it's for the cause of advancing our knowledge of magical forensics..." She spread her hands.

"Absolutely." Jenny led the way down to the ritual lab in the basement.

Unlike the cluttered workstations filling most of the offices, the small square table in the centre of this room stood bare. Etched into the concrete floor around it was a ritual circle, bounded by concentric rings of symbols. On the ceiling above was painted an exact duplicate. Containment circles, there to trap anything that might be raised here; Pierce was careful to stay well outside the bounds.

An industrial refrigerator hummed away to itself in the furthest corner of the room. Beside it stood a row of fireproof cabinets. Jenny fished a key out of her pocket to unlock the leftmost, rooting briefly through shelves of labelled boxes and plastic bags. "Ah, here we go," she said as she retrieved a cloth-wrapped bundle.

She tugged the cloth aside to reveal a crudely made bowl on a metal stand. Oval-shaped and fitted with a metal rim, the polished but uneven surface was the colour of ivory... or bone.

"Is that a skull?" Pierce said, raising her eyebrows.

"Yep." Jenny gave an impish grin as she held it up beside her own head to illustrate the angle at which the skull had been sliced. "Brains not included, I'm afraid, but he does have mystical powers of divination to make up for it. And don't worry—whoever he was, he's a couple of hundred years outside your jurisdiction." She turned the bowl over so Pierce could see the symbols painted inside. "This is a Magnus bowl."

"How does it work?"

Jenny grinned wider as she set the bowl down on the table. "Ah," she said, raising a finger as she moved to the refrigerator. "That's where the goat blood comes in."

"Always reassuring words," Pierce noted as Jenny came back to the table with a beaker of thick red fluid. She set it down next to the bowl, then retrieved a wax candle and a ritual knife from a drawer.

"Right, now, I wasn't kidding about this being an experiment," she said. "We've tried this with hairs from live humans, but where fur from an enchanted shapeshifting pelt fits in, God only knows. *Assuming* that it's viable at all, our best bet is probably divining something that's a common truth for both panther and man. Location of their home, for instance."

"That'd do me."

"Okay. So, I'm going to carve what is *hopefully* the right symbol for home into this candle..."—she made a few precise incisions with the knife—"and then add the magic focus..." She made a deeper slit in the base of the candle and carefully inserted the hair. Then she stood it up in the middle of the skull bowl, and poured blood in around it. "All right," she said, and took a slow, deep breath. "The next step is to light the candle." Her eyes flicked to Pierce. "This might be a good time to mention that if this spell interacts badly with the one on the pelt, it could well blow our heads off."

"Good to know," she said wryly, but made no move to leave.

Jenny fetched a box of matches from the drawer, then

shuffled back to arm's-length distance from the table. "Well, here goes." She lit a match and stretched forward to touch it to the candle.

The wick went up as if it had been soaked in lighter fuel. Jenny yelped and scrambled backwards as the candle flame leapt high, burning a dark, vivid red that filled the space with shadows. The wax melted like butter, shrinking rapidly, while the atmosphere inside the closed room grew heavy and greasy. As the sinking flame drew level with the blood filling the bowl, it flashed into a hissing cloud of steam. Pierce flinched back, shielding her eyes from the scalding red mist that boiled outwards.

When she lowered her arm a fraction later, the steam had faded and the candle burned out, leaving behind a nauseating smell like burning flesh. The thick tension that filled the air gradually leaked away.

Beside the table, Jenny rose from her defensive crouch, and let her breath out in a sheepish huff. "Well," she said, half to herself, "let's see what that did."

Moving closer, Pierce saw that the inside of the skull bowl was caked with sticky black clots of dried blood. Random splashes, to her eyes, but Jenny seemed quite satisfied as she hauled over a big book from on top of a cabinet. She paged through the long lists of symbols inside, occasionally pausing to jot one on a notepad.

"Right," she said, after a good deal of rifling back and forth. "Amazingly, I might actually have something for you." She indicated a blood splatter at the centre of the bowl, a crescent moon shape with a cluster of dots. "That's definitely a number—twenty-two, I think. It could be thirty-two." She moved her pen to point at to another misshapen blotch. "And this one I know for sure: that's the symbol for 'path' or 'way.'"

"So it's Twenty-Two Something Way?" That sounded promising.

Jenny raised a hand in a half shrug. "Could be 'Way.' Could be 'Road,' could be 'Street.' It's not an exact translation." She tapped two other clusters of blood spots with her pen. "Which is what makes this part tricky to decipher. So far as I can tell, these are the symbols for 'antlers' and 'wood.' Wood as in planks of, not a forest."

Pierce mulled that over. "Antler-timber." Not the most common street name, she had to admit. What else could antlers stand for? Deer. Stags. Reindeer. Horns. Hornwood? Horntree? She had it. "Hornbeam!" she said aloud. "Twenty-Two Hornbeam Way?"

"You should do cryptic crosswords," Jenny said.

"Ha. I prefer my clues to end with arrests and convictions." She was already heading for the door. "Thanks, Jen," she said.

"I did nothing, I saw nothing, I was never here," Jenny called after her.

CHAPTER FOUR

A LITTLE SLEUTHING turned up the most likely match to the partial address, and Pierce left Deepan in charge of the rest of their caseload while she drove over to check it out.

It proved to be an ordinary residential street, narrow semi-detached houses with small gardens out front. Number Twenty-Two was no different to any of its neighbours, no obvious signs of neglect or suspicious activity to draw attention. There was a car on the drive in front of the garage; bog standard silver Ford, neither new enough nor old enough to be distinctive.

The curtains were closed. Either someone inside didn't want to be seen, or nobody had been home since they'd arrested the shifter.

It was a big house for a single man living alone. Maybe there was an ex? She'd have to ask the neighbours. Considering she was no longer officially on the case, it could be tricky to find an excuse to get inside the house. But there might be someone on the street who'd seen something of use. If the shifter's car was still here, then he must have got a lift, or else he owned a second vehicle. The white van at the barn? Maybe she could get a registration.

Pierce drove on past the house and parked further up the street. No need to betray her interest in the house too soon. One advantage of coming alone was that no one suspected a middle-aged woman in a suit of being police.

It could quickly turn into a disadvantage if someone was lurking behind those curtains. It was a chill October day during normal working hours, and the street appeared entirely deserted. The odds of someone coming to her aid if she called for help were on the anorexic side of slim.

Best not to get in any trouble, then.

She strolled past the front hedge, taking a casual glance up at the windows. Not enough gap round the edges of the curtains to be able to steal a peek. The narrow windows in the door were smoked glass, revealing no more than a useless blur. Pierce pressed the bell, and listened to it buzz faintly inside. No sign of movement.

A second attempt proved just as fruitless. She peered in through the letterbox. There was nothing to see except the foot of the stairs.

Balls. Time to try the neighbours, then.

No one answered the door at the houses to either side, but the old lady opposite proved to be a goldmine—and not just because she offered tea and biscuits.

"Oh, yes, that's Joe and Lisa's house," she said, as she settled down in her armchair with a creak of bones that made Pierce wince in sympathy. "Well, I say Joe and Lisa's. I think Lisa might have moved out, but I could be wrong."

"Oh?" Pierce cocked her head in encouragement as she eyed up a custard cream. There wasn't much need to employ interrogation skills; the woman was clearly delighted to have a chance to chat.

"That's her car, you see, out there on the driveway," she said. "Joe has his own—well, it's more of a van, really, I suppose."

"Do you know the make and registration?" She reached for her notebook, not all that hopeful.

"Oh, I'm sorry, love." The old woman shook her head. "I've never been much of a car person. It's a white van, but that's all that I can tell you." The teaspoon clinked in her cup as she stirred it reflectively. "I think he's a builder or a plumber, something like that—Lisa was always a bit vague. She was the one that I usually spoke to; Joe always kept himself to himself, you know the type."

"But it's been a while since you last saw Lisa?" Pierce pressed her.

"Well, now I come to think of it, it must be a couple of months." The old woman frowned over her cup and saucer. "I asked Joe—I thought she might be ill, you see, or maybe her car was broken down, with it just sitting on the driveway all the time. He told me she'd moved out, but, well, she's done that before, you know." She arched her eyebrows meaningfully. "They were always fighting—not that it's any of my business, of course. I thought she'd be back within the week, but perhaps this time she's thrown him over for good." She took a thoughtful sip of tea and frowned again. "Funny that she wouldn't take her car, though."

"Funny," Pierce agreed with a tight smile.

* * *

IT WOULD BE pushing it to claim she believed that lives were in imminent danger, but Pierce thought she'd learned enough to justify poking about. It wasn't impossible to think Lisa could be a prisoner, and if so her captor wouldn't be coming back. She'd be neglecting her duty if she didn't at least take a closer look.

A little investigating proved that the gate at the side of the house was only held closed by a bolt, easily jiggled loose. Pierce rounded the building, warily alert. It *felt* like an empty house, but even in more mundane police work it was a bad idea to trust appearances. Jumping at shadows was a small price to pay to avoid shadows jumping at *you*.

The house's small back garden was more overgrown than the front, but offered nowhere for a criminal to hide. A magpie watched her passing with a suspicious eye, but she was pretty sure shapeshifters couldn't shrink that small. The skinbinder's eagle wings made him a man-sized bird: not exactly inconspicuous in daylight. He'd need somewhere to hole up for the day in human form.

Was this the place?

The house had patio doors, unsurprisingly locked. Pierce looked in on the empty living room. Nothing of note to be seen, except for the fact that the three piece suite had been pushed to the wall as if to clear more floor space. The carpet looked rucked up, and she itched to be inside where she could lift it up to check for evidence, whether criminal or ritual.

No warrant: no such luck. She moved on towards the rear of the attached garage instead. There was a back door, and she halted as she saw that it wasn't completely shut; it had been pushed to, but wasn't quite flush with the edge of the frame.

Just a door swollen by damp that wouldn't close—or was someone still inside?

Her hand went to the malodorant spray fixed to her belt. Wouldn't work so well on humans as on more sensitive noses, but it was still a vile stink that ought to shock anybody enough to give her time to run and call for backup.

She should call for it right now, but she was hesitant to do it, unwilling to blow her cover before she knew that somebody was there.

Exactly the kind of reasoning that got officers killed. Pierce guessed it was good she was old and wise enough to recognise the stupidity of the move—right before she went ahead and did it anyway. She unclipped the spray from her belt, holding it in her pocket ready to whip out. Then she took hold of the doorknob. The door was stiff in the frame, scraping along the ground with a rasp that ruined her efforts at stealth.

Inside, the garage was musty, and dark aside from the light that followed her in through the door. She fished for the penlight that she had attached to her keys, wishing she'd stopped to grab her full-sized police torch from the car. If she hadn't been kicked off the case, she wouldn't need to be sneaking around without proper backup or equipment.

The penlight's narrow beam did little to illuminate the space, only highlighting isolated spots as she flicked it around. Workbenches, tools hanging up on the walls; this garage was clearly never used to store a car. It was crammed with old pieces of furniture and garden tools that filled the space with odd-shaped shadows.

Pierce edged her way in past a rusty, grass-stained lawnmower, moving a folding chair out of her way. The garage smelled faintly of petrol, and under that another, subtler scent that raised her hackles. A rolled tarpaulin lay to one side, and she unfurled the plastic sheet as well as she could in the tight space. Dark streaks and drip stains marred the wrinkled fabric. Oil? She knelt down on the concrete to shine the torch beam closer.

Not oil. Even by the penlight's feeble glow she could see the faint reddish tint to the stains. Blood—but was it human or animal?

A clunk and creak from the front of the garage made her whirl, and she saw the door starting to rise. The sunlight that poured in beneath was blinding, and she squinted to make out the figure silhouetted outside as she fumbled to pull the spray out from her pocket.

Before she could bark out a warning, the man in the doorway spoke. "DCI Pierce." She recognised the cool, calm voice at once. "Perhaps you didn't fully understand my meaning when I told you that your team was off the case."

MAITLAND MIGHT HAVE caught her red-handed, but Pierce was pretty sure he was in no hurry to start disciplinary proceedings. Whatever his mysterious little group were up to, she doubted they could spare the time or stand the added scrutiny.

So she stonewalled to the best of her ability. "I received a tip linking a shapeshifter to this address," she said. Perfectly true, as was the fact she'd promised to protect her source; no need to delve into the details further. "Unauthorised shapeshifting falls under our jurisdiction."

Maitland gave a pleasant smile that didn't touch his eyes. "Of course. Nonetheless, given that you knew my team was working on a similar case in the local area, it might have been wiser to keep us informed."

"It was an unreliable tip," she said. "Might easily have been nothing." She hadn't risen through the ranks to DCI without mastering the art of obfuscating without lies.

"Nonetheless," he repeated, still smiling.

The whole exchange was utter bollocks and both of them knew it, dancing round the subject to avoid complications.

Christ, she hated politics.

She left Hornbeam Way no more enlightened, and considerably more pissed off. Whatever evidence might be found in the dead shifter's home, Maitland and his team wouldn't be sharing.

So what was it about this case that had drawn the attention of Counter Terrorism? She'd yet to see any evidence there was more to it than illegal skinbinding and maybe murder. It rankled to think that she might have to let the case go without even knowing what it had been about.

Pierce stopped at a café to beat her mood into submission with chips. While she was waiting for her food to arrive, she called Deepan on her mobile.

"Nothing new, Guv," he reported. "Just paperwork and cold cases. I let Tim go off to the hospital to visit Sally—he wasn't getting a thing done."

"Sally's doing all right, then?" she asked. At least that was one glimmer of good news.

"Husband said she's doing well." Deepan hesitated. "Sergeant Henderson didn't make it through the night, though. Sorry, Guv."

"Damn." Pierce closed her eyes. She hadn't even had the chance to learn the man's first name.

She felt another sharp stab of resentment towards Maitland. It was her request for Firearms Support that had put the team in harm's way, and now she couldn't even tell them for sure that the sacrifice had been for a good reason.

She took a slow, deep breath. "Okay, thanks, Deepan," she said. "I'll probably drop in to see Sally on my way back, if you're all right holding the fort. No trouble from Palmer about the incident in the cells, I hope?"

"Haven't heard a peep, Guv," he said. "Don't even know if there's going to be an investigation our end—looks like Counter Terrorism are going to handle it internally."

"Brush it under the carpet, more likely," Pierce said with a grimace. "All right," she said, after a moment. "Call me if anything comes up."

The meal could have been five star dining, and it still would have sat poorly in her stomach. She arrived at the hospital to catch Sally's husband picking at a sandwich in the lobby café with the same lack of enthusiasm. He looked exhausted, face papery grey, though he summoned up a wan smile as she crossed the room to greet him. She'd met him before at various work dos, but she still had to dredge for the name.

"Hi, Mike. How's she doing?"

Mike let out a breath as he rose and collected up the debris of his meal, seeming glad to have an excuse to abandon it. "She's doing well, they said. Came out of surgery all right. She was awake for a little bit earlier. Still a bit out of it, though."

"Not surprising."

"She can't talk at the moment, but they've given her a whiteboard," he said, leading the way over to the lifts at the far side. "She wasn't really up to writing anything this morning, but I think she appreciated my artwork."

She smiled and nodded. Oppressive silence fell as they waited for the lift to arrive. As they stepped inside, the doors swished closed behind them, Mike spoke again, abruptly. "Did you catch the bloke?"

It took a moment for her to switch mental gears. "The attacker? Yes. Yes, we did." She wasn't about to mention that he'd died in police custody, or that a second suspect had escaped.

Mike seemed to draw some comfort from it anyway. "That's good to hear." The lift doors opened with a ding and he straightened. "This is it."

He led the way along the antiseptic-smelling corridor, shoes squeaking on the tiles. As they passed through the double doors into the ward, Pierce spotted Sally in the second bed.

She'd looked better. The tracheostomy tube sticking out of her neck was a stark reminder of the severity of her injuries. Wound dressings disappeared below the scoop neck of her hospital gown, and her head lolled back against the pillow. At first Pierce wasn't sure if she was actually awake, but then she turned her head to face them as they approached, managing a fraction of a smile.

"Hello, love," Mike said, dropping a kiss on her cheek. "Feeling a bit better this afternoon?" He turned to Pierce. "I'll just go and get us some chairs."

She couldn't really afford to stay for very long, but it was easier to let him go than try to protest. As he headed back out into the corridor, she turned her attention to Sally.

"You look like hell," she told her. "If you wanted to get out of the post-raid paperwork, there are easier ways." Sally gave another pseudo-smile, clearly a painful effort with her neck in its current state.

As her husband returned with a pair of stacked plastic chairs, she held out a hand towards him and made a flapping motion. "You want the whiteboard?" he guessed. "Hang on. Let me just move the table closer so you can grab it."

He wheeled the small table over to her bedside, and Pierce saw a miniature dry erase board resting on it, with a pen on a string. Sally started to try to sit up to reach for it, with obvious difficulty.

"Whoa, don't strain yourself, love," Mike said. "Give me a second and I'll raise the bed for you."

It took lot of faffing to get the bed raised up and Sally comfortable, but she seemed to have something she was determined to communicate. When Mike uncapped the pen and handed it to her, she scrawled CASE? across the board in shaky letters.

"We caught the shifter," Pierce told her, avoiding more complex explanations. She hoped Sally didn't remember to ask after Henderson. "The other one got away." She didn't want to reveal too much detail in front of Mike, but she couldn't help but press for more information. That glimpse beneath the tarp Sally had taken was the only look at the evidence they'd got. "Did you have something to say about the scene in the barn?" she asked.

Sally started to nod, then winced in pain. Her shoulders were tense and the motions somewhat jerky as she scrawled another word on the whiteboard. This one was considerably less controlled than her previous letters, but the message was still legible.

HUMAN.

Mike smiled fondly and patted her arm. "Believe it or not, love, we already realised that you were only human."

But it was Pierce that Sally locked eyes with, willing her to understand.

A cold ripple slid down her spine as the words clicked together in her head. The last thing Sally had said before the panther had attacked them.

Guv, we've got skins here. But I think they're—

Human?

CHAPTER FIVE

PIERCE DIDN'T LINGER at the hospital for long; Sally was obviously too exhausted to take much more, and her own mind was spinning with the implications of that scribbled word. She couldn't ask for direct confirmation with Mike there, but she was sure she'd understood what Sally meant.

Under the tarpaulin in the barn had been human skins.

They couldn't be shapeshifting skins—at least, not working ones. People had been trying for centuries to bind the enchantments onto human skin, and never had more to show for it than an ugly, bloody mess. The skinbinder they were after must be one more in the long line who'd attempted it and failed.

And yet, if that was true, then why was Maitland after him? There was no reason for the Counter Terror Action Team to take an interest in an RCU case. Not unless it had implications for national security.

Implications like the existence of a ritual that would

allow a person to be murdered, skinned, and seamlessly replaced by an impostor. Could it be possible?

She drove on autopilot as she left the hospital, pulling into an empty lay-by when she was a few miles on. This was one conversation she'd rather not have overheard and spread all round the social networks. She pulled out her phone and called a former colleague who'd moved down to RCU Oxford.

"Phil. Got a moment to talk?" she asked when he picked up.

"Well, I'm knee-deep in dismembered bodies right now, but for you I suppose I'd be willing to tear myself away." Phil's broad Yorkshire accent came through just as strong as she remembered, undiluted by his years spent living down south. "Hold on." She heard a few rustles of background noise and then the sound of a door closing before his voice returned, a little clearer now. "What's up?"

"That book you were collecting notes for on human-to-animal transformation. You get anywhere with that?"

"What, in the copious free time I have for writing? No, it's on my list of a million and one things to do when I retire. Why, are you after a reference text? I could probably recommend a few, but nothing you wouldn't have heard of."

"Just wondering if you'd been keeping up with the latest research in the field. Anything new popped up in academic circles about human-form shifting?" New occult texts, whether real or fake, were always guaranteed to spark off a fad for attempts to recreate the rituals.

"That old chestnut?" Phil laughed. "No, nothing new that I've heard—just the same old balls being recycled.

Always some idiot convinced they can outdo a thousand years of failures with a ritual knife they bought for twenty quid on eBay."

"Mm. All right, thanks, Phil. Probably just another wannabe with more ego than support for his ideas. Nothing for you to worry about."

But as she hung up the phone, she couldn't help but wonder. In the months they'd been chasing the skinbinder, he'd turned out pelt after pelt that matched the quality of any antique piece that she'd seen. It might just be pure arrogance that led him to believe he could succeed where countless others had failed through the centuries—but what if he was right?

The only way to know for sure was to get a proper look at the skins from last night's raid. Sally hadn't had time for more than a brief glimpse, but closer examination ought to show if they were viable skins or just the remnants of attempts that hadn't worked.

She pressed her lips together. Maitland might have his own forensics team and magical experts, but it would still have taken them a while to process the scene. They wouldn't want to risk damaging the skins by moving them in haste—in fact, why move them at all? The farm was safely isolated and the owners off in Spain, and the skinbinder might well return if they left him the bait. Odds were that Maitland's people hadn't left.

She sent Deepan a deliberately vague text about checking out a lead, and drove back to the farmhouse.

Pierce could tell that she'd hit paydirt when she turned down the farm road. There were unmarked vans still parked there, and when she pulled up beside them, a serious man in a suit hurried over to stop her.

"I'm sorry, this is a crime scene," he said, holding up his hands. "I'm going to have to ask you to get back in your car—"

"RCU consultant," she interrupted, showing her badge and stepping around him without slowing her stride. "I'm here to look at the evidence from the barn—are you cleared to know about this, son?" She gave him a scrutinising look. Nothing cemented credentials quite like challenging other people's.

It put the young guard on the wrong foot, and he faltered, scrambling to keep up with her pace. "Er—Um, I wasn't told—"

"No, I don't suppose you were," Pierce said brusquely, heading straight towards the barn. "Clear it with Jason Maitland—he's the one that called me in. Now, excuse me, son. I have a job to do." She left him hovering uncertainly behind her. Even if he called her bluff and did as she suggested, it would still take time to make contact and find out she was lying. All she needed was a chance to get inside the barn and have a look underneath that tarpaulin.

There were a few people inside, all wearing suits rather than coveralls. Convenient for her chances of blending, but suspicious. They clearly weren't concerned about contaminating evidence; either they already knew the skinbinder's identity, or they were confident that nothing in this barn could help them find out.

The whole setup stank to high heaven. Maitland had to have known that the skinbinder was here before last night, yet he'd kept his people back and let her team shoulder the dirty work. She scowled.

It gave her just the unapproachable aspect she needed to avoid questions as she entered the barn. The space inside was gloomy even with the daylight that poured in through the window at the rear. The dirt floor was still scuffed with the footprints from last night, but the bloodstains only drew her eye because she knew where to look.

She didn't look too long, aware that every moment she gave Maitland's team to think increased her chances of getting kicked out. "So where are these skins?" she barked at the nearest person. "Here?" Without waiting for an answer, she moved to grab the corner of the tarp that she'd seen Sally lift last night.

What lay piled beneath it could have been taken for pigskin at first—until, like an optical illusion, details emerged. A clump of matted dark hair, the curve of a human ear... Pierce gagged and covered her mouth, visceral horror overcoming even her police training. Violent death was nothing new after her decades on the job, but the thought of the callous indifference that it took to peel skin back from flesh and bone and stitch it into a costume for someone else to wear...

She turned her head away, swallowing bile. Her eyes fell on the bloody meat hook where the wolf had hung last night. The half-skinned carcass had been pulled down and covered up with a sheet, but in her mind's eye she saw a human corpse in its place.

She hoped like hell the victims were dead before the skinning began.

She took a slow, deep breath, regaining her composure, and used it as a chance to scan the barn. Her eyes fell on the silver skinning knife below the window, dropped there so the skinbinder could transform and make his flight. He wouldn't have abandoned it by choice; it must have been custom made and difficult to replace. She rose to get a better look at the blade.

Before she'd fully straightened, Maitland's voice spoke from behind her. "Chief Inspector." For the first time he was starting to sound sharp in the place of his previous calm. "At this point, I'm not sure if I admire your persistence or if I should just have you arrested right now."

Pierce swivelled on her heel, refusing to betray her jolt of surprise at his presence. "How about you just give me the answers that I'm looking for?"

"I'm afraid that's not possible. But we should talk." He extended his hand in an invitation that was clearly an order. "This way, please."

As soon as he'd led her out of earshot of the others, Pierce turned to face him. "Human skins. You knew about this?"

Maitland gave a slightly pained looking grimace, the first real expression she'd seen on his carefully composed face. "Perhaps now you appreciate why this is a matter of national security," he said in a low voice.

"They're functional?" she said, still sceptical despite his tone. A collection of convincing-looking skins didn't prove human-form shifters could exist.

"Our information says yes."

Pierce narrowed her eyes. "And where do you get your information? If this is for real, the RCU needs to know about it. This contradicts a lot of things we thought we knew for sure. We can't do our jobs if we're kept out of the loop."

"On the contrary," he said, still keeping his voice down. "It's *vital* that this information be contained. Right now, we don't believe that our target has spread the news, and if he has, it's easily dismissed as empty bragging. But if your department is seen to be reacting to a genuine threat, intelligence agencies and terrorist groups all over the world will take notice. We *must* have the skinbinder under our control before this leaks out."

"'Under control.' As opposed to 'under arrest'?" She shook her head in disgust. "This man is linked to God knows how many assaults and murders—if not by his own hand, then as part of a conspiracy. I doubt these skins come from volunteers who donated their bodies. Did you know that the panther shapeshifter's ex-girlfriend has gone missing?"

"You can conduct an investigation after we've secured the suspect. But evidence of human shapeshifting can't go to trial, and if any of your team saw the skins, they should be informed that they were unviable, failed attempts."

Pierce gave a thin, humourless smile. "You mean you'll trample all over the evidence, and then let us sweep up the loose ends while the real criminal goes free."

Maitland showed off his pearly white teeth in a cold smile of his own. "Not free. I assure you, the skinbinder won't escape us."

"Won't escape incarceration, maybe," she said, holding his gaze. "But what about justice?"

Oh, she didn't doubt that Maitland's team would lock the man away. He'd spend the rest of his life stuck in some top secret facility, earning good behaviour points by putting his skills to work. But what about the victims of his crimes, the people who'd lost friends and family to his blade? They would never learn the truth of what had happened to their loved ones, left to wait in vain for people who were never coming home.

Maitland let out a faint sigh. "Justice is best served by ensuring this man's skills don't fall into the hands of our nation's enemies. As I'm sure you'll realise when you've calmed down from your reaction to last night's events. But I'm afraid that in the meantime I really can't afford to have you interfering in this. Consider yourself placed on leave until further notice."

Pierce held his gaze. "Yes, sir," she said with perfect crispness.

She was pretty sure he understood *exactly* what those words meant, but he just smiled and offered her his arm. "Now, allow me to escort you to your car, just to make sure you don't get lost on the way."

PIERCE DROVE AWAY from the farm—but she didn't head straight home. Even Maitland couldn't object to her using her time off to get a bit of shopping in.

Leeds Occult Market seemed like the perfect place. She drove into the city and found a place to park before taking a stroll through the covered market.

There was always a certain sense of stepping back in

time on passing through the stalls to the occult section; leaving behind familiar brands and garish modern logos for strange little stands selling handmade things covered with obscure symbols. A heady mix of scents filled the air: acrid herbs, sweet incense, perfumed oils. She passed stalls stacked with thick leather-bound books, and others loaded with trinkets that claimed to be magic charms.

Most of the goods were cheap knock-offs and silly New Age nonsense: at best just pointless quackery, at worst actively dangerous to use in a real ritual. None of that was the RCU's problem. They had their hands full just dealing with genuine artefacts; Trading Standards could handle the rest.

Occult markets were a con-artist's paradise, but an experienced eye could pick out the real thing from all the junk. Pierce cast a glance over each seller's wares as she passed by, alert for anything illegal even if she was formally off-duty.

A few of the regular stallholders here knew her by name, or at least well enough to share a nod in passing. It was the first place the RCU looked for illegal sales; there weren't many places outside Leeds and London where the occult markets were big enough for criminals to lose themselves in the crowds.

The knife stall was a frequent port of call, for all that its sales were above board. Anyone over eighteen could buy a ritual knife; they were rarely used as weapons outside of your average domestic, since those with premeditated murder on their minds had plenty of cheaper stabbing tools to choose from.

But for ritual preparations, you couldn't use just any old blade. The materials, the shape, the conditions under which it was made, the symbols worked into the blade and handle... all of them made a difference to the kind of enchantments it could be used for. Anyone with half an inkling of what they were doing would have a very specific set of requirements.

And that made knives a very fruitful avenue of enquiry. *If* the seller was willing to cooperate.

"Our Lady Pierce," Harry Draper said wryly as she approached his stall. "Come to harass an innocent businessman again?" He was a big burly bear of a man, the kind that even the most opportunistic thief would think twice about trying to wrestle a knife away from. Six foot and change—lots of change—with a beard you could lose a small pet in, he was close to being literally twice her size.

Pierce wasn't intimidated. In her experience, it was the scrappy little guys with lots of practice taking punches that were the ones you had to watch for in a fight. "It's your guilty customers I'm more concerned about," she said. "I need you to consult your records for me."

He cocked his head, unimpressed. "Got a warrant?"

"Have a heart, Harry," she said, stepping closer as she saw a girl in a green hoodie pause to give them a curious stare. "I've got one officer dead and another badly injured. There was a skinbinder involved, and he left his knife on the scene. Anyone come in today to buy a silver skinning knife?"

"Not that I recall," he said, stonewalling maybe just as a matter of principle. She'd heard that Harry had been in trouble with the police back in his youth, a hazard of being the biggest man still conscious at the scene of a few bar fights. Hard to say if he was covering for a customer right now, or yanking her chain purely for the hell of it.

She pressed on anyway. "Or what about the original knife, do you remember that? A silver skinning knife with a curved blade; would have been sold maybe six months ago to a young man, twenty, twenty-five, with dark hair and rune tattoos on his arms."

"I wouldn't remember that far back," he said. "Old man like me? The memory goes."

He was ten years younger than her if he was a day— but it wasn't Harry's reaction that grabbed her attention. The girl in the green hoodie had jerked at the description, more response than she'd given to the talk of crimes and dead police officers. Pierce swung towards her, scenting a possible lead. "You know someone who looks like that?" she asked.

The girl turned and ran.

CHAPTER SIX

FIRST RULE OF police work: when someone runs away from you, run after them. Second rule: don't be an idiot about it.

The first part was always easier to manage than the second.

Pierce was reaching for her radio to call in for backup when she remembered that she was alone and technically off-duty. *Balls.* She'd better keep up with her suspect.

The crowds that thronged the market worked against her on that front, shoppers still aimlessly drifting or looking around for the source of the commotion. "Police! Stop!" she yelled, which achieved nothing except wasted breath.

If the girl had slowed to a walk and shrugged off the green hoodie, she could have disappeared into the crowd without a trace. Luckily she didn't stop to think but just took off, the clatter of her feet and startled squawks of bystanders betraying her direction. Pierce elbowed her way past gawkers in time to see the girl run through the automatic doors and out onto the street.

She gave chase, though her chest was starting to burn from the effort. Should have had a healthy lunch instead of the most greasy option—and not just today, either. The girl was pulling ahead, youth and fitness on her side, but her boots weren't made for running and the awkward bulk of her shoulder bag was slowing her down.

"Police! Stop!" Pierce yelled again. A lot of bloody good it did. The girl dodged around the bollards at the end of the pedestrian strip and ran out across the road without stopping to look. Pierce winced, anticipating squealing brakes or even worse, but luck carried the girl across the street without disaster.

A big lorry arrived just as she reached the kerb, but she saw the girl veering right, and kept pace with her on her own side of the road. The line of shoppers at the nearby bus stop gawked at them both; Pierce cut across the road in front of their bus as it pulled up.

The pavement on the other side curved round a sharp corner where the road merged into another. The girl ran straight across this road as well, this time earning a blare of horns from a swerving driver and the tail of traffic slamming on their brakes behind him.

On the far side, hoardings closed off a partly demolished building. The girl slung her bag over the top, jammed a foot between the crumbling bricks of the adjacent shop front, and hauled herself up after it. As she stretched up, the sleeve of her baggy hoodie fell back, revealing a ring of runes tattooed around her wrist. Another skinbinder, or at least a wannabe.

"Shit," Pierce said with feeling. Now she had even more reason to copy the gymnastics.

It wasn't pretty. The last time she'd scrambled over a fence had been back in her uniform days, and she'd put on a lot of years and weight around the middle since then. As she dragged herself clumsily over the top, after several false starts, she hoped no one was videoing this from an angle that would show her face.

On the other side of the fence was a patch of rubble-filled waste ground, overlooked by the boarded shell of the abandoned building. The girl hadn't run any further, but stood waiting warily a little further up the slope. Behind her lay a collection of piled wooden boards with symbols chalked and spray-painted all over them. This was clearly a hangout for those who practised the less legal kind of ritual, without the money and resources to keep it behind closed doors.

There was only one thing more dangerous than stupid kids playing with rituals they didn't understand—*smart* kids playing with rituals they *almost* understood. Pierce eyed the girl, wondering which category she fell under.

She was a scrawny kid, somewhere between her upper teens and middle twenties. All sharp angles, not enough meat on her bones for proper curves, with sunken cheeks and hair the grubby blonde of a cheap dye job.

"Who are you?" she asked, watching Pierce with fierce suspicion. "You really police?"

She reached for her badge. "DCI Pierce, Ritual Crime Unit. How about you? You got a name of your own?"

She glanced around the site, wary of having been lured into an ambush, but there weren't many places to hide. Most of the entrances to the derelict building were boarded up, and on the right-hand side a maze of scaffolding would prevent all but the most determined of efforts to squirm through.

"Julie," the girl said tersely, after a lengthy pause spent playing with the drawstrings of her hoodie. Not likely to be her real name, but Pierce had bigger fish to fry than a young would-be skinbinder who might never have done more than talk the talk.

"You recognised that description that I gave to Harry Draper," she said, holding the girl's gaze. "And it meant something, or you wouldn't have tried to run. Who is he?"

It was a worthless description really, nothing more distinctive than the mention of tattoos that almost any skinbinder would have. The fact that Julie had run meant she already had someone in mind, someone who she'd found suspicious even before she'd heard a description matching him.

She gave a defensive shrug. "Look, I don't even know him. He's just some bloke who used to hang around here sometimes. I haven't seen him for months!"

"You know his name?" she pressed.

Another sullen shrug. "Sebastian. That's what he said, anyway. Like I say, I don't know him. Somebody invited him because he had all these books about skinning and stuff, but nobody really liked him. He was a creep."

"He have other friends?" Pierce asked. She tapped her foot when Julie hesitated. "Look, this guy's not your friend, so what do you care? Just tell me what you know, and I'll get out of your hair. I'm not interested in what you and your mates get up to." Not right now, anyway.

"He didn't have friends," Julie said, wrinkling her nose. "But there was this bunch of blokes who turned up at our meetings—dunno who they were, none of us invited them. Craig reckoned they were government and they'd hacked our phones or something, but it was probably just some twat put the meeting up on Facebook." She snorted and shook her head. "Anyway, they showed up, and they were asking all these questions about human transformation— had we tried it, did we know anyone who'd done it and all that shit. They had this book that was supposed to be the ritual for it."

"And what did you tell them?"

"We told them to piss off!" Julie said in a sudden burst of animation. "Human skins? That's psycho stuff. It's all a load of bullshit, anyway. Doesn't work. We figured it was the police trying to fit us up for something dodgy." She glared at Pierce with fresh suspicion.

"But Sebastian was interested in what they were saying?"

And now they were back to the noncommittal shrugs. "I dunno—like I said, he was a creepy bastard. And after those blokes came round, he stopped showing up, so we all reckoned he must have gone off with them. That was about Easter. Haven't seen him since then, so I can't help you, all right?"

Easter: six or seven months ago, roughly the same timeframe in which their skinbinder had become super-active, churning out pelts as if he had a whole menagerie at his disposal. Their efforts to track the source of the animals had got them nowhere; no zoos or wildlife sanctuaries missing anything major, no evidence of an increase in smuggling. Backers with money and connections explained a lot.

That might be why Maitland's team had been holding off before they brought in the skinbinder... but if so, why not keep her department informed and have them call off the raid? It was hard to escape the suspicion there was something shady going on.

Behind them the scaffolding creaked, and Julie whirled to look at it, jittery as a cat. "Look, that's all I know, all right?" she said, tucking her hands up inside the long sleeves of her hoodie. "I don't know who those blokes were, I don't know where they went, and I definitely don't know anything about dead coppers. Can I go now, please?" She tensed, clearly ready to bolt regardless of the answer.

"Who else might know something about Sebastian?" Pierce asked. "You mentioned a Craig...?"

Julie stepped back, shaking her head. "I—"

Another groaning creak sounded from the building behind them. The scaffolding gave an ominous rattle, and Pierce looked up in time to see a dark shadow detach from the edge of the roof. For a moment she thought a chunk of masonry had torn loose—and then her eyes made sense of the falling shape.

Not falling—leaping. "Shit!" She scrambled back towards the fence.

Julie barely had the time to look bewildered before the shapeshifter crashed down beside her in a cloud of brick dust. It was a huge black dog, a mastiff—but no normal dog would have made such a suicidal jump, or bounced up from it unharmed.

It lunged for Julie, and she shrieked, smashing at it with her bag. The dog tore it out of her hands with a toss of its blunt head, scattering the contents across the ground. "Get back, get back!" Pierce yelled at her, but instead she snatched a chunk of broken brick up from the ground to hurl at the shifter. It bounced off like a pebble.

Pierce grabbed for her malodorant spray, but before she could get close, the dog shifter gave an echoing bark and snapped its teeth at Julie. Her shrieks of fear became a howl of agony as the massive jaws clamped down around her arm.

"Christ!" Pierce fired off the spray, a sulphuric stench that made her gag and her eyes start to stream.

The big dog reeled back, swinging Julie with it, like a toy held in its mouth. She hit the scaffolding with such force that the metal bars jarred loose, and the framework collapsed in on itself in a jangling cascade. The creature dropped Julie's limp body and bounded away, snarling and shaking its head as if to try to dislodge the smell. Chunks of brick and slate roof tiles rained down from the building behind.

Pierce's nausea rose higher as her ears rang from the avalanche, but she swallowed it and ran forward to grab Julie's dropped bag. If she was a skinbinder, she should have the tools of her trade in there.

She cursed as she dug through it, finding only make-up, books and junk. A glance up showed the big dog was turning around to come back, its human mind wresting control back from animal instincts. More discipline than most humans would have shown in a fight—but then, these shifters weren't the usual bored thrill-seekers. She was dealing with people who had killed, and would do it again.

Inside the satchel, her hand closed around a sheathed knife.

The ritual blade that she pulled out was smaller than Sebastian's, lacking the wicked curve and not half as ornately made. But in one important aspect, the two skinning blades were twins—both made of solid silver.

Pierce fumbled to unfasten the leather sheath and release it as the big dog came thundering back towards her. She hadn't trained to fight with knives, only against those wielding them, but all she needed was to do some damage to the pelt.

And not get killed. That would be the real trick.

As the shifter lunged towards her, she kicked the bag its way, but it just flopped over, the undone flap flying up in the dog's face. The moment of obscured vision gave her time to dive away, escaping the snap of its slobbering jaws as she stumbled on a loose brick. Rubble shifted under her feet and she skidded down the slope, swinging the knife in a wide arc as she turned back.

The dog leapt at her, its true size apparent for the first time; the huge frame stretched out longer than she was tall. Pierce lunged forward to meet it, stabbing upward with the blade.

The shifter's own momentum drove it onto the knife, and she felt the shift in pressure as her thrust into solid flesh became a slice through layers of fur and cloth. The body that slammed into hers was a man's wrapped in fur, still heavy enough to knock her off her feet, but with teeth that clicked together harmlessly beside her ear, no longer the dog's mighty crushing jaws. Before he could recover from the jarring shock, Pierce clouted him across the head and shoved him off of her, snatching for the handcuffs from her belt.

"Police!" she shouted. "You're under arrest! Stay down on the ground!"

He ignored her words, or didn't understand them, mind still not caught up to the shift in shape. Instead he staggered backwards, unbalanced on two legs, and tried to bark at her with vocal cords that wouldn't make the sound. The face beneath the mastiff pelt was at odds with the snarl, clean shaven and well groomed like any bland young office worker.

"Stay where you are!" she said again, but it only seemed to snap him out of the haze, his eyes growing more focused as the situation sank in. He turned and ran towards the fence.

"Shit!" Pierce chased after him, but she was too winded to catch up, and he leapt to grab the top of the hoardings and haul himself up. As he swung over, the mastiff pelt flapped away from his back, and she glimpsed the maker's rune tattooed beneath. Just a glimpse—but enough for her to see that it wasn't Sebastian's mark. The pelt had been made by another skinbinder.

What the hell?

For a brief instant she almost contemplated climbing after, but she knew she was too worn out from the previous chase—and that reminded her to think of Julie.

She turned to look around for the young skinbinder, and saw her still lying slumped underneath the fallen scaffold.

"Shit," she said again, more heavily, and hurried over. She brushed brick dust off unmoving flesh, and felt for a pulse.

No miracles today. The girl was dead.

CHAPTER SEVEN

PIERCE LEFT THE waste ground over the back fence, with a last apologetic look at Julie where she lay beneath her scaffolding cairn. It stung to flee the crime scene without waiting for the police, but she couldn't afford to get bogged down in the red tape right now—or worse, let Maitland find out she was still on the case. She'd stumbled on something bigger here than one rogue murderous skinbinder, and she wasn't about to let the trail go cold over a jurisdictional pissing contest.

If that was all this was. Counter Terrorism had their own motives for seeking Sebastian, and she couldn't trust their interests were in line with hers. Sebastian clearly had powerful backers, and it was all too easy to believe Maitland would be willing to cut them a deal.

And now it seemed there was a second skinbinder in the mix. The maker's mark she'd glimpsed on the mastiff pelt wasn't used by any of the country's licensed skin shops, and she didn't recognise it as an antique. Of course, that was Sally's field of expertise, not hers. Pierce grimaced. She couldn't drag a woman who was still recovering in hospital into this morass.

In fact, it was better if she kept the whole of her team out of it. Maitland might have been content to just warn her off so far, but he could easily cause trouble if she kept investigating. Pierce was willing to take that risk, but she wasn't about to drag the rest of the RCU down with her.

When she got back to the car, she grabbed her notebook, and sketched the maker's rune as best she could recall it. Part of the design had been obscured, but if she assumed basic symmetry...

As police sirens wailed in the distance, she capped her pen and frowned over the inked scribble she'd produced. A little like an ankh with wings surrounded by a halo; not high art, but at least it was a lead.

Now she just needed someone to decipher it—and luckily, she had someone in mind.

GARY HOLLAND WAS strictly a small time crook, and even that was pushing it. In truth he was mostly just an enthusiastic collector, with a bad habit of getting carried away when it came to purchases that didn't quite square with the law.

He looked distinctly wary as he opened up the door of his small terraced house to let her step inside. "Chief Inspector," he said, with a strained smile. He was an awkward little man, somewhere in his early thirties, with a bald spot and a taste for knitted jumpers that prophesied the old man he'd become. "Now, I don't know what you're looking for this time, but I can assure you, my collection is completely clean. No more Libyan scorpion sting charms for me!"

It was hard not to feel a bit sorry for him. His twitchy mannerisms always made him appear guilty even when he was telling the truth—which he genuinely might be, this time round.

Or maybe not. As she stepped into the house, Pierce was immediately reintroduced to the collection that cluttered every inch of space. If anything, it seemed Gary's hoarding tendencies had grown since last she was here.

Even the narrow hallway was lined with rows of shelves; she had to squeeze her way along. The contents made for a disturbing display: a mangy looking badger paw holding a candle stub; the skeleton of an eel with its eyes replaced by black stones; a taxidermied owl that had seen much better days. If there was a ritual artefact that had once been a live animal, Gary had it, or a framed, authenticated photo of it, or at the very least a set of books and articles about it.

Shapeshifting pelts he didn't have a licence to keep, but that didn't stop him tracking down all there was to know about them.

"You're in luck, Gaz," Pierce told him. "I'm not here to inventory your collection this time." Though no doubt if she did, she would find more than a few things that shouldn't strictly be there. "I'm here for your expertise."

She almost regretted the words when she saw how he puffed up. She suddenly imagined decades of fielding calls from him offering the RCU his expert guidance.

Of course, the way things were going, Pierce might not be part of the Unit long enough for that to be her problem. And besides, right now she needed information, and she couldn't go to anyone that Maitland might be watching.

Gary ushered her through to the living room, as musty and cramped as the rest of the house. There was only one actual armchair, the rest of the space taken up by glass display cases and shelves. He scurried off to fetch a chair from the dining table. "Can I get you something to drink, Chief Inspector?" he asked from the doorway. "Erm, I've only got Diet Coke or soya milk, but..."

Pierce demurred, not least because she didn't want to contemplate what he might serve it up in. As she sat in the armchair, she found herself facing a goat's head with both of its eyes stitched closed. It managed an accusing stare despite the lack of eyeballs. She was pretty sure that if she started asking about import certificates and licences for some of the more dodgy-looking items on display here, their owner would be in a world of trouble.

Best to steer clear of that can of worms right now.

Gary returned to the room with a straight-backed chair, setting it down close enough to hers to make eye contact uncomfortable. "So what can I do for you expertise-wise, Chief Inspector?" he asked with a nervous giggle.

She decided to treat him like the professional he wanted to be. "I need to know more about shapeshifting pelts. I understand you're an expert on maker's marks."

He lit up at the words. "Oh, yes. I've read all the books— *Foston's Guide, European Skinbinders of the Middle Ages, Lost Artefact Pelts of the Ancient Masters...*"

"It's a modern mark I'm looking for," she interrupted. "Could be someone new on the scene. Would you know about that?"

She wasn't sure Gary would have known 'the scene' if it bit him—something it was quite likely to do—but he nodded enthusiastically all the same. "I'm on all the forums"—he remembered who he was talking to—"well, all the *legal* forums, obviously, heh, nothing dodgy." His forehead crinkled and his eyes took on a hunted look.

"Of course," she said, suppressing a sigh. No point hoping that Gary was ever going to learn. She drew the sheet of notepaper from her pocket and unfolded it. "This is the rune. Do you recognise it?"

He took the paper with a confident smile, but after turning it towards him he visibly paled. "Erm, this is a difficult one..." he hedged, and swallowed. "I'm not sure I can help you with this, Chief Inspector." He looked pained.

It could have been just the fact that his claim to expertise had foundered—but that didn't fit the Gary that she knew. He would have prevaricated, *ummed* and *erred* a lot more and come up with creative reasoning to excuse his ignorance. Pierce narrowed her eyes.

"Come on, Gary," she said. "It's not like you to be without a theory. Are you sure you haven't seen it somewhere? Heard somebody mention a new skinbinder on the forums? If anyone would know, it's you." She held his gaze.

Gary tugged uneasily at the collar of his jumper. "Er, well, as I say, it's a bit of an unusual one... No, sorry, never seen it before," he babbled, voice rising to a squeak by the end. He really was a quite appalling liar, but that never seemed to stop him trying it on.

Time to play bad cop. Pierce leaned forward, putting some steel in her glare. "Come on, Gary! I know this is your area. People are hurt!" She opted not to mention that some of them were dead. She didn't know what he might be scared of, but something had him spooked. "Sally Keane's in hospital because of this case!"

"What, Constable Sally?" His eyebrows furrowed in dismay. "Is she all right?" It was Sally they usually sent over to give him a talking to; she had more patience for him than the rest of the department.

"She'll live," Pierce said brusquely. "But it was a close thing, and she's not going to be the only victim if these people aren't stopped." She already wasn't. "If I find out you have information on this and you're keeping it concealed, there could be very nasty consequences."

Gary squirmed for a moment, then collapsed like a heap of blancmange. "You can't tell anyone that I told you," he said in a rush. "They'll come after me. I'll be assassinated. I'll be banned from the forums for life!" It was hard to tell which he considered the more dire fate.

"I'll credit you as an anonymous source," she promised.

He brightened at that, and leaned forward to speak in a conspiratorial whisper. "They're men in black," he said. "Government stooges. That rune is the symbol of a top secret government department. They do all these assassinations, made to look like it's just dog attacks. If you ever see those newspaper articles where people supposedly get killed by their own family pets? It's them."

She should have guessed it would be that kind of conspiracy theorist bollocks. But still, perhaps there was a small grain of truth beneath. Somebody somewhere had once had a reason to connect this rune to a government group.

Like the Counter Terror Action Team, for instance?

Pierce's thoughts were grim as she left Gary's house. It might be just the ravings of a few online conspiracy nutters, but it tied with what her instincts were telling her: Maitland was up to no good. Could he have sent the mastiff shifter to deal with some loose ends who knew too much?

Either way, it seemed clear that he and his team were willing to let innocents die if it helped them achieve their goals. They'd had the opportunity to arrest Sebastian before last night, but instead they'd left him free to keep plying his dark trade until the RCU raid had forced their hand. Had they hoped to study him and learn his secrets before they took the risk of moving in?

Or were they the ones who'd placed him at the farm in the first place?

Her blood was boiling as she drove away. She was sure Maitland was dirty in some way, but what was she supposed to do about it? Take it to the Superintendent? He'd already admitted Maitland's influence extended over his head. Pierce had no personal allies up there where the air was thin, and certainly not anyone who would take her word without proof.

Where and how the hell she could get that, Pierce couldn't begin to imagine.

She was driving without any real destination in mind when she heard her phone ring from the passenger seat. She parked down the nearest side street and picked it up to check the display. Tim. Her stomach flipped. Why would Tim be calling her instead of Deepan?

There could be any number of innocent explanations, but dire thoughts still circled through her mind. Something had happened to Sally. Something had happened to Deepan. Something had happened to *Tim*. "Tim?" she said as she picked up. "What's going on?"

A stomach-clenching pause before he spoke, voice low and hoarse. "DCI Pierce?"

She thought she'd trained him out of being so formal.

"What's wrong? Is Sally all right?"

Another pause. "Er, yeah, she's fine. We're all okay." But he was still speaking barely above a whisper. "But... I need to speak to you. There was a body found in Leeds, a female skinbinder. Chief Inspector... they think you had something to do with it."

Pierce tensed, but she kept her voice level. "Who's 'they'?" she asked, though she had a pretty good idea.

"Um, the Counter Terror Action Team. They took all our files. They said we were compromised. They're listening in on Sergeant Mistry's phone now to see if you make contact, but I managed to sneak off."

"Smart thinking," she said, but inside she couldn't help but wonder. The stilted, careful way that he was speaking, the overly formal terms of address—was it just nervousness at the situation?

Or was someone else listening in on the call?

He might be calling under duress, or simply have been persuaded it was the right thing to do. Tim hadn't been with the Unit long enough for her to expect the kind of loyalty she might from Deepan or Sally. She couldn't blame him for taking orders from people who outranked his superiors.

But if this was a trap, she might be able to spring it to her own advantage. She needed proof beyond doubt Maitland was playing dirty; this might well be her best chance to get it.

All she had to do was make sure that she said all the right lines. "Listen, I had nothing to do with that girl's death," she said. "Someone's trying to fit me up, and I'm pretty sure I know who and why. Are they watching my house as well as the station?"

"They're watching all our homes—but I know where we can meet."

Bingo. Pierce smiled grimly to herself. "Tell me."

There might be an ambush waiting there when she arrived... but it wasn't going to take her unawares.

CHAPTER EIGHT

THE ADDRESS THAT Tim gave her was for an industrial estate, sure to be safely devoid of witnesses after the close of business. It was still just faintly possible the meeting was for real and not a trap, but Pierce wasn't prepared to bet her life on it. After Tim hung up, she considered her options.

Contacting Deepan was out, and the same went for pretty much everybody at the station. There was no way to know who Maitland might be watching. Sally was out of the office, but in no condition to help—if anything, she might well be in danger herself. She'd seen the human skins in the barn, and if that mastiff shifter had been sent to deal with witnesses who knew too much...

She cursed. Sally was a sitting duck at the hospital, and Mike wouldn't be much help. There were a thousand and one ways to arrange for her to suffer a tragic accident, or even a death that looked like natural causes. Pierce wondered now if Henderson had truly died of his wounds, or if someone had taken advantage of his condition to get rid of somebody who'd seen the skinbinder's face. She still hadn't had a chance to speak to Leo.

Maybe she should do that now.

This time she was in luck, and he was there to pick up the phone after only a couple of rings. "Grey."

"Leo, it's Claire Pierce," she said. "Are you free to talk?"

She heard a rustle of papers over the phone. "Yeah, I'm in the office. Go."

First things first. "Sorry to hear your man didn't make it. He was a good officer. Saved all our backsides in there."

A brief pause that she knew was all she would get in the way of a show of emotion. "Appreciate the words," he said, voice as gruff as ever. "Especially since I hear that you've got plenty on your plate. Something going down at your headquarters?"

"Something that stinks to high heaven. Our friend Maitland who took over at the farm might not be what he seems. Turns out that skinbinder we're after has learned some nasty tricks, and Counter Terrorism are willing to do whatever it takes to make sure news doesn't get out. The skinbinder might even be one of theirs."

"Huh," he said, after a brief pause. "Well, that's only the second wildest tale I've heard today, but to be fair, the other one did involve you being wanted for murder."

"I've had a busy day. And it's not over yet. Listen, I need a favour. Can you send someone you trust to keep a watch on Sally? I can't risk showing my face at the hospital again, but it's possible that she could be in danger."

"Where are you going?"

Paranoia held her tongue. She knew Leo would never work with someone willing to sacrifice his people's lives, but that didn't mean that she could trust that his phone wasn't bugged.

"Private meeting. If you need me, ask my team where to start looking." It was as much of a clue as she dared give.

A pretty thin excuse for a safety net, but it beat being wholly alone. She checked the time on her phone after hanging up. Early yet for heading to her meeting with Tim, but if she could scope out the lie of the land before trouble caught up, all the better.

Post-rush hour traffic clogged the roads on her drive back from Leeds, but as she turned off towards the industrial estate she shed most of the company. Isolated cars swished past as she drove down back streets lined with metal fences and near-empty car parks. The buildings were ugly square blocks with small, dim, grubby windows, no sign of anybody still inside. She passed an overgrown, abandoned stretch, strewn with plastic bags and piled with dumped tyres.

It would be an equally good place to dump a body.

Maybe it hadn't been the smartest move in the world to come out here alone, but she was nothing if not stubborn. She took a left onto the industrial estate, passing under a raised barrier and into a cul-de-sac lined with shuttered units. Tim had given her the number of a unit where they could meet; how he'd managed to get access to the place, he hadn't said.

More points towards this being an ambush. But then,

she'd still turned up to meet him anyway, so maybe they weren't as stupid as all that.

The potential need to make a quick escape outweighed her desire for stealth, and she parked directly in front of the unit. No sign of Tim's car, but there was a white van parked nearby with a nondescript logo for a company called Solomon Solutions. Could be legit, could be Maitland's people. There was no way to know.

Pierce checked her watch. Six-thirteen—earlier than they'd agreed.

But was she the first one to arrive?

She left the car unlocked when she got out, and kept the keys clutched in her hand. Both the ticket to her quick getaway and a makeshift weapon; she closed her fist around the key fob, leaving the keys sticking out between her fingers. That old classic of self-defence, not much use against someone well-trained and maybe armed, but enough to buy her time to get away.

The door beside the closed shutter had a padlock, but a closer look showed it had been left unlocked. Rather than let herself in, she lifted the letterbox to steal a peek through. It gave a rusty creak, betraying her arrival, and all that she could see was blackness beyond.

"DCI Pierce?" a faint voice said from within. Recognisably Tim, even with the raspy whisper.

Didn't mean it couldn't be an ambush, but hopefully a sign it wouldn't be a fatal one. Two RCU members killed on the same night would draw more attention than she thought Maitland wanted.

Keys still readied, but tucked inside her pocket, Pierce

turned the door handle with her left hand. She opened it only halfway, keeping the door between her body and potential attack. "Tim?" she said warily.

"It's just me," he said, though he still spoke in a low voice. He stepped out from the shadows into the dim light spilling in through the door.

He looked terrible, years older than the baby-faced twenty-something she'd left behind at the station just that morning. His face was grey and waxy, and behind the glasses his pale eyes were glazed. Even his hair looked limp, lacking its usual sculpted spikes. Christ, he looked worse than *Sally*, and she'd just had her throat slit.

"Jesus, kid, what did they do to you?" she said, stepping inside.

"I'm all right," he said tonelessly, but she couldn't quite believe it. Not looking like that; not with his face so slack and lacking any of its usual animation. She glanced around, wondering if they were under observation, but the empty unit had been stripped of any fittings that might provide concealment. For now, at least, the two of them were alone.

All the same, Tim moved to close the door, shutting them in together. Pierce shifted her grip on the keys to flick the penlight on instead, the narrow beam providing only just enough illumination to pick out Tim's face.

In the dark, the echoing space abruptly seemed close and confining. A musty smell like something rotting battled it out with the stink of Tim's deodorant. It wasn't like him to take a bath in the stuff; he was clearly nervous about something.

Pierce shone the penlight on him. "Why bring me here?" she asked. "What's so important that you couldn't say it over the phone?" He didn't say a word, just stepped closer. "Tim?" She couldn't read his face, bleached even paler in the harshness of the torchlight. His eyes were blank.

A second later, he was swinging for her head.

No flicker of expression telegraphed the action; the first thing she knew about it was the fist that cracked her across the jaw. She reeled backwards, stunned not just by the impact, but by the source of the attack.

"Tim, what—?" There was no time to gasp the question as a gut punch smashed her breath away. "Jesus—" She barely blocked the next blow with her elbow as she flinched back.

She raised the penlight, trying to get a good look at his face. Completely blank, no sign of murderous rage, panic, or any hint of regret. He was relentless, coming after her in total silence.

It made no sense. Tim wouldn't just *attack* like this, even if he thought she was a killer. He had police training, he was a sweet kid—she would have sworn there wasn't a violent bone in his body.

The fist that flashed towards her head called her a liar. Pierce ducked away from him, retreating, moving further away from the door. It might have been smarter to try to get past him and make a break for her car, but she couldn't leave without finding out why. Was Tim being pressured into this—bribed, threatened, blackmailed? She swallowed the urge to demand he explain himself again. She needed all her breath just to keep dodging.

It was hard to pinpoint Tim in the dark unit. All she heard were soft rustles and her own breathing. She flicked the penlight about, the beam lighting up damp-stained walls, support pillars, the murky shadows.

A faint sound. She spun, just in time to catch him with the beam as he lunged and wrapped his hands around her throat. "Shit!" The word became a wheeze as he dug in with his thumbs. When did Tim get so damn *strong*? Pierce slammed the heel of her hand into his stomach, but it felt like she'd hit a wall of pure muscle. He might look like a gawky kid, but he had reach and youth on her, and she didn't have the strength to force him off.

"This isn't you, Tim," she squeezed out around the crushing pressure.

He gave a guttural laugh. "Oh, you have no *idea*, you stupid old bitch," he said, and now there was nothing in his voice of the Tim she knew at all.

It made it easier to thread the keys between her fingers and slash at his face.

She couldn't miss at this range, with his hands wrapped around her throat, but her strike cut even deeper than she'd aimed. The key's serrated edge tore through his cheek, and he let her go as he reeled back, clutching his face and swearing. The penlight hanging from the keys swung wildly, picking out parts of the room in confusing splashes of light.

Pierce kicked at Tim, but missed him in the darkness, throwing herself off-balance. He shoved her and she went sprawling across the concrete floor, the handcuffs at her belt digging into her side.

Her cuffs. She fought to tug them out as she scrambled back to her feet, belatedly remembering police training. Tim kicked out at her midsection as she fumbled with them, almost knocking her right back to the floor. She wheezed, muscles protesting as she rose and staggered back. She was too old and tired to take much more of this.

She raised the penlight as Tim came towards her. A flap of skin was peeling down from his cheek where she'd slashed it, but in the weak torchlight she couldn't see any blood. A pained rictus distorted his face as he stumbled after her, movements clumsy even though she could swear that she'd barely touched him.

Pierce shone the light straight into his eyes, reflecting off his glasses, and he raised his arm to shield them with a snarl. In the moment he was blinded, she punched out with the cuffs held looped around her fist like knuckle dusters. It jarred her hand, but Tim fell backwards, clutching his nose with a howl. Before he had any chance to recover from the blow, she lunged forward, snapping the silver cuff tightly around his left wrist.

"Right!" she barked, yanking on the cuffs and shining the light in his eyes. "Enough pissing around! What the *hell* is going on, Tim?"

But the face that she lit up wasn't Tim Cable's at all.

CHAPTER NINE

PIERCE RECOILED IN shock at the sight of her prisoner. Dead skin was peeling away from his face in ragged strips, as if he was about to slough it all off like a snakeskin. Her first thought was another suicide rune, her captive withering before her eyes.

But beneath the peeling outer layer of skin was a whole, unblemished face—a face that wasn't Tim's. A flatter nose, dark-stubbled cheeks, a blunter chin... It was as if Tim's features were a latex mask, pulled on to cover a different face and now disintegrating.

Only it wasn't latex. Not latex at all. Her stomach lurched, and she gagged in horror as she realised what she was seeing.

"*Tim.*" Tears sprang to her eyes, and she turned her head away, half-sure that she would vomit. "Oh, my God, *Tim.*"

Such a sweet kid, an overeager puppy of a constable who hardly seemed old enough to be part of the police force... and now the man who stood before her wore his decomposing remains like some sick parody of a Hallowe'en costume. The real Tim had been murdered, skinned, callously slaughtered just to provide a temporary disguise.

Monsters. Call it skinbinding, shapeshifting, magecraft; however you termed it, the fact remained that she was dealing with monsters.

The shapeshifter made the mistake of taking her grief-stricken shock as a chance to make a break for it. Pierce yanked on her end of the cuffs to pull him up short, not caring how much the metal dug into his skin.

"I wouldn't," she said hoarsely, finding determination despite the sobs catching in her throat. "Enchanted silver. They'll take your hand off before you get out of them— and believe me, I'd be glad to see you try."

"Bollocks," the man said. His voice was nothing like Tim's now, the cruel mimicry of the skin broken by the effect of the silver cuffs. "You're police, you can't do that kind of shit. I've got rights."

"Yeah?" Pierce slammed him back against a pillar. "Bad news, kid. The RCU has a lot more discretion when it comes to magical threats... and in case you didn't hear yet, your friend Maitland just put me on leave. Right now this is strictly personal." She yanked his arms around the pillar and cuffed him there, with his face hugged against the concrete. At least now she could step away and not have to be so close to the evidence of the horror of Tim's death.

"Maitland?" he said, struggling without success to turn

his head to face her as she stood behind him. "Who the fuck's that supposed to be?"

"You don't know Maitland? How about Sebastian? That name ring any bells?"

He clammed up, smugly silent, and she was forced to circle round the pillar to see his expression. She shivered with revulsion at the sight of the decomposing skin mask clinging to his face. The features had degraded to the point where she could barely recognise them—a mercy, until she started thinking of the implications. The skin must have been made with extreme haste. Just when had Tim been replaced? Earlier today? Last night? Her gorge rose as she realised that she couldn't even be sure if it was the real Tim she'd seen that morning.

She didn't let her mind linger on it, forced her eyes to look past the peeling skin to the prisoner beneath. If she let herself think of it as part of Tim, she would just lose it.

Playing interrogator was always a type of acting, and right now Pierce needed to sink into the role like never before. She gave her prisoner a cold smile and then moved around the pillar and clasped her hands around the loops of the cuffs. "Oi, what are you doing?" he said, struggling against her grip.

Instead of answering, she gripped the metal tighter, and muttered a low stream of guttural words. The silver already felt warm beneath her touch.

"What the fuck was that?" he demanded as she stepped back. "Hey! What did you just do?"

Pierce didn't answer, walking two slow circuits round

the pillar as he squirmed. "Feeling warm yet?" she asked in a conversational tone.

"What did you just *do*, you bitch?" he repeated, metal scraping against concrete as he pulled against the cuffs.

She kept pacing in circles, forcing him to try to twist his neck to follow her. "Just a little enchantment we have on the cuffs for awkward prisoners," she said. "Don't worry, it's harmless—as long as it's stopped in time." She smiled again. "Tell me if it starts to get too hot."

He spat obscenities.

Pierce kept walking, watching as his struggles against the cuffs grew more frantic. "Of course, we don't *really* understand how the spell works," she said. "Magic's funny like that. We know the cuffs will keep on getting hotter until someone deactivates them—but what if they don't?" She gave a theatrical shrug. "No one's ever toughed it out long enough to find out. It could be that the cuffs'll melt, or maybe they'll even get all the way up to cremation temperature... Hell, maybe the spell's got a built-in limit and it'll shut off before you lose your hands." She grinned. "Ready to risk it?"

"Fuck off," he said, but she could see the way that he was fidgeting. Those cuffs had to be pretty warm by now.

Well, naturally. They were silver, after all: guaranteed to cause a reaction with the enchantments on shapeshifting skins. And while a properly made pelt would insulate its wearer from the worst effects of silver burn, she'd seen what happened with the shoddier ones before. This one was disintegrating fast, and whatever protections it might have had to start with, they were failing now. The longer he wore those cuffs, the more the touch of the silver was going to burn.

There was no magical activation phrase to cause it, and it wasn't likely to get much worse than a sunburn or a bite of too-hot pizza—but the power of suggestion was an amazing thing.

"Take your time," Pierce said. "I've got all night. I'm sure that you can take a little pain. Of course, the nerve damage might be a bit tougher to deal with, but—"

"Look, just get these things off of me!"

She dropped the pleasant smile, deadly serious now. "Tell me who you're working for. Tell me where to find the skinbinder who supplied you with that skin. And tell me why you killed Tim Cable!" Her voice broke a little on the last demand.

Her prisoner grinned nastily. "Oh, was that his name?"

She yanked on the handcuffs, pulling him against the pillar with a thump.

"Listen, you moronic little shit," she said, leaning close. "You're dependent on my goodwill not to die a painful death, and let me tell you now, my feelings of love and joy towards all God's creations are not at their highest. You'd better *hope* you've got information worth deactivating those cuffs, because the price tag on that is going to keep rising higher with every moment you dick me around."

He gave a sulky grimace, and Christ, she could have killed him then and there just for that look. Tim had *died* to give this little shit his chance to come after her, but it was clear that he was no fanatic ready to take his own life like the panther shifter—just a petty thug who pouted when things weren't going his way.

A couple more seconds of resentful squirming, and he cracked.

"Look, I didn't kill anybody," he said. "They just gave me the skin and told me to keep you out of the way. I don't *know* why they picked your mate! He was probably just there. They needed somebody police so you would listen to them."

'Probably just there.' Hell of an epitaph for a good man who'd died far too young and in the most horrible way. Had he been alive when the skinbinder had—No. Don't think about it.

"Who's 'they'?" she demanded.

"I don't know, do I?" he said with as much of a jerky shrug as he could manage. "Bunch of blokes from some company doing research into all that ritual shit. I didn't go round asking people's names. A mate of mine got me some work with them before—driving vans, unloading stuff after dark, that kind of shit. I didn't have anything to do with the magic side of it. That was all that freak Sebastian's job."

"The skinbinder." A private company, conducting their own research into binding human skins... then where did Maitland fit in? What about the government dog that had come after her?

"I don't know anything about that kind of shit," he repeated, and rattled the cuffs. "Look, can you get these things off of me?" he whined. "My hands are on fire!"

"Not yet, they're not," she said, without the smallest

pang of sympathy. "This company you were working for—what were they called?"

"I don't know!" he said. "Just one of those stupid business-speak names that doesn't mean anything. Sole... solutions? Something like that."

The van she'd seen parked outside. "Solomon Solutions?"

"Yeah, that's it. They've got a place just up the road." He jerked his head. "Look, that's seriously all I know, all right? Now get these fucking cuffs off me before—"

The door rattled. Pierce spun to look, shielding her eyes against the bright beams of the headlights that shone in from outside as it swung open.

She wasn't really surprised to see who stepped in.

"Maitland," she said grimly.

"DCI Pierce." He inclined his head. "Do I trust, now, that you finally believe the two of us are on the same side?"

Pierce still wasn't convinced he was on anyone's side but his own. She stayed silent as a number of men in dark clothes followed him in.

"We'll take custody of the prisoner from here," he said.

"And then what?" she demanded, standing her ground. "He'll just disappear? He's involved in the murder of one of my men!"

"An unfortunate incident that would never have happened if you'd done as you were asked—*ordered*, in fact—and avoided any further involvement in this case."

The cool statement was enough to gut her like a knife, laced with just enough plausibility to keep her up at night. Would Tim still be alive if she hadn't pursued this?

Pierce took a deep breath and then let it out. "Well, I'm involved now," she said. "So I guess it's a little bit late for regrets."

"Quite so," he said, and gave a tight-lipped smile. "You've certainly followed the trail with impressive persistence. But now that we've learned where our targets are based, I'm going to have to ask you to step aside and let my team work." He narrowed his eyes. "In fact, given your track record with following requests, I'm afraid I'm going to have to insist." He turned to address his men. "Remove the prisoner, and have her cuffed in his place. Standard cuffs—keep the silver ones on the shapeshifter."

"Hey, no way!" the shifter blurted, struggling in vain against Maitland's men as they pulled him away from the pillar. "I want these fucking things off me!"

Maitland ignored him, turning back to Pierce. "If you please," he said, inclining his head towards the pillar. She knew the seemingly polite request would soon change tenor if she disobeyed. With a glower, she wrapped her arms around the pillar and allowed herself to be cuffed in place.

"Take her car keys. And her phone," he directed his men. She tensed as brusque, impersonal hands pattered her over, removing the offending items from her pockets.

"You'll be released when the skinbinder is secured," Maitland told her. "Until then, I'm afraid, it's just too much of a risk to let you run free." He dipped his head, though he didn't look the least bit sorry. "My apologies, but you brought this on yourself."

Pierce scowled, but kept her mouth shut; there was

nothing she could say that would make him change his mind, and plenty that would get her in worse trouble.

The captive shapeshifter protested as he was hauled towards the door. "Hey, wait, that bitch is the only one who can get these fucking cuffs off! I've got second degree burns here. This is police brutality! I'll sue!"

Maitland turned to her and raised a sceptical eyebrow. "Just how much danger is he in from wearing those?" he asked.

"Might get a skin rash," she said, with as much of a shrug as she could make while handcuffed to the pillar. "Maybe some minor blisters. It's just silver burn—so far as we know, it's completely harmless."

The shapeshifter's furious explosion of swearing as he was dragged away provided a small spot of consolation in what was otherwise a deeply shitty day.

CHAPTER TEN

BEING CUFFED TO a concrete pillar hadn't started out much fun, and it only got less comfortable with time. It was cold inside the unit, and almost pitch black, only the crack of light creeping under the door breaking the illusion of an airtight space. The scent of rot she'd noticed earlier was fainter but still there, and her stomach rolled as she realised it must be the smell of the decaying skin.

Tim's skin. Now that she was alone in the dark with nothing to do except wait, it was impossible to maintain the professional detachment she'd held onto until now.

Christ. Tim, dead. Tim, who they'd teased for being the baby of the office, who'd still carried his spare clothes into work in the battered old backpack that he'd worn to school. Tim, who bought stupid fancy coffee because he didn't like tea—who'd ever heard of a copper who didn't like tea?—and fixed the computers for the rest of the office when the updates clogged the system.

That goofy kid, who hadn't even been born when she

first joined the police force, dead and skinned to make some idiot a useless disguise. Pierce tried to rub her eyes with her arm, aware that Maitland's men might come back in at any moment, but in the dark the tears leaked nonetheless.

The minutes ticked past. There was no way to tell how long it had been; she couldn't move her arms round far enough to look at her watch, and the unchanging darkness gave her no clue. She was able to slide the cuffs far enough down the pillar to sit on the floor, but it was far from comfortable, and the cold concrete only made her more aware of all her aches and bruises.

Was anyone still outside, or had they left her here to rot? Only pride stifled the impulse to thump and shout and demand an answer. Maitland had to come back for her sooner or later. If he wanted her dead, he'd have had her killed directly, not left her to a slow death in a place where she could easily be found.

Of course, that assumed he and his men hadn't all been killed by the skinbinder. Pierce counted seconds, making bargains with herself. She could wait a few more minutes before shouting for help. She could wait another couple after that...

An unknown eternity passed before she heard the sound of a car engine approaching. She pushed herself up from the floor, stiff muscles aching in protest. Her heart beat fast. Were they coming to let her out... or to dispose of her now she was no longer needed? In handcuffs, there was nothing she could do to fight back. She took a slow, deep breath, determined not to let her trepidation show.

The door creaked open, and a dazzling torch beam lit the space. She flinched despite herself, her eyes streaming in the sudden brightness. She squinted uselessly, unable to even raise an arm to shield them.

"Claire?" The low whisper of her first name made her jolt in surprise. Not many people used it—she was always 'Guv' to her team, 'DCI Pierce' to most others; only a few longstanding colleagues were on first name terms.

And she recognised that gruff voice even at a muted whisper. "Leo?" she said in disbelief, trying to blink her eyes clear.

"It's me," he said, stepping forward to play the torch beam over the pillar she was chained to. "Are those your handcuffs?" he asked, raising his eyebrows.

"Do they look like silver to you?" she shot back, before paranoia reminded her he might have good reason to care. She tensed. "Prove that you're really Leo Grey."

"What?" The way that his brow crinkled almost seemed like confirmation; an impostor would know why she was so wary. But that was wishful thinking—she needed proof.

And that bastard Maitland had taken the silver cuffs she could have used to test him.

But maybe that wasn't the only silver around. "Got your silver bullets with you?" she asked.

"I brought my Glock and the rest of the silver-points," he said with a curt nod. "And I'd damn well better get your signature on the paperwork to say you authorised it, because I'm taking your word that the chain of command is compromised."

"Could be far more compromised than I was guessing,"

she said. God, if they'd got to Tim, who else? "Get one of the bullets out and show it to me."

Leo shook his head, more in bemusement than refusal. "This isn't the best way to convince me that you're not losing it," he warned, but he stepped back and turned away to draw his gun, releasing the magazine with a click. He pushed the topmost round out from the stack, holding it up between his thumb and finger. Even in the half-light, she could recognise the anti-shapeshifter rounds they used, customised hollow-points with cast silver tips. "Satisfied?" he said.

It was only a small amount of silver, but he held it with bare fingers, showing no sign of discomfort. And besides, he sounded a hell of a lot more like Leo than the shifter had been able to impersonate Tim. Pierce let out her breath in a rush and sagged against the pillar.

"All right. I'll believe you're you. Now please just tell me you've got a cuff key with you."

He reholstered the gun and drew his key to let her out. Her arms felt numb and heavy now that they were finally released from the restraints.

"Okay. You want to tell me what that was about?" he asked as she stretched stiffly, massaging her wrists.

"Short version? Shapeshifters in human skins."

Leo frowned. "Thought that was impossible?"

"That's what we thought, but it looks like we're behind the times. I saw it with my own eyes." Despite her best efforts the repressed tears leaked into her voice. "They killed Tim."

It took him a moment. "Your Tim? Cable?"

Pierce nodded, and drew a slow steadying breath. She could fall apart when she got home; right now there was work to do.

"They made a skin of him and used it like a puppet," she said, her fury boiling up as she spoke the obscenity out loud. It gave her a fresh surge of strength and determination after the depression of the dark. "It was falling apart by the time I saw it, but maybe they were just rushed for time. We have to assume they can make skins that allow for a perfect impersonation."

"That's not good," he said, and she barely smothered a painful snort of laughter at the understatement.

"No, it's not. Maitland and his gang went to apprehend the skinbinder, but I don't trust them as far as I can throw them. I don't even know if they've managed to find him. They were supposed to be coming back for me, and that was—" She checked her watch and shook her head, uncertain. "A while back." She focused on Leo, wondering for the first time how he'd even known to look for her here. "How did you find me?"

"You told me I should ask your team," he reminded her. "I called Sympathetic Magic, had them put a trace on you." He cocked his head in response to her look. "That not what you meant?"

"Smarter than what I meant. We might still have a chance to catch up to Maitland, if he hasn't just decided to leave me here for dead. Did you pass a place called Solomon Solutions on your way here?"

A quick search on Leo's phone revealed a suspicious lack of internet presence for any local company by that name. But she'd seen the logo on the van, which was at least proof that some kind of front existed.

The van was gone from outside the unit when they left; most likely it had belonged to the shapeshifter, and Maitland had taken it as a cover.

"Find that van, and we'll find the place we're looking for," she said to Leo. "The shapeshifter said it was close, and I doubt he cared enough to bother lying. We'll just have to scout around until we see it." She eyed the lurid markings of the Armed Response Vehicle that Leo had arrived in and sighed, mourning her confiscated car keys. "On foot," she added wearily. Best not to go flying full police colours until they knew just what they would be facing.

Leo went over to exchange a few words with the officer in the driver's seat of the ARV. Without something immediate to focus on, Pierce felt weariness slump over her like a heavy coat. The day had been far too long, especially coming on the heels of a late night raid.

And it wasn't over yet. As Leo returned from the car, Pierce straightened up, trying to will herself back to alertness. Right now she would have welcomed the North Yorkshire Police's awful coffee—she'd have welcomed dishwater, if it had added caffeine.

"Baker's going to wait here with the car until we call for him," Leo said, though he didn't look all that happy about it. He shook his head. "If Henderson was here, he wouldn't be letting me do this. Nobody in Firearms should be running around playing cowboy without authorisation—and don't tell me I've got yours; it's not worth the paper it's printed on right now."

But Pierce wasn't the only one who'd lost a colleague to this skinbinder and his allies. "If Henderson was here, you wouldn't need to," she said, holding his gaze. "These people are killers, and they *will* kill again. And I don't trust that Maitland cares nearly enough about stopping them from doing it, just as long as he gets what he wants."

He grunted. "That's why I'm coming with you. But I'm not going in shooting without a damn good reason, and if this goes bad, I'm calling for backup."

"Agreed," she said without hesitation.

They started away from the cars and out onto the main street. Pierce stretched her arms, still sore from where she'd been pinned in place around the pillar. She'd kept the cuffs as a replacement for her own: not silver, but still strong enough to restrain a normal human being. Maitland would be a favourite.

"You eaten?" Leo asked her as they walked.

"In one of my past lives, maybe." Her stomach growled.

"Figured. I stole Baker's midnight snacks for you." He offered her a chocolate bar from one of the pockets of his vest.

"Marry me," she said, diving in before she'd even fully opened up the wrapper.

"I think my wife would object," he said, without cracking a smile.

"Well, that's just picky."

The brief boost to her mood from welcome sugar and good humour gave her the energy to keep on walking. The road was deserted, the widely spaced streetlights casting diffuse pools of light that were just enough to give shape to the darkness. A slice of moon showed through the heavy clouds cloaking the sky.

Just past full moon; still a powerful time of the month for lunar rituals. The skinbinder's backers wouldn't want him to miss out on a night's work, and she wasn't sure that Maitland would make too much effort to stop it either. He'd kept a hands-off approach back at the farm, apparently content to watch and learn. Who knew how many murders he might have turned a blind eye to before Pierce had thrown a spanner in the works?

If she had her way, she would throw some more before the night was over.

The businesses they passed were all in darkness, and she had to squint to make out the names on the signs; her penlight was gone with the confiscated car keys, and they didn't want to court too much attention with the bright beam of Leo's police torch. There were fewer vehicles remaining in the private car parks, and she saw no sign of the Solomon van. For all they knew, their quarry was long gone.

"Which way?" Leo asked softly as they reached the end of the road.

Buildings were clustered to their left; more promising than the trees she could see off to the right. She nodded that way. As they rounded the corner, the sound of a car approaching from behind made her tense up. No place to hide; she could only try to move to block the driver's view of Leo in his police gear.

Bright headlights swept over them... and moved on

without pausing. Just an innocent passer-by driving down the road. Pierce breathed out.

They followed the rusty fence along. On the opposite side, an access road disappeared around the back of an old yellow brick building. She looked at Leo. "Let's check it out."

The access road lacked street lamps, and the glow of the light behind them diminished as they walked along. Partway down the road metal gates should have barred the way, but despite the late hour they stood open. A security light flashed on as they approached, and Pierce froze in the glare. An angled CCTV camera peered down like a curious robot, but closer inspection showed that it was only the casing, the camera removed from the inside.

Tension coiled in her stomach. This had to be the place.

"Camera thief in this area, apparently," she said. She cocked her head at Leo. "We should probably pop in and check that nobody's in danger, don't you think?"

He grunted in response, his posture shifting subtly into something more alert, more dangerous. He was too much of a pro to draw his gun without good reason, but she sensed the mental switch from a policeman on patrol to a Firearms Officer ready to go in.

She let him take the lead as they continued up the hill. They were hemmed in by a steep bank on the left, a line of metal fencing on the right. It made her think of animals being herded towards slaughter pens. Loose gravel on the rough road surface crunched under their feet.

The light clicked off behind them, plunging them into darkness. She didn't argue as Leo pulled out his torch and switched it on. The element of surprise might have been helpful, but only if it wasn't turned on them. They didn't know who or what might be waiting in ambush.

They crept along the road. No signs of life so far, a fact that only made her nervous. If this was the place, then there should be the chaos of a raid in progress, or else they should have found the scene sealed off against intruders. This dark, stifling silence wasn't right.

The road curved round a corner towards a large brick warehouse. There were vehicles parked up on the verge to the right. Two black vans, and in front of them another with the Solomon logo. Maitland's team?

There were no engines running and no lights on. Had they abandoned the vehicles? She motioned to Leo, and he shone his torch into the window of the nearest.

Empty. They moved on to the next one. Also empty. An odd move to leave their transport unattended. Had the team been overstretched, called the drivers in for back up when they ran into resistance?

Leo went to check the Solomon Solutions van, then paused, shining his torch beam on the back end of the vehicle. "Door's not shut," he said. The windowless white rear doors were a fraction out of flush, the left allowed to fall back into place instead of slammed shut.

Pierce glanced at him. He gave her a nod and drew his pistol, taking up a position to the right of the doors. She stood to the left, out of the line of fire, and rapped on the door. "Police! Identify yourself and come out of the vehicle with your hands up."

No response.

"I am armed and prepared to fire if you make a hostile move," Leo said loudly. "If you cannot speak for some reason, then make a noise to let us know you're in there."

Still nothing. Could be empty—could be trouble. Her chest was tight as she took hold of the door handle. She waited for Leo's acknowledging look, then mouthed a countdown to him. *Three. Two. One...* She yanked the door open and leapt out of the way.

Something dark flopped down from inside of the van. She flinched, anticipating the sharp bark of the Glock, but Leo didn't share her trigger-happy instincts. He let out a slow breath and reholstered the gun as she registered just what had fallen out.

A dangling arm, attached to the body that lay slumped on the floor of the van.

Emphasis on the word 'body.' Judging by the bloody wounds that had made rags of the man's clothes, checking for a pulse would be a waste of time.

Pierce climbed inside the van to do it anyway. The only heartbeat to be found was hers, thumping hard enough in her chest she'd swear it echoed in the closed space. She turned to look at Leo, shaking her head. "Dead." Probably one of Maitland's men. He was dressed all in black, outfitted for a stealth infiltration.

Clearly hadn't been stealthy enough.

Leo reached for the radio on his vest. "Okay, this is the point where we stop doing things off the record," he said. "I'm going to call Baker to bring the car up, and—" He broke off, aware that she'd stopped listening. "Claire?"

Her eyes were on the shadowy shape of the black van

behind them; a shape that had suddenly grown deformed as *something* huge and grotesquely misshapen rose from the roof.

"Leo, look out!" she shouted as it sprang.

CHAPTER ELEVEN

LEO BARELY HAD time to turn before the monstrous beast slammed into him. The impact knocked him backwards into the van, and he sprawled across the corpse. Pierce grabbed his ballistic vest to drag him along with her as she retreated towards the van's front seats. The torch clipped to his vest bounced all around, light flickering across the nightmare creature crouched outside.

The pieces the light revealed looked like nothing that should be part of a whole. A bulky, bear-like body, feline paws, vicious curved horns... no creature that had ever walked the Earth had looked like this. Pierce would have sworn out loud if she'd had any breath to do it.

A chimaera pelt. They were the stuff of legend; the one supposed real-life example that she'd seen was a threadbare museum piece most people thought was a hoax. There might be stories of skinbinders with the skill to stitch multiple animal skins into single working pelt, but no reputable source could claim they'd ever seen it done.

Well, if she got out of this alive and with a sliver of her reputation intact, that had changed.

Leo gave a sharp grunt of pain as the thing's claws raked his leg, and she cursed as she hauled him frantically backwards. He wasn't a big man—she doubted he outweighed her—but that didn't make him easier to move. There was no space in the van with the corpse slumped on the floor and the beast swiping at them through the doors like a cat with a cornered mouse.

Her elbow hit the headrest of the passenger seat. "Shit!" She turned to squeeze between the seats. "Leo, come on!" she said. They were sitting ducks inside the van. "We've got to get out of here!" He struggled to rise, and she grabbed his arm to pull him after her.

The whole vehicle lurched, tipping backwards as the chimaera set a paw on the bumper to try and crawl in after them. Its snorting, wheezing breaths filled the inside. Pierce clambered between the seats and dropped into the driver's seat, bashing her knee on the steering wheel as she hauled her legs up after. She cursed as she felt around in the dark for the door release.

Leo's hand groped her shoulder as he fought to keep from falling backwards. There was no chance for him to go for his gun, and firing it inside the metal cage of the vehicle would only put them in more danger. They had to get out of the van.

As the vehicle rocked, Pierce finally managed to grab the handle and throw the door open. Gravity tried to slam it shut in her face, but she shoved her way out and dropped down outside, narrowly escaping being crushed against the fence as the van wheels bounced down after her.

"Leo, come on!" She shoved a hand back through the closing door to help him. He let out a gasping curse as he shouldered his way out, his left leg dragging behind him, maybe clawed up, maybe broken.

There was no time to treat the injury gently. She hauled him with her through the tight space between the vans and the fence. Yet more rusty metal fencing, like the bars at some long-neglected zoo—except the prize exhibit was loose, and they were the ones trapped in the enclosure.

As they ran towards the dark cluster of brick buildings ahead, Pierce stumbled over something soft and yielding. She cursed in startled disgust as she realised that it was another body. Too little light and time to register the cause of death, or even confirm that the man was dead. If any of Maitland's team had survived the chimaera's attack, she was in no position to help them right now.

Just keeping her and Leo alive seemed like a lot to ask. Behind them, the chimaera pulled free of the van with a groan of stressed metal. It gave a strangled, howling roar that didn't sound like any natural creature Pierce had ever heard. Christ knew what kind of jumbled mess of internal organs might exist under that patchwork pelt. It was amazing that the thing was even capable of moving.

And yet it didn't seem to have any trouble persuading its disparate parts to focus on its objective. *Kill.* It scrambled after them at an alarming speed, despite its mismatched limbs.

Beside her, Leo let out ragged gasps with every limping

step, but he still fumbled to draw his gun and aim. "Take the torch!" he yelled to her. "I need a clear shot!"

"What, and you think I can help?" At the rate they and the beast were running, she'd be lucky to even find it with the torch beam, let alone hold a steady light on the thing. All the same, she reached for the torch on his vest and struggled to unclip it, turning their already staggering run into a three-legged race. As they reached the corner of the buildings she finally wrenched it free, and turned about to shine it on the beast.

It was barely the length of a lorry away, and crossing the distance fast. In the glow of the torch she glimpsed the thing's eyes, shockingly human amid alien features that blended bear and lion with the curved horns of an ox. The bark of the gun from beside her made her jump. It was followed by a second gunshot, then a third. She flinched, expecting more, but Leo yanked on her arm instead.

"Come on!" he bellowed, the words only half-heard through the ringing echoes in her ears. "Got to get behind cover!"

"Did you get it?" she shouted, and looked back to check for herself. The thing was lurching along now, halfway dragging itself, but it wasn't down, and it hadn't reverted to human. Chimaera skin, shit—it must have more runes, too many layered enchantments for one silver bullet, or even several, to destroy. What would it take to bring it down?

They rounded the edge of the building, hustling as fast as Leo's injured leg would take him. He was stumbling now, relying on the wall and her shoving him from behind to keep him upright as pain began to drown out the panic boost of adrenaline.

Pierce wasn't sure how much more running she could take herself. She was battered, exhausted, and far too old for this. Her breath was rasping in her chest like sandpaper.

She stole another look over her shoulder. Wounded or not, the chimaera still chased. Its back end dragged, no longer fully under its command, but a human mind was still calling the shots; they couldn't rely on it being scared off or convinced to slink away and lick its wounds. It might not be moving too well, but then neither were they, and those jaws and claws and vicious-looking horns could more than compensate if it caught up.

She turned back, and the torch beam swung across a steel door a short distance ahead of her. "Leo!" The door had a security keypad, but it looked as if it had been left ajar. The work of Maitland's people, or maybe left that way in a hasty evacuation.

Deserted or not, the building was their only hope now. She ran ahead of Leo and shoved the door open. Inside, stark fluorescent strip lights lit empty corridors with the institutional look of an old-fashioned school or office.

Not quite empty. A body lay collapsed on the floor in a doorway ahead of them, one slack hand outstretched as if someone had unfurled the fingers to take something from them. Pierce ran forward, crouching over the man to take a pulse, but the glazed eyes and blood-stained mess of his shirt told the story before her fingers could confirm it.

Behind her, Leo leaned against the wall just inside the door, clutching his thigh as he shouted directions into his radio. "Get every Firearms unit in the region that's available. Silver-point rounds if they've got them. Contact Sergeant Mistry at the RCU—get Oxford RCU on the line as well. We might need them to consult. We have no idea how big this—"

The metal door slammed open, crushing him back against the wall as the chimaera burst in. It was almost too big to make it through the door, the doorframe splintering around it as it forced its way through.

"Leo!" Pierce yelled as she heard him cry out in pain. He sagged to the ground as the heavy door rebounded, falling back against the wall. The chimaera snarled and turned on him, clumsily dragging its back legs behind it. She could see that the bearskin that made up the back half of the pelt was splitting, coming apart where Leo's bullet had taken it in the flank. A bloody mess of flesh and muscle oozed out from between the fraying joins.

The beast was wounded, maybe dying—but not nearly fast enough.

"Leo!" she yelled again, unable to see past the bulk of the thing to tell if he was moving. Was he still conscious? Still alive? She cast around for something, anything, that might work as a weapon, but what could even hurt a shapeshifter that big? She didn't have her silver cuffs or malodorant spray, not even something heavy she could throw. She yanked the corpse beside her closer, searching for a gun or knife.

No weapons. She cursed in desperation.

Pinned in the corner, Leo shifted weakly, trying to rise. The barrier of the door gave him a little protection, but the beast was fishing behind it with its feline front paws. He gasped in pain, and it let out a strangled snorting snarl.

Pierce ran forward, not sure what she could do to help, but determined to try. She lunged to grab the creature's stubby bear's tail, yanking back on it with all her strength. No sound of pain from the beast; this part of the pelt was dead, and it felt like dragging on a heavy fur coat. Stitches tore, the seams never meant to take the strain of joining lifeless fur to animated flesh. Shapeless entrails and tangled, twitching muscles spilled out from the rips, caught in some twisted state halfway between man and beast.

Pierce doubted that she'd hurt it—how would it even recognise a pain signal in that state?—but she'd sure as hell succeeded in getting its attention. The chimaera roared and tried to turn in the tight space, hampered by its unresponsive back legs. She ducked away from the thing's horns; they should look ludicrous on a crossbreed of bear and lion, but the points were too damn lethal to appreciate the joke. Even a sidelong blow could crack her head open.

She was too busy watching the horns to pay attention to the claws. The paw that whipped out to rake her hit with enough force to slap her across the hallway as it sliced her arm open.

"Shit!" She clutched the wound. Not deep, or if it was, the shock was still too fresh to feel it, but the pain was sharp enough to leave her stunned and gasping for breath. She staggered back, leaning against the wall.

No time to rest. Another deadly paw slashed out towards her. She ducked, but not in time to avoid a cuff to the head. Her skull, already ringing with echoes of the gunshots, felt like it was about to break apart. She pressed a hand to her head, struggling to think, unable to plan anything more than a blind retreat. She scrambled back—and tripped over the body in her path.

She caught herself, but her sliced arm buckled beneath her. She hit the ground with a grunt, no breath left for witty last words or even to swear. The chimaera reared over her, its fanged jaws opened wide—

A shot rang out, followed in quick succession by three more. The thing's head jerked backwards, and it toppled like a felled tree. Pierce rolled out of the way just in time as it hit the ground like a sack full of entrails. Inside the loose wrapping of the pelt, the shifter's innards had disintegrated into a shapeless, twisted mass of disconnected organs, meat and bones. There was no way to tell if it was human, animal, or both.

Pierce gave the thing a sharp prod with her shoe as she got up, but it was obvious that it was going nowhere until someone scraped the mess up with a shovel.

That jumble of unidentifiable body parts must have been a human being once. Could the shifter have survived the transformation back if the chimaera pelt hadn't been damaged? No way to know. Messing with untested rituals was never risk free.

Right now she had no pity to spare for the killer who'd worn the chimaera skin. She skirted round the ruins of the corpse and ran across to Leo.

He'd set the gun down on the tiles by his side, the effort of reholstering it obviously too much. His eyes were closed, and his head had fallen back to rest against the bricks. Only his laboured breathing confirmed he was still in there.

Pierce leaned over him uncertainly. "Leo, you all right?" she asked. A bloody stupid question. His slumped position concealed broken bones at least. There was no way that it would be safe to move him.

"Great," he rasped, opening his eyes to narrow slits. "Mind if I... rest here for a while?"

"Long as you're not planning on resting in peace." There were too many people dead already, thanks to this case.

Pierce scrutinised him with concern. She didn't want to leave him, but the building wasn't secured, and there was still a chance the skinbinder was here. "Backup's on its way?" she asked.

Leo made an attempt at a nod that ended with a gasp and grimace. Broken ribs, more than likely. *Fuck.* Not much she could do about it here and now. He licked his lips and took a long, painful pause before he spoke. "Baker's... on his way here," he said with a wheeze, "and I told him to call for..."

"Okay." She cut him off, not wanting to force him through more strained words. "You've got your radio. Just... try to hold it together until help gets here." She patted his arm very lightly, trying not to jar anything that hurt.

He raised his chin as she stood, clearly fighting to say something. He tipped his head towards the pistol by his side. "Still one... silver-point round. You should take it."

She balked, shaking her head. "Leo, I don't have your training," she reminded him. Never mind the regulations—and the *laws*—it would be breaking; they were far enough off the reservation by now that one more rule breach wouldn't make much difference.

Leo shifted his leg as if to push himself further upright before thinking better of it. He focused on her in a squint. "But you've had some?" he said, halfway between statement and question. "Nightstalker Initiative, right?"

"Christ, Leo, that was decades ago!" she said. But he was right; she'd been with the RCU back in the less regulated days when the team still had its own firearms in the office safe. Too many questionable shootings had seen regs tightened up before she'd even been issued a weapon, never mind had to use one in action—thank God—but she'd had the training nonetheless. Such as it was.

Back in those days, wasting expensive ammunition had been a much bigger concern than whether the trainees could hit the broad side of a barn. The old revolver that she'd learned to shoot with didn't much resemble Leo's modern semi-automatic, and her reflexes and eyesight sure as hell weren't the same as they'd been in her twenties. She knew enough not to take her own foot off, but that was about as much as could be said.

Besides, if there was another shifter around, she wasn't the one who was most defenceless right now. "You should keep it," she said.

Leo shook his head, a weak wobble from side to side. "I'm in no state to have a gun in my hand. Just... keep your finger outside the trigger guard unless you want somebody dead." He breathed out in a sigh and held her gaze. "Don't let them get away."

For Henderson's sake, and for Tim's, and for who knew how many other innocents. Pierce took a deep breath of her own and nodded slowly before bending down to take the gun. She hoped to hell she didn't have to use it—but one way or another, she had to bring Sebastian down tonight. Too many people had been hurt to let him walk free from his crimes.

"Stay safe," she said, and turned to go, hoping that this wouldn't be the last time she saw Leo alive.

CHAPTER TWELVE

THE SILENT HALLWAYS of the building were deserted, but signs of the recent struggle were everywhere. Pierce passed three more dead bodies, two of them members of Maitland's team, the third still dressed up in a bullet-riddled wolfskin. Apparently Maitland's people had brought their own supply of silver bullets.

No sound of distant shooting reached her ears; there was no sound at all, beyond the click of her shoes on the floor tiles. If backup was coming, it was still too far away for her to hear the sirens. Without her radio, she couldn't listen out for reassurance, or even check Leo was still alive.

She could have been entirely alone. Maybe she was. But the quiet only wound her nerves still tighter. She checked each doorway as she passed, the gun a deceptively light weight in her hands, almost as threatening as the brooding stillness around her. She had to fight her instincts every time not to let her finger slip towards the trigger, not to point the thing ahead of her with no idea yet what she might be facing.

She should never have agreed to take the thing; she wasn't trained for it, and she was almost more afraid of putting a hole through an innocent than she was of what might leap out from the shadows. Almost. Her hands sweated on the grip.

The rooms she passed looked like workrooms and labs: books, files and computers everywhere. A field day for the Arcane Documents team, assuming they had the chance to secure the site and seize all this as evidence. Through one door she glimpsed a large storage room, suspicious trophies bagged and tagged and organised on shelves. Pierce itched to get in there and catalogue the artefacts, but now wasn't the time.

As she turned the next corner, the faint murmur caught her ear. Even before she could make out the words, she recognised Maitland's calm voice. She should have known he would have found a way to sidestep the slaughter. But was he her ally or her enemy right now?

That might just depend on who he was talking to.

She crept closer to the voices, straining her ears to pick up the words.

"How far do you think you'll get if you run?" That was Maitland talking, still sounding relaxed. "Your allies have packed up and fled by now, and they won't risk themselves by coming back for you. You've run out of shapeshifters to defend you."

"I can make more." The second voice was low and rough, with an arrogant edge.

"Can you?" Maitland was just as self-assured. "You might have the skills, but you don't have resources. Where do you plan on getting the animals to make pelts? This is England. Missing wolves and tigers draw lots of attention."

"I can do better than wolves and tigers," the other man said, and Pierce's fingers tightened around the gun. This was their man. But what was Maitland playing at? She edged closer to the corner to try and see. The harsh fluorescent lights and bare corridors left few shadows to conceal her movements.

"Maybe," Maitland said matter-of-factly. "But too many missing people will bring even more trouble than wolves. You won't last long without a patron to protect you. Turn yourself in."

"Or what, you're going to make me?" The skinbinder snorted. "You and what army? The one my monsters ripped to pieces?"

Smug youthful bravado, but he had ability to back it up. Pierce stole a cautious look around the corner.

The short corridor beyond led to an emergency exit that must come out at the rear of the building. It had a push bar that would set off an alarm when it was opened, probably the only reason Sebastian had hesitated long enough to cause this standoff. Maybe he wasn't as sure as he'd claimed that Maitland's team were all dead, but so far as she'd seen, he was probably right.

Did Maitland know that?

Right now he was standing a safe distance from the skinbinder, hands slightly raised to signify that he wasn't a threat. Sebastian had his eagle wings strapped to his back again, and he was closer to the door. He could take his chance with the alarm and flee; what was he waiting for?

"I can see you're not the kind to be intimidated by threats," Maitland said. "You're too smart for that—and you're smart enough to realise we can be useful to each other." He held the young man's gaze. "You have abilities we want, and we're prepared to bargain with you for their use. We can help you just as much as you'd help us."

"Oh, yeah?" The skinbinder lifted an eyebrow, the bird wings shifting with his shoulders as he shrugged. "Like how?"

"Amnesty for all your crimes," Maitland said. "A facility—better than this one—with other skinbinders to work as your assistants. The freedom to conduct your experiments without censure or risk of punishment, in return for doing certain jobs for us."

Sebastian cocked his head, smirkingly noncommittal. "That all?"

Maybe he wanted Maitland to offer him more, but Pierce had heard more than enough. She stepped out from the corner, gun in hand.

"How about a counteroffer?" she said. "No bargains, no amnesty: you're under arrest." She swept her eyes coldly over Maitland, standing unruffled in his immaculate suit, untouched and undisturbed by the life and death struggle that had left at least four of his team dead. "*Both* of you."

She didn't give a damn what kind of authorisation Maitland thought he had. Once he'd started offering amnesty for the darkest kind of murder, he'd lost his right to claim he was on the side of the angels.

Maitland turned towards her with a wry smile. "DCI Pierce," he said, with a faint breath that was almost a sigh. "I should have guessed that you'd turn up sooner or later." He shook his head. "Your resourcefulness does you credit—but I'm afraid you've overstepped your bounds. Even if you've forgotten the fact that you're currently off-duty, you don't have the authority to hold me." His eyes flicked pointedly towards the gun in her hand. "And you definitely don't have authorisation to hold *that*."

"Looking after it for a friend," she said, baring her teeth in a smile. "He decided he was in no state to be in charge of a gun, so he sensibly handed it in to the nearest police officer." She shifted her grip, still pointing the gun at the ground but adjusting her hold as a silent warning. "And I'm pretty sure I have the authority to arrest anyone I believe is breaking the law. Now, both of you—"

The skinbinder made a lunge for the doors, shoving the bar and setting off a head-splitting wail that filled the hallway. Pierce lurched after him with a curse, but her fingers only just grazed the trailing feathers of his wing as he ran out into the night. The ringing in her ears rose to a deafening crescendo as the howl of the alarm sang counterpoint. Maitland shouted something at her, snagging her arm, but Christ only knew what it was he'd said. Pierce shook him off and shouldered the swinging door aside to follow the skinbinder out.

He was running, his head awkwardly hunched forward as he raised his arms—

"Stop right there!" she bellowed after him. "Do not transform, or I will shoot!" She raised the gun, trying to remember how to take up a firing stance. The memories were far too vague for her to be confident of making the shot at anything more than point blank range.

Sebastian paid no attention to her words. Pierce saw his body start to shift, joints stretching and refolding into new, unnatural angles. She should fire—but she hesitated, reluctant to pull the trigger on a suspect who was fleeing rather than fighting. He was a murderer who wouldn't hesitate to kill again, and once he took to the air there would be no way to chase him, but all the same...

"Don't shoot!" Maitland ordered from behind her. "We need him alive!"

It was just the push she needed to remind her of the consequences if the skinbinder escaped to sell his talents to the highest bidder. She held her stance, aimed the gun as best she could. Sebastian was in full eagle form now, fighting to clear the fence...

Don't overthink. Just *shoot*. She squeezed the trigger.

The recoil jerked her hands up and backwards, the bark of the gun so close making her flinch and stumble. Even if she'd had a second bullet, she wouldn't have recovered in time to take the shot. The skinbinder was lost against the shadows of the trees beyond the fence as he dropped from the sky—hit, or just stooping to evade further gunshots? She strained in vain to try and make him out.

Maitland grabbed her shoulder, yanking her further off balance. "If he's dead, I'll see you thrown off the force!" he shouted in her face.

Pierce swung around, throwing her full momentum into a right hook across his jaw. Maitland staggered back, clutching his mouth and spitting muffled swearwords.

There was no time to stop and bask in the satisfaction of the moment. The skinbinder could be getting away.

She ran towards the fence. There were no streetlights back here, and the light of the moon was just about enough to paint the night in shades of charcoal. She should have brought Leo's torch, but she hadn't thought to ask for it while they were still indoors.

She hoped like hell Leo was still all right. If something had gone wrong after she'd left him...

But this wasn't the time to get distracted second-guessing things she couldn't change. Sebastian was out there, and he might not be alone. She couldn't be sure if Maitland's people had properly swept the grounds before they were killed.

If only that idiot had been willing to work with the RCU and the local police, then maybe tonight's bloodbath could have been avoided. But Maitland was playing his own game, and she had to secure the skinbinder and turn him over to the real police before the Counter Terror Action Team could get there first.

The fencing was tipped with lethal spearpoints, too dangerous to climb even if her battered body could have done it. She jogged along the boundary as fast as she could manage, looking for signs of movement in the shadows. On the other side, the hill sloped steeply down to a copse of trees.

Where had Sebastian fallen? Had he fallen at all? She couldn't see a damn thing through the long grass.

She spotted a gate in the fence ahead, and ran towards it at a downhill stagger. As she drew closer, she could see a dirt track, almost concealed by darkness and the grass. The Solomon team must have evacuated this way, and left the gate thrown open when they went. She hadn't heard a vehicle; with any luck, that meant nobody had stayed behind to wait for the skinbinder.

Of course, if he could still fly, that meant exactly nothing. Pierce scanned the cloudy sky for wings as she passed through the gate; a man-sized eagle should be possible to spot even in the darkness. She'd hear the beating of his wings if he took off from nearby.

So where the hell was he?

She left the dirt track to make her way through the long grass, the gun still held in her hand. Empty now, by Leo's count, but she carried it as if it wasn't, a safety precaution and a bluff. Sebastian most likely wouldn't know how limited a stock they had of silver bullets.

Pierce made her way down the hill, alert to every sound. The knee-length grass tangled around her legs, concealing dips and sudden slopes in the steep hillside. Humps of vegetation made false outlines in the dark. She kicked out at a silhouette that looked like a crouching shape, but it was just a hummock in the grass. The cool night breeze had picked up, and the grass bounced and waved around her.

Except in one place a short way ahead, where it stayed flattened to the ground. Her instincts prickled and her footsteps slowed. A wide furrow had been ploughed through the grass here, as if something large and heavy had been dragged down the slope.

Something there, caught in the weeds: a broken feather, far too large for any native bird. Her chest grew tight as she inched closer. Her eyes could now pick out the dark shape slumped on the ground ahead. Sebastian, lying sprawled out on his stomach where he'd fallen, the false wings still outstretched, though one was bent back at an uncomfortable angle.

The silver bullet must have at least clipped him, enough to make him revert back to human. Shit. Her stomach lurched. She'd shot a man with a gun she wasn't authorised to carry, and the fact it had seemed the right thing to do at the time wouldn't help her case much. She couldn't ask Leo to cover for her and claim he'd made the shot himself, and no one would believe he'd been mobile enough to do it anyway.

She approached Sebastian's still form with caution. Was he dead? Unconscious? Just winded? She halted a few feet away. "Don't make any sudden moves," she said, aware she could be giving the warning to a corpse. "I have a pistol full of silver bullets, and I *am* prepared to fire if you make a hostile move. Can you stand up?"

No response. Pierce edged a little closer.

"If you're injured, I will see that you get medical attention. Are you able to speak? If you can make a noise, or move any part of your body, do so now to show me that you're conscious."

She held her breath, but all was silent and still except for the sigh of the wind. She thought she might have heard the distant rise and fall of sirens, but it might just be the ringing in her ears.

Sebastian hadn't so much as twitched. She couldn't tell if he was even breathing. His head had fallen forward in the grass, the curtain of his hair obscuring any clear look at his face. She transferred the useless gun to her left hand as she inched past the wing stretched out in the grass.

Still no movement. Pierce bent forward to check the pale neck for a pulse. As she did, she noticed that the straps that bound the wings to his back had come untied, leaving one of them draped loosely across his shoulder.

A hand shot out from under the wing and grabbed hold of her wrist. As she jerked back, Sebastian reared up, his other hand darting out from underneath his body, holding a knife. She just had time to see the glint of moonlight off the silver blade before it flashed out towards her heart.

She twisted away, but the knife still bit deep into her shoulder. "Fuck!" She stumbled back, the empty gun dropping from her numb fingers as she clutched at the knife hilt jutting out from the wound. How the hell had he carried the knife in eagle form? Some kind of pouch that protected him from the direct touch of the silver? Her mind stuck on the pointless question, her thoughts hazed by the cold shock of a pain she knew she wasn't fully feeling yet. Blood soaked out beneath her fingers.

But she still had a prisoner to secure. As the skinbinder scrambled up, shrugging off the discarded wings like an unwanted blanket, Pierce lunged after him, slamming into his back. He might be younger, faster, more athletic, but she still had the skinny bastard beat on bodyweight.

He went down and she followed him, the hill steep enough to send both of them tumbling. Sebastian hit the rough ground with a sharp cry of pain, and she crashed down on top of him, jarring her wounded shoulder even further.

Her eyes screwed shut in agony, and she didn't see the bony elbow coming as it cracked her across the jaw. Sebastian tried to wriggle away from her, but she caught him by the arm to haul him back. Something in her shoulder felt like it was tearing, and she sobbed with pain, but didn't let him go.

"Get back here, you little bastard," she said through gritted teeth, reaching for the handcuffs on her belt. Not silver, but the standard pair that she'd taken from Maitland would still do for this job. She leaned her weight on him as he struggled and spat and swore.

"You do not... have to say anything," she wheezed, fumbling with the cuffs, "but it may harm your defence"—she snapped the left loop closed around his wrist, strained tears leaking from her eyes—"if you do not mention when questioned.... something which you later rely on in court." He bucked beneath her, almost throwing her off, but she rolled back to pin him down with her knee. "Anything you *do* say..."—with a final gasping grunt of pain, she yanked his other arm into position to snap the second cuff in place—"may be given in evidence," she said, panting for breath. "Understand me?"

He burst into a furious string of swearwords.

"I'm going to... take that as a yes," Pierce said, and slumped down wearily to sit beside him on the hillside. "Now... stay where you are. You're under arrest."

She swallowed as she turned her blurry gaze to the knife

hilt still sticking out from her shoulder. The sound of sirens was drawing closer, definitely real this time. All she had to do was stay conscious until backup arrived.

Easier said than done...

CHAPTER THIRTEEN

INJURED AND RUNNING on empty as she was, Pierce had little choice but to turn the skinbinder over to the custody of the local police. She spoke to Deepan, and instructed him to make sure Sebastian turned up where he was sent, no unexpected detours. She also had to break the news about Tim, though she shied away from the full ugly details.

Maitland, it emerged, had disappeared into the night, and taken any of his surviving teammates with him. The police who raided the site found no one else to arrest, just more corpses, some still wearing shapeshifting skins.

Analysing exactly what had happened tonight was going to be a hell of a forensic job, but it was one that Pierce was in no condition to oversee. She was too exhausted and in too much pain to protest being sent away from the scene in an ambulance as soon as she'd spat out the most important explanations. She turned out to be sharing it with Leo, clearly in a bad way even before hospital x-rays could confirm it.

At least he was still alive.

It was hard to celebrate her own survival with enthusiasm once adrenaline and triumph faded. Shoulder surgery, and a long program of rehab to look forward to, plus all the lesser scrapes and bruises she'd picked up along the way. It would be a long, grim and painful recovery, without even the indulgence of self-pity when so many of the people who'd been involved in this mess had come out a whole lot worse.

Few visitors came to see her in hospital. Tim was dead, two good friends were hospitalised themselves, and Deepan was stuck doing everybody's job including hers. The RCU was undersized and overworked as it was, and now it was down by three quarters of its manpower.

So she was surprised when she received a visit from Superintendent Palmer, who she'd always believed to be attached to his desk by an umbilical cord. She was even more surprised that he didn't seem to be there to give her a bollocking.

In fact, he was unusually reluctant to get to the point, avoiding her gaze as he adjusted the front of his uniform shirt. "Ah, Claire," he said, with unaccustomed hesitation. "Shoulder improving?"

"So they tell me," she said. "I'll let you know when the painkillers wear off." At least she was sitting up in the chair instead of lying down; entertaining the boss while still in bed would have been awkward. Pierce really hadn't anticipated a personal visit from him; an elegantly penned Get Well Soon card was really more his style. "Everything all right back at the office?" she asked.

"Er, yes, yes," he said with a nod. "Your... sergeant is doing very well. And there will, erm, be an official investigation into the Counter Terror Action Team's handling of this case. Rest assured that the skinbinder you brought in will be appropriately punished for his crimes." He grimaced, as if aware she wouldn't like what he had to say next. "But it will, of course, have to be handled discreetly. You understand that word of this young man's work can't be allowed to get out."

Perhaps he expected an explosion, and if she'd been healthy he might well have got one, but right now she was too weary to give both barrels to the debate. Secret courts were nobody's friend in her eyes, but politics was what it was, and those kind of decisions took place far above her head. At least she knew she could trust Palmer to be a straight shooter, far more so than Maitland.

And talking of shooting... there had been curiously little mention of her less-than-legal part in bringing the skinbinder down. Was it all being swept under the rug as part of the general cover-up? The thought didn't sit entirely right with her, but now was hardly the time to go falling on her sword. With Sally in worse shape than she was and Tim dead, the RCU couldn't afford to lose its DCI in charge as well.

Pierce grimaced at her own thoughts. A convenient excuse why 'just this once' the rules had to bend. *That* was a hell of a slippery slope to start down.

Palmer's uncomfortable squirming drew her out of her darkening thoughts. "Well, erm, that's all the news you need to worry about right now," he said. "I should probably get back to the station." He made an abortive move to check his watch, lowering his arm rather awkwardly as a flash of bare wrist was revealed. Things *must* be hectic back at the office if even her immaculately pressed boss was getting ready for work in that much of a hurry.

Or maybe not. Her amusement iced over as she remembered the watch the Superintendent usually worse, the kind of status symbol that immediately marked him out as someone who did his policing from behind a desk. Her own taste in watches ran to the cheap, plastic, and shockproof, but Palmer's favoured wristwatch was far more ostentatious...

And made of sterling silver.

Her eyes snapped up to study his face, but he was already turning to move away. "I look forward to seeing you back at the office," he said over his shoulder.

He looked like Palmer, sounded like him. Her doubts had to be no more wild paranoia.

They had to be... but how could she be sure?

His footsteps faded away into the background hubbub. Pierce shivered in her hospital gown, goose pimples crawling over her skin. She was surrounded by the noise and bustle of the busy ward... but right now, she felt very much alone.

PART TWO

CHAPTER FOURTEEN

THE NEXT TIME Pierce got stabbed in the shoulder by a suspect, the bastard had better have the decency to do it in the summer. Bad enough to have spent weeks in a sling and more doing rehab without the shitty weather and joint aches to contend with. She was cleared to drive by now, but still wary of her shoulder; the December roads were icy after last night's rain, and the last thing she needed was to crash the car on the way to her first day back at work.

The station hadn't got any prettier in her absence. A squat, shabby red brick building, it hosted the local police team first, the Ritual Crime Unit crammed in as a vague afterthought. Promises of new facilities had never come to anything; the budget always went on Oxford branch or RCU London. Here up north, they made do.

Pierce parked outside and walked in. On duty at the front desk, Jill Lyons gave her a nod. "Dragged you back already, have they?" she asked. "So much for the season of goodwill."

"Needs must when the budget drives," Pierce said. In truth, she could probably have swung the extra leave to stay off till after Christmas, but one more week at home and she'd go spare. After years of vaguely dreaming of having more time off, it turned out she had bugger all to do with it. Her duff shoulder had put the kibosh on fixing up the house or garden, and most of her social connections had withered on the vine after years of the job getting in the way.

The problem with being married to your work was that eventually there came a point when you had to get a messy divorce. Pierce grimaced as she climbed the stairs up to the RCU. She might be out of shape from her time off, but at almost fifty-five, there was a limit to the shape she could get back into.

Not that she had any business feeling sorry for herself. She'd been lucky to come out of her last clusterfuck of a case with no worse than a stab wound: shutting down a ring of illegal shapeshifters and the skinbinder supplying their pelts had left one of her officers critically injured and another dead.

Pierce hesitated in front of the double doors onto the office, steeling herself against the inevitable ache of the missing faces. The RCU's work was always high risk, but there had been something rotten in the state of Denmark this time round: too much information held back from her team when they needed it, too many special interests playing politics with people's lives. There was no way she was shuffling quietly off to retirement when there were forces above her head in the police and government who thought they could manipulate the RCU and the law.

At least there was still one familiar face left to greet her. As she pushed through into the RCU's open-plan office, Sergeant Deepan Mistry jumped up from his computer with a smile. "Guv! Come back to take the reins at last?" he said.

Despite the boyish grin, the detective sergeant looked older than when she'd seen him last. Even now he'd hit thirty, Deepan had a chubby-cheeked baby face and a penchant for hair gel that had always made him seem barely out of his teens to her; right now, though, the clear signs of tiredness were etching more years on his face. October's bloodbath had left him in the lurch, the only RCU member still standing after the carnage cleared.

But Pierce was back now, and hopefully able to lift some of the weight of shepherding the rookies off his shoulders. "Looks like my reign's not over yet," she said, glancing around the office to see what was new. Not much, except her *Team Leader: DCI Claire Pierce* sign had been supplanted by a sheet of printer paper that read *Acting Team Leader: DI Graham Dawson*. She supposed it would be petty to walk right over and tear it down, though it didn't seem that the man himself was around to see it.

The room's only other occupant was a smartly dressed young black woman with her hair pulled back into a bun, fresh-faced and eager and not looking a day over twenty-five, if that. Pierce felt a twinge as she remembered the last equally youthful soul to occupy that chair, and why he wouldn't be there anymore.

She kept that thought off her face, and gave their new recruit a nod and smile. "You're one of us now, I take it?" she said.

"That's right, Guv." The woman nodded crisply. "Constable Gemma Freeman—I took the PRMC certificate with Greater Manchester Police."

The PRMC exam was required to work in Ritual these days, though Pierce wasn't convinced it was much more use than her own on-the-job orientation, which had largely been on a theme of, "Assume nobody has a clue what they're doing and everything can kill you." Even in these twenty-first-century days of global information networks, magic was still too difficult to reproduce and too deeply surrounded by fakery and bullshit to have more than a trial-and-error approach to understanding what it could do. The only training they could give their people was to toss them in at the deep end and hope they either swam or clawed their way out without drowning.

Probably not an effective pep speech, that.

"Well, welcome to the team," she said, instead. "I don't doubt Deepan's done a good job showing you the ropes while I was off." She turned back to him. "Where's DI Dawson?"

"Out at a scene, Guv, with our other new DC."

"Two new constables *and* a DI?" Pierce raised her eyebrows. "Good Lord. Rock star treatment." Maybe having three out of four of the team dead or injured in a span of days had finally woken somebody up to the fact that they really did need the extra personnel they'd been requesting for years.

Or, more likely, her superiors had expected her to conveniently retire after the disaster of the shapeshifter case. Well, they were out of luck: Pierce had never been one to take subtle hints, and there were too many unanswered questions for her to step down now. She might have arrested the skinbinder, but they still only knew him by the possibly false name of 'Sebastian,' and the group who'd funded him remained a mystery. With the Counter Terror Action Team muscling in on her case, all the evidence had been seized before she'd had the chance to follow up.

That didn't mean she was prepared to let things go without a fight—so if Dawson was planning to ascend the ranks and take her place, he was going to have to be a patient man. Pierce had hoped to have the chance to meet with him and make their positions clear right from the start, but she supposed it had been too much to ask that the RCU's never-ending caseload would give everyone the day off to throw a welcome-back party.

"All right. If Dawson comes in, tell him to come and see me," she said to Deepan. "Figure out which cases I need to know about, and get me copies of the files." The RCU was always snowed under with reports on every squiggle of suspicious graffiti, self-described magician and fancy dress party north of the Watford Gap; if she tried to read up on everything that had come in while she was away, she'd be here till Easter. "I'll be next door."

That loose term covered the assorted offices of the Magical Analysis department: what passed for forensics when it came to the occult, though anybody who worked in true forensics would hate the comparison. Even after decades of development, police magical research was still largely at the level of 'poke it and see what happens.' They could get results, sometimes even repeat them, but finding something that could be relied upon in court was like winning the lottery.

Hence the fact that the RCU's research department was made up of a hodgepodge of eccentric specialists, crammed into tiny offices and working on a hundred things at once. Pierce poked her head into one particularly small room, so close to literally overflowing that there were books and files stacked on the floor outside the door. She waved at the woman just about visible behind the wall of file folders.

"Jen! How's Sympathetic Magic treating you?"

"Claire! You're back! Not very sympathetically." Jenny Hayes rolled her chair round the end of the desk, or as far as it would go before the wheels struck yet more boxes, and leaned out to wave back. "Your new constables are wee sweet little lost lambs, but somebody really needs to teach them that they don't need to send me every hair and fibre from within fifteen miles of the crime scene."

"I approve of thorough," said Pierce. Always better than slapdash.

"Yes, I know you do, since you're not the one who has to process it." But Jenny grinned. "Good to have you back—place hasn't been the same without you."

"Is that in a good or a bad way?" she asked dryly.

"It's been awful," Jenny said, composing a piously straight face. "I hope you realise I've had to pretend to be a proper grown-up professional every time your new DI drops by. Had to put my shoes on and take my feet off the desk and everything."

"Terrible," Pierce agreed. "Dashing, is he?"

"Only in the sense of moving places fast." She arched her eyebrows over her glasses. "Bit of a bulldozer, that one. Wants things done his way and fast, doesn't want to hear about the details."

"I know the type." And it didn't bode well for harmonious cooperation; still, plenty of those who pushed the support staff around weren't quite so eager to bark at the boss. She'd see. "Right, better push on and act like I'm doing something useful around here... I'll see you later, Jenny."

"We should go down the pub sometime, celebrate you coming back to work," Jenny called after her as she left.

"We should." A nice plan that was never going to happen, given how much Pierce had to catch up on. All the same, it was good to be reminded that even with half the detective branch gone, there were still people here that she knew and trusted. She'd felt isolated and ineffectual, stuck at home recovering, but now she was back on her own turf.

She dropped in on each member of the research team to let them know that she was back and see what kind of workload they were up against. Without exception heavy, but that was nothing new: they'd always had a backlog on their backlog. Pierce was fairly sure there were some evidence lots still waiting to be processed that had been around since she was a DS.

The Enchanted Artefacts department had the biggest backlog of all. The literature on magic was still such a patchwork of guesstimates and myth that it was tough to certify *anything* as definitively free from enchantments: all they could do with mystery items seized from ritual scenes was keep prodding to see if they went boom.

As Pierce approached the lab at the end of the corridor, she became aware of a faint but insistent hum on the cusp of hearing, like a machine running somewhere in the distance. As she pushed the door open to step into the Artefacts lab, the hum grew louder, but no more distinct.

Clifford Healey popped up from behind a lab bench to greet her, wearing a pair of clear plastic goggles and a set of headphones. He was a big man with a broad face like an affable potato, and hair that had migrated into two greying clumps on either side of his head. He raised a finger to beg for a moment's pause as he struggled to retrieve his mp3 player from a pocket under his V-neck and disentangle himself from the headphones.

He beamed at her. "Claire!" he said heartily. "Back in our neck of the woods? I was beginning to fear we might have seen the last of you."

"You should be so lucky," Pierce said. The humming hadn't stopped with the cessation of whatever music he was listening to, and she found she was talking too loudly to compensate. "What's that noise?" she asked with a wince. It was hitting the perfect frequency to drill right through her head.

"Ah!" Cliff said, holding up his hand. "Turns out today is quite the day for blasts from the past." He bounded across the lab to the racks of metal shelving on the far side and began to peer at the labels on various storage boxes.

"You calling me an old fart, Cliff?" she said, leaning against the doorway.

"We can both be farts together, my dear," he said,

smiling at her through the shelves as his box-shuffling created a gap.

Pierce couldn't help but snort. "You really know how to charm the ladies, you do."

"And now here I come bearing gifts." He moved back to the table with a large plastic storage box, removing the lid with a flourish. "Recognise this handsome fellow?" he asked.

She leaned in to get a look at what seemed to be an intricately made, if hideous, cast iron lantern. The eight sides were fashioned into faces, devilish masks with wide gaping mouths, each sharing one eye with each neighbouring face so they blended into one unbroken chain. It had an iron ring on top to hang it up, supported by metal bands that gave the faces the impression of horns.

"Looks like a bloke I went out with in the 'nineties, only he had a bigger mouth," she said. She was aware of a change in the quality of the hum as Cliff lifted the thing out of the box. "Although it does seem to be blowing a lot of hot air. So where did we get this thing, and should we be worried that it's humming?"

"We've had it for years, and... who knows?" he said, with the airy shrug of one who spent his days playing with volatile enchanted objects to see what he could make them do. Sometimes Pierce suspected their research department had even less sense of self-preservation than the detective branch.

He moved the box onto the floor and stood the iron lantern on the lab bench. "This was seized evidence from the Collingate murders," he said. "I don't know if you remember?"

It rang a vague bell, though she thought it had been somebody else's case back in the day. "Big posh house, son tried to summon something nasty to murder the father, ended up getting more nasty for his money than he was expecting?" she said.

"Something along those lines," Cliff said with a nod. "The father was a collector—had a lot of unclassified artefacts that weren't directly involved in the murder itself, but were judged potential class three and four violations. We seized the lot, and haven't done much with them since. However, Nancy was down at the long-term storage facility the other day and noticed that our devilish friend here had started making a noise—gave her quite a start, I should imagine. And so... here we are." He spread his hands.

Pierce bent down to peer closer at the lantern, holding her palm in front of each of the mouths to see if she could feel any motion of air. Nothing obvious. "And do we know *why* it's making a noise?" she asked, looking up at Cliff.

"Well, we have theories," he said. "I've been doing some research, and I believe our friend here is probably a watch lantern. It's his job to let his owner know when something nasty approaches—nasty, in this case, most likely meaning some form of supernatural beastie with ill-intent. Quite the thing among feuding spirit-raisers a few centuries back."

Pierce stepped back, reflexively looking around even though she didn't know what she expected to see coming at them in the middle of a police station. "So what is it warning us about?" she asked.

Cliff pursed his lips, as close as he ever seemed to get to an actual frown. "Well, that's the question, isn't it?" he said. "Now, it may be something as simple as proximity to another artefact that's set it off, or it may be something in the greater area. In theory, if his light was lit, he might be able to give us more of an indication of where it was coming from. Here's where the science gets a bit fuzzy, though, I'm afraid: the signals were not really standardised, and I haven't been able to dig up any specific information on the provenance of this particular model."

"Any risk to lighting it up?" she asked.

"Well, there shouldn't be. I was planning to get around to trying it sometime later today, but there's no reason we can't do it now, if you'd like to watch. It never hurts to have a second set of eyes to check my observations."

Pierce stood back. "Go on, then. Dazzle me."

Cliff smiled, and patted several pockets before coming up with a cigarette lighter.

"Thought you quit," she said, as he bent with a slight groan to pick up a big box of candles from the floor.

"Well, I *did*," he confessed, "but it's so convenient to have the lighter for work, and when you've got it right there with you in your pocket..."

"You should get a job that doesn't require setting things on fire," she said.

He grinned as he opened up one latched side of the lantern to place a candle inside, causing a shift in the atonal hum. "Now, where's the fun in that?" he said. He closed the lantern hatch again and retrieved a pack of wooden tapers, shaking one out and setting the end of it ablaze with his lighter. "All right," he said. "Best not to get too close, but do watch carefully. Any subtle action of the flame could well have some meaning."

Pierce nodded and held still as he brought the taper to the candlewick. It took a moment to properly catch, and then the humming noise that she'd been hearing all along took on a new, more piercing quality, like wind blown over the mouth of a milk bottle. Her hair fluttered against her forehead as if caught in a breeze, and the wooden taper in Cliff's hand puffed out.

She raised her voice above the sighing howl of the unnatural wind. "Is this—?"

The candle flame abruptly flared, as if someone had poured petrol on the fire, and she jumped back as tongues of flames spewed forth from the devilish mouths.

"Oh, dear," said Cliff, turning to reach for the wall-mounted fire extinguisher with an air of calm resignation. "I think we should probably—"

The flame leapt again, showering sparks, and thick black smoke began to billow forth, filling the room at an alarming rate. Pierce covered her mouth with her sleeve and grabbed for the door handle behind her, winning a twinge from her still-healing shoulder.

"Cliff!" She meant to order him out, but her next words were swallowed by a cough. She turned to look at the door she was groping at—where the *hell* was the bloody handle?—but another flare of the candle flame at the corner of her eye made her turn to look.

The room was already a shadowy haze, the grinning devil's mask of the lantern leering at her through the growing smog. "Cliff?" She coughed harder, squinting through streaming eyes. A metallic *thunk*—the fire extinguisher striking something. Had he fallen?

They had to get out of here. She slapped again at the door and finally managed to grab the handle, yanking it open and sending dark smoke coiling out into the corridor. She flapped her arm, ineffectually trying to waft more of it away. "Cliff! Get out of there!" She held the door open for him to follow, still coughing.

"Hang on! Just let me—" His words collapsed into spluttering, but she heard the spurt of the fire extinguisher, and then the metallic clang as he let it drop to roll across the floor. She stepped back into the room and stretched to grab his arm, yanking him with her towards the door.

"Go!" She shoved him out and then followed, pulling the door shut behind them to close off the smoke. They both collapsed against the wall, panting for breath. "All right?" she asked him, with a sideways glance.

Cliff nodded, red in the face as he drew in sucking gasps of air.

"Notice any subtle signs?" she asked him.

He laughed, then doubled over, coughing. As office doors along the corridor cracked open, the fire alarm above them began to blare.

Looked like work was going to be business as usual.

CHAPTER FIFTEEN

MEETING HER NEW boss at the fire assembly point outside the building probably wasn't the best start their working relationship could have had, not least because it meant there were witnesses when he ordered her to accompany him to his office. The fact the looks were by and large sympathetic rather than smirking was more of a warning sign than a reassurance; apparently Superintendent Snow had made his own dubious first impression in the weeks that he'd been in charge.

Pierce could well believe that; she'd known the man all of ten minutes, and already she wanted to punch him.

Robert Snow was a tall man with an aquiline nose and hair that was well on its way to matching the surname. He had an upright, imperious bearing, and a long stride that he didn't moderate to allow for her shorter legs as he led the way through the building. Pierce refused to scurry to keep up, following along at a comfortable walking pace. She was too old to get dragged into status games.

If only that stopped other people from playing them at her.

They reached the office that she still thought of as Superintendent Palmer's. "Close that door, please," Snow directed, taking his chair without explicitly offering her a seat herself. He straightened the papers and took out a pair of rectangular-framed glasses to set on his nose. Delaying tactics meant to remind her of her place, but Pierce was glad of the chance to compose a neutral face and take a glance around the office.

It had been stripped of any trace of its former occupant's personality—not that Palmer had ever shown much, a petty bureaucrat down to his toes. But she'd known the man more than a decade, and despite his regular griping about the RCU's budget and its methods, he'd always had her back with his superiors when it counted.

She'd been told he'd taken early retirement while she was on leave, and she was sure anybody she asked at the station would confirm it. The problem was, she wasn't sure that the man they'd seen retire was the real Howard Palmer. When he'd visited her in the hospital... well, maybe it had just been paranoia to think that he wasn't himself, to wonder at the absence of the silver watch he'd worn for years. But when her last case had proven that shapeshifters stealing others' faces was more than just a myth, it was easy to be paranoid.

A ringer masquerading as Superintendent Palmer could have done any amount of damage, making sure that unwanted evidence vanished, shutting down important lines of investigation before they could get anywhere. But with him already gone before Pierce could seek proof of her suspicions, she was left with a new and no less pressing question: just who was Robert Snow? A co-conspirator in the imposter's cover-up, or just an innocent replacement brought in after the dirty deeds were done?

Pierce studied his face, but it offered nothing except the stern patrician look of a man used to being the main authority in the room. He seemed to be waiting for her to speak, so she obliged him. "Did you have a chance to speak to Superintendent Palmer before he left, sir?" she asked. "I was wondering if you might know where he'd moved on to."

Snow's face tightened just a fraction, nostrils flaring, though she wasn't sure if it was a sign of tension or just irritation at the fact she was invoking his predecessor. "He retired, as I understand it," he said coolly. "I believe after the loss of much of the RCU's detective branch it was felt new leadership might be in order."

Was that dig aimed at her or Palmer? Probably both. Pierce gave the blandly neutral smile she'd perfected for senior officers. "Did he leave the area?" she asked. "Only I've been trying to get in touch with him, and he doesn't seem to be at his old house." Repeated phone calls and eventually a visit had brought her to an empty property. He'd been a single man: she hadn't known him well enough to be aware of any friends or family, or if he had an ex-wife stashed somewhere, who might have been informed of any move.

Her new boss's blank indifference gave her nothing to latch on to. "I was told he stated his intention to move to the south of France," he said, sitting back. "Now—"

Pierce narrowed her eyes. "Really? I would have thought they'd want him to stick around for the investigation." Police internal inquiries never moved that fast: not unless there was a cover-up. "Did he leave a forwarding address?"

"Not with me," Snow said, a curt, impatient close to the discussion. "Fortunately, his notes were very thorough. It seems he kept a tight rein over the officers under his command—although your department seems to have been a frequent exception."

"Well, we do handle exceptional situations, sir," she said, focusing on the wall past his head rather than meeting his gaze. Snow had already managed to put up some framed photographs of himself with various local dignitaries.

"I'm sure you do." The faint curve of the superintendent's thin lips made the neutral tone sceptical. "Nonetheless, however, you are a police unit, and there are regulations to be followed. The test this morning should never have been conducted without authorisation. We had to evacuate the building!"

Pierce tried not to grimace. "Sir, the behaviour of magical artefacts is always going to be unpredictable," she said.

His bushy eyebrows crunched down low over his glasses. "Then perhaps tests with unpredictable outcomes should not be conducted within the environs of a working police station," he said acidly.

Aha, familiar ground. "Well, sir, we've asked repeatedly for the research division to be given their own dedicated building with an on-site storage facility." Not to mention a million other things that also weren't going to happen.

"Perhaps if you could put in a word with your superiors about the necessity—"

As she expected, he cut her off with a *harrumph*. "Yes, well, that's simply not practical. I'm afraid with the scale of the operation you mounted to catch this, er, shapeshifting pelt-maker last October—"

"Skinbinder," she supplied. He gave her a cold look over his glasses, as if more irritated than appreciative of being corrected on the proper term.

"Quite. Well, with the expense and disastrous consequences of that operation and the addition of a new DI to the department, the RCU is not in any position to be requesting any further budget increases for quite some time."

Great. A budget injection just when she'd been in no position to advise on its distribution, and now she was stuck with an unnecessary DI clogging up the chain of command when she could have had two constables for the money.

Was he expecting a response? Probably: Snow seemed like the type who liked to make his subordinates acknowledge him. "Yes, sir," she said.

He nodded wisely. "Now, as to the matter of the research department's unpredictability, perhaps a greater degree of oversight is the answer. I understand the artefact being tested was not even part of an ongoing investigation?"

"No, sir, but given the volatility of some enchanted materials we handle—"

"Prioritise," he said curtly. "I expect you to cut down on unnecessary experimentation: only research pertaining to open cases should be performed."

Which meant they'd never bloody learn anything new or useful that they could use *to* solve those open cases, but she could already tell that argument would get her exactly nowhere.

"Yes, sir," she said, instead.

NOT THE MOST enlightening of interviews. Pierce couldn't tell if Snow was stonewalling her for a purpose, or he was just your common-or-garden pain in the backside administrator. Lord knew she'd worked for more than a few, Palmer himself no exception. She'd respected the man more than she'd liked him—but nobody deserved the kind of fate that she darkly suspected he'd come to.

Skinned so a shapeshifter could wear his face like a mask. It had happened to one of her officers, a lad no older than their latest squeaky clean rookie. At least she'd had the thin consolation of putting the skinbinder responsible behind bars.

If only the same could be said about those who'd aided and abetted his crimes.

Pierce was glad to step back into the RCU office, never short of teetering piles of work to keep her from dwelling on her thoughts.

"Fire out now, Guv?" Deepan called with a cheeky grin as she arrived.

"Metaphorically or literally?" she said, pulling out a chair. She'd never really had a formally assigned desk to be returning to; the office was always such a mess it was usually just a case of grabbing whichever position could be dug out with minimum excavation. "In both cases, mostly just a lot of smoke."

Probably best not to venture any more direct opinion of their new superintendent with Constable Freeman in the room. "So when did old Palmer retire?" she asked instead, keeping the inquiry deliberately casual. "Always thought he was Sellotaped to that chair."

She trusted Deepan, but she hadn't told him of her suspicions. Even to her, it sounded like the vivid imaginings of someone who'd had a crappy week and too many hospital painkillers the last time she'd seen the man, and as time passed, her original certainty grew thinner. She needed proof before she went off spouting wild conspiracy theories that would make even her true friends think she'd lost it.

Especially since there was always a chance that she had.

"He was pretty stressed after you went on medical leave, Guv," Deepan said. "Two large-scale busts within a week, officers killed and injured... There was a whole big inquiry. I swear we had new sets of people in asking us questions every week." He shook his head. "I don't know if they pushed him out or what—nobody really had much clue what was going on. We had some people in from Oxford RCU to hold the fort for the first month or so, except of course they didn't know anything about our systems, and Oxford were pushing the whole time to get them back because *they* were understaffed... I don't blame him for doing a runner. I'd probably have quit as well if I didn't have two kids and a mortgage."

Pierce swivelled her chair around to face him. "Well,

you don't look like you've done too badly for yourself," she said, with a nod that also encompassed Freeman. The young constable was sitting at her computer and doing a good job of looking like she was diligently working, but no doubt was earwigging as any smart detective should. "I know you got dropped in at the deep end, but it looks like you managed to keep the place from burning down around your ears."

"Unlike you, Guv," Deepan said with a grin.

"Unlike me." She clapped her hands together. "All right. Give me a rundown of what we've got going on right now."

"Mostly, it's been pretty small change, luckily," he said. "Ritual graffiti, curse threats, small-scale dealing in restricted artefacts... we've acquired a bunch of druids who keep ringing up because some company bought up the land they use for their traditional solstice rites. Obviously a government conspiracy."

"Well, it wouldn't be RCU without the cranks," she said. Better watch she didn't get a rep for being one of them.

"We do have a couple of ongoing investigations, though," he said, picking up a small stack of file folders and opening the topmost before handing them to her. "The main one is a string of artefact thefts, fairly professional jobs—they've hit a couple of museums and some well-guarded private collections. Definitely after reputedly magical items rather than in it for the money—they've left some more valuable pieces untouched, and none of the ones they've stolen have resurfaced on the market. Leads have gone cold, but we're expecting them to strike again sooner rather than later."

"Interesting..." she mumbled, taking a glance through the contents of the first folder. Could just be a fanatical collector after pieces not on general sale, but in her experience, when you had some nutter collecting ritual artefacts, they were usually planning to do something with them.

"This case DI Dawson's just gone out on might be something, too," Deepan added. "Possible ritual murder."

"Oh, yeah?" Pierce looked up from the folder she was reading.

"Dog walker found a buried skull early this morning," he explained. "Local police took a look, saw some signs that they thought might indicate ritualised burial, and called us in."

"Did they, now?" She set the folder down and stood up. "Well, I need to talk to Dawson anyway, and I'm sure you don't need me getting in the way here while I catch up. Where's the scene?"

THE SKULL HAD been found in a field north of Bingley. Pierce could have identified the place by the sheer number of cars parked alongside even if some hadn't had police markings. Small chance of finding witnesses to a spot of literal skulduggery out here amid the fields, at least not in December; come the summer, and you never knew your luck when it came to packs of ramblers stumbling over criminals.

Too bloody grey and windy for anyone to be out walking today, if they had any choice in the matter. Pierce flashed her warrant card at the miserable looking PC by the dry stone wall and let herself in through the field gate.

It was a struggle to drag it past the tall weeds that had grown up on both sides. Not used often, then. Certainly, there was bugger all of note about the field aside from the police presence near the trees at the far end. As she started up the uneven slope to join them, a youngish ginger-haired bloke in a cheap suit broke away from the pack to intercept her.

"Um, excuse me, madam, but this is a crime scene," he said, revealing an unmistakably Brummie accent.

Was it uncharitable to bet that a male officer in plainclothes wouldn't have been stopped and questioned? Though he bloody well ought to have been, so no point biting heads off. She'd kept the warrant card handy for this eventuality. "DCI Pierce. RCU," she said.

The young copper paled a bit. "Oh! Sorry, um, we thought you were going to be off until after Christmas," he said.

For a moment Pierce wondered if she'd become so notorious across the local forces they were keeping tabs on her medical leave, but then she caught on. "You're one of the new RCU officers?" she said.

He nodded hastily, obviously worried he'd made a bad first impression. "Constable Ed Taylor."

Oh, well, earnest and overzealous beat sloppy and cocky. She waved him on ahead of her with a nod. "I'm just here to check in," she said. "Is DI Dawson around?"

"Er, yes, ma'am, he's overseeing the search for more remains."

Overseeing. Blimey. Maybe Taylor wasn't the only one who was being a tad overzealous. Unless they'd turned up greater evidence of an imminent threat than a skull with a few ritual markings, the RCU's role in the case should be purely advisory. Local police forces tended to get more than a bit shirty when you stomped in and started ordering their officers about, and the RCU was far too dependent on outside manpower to try playing ten ton gorilla.

She followed Taylor up the hill towards the trees, where a group of police and forensics bods stood clustered around a marked-off excavation. Which one was Dawson? Her money was on the ruddy faced bloke with the receding crewcut who looked like he had an equal amount of fat and muscle stuffed under the tight-collared suit. The man next to him had a face like he'd just found a wasp in his chewing gum, so she pegged him as having been the officer in charge prior to RCU involvement.

Taylor's pointing finger confirmed it. "That's Inspector Dawson, ma'am."

Which meant now came the joy of playing politics. Stop and introduce herself to Dawson first, with the attendant likelihood of ruffling the feathers of the local police even further as she ignored them, or snub Dawson and run the risk of him being the type to hold a petty grudge for the rest of their working career?

Fortunately, she was spared having to pick option A or B by a shout.

"Sir!" one of the PCs called from further off in the trees. "We've got another skull!"

CHAPTER SIXTEEN

IN THE GENERAL scramble to relocate to the second find, Pierce managed to get the chance pull her new DI aside.

"Dawson?" She offered him a handshake. "DCI Claire Pierce."

Seemed he wasn't the kind of idiot to try making a point by crushing her bones, but he definitely had a hearty grip. The strong scent of cigarettes clung to his coat. "DCI Pierce," he said with a curt nod. "I was told you had another week or two of leave."

"So was I, but I'm not one to sit around," she said. "What's the situation here?"

"Man walking his dog took a shortcut through the field. Dog ran off and started digging, uncovered a human skull." He indicated the original excavation, where forensics had carefully cleared out the earth from around the skull. "Local bobbies had a look and then called us in. I told them not to move it till we'd had it analysed."

Pierce moved in for a closer look at the skull down in the

pit. Not hard to see why it had been flagged as the RCU's business: the skull was daubed with complex geometric patterns in what looked like blood, and a rolled parchment scroll tied up with black ribbon was tucked between its jaws. Around it, the excavation had uncovered a ring of nine small flat stones, each one etched with a different symbol.

Not one of the common sets of runes, but that didn't mean much. The world—and these days the web—was awash with alleged occult texts, far too many for the police Arcane Documents Network to try to compile. Only a tiny fraction might be legitimate, but the real bugger was telling that fraction from the rest. The general public mucking about with magic were the infinite monkeys with typewriters who only needed to strike it lucky once; the RCU had a handful of overworked monkeys and a limited budget for typewriter ribbons.

Pierce straightened up and looked around. No obvious landmarks to suggest this field had any particular magical significance: not even a distinctive hill or suitably ancient tree. The choice of field might indicate some sort of curse targeting the owner, or it could just be a conveniently out-of-the-way location for the ritual burial.

Dawson had moved on without waiting for her, but DC Taylor was still hovering, probably in a state of existential confusion over who was technically in charge. Pierce motioned for him to walk with her as she followed the others over to the trees. "What do we know about the owner of the field?" she asked.

He hurried to consult the pages of his notebook. "Er... Jane Hockney. Local, seventy-two... keeps cows. Used to use the fields to... graze them, or something?" He gave a confused shrug. "City boy, me. But apparently she's been selling off most of her animals since her husband died two years ago, and this field hasn't been in use for quite a while."

Not the most likely avenue of investigation. Still, best to be thorough. "What happened to the husband?" she asked as they moved into the shade of the trees.

"Throat cancer," he said, with a sympathetic twist of the mouth. He ducked under a tree branch and held it back for her. "Nothing suspicious. And he was cremated, so, probably not his skull."

"Not unless he had two heads, anyway," she said, as they caught up to the others, clustered around a newly marked off area where one of the forensics team was crouched. As the woman brushed dirt away from the crown of a second skull, Pierce could see a similar set of blood-daubed patterns emerging from the soil.

"Looks like more of the same," Dawson said, stepping back. He raised his voice to address the whole assembled group. "There may be others! They're probably arranged in a pattern. Measure out the distance between the two skulls, and start searching in an equivalent radius around them. If you find a patch of disturbed earth, let forensics dig it out—it may be dangerous to move the skulls." He clapped his hands. "Go!"

Pierce hid a grimace at the supercilious tone. The local officer in charge didn't bother, scowling openly at the order even as he reluctantly endorsed it. "All right, do what the man says, lads, come on," he said. "The sooner we get this scene mapped out, the sooner we can leave the RCU to do their thing." *And go back to proper police work* was silently implied.

Dawson definitely wasn't winning friends and influencing people here, and that would be a real pain in the buttocks if they needed more assistance from the locals later on. Maybe he was used to having enough clout to run things his way, but the RCU didn't have the resources to operate like that. They'd have been here till February if they had to process a scene this size with no outside help.

But stepping in herself wasn't likely to smooth any feathers, only ruffle Dawson's, so she let him go off and direct the operation as he would. The attitude problem might not be wholly on his side this time, she supposed; if it turned out to be a pattern of behaviour, she could address it later.

Instead, she turned her attention to her other, newer and more malleable young recruit as he joined her in watching the painstaking excavation of the second skull. "All right, Taylor, what's your opinion on this?" she asked. He blanched, but Pierce only had a limited amount of pity to waste on nervous newbies. RCU was a specialisation where you had to think on your feet.

At least he rallied fairly quickly, even if he retained the deer-in-the-headlights look. "Er, well, the... presence of multiple prepared skulls suggests... it's not just a ritual burial. It's more likely that the skulls themselves are an... ingredient, if that's the word? It's skulls because the ritual requires skulls, not just because the perpetrator had bodies to dispose of."

She gave a noncommittal *hmm* and a single nod, encouraging him to go on.

His eyes darted down to the half-buried skull for inspiration. "Erm... the elaborate setup and use of sigils suggests this is something copied from an occult text rather than the caster's own invention, which means it's worth researching from that angle."

'Worth it' more in a hypothetical sense than in terms of the needle-in-haystack odds of finding the right text, but she'd allow the optimism.

Taylor was sweating now as he struggled to come up with anything else. "Um... the tied scroll in the skull's mouth most likely has a written enchantment. Untying it might break the ritual, or it might set it off. Skulls... suggest some kind of death-related symbolism, so..."

And now they'd reached the point where he was just desperately parroting any old bollocks from the textbooks, so she raised a hand to stop him. "Lots of symbols in magic, true, but don't assume it's that straightforward," she said. "Blood and death equate to power, and just because a ritual uses them for juice doesn't mean it's intended to kill." Though it was probably a safe bet that it wasn't meant to bring great joy and happy bunnies.

Still, decent effort on Taylor's part. Pierce gave him a nod. "Not a bad analysis, just don't take it too far," she cautioned. "The most important thing to know in this job is that most of the time we actually know bugger all. Always better to admit you haven't got a clue than assume you know what you're dealing with when you don't."

She straightened up, beginning to get a crick in the neck

from watching the excavation. "All right," she said. "Let's see what's going on with this search."

FULL EXPLORATION OF the site, or at least as wide a region as it was feasible to search, uncovered a total of three skulls, arranged in a triangle. The locations were interesting, one tucked away under the trees, the third one close to the base of the dry stone wall. Awkward places to dig, not the nice convenient patch of open ground that you'd pick if you were free to site your ritual anywhere you chose. It suggested that the arrangement had some significance, but that didn't necessarily mean it was tied to the field itself or the people who owned it or lived nearby.

Magic. Always more questions than answers.

Pierce watched enough of the excavation of the final skull to confirm it matched the others, and then went to join Dawson. He'd moved away from the rest of the group to make a phone call, but as she approached, he lowered the phone from his mouth and pocketed it. She tried not to give in to the momentary flash of paranoia. No reason to think he'd been talking about her, and even less to assume it was more than bitching about the boss being back if he had.

"So what's your plan from here?" she asked, careful to take less of an assessing tone than she had with Taylor. She didn't need to be at war with her DI, especially since he'd had weeks to establish his claim on the loyalties of the two new constables she'd barely met.

"I'm treating this as a potentially serious ritual curse,"

he said. "We need to learn more about these skulls before we try to move them. I've called in a necromancer—"

"A necromancer? Who?" In Pierce's experience, those who claimed they had an affinity for raising the dead were either fakes, or worse, the kind of dangerous dabblers who knew just enough to get a result but not what to do next.

Dawson's eyes narrowed fractionally at the challenge. "Man called Martin Vyner. He's a local."

"Never heard of him." She frowned.

"No? Well, you've been out of the game for a while," he said. The dismissive tone set her on edge.

"Maybe—but I've been in it for long enough to know that trying to raise the dead rarely makes a situation better," she said sharply. "We've got the site contained and there's no immediate danger. No need to escalate things by bringing more magic into the mix."

"Not so sure about the lack of immediate danger," he said. "This is no amateur effort. We need to know what we're dealing with."

"And there are ways to find out without leaping straight to the nuclear option."

"Not quickly." He held her gaze with a challenging stare.

Pierce would have had plenty more to say, but the DI in charge of the local team, Bowers, was heading towards them. She made a conscious effort to relax and step back, aware that even if he wasn't close enough to overhear, he could more than likely recognise the body language of two officers having a barney.

As it was, Bowers seemed to have built up a head of

steam of his own. "Some bloke with no police credentials just showed up at the gate saying that you called him in," he said with a glower. "Who is he? Is he one of your lot? If you want us playing rent-a-guard while your people ponce about, the least you could do is keep us bloody informed."

"Outside consultant," Dawson said. "I called him in to perform a ritual for us."

"He's cleared for RCU work," Pierce put in, and hoped Dawson wasn't making her a liar. He must have had this bloke vetted before using him at scenes, surely.

"Oh, is he, now?" Bowers was not appeased. "Well, maybe your work involves farting about doing rituals, but we have actual police work to get done. Forensics have done their job, or as much of it as you'll actually let them do, so how long before we can remove the skulls? We can't keep this place cordoned off for you all day."

"That depends on the outcome," Dawson said, looking past Bowers to where DC Taylor was approaching, accompanied by a tall, cadaverously thin gent with a dark Van Dyke who was carrying a duffle bag. He wore a suit jacket over a black T-shirt with a pentagram design, and small round glasses with yellow lenses.

Pierce could have picked him out as the necromancer in a crowd without even being told she was looking for one. She doubted he could do anything except make matters worse, but she couldn't send him away now without making the RCU look like they didn't know their arses from their elbows.

Not that they had much credit to lose with Bowers on

that front. He looked as if he was about to burst a blood vessel as Dawson strode off without a backwards glance to hail the new arrival.

"Mr Vyner! Thanks for getting here so quickly." So her DI *did* have manners, he just didn't think the local police they had to work with day-in, day-out merited them. Bloody wonderful.

She could sympathise with Bowers' visible headache, but she doubted he'd appreciate the commiseration. "'Scuse me," she said politely, more to stick it to Dawson than out of any hope of papering over the damage he'd already done, and went to join her subordinates with Vyner. She just hoped that this alleged necromancer could manage some sort of performance that wouldn't leave all them looking like idiots.

The necromancer had a soft, dry voice that was made for snooker commentary, and a penchant for stroking his beard as he listened. "Hmm, yes, I see, I see," he was saying as Dawson outlined the situation. "And these skulls haven't been moved from their resting place?"

"Excavated by police forensic specialists," Dawson assured him. "They're very careful not to disturb anything from its original position."

"Excellent, excellent." Vyner nodded. "An unquiet spirit builds a connection to the soil in which it's interred; the raising will be easier if the bones are still in place."

Constable Taylor looked like he was drinking this all in, but Pierce preferred to talk practicalities. "So what's the plan?" she asked bluntly. "What can you do, and what do you need to do it?"

Vyner turned to face her, eyes rendered uncomfortably unreadable behind the tinted lenses of his glasses. He had the kind of calm composure that *could* indicate confidence—or just a plain old con.

"If the soul died in pain or spiritual distress, then I should be able to call it forth and command it to speak," he said. "But I can't guarantee it will have any story to tell. Spirits are no more than lingering impressions, the psychic stain left behind by the victim's final memories. They fixate, and rarely retain enough self to offer more than one or two repetitive thoughts."

Genuine and smart enough not to promise too much, or covering for the fact his so-called ritual wouldn't do a damn thing?

"We'll start with this one," Dawson said, leading the way to the first skull they'd uncovered, out in the open.

They stood and watched with varying degrees of scepticism as Vyner made his preparations. He laid out a carefully measured ritual circle around the excavation using poured salt and powders, then drove metal stakes into the ground at points around the circle, joining them together with taut strings. He set out various items on a cloth beside him—a knife, a set of brass scales, a mirror—and planted seven blood red candles around the circle. All the way through, he kept up a low chanting under his breath, the rhythmic words indistinguishable.

At last, when he was satisfied, he sat back on his heels. "If I could have silence, please?" he said. "Everyone, be careful not to come too close to the circle—it's vital that the line remain unbroken."

Vyner struck a match and raised it to light the first of the candles. "Spirit, I call to thee," he said, the low words loud in the thick silence. The flame leapt high, burning a deep indigo blue, and the stench of sulphur filled the air. "Spirit, I call." He lit the second candle, bathing his face in blue light. The atmosphere seemed to chill and the field become darker; Pierce looked up at the sky, but the sun still squinted out between the hazy clouds just as brightly as before. Somehow it seemed to be further away.

"I call to thee," Vyner repeated as he lit the third candle. The dark smoke rising from the candles filled the air above the excavation with a haze, and his voice now sounded hoarse. "I call to thee." The fourth candle. The world beyond their little knot of observers around the circle had receded, sounds hushed, the wind calming into stillness, though she could see tree branches moving on the other side of the field.

He lit the fifth candle. "I call to thee." The sixth. "I call." At the lighting of the seventh, his voice rose abruptly into a booming roar. "Answer the call!"

The atmosphere sizzled and cracked, like a lightning strike without the flash and bang. Pierce felt her ears pop, and the short hairs at the back of her neck rose, as much from static as the rippling chill. They all held their breath as the candle flames died back down, and the smoke over the excavation slowly drifted away to reveal...

Nothing.

The long moment of waiting began to tip over from tense into awkward.

Bowers was the first to break the silence. "That it, then?"

he said, folding his arms. "Well, if you've quite finished arsing about, I'm going to—"

Vyner snatched up a bone-handled knife from his kit and threw himself forward, face contorted in an animal snarl as he lunged towards Bowers.

CHAPTER SEVENTEEN

THE NECROMANCER MOVED too fast for anybody to react, slamming into Bowers and sending the DI staggering backwards. Vyner's spindly limbs were flailing in a frenzy, the knife he clutched in one hand already half forgotten as he tried to attack with his whole body at once. He was snapping his teeth, kicking, clawing, trying to headbutt... It was as if he was too crazed to try to think.

As if he wasn't the one doing the thinking.

"He's a fucking psycho!" Bowers choked out, trying to ward off the flurry of attacks. He didn't have a stab vest; he was a detective visiting a potential body dump, not a uniformed officer expecting trouble on the beat.

Dawson was equally defenceless as he grabbed at Vyner around the middle, trying to haul him off the other man and getting the back of Vyner's head to his jaw for his trouble. One lucky swipe of that wildly swinging blade, and there'd be arterial blood flying. Pierce could see uniform officers running to join them, but they were too far off, and they didn't know what they were dealing with.

She had no more bloody clue than they did, but she had enough of one to realise there was more at work than an aggressive nutter.

"Taylor, get that knife off of him!" she barked, lunging for Vyner's kit. Think, think—if he'd raised something he hadn't meant to, how did she put it down? She scrabbled through the contents of the duffle bag, upending it: books, books, jars, candles, nothing fucking labelled, fucking *idiot*—

A yell of pain split the air, and she looked up to see Bowers clutching at his ragged suit sleeve, gushing blood welling beneath his hand. Dawson's attempt to tear Vyner away from him sent all three men staggering through the tangle of pegged strings and down into the excavation pit, scattering the salt and powder lines and kicking candles everywhere.

Taylor scrambled after them, lunging for Vyner's waving knife hand but jerking back as the blade swung towards his face. As Dawson grabbed to try and restrain Vyner's snapping teeth, his hand knocked the necromancer's glasses away. Pierce glimpsed the eyes behind, narrowed with rage, and red as clotted blood from edge to edge.

She doubted they were coloured contact lenses.

"Shit!" Scrabbling more frantically through the detritus of the dumped out duffle bag, Pierce tried to find anything that might help reverse a possession. Why hadn't Vyner taken some kind of—

Or maybe he *had* taken precautions. Cursing herself for an idiot, she abandoned the duffle and ran back to the remnants of the ritual. If he'd had anything on him to deal with things going bad, he would have kept it close to hand, not shoved at the bottom of a bag.

As she reached the crumbling edge of the excavated hole, Vyner tore free from the three men trying to hold him. He sighted her, and snarled like a beast catching a new scent, blood red eyes glaring over the yellow lenses of his lopsided glasses.

Tinted glasses. Who wore bloody tinted shades on grey days in December?

Someone who was trying to avoid meeting people's eyes. Snippets of questionable magical trivia she'd picked up over the years flashed through Pierce's mind: mesmerising gazes that had to be avoided, turning power back with a reflection. And one of the things that Vyner had laid out for the ritual had been a silver folding mirror...

As he came lunging at her, Pierce cast around for the case on the ground. A glint of silver there on the grass— Fuck! She jerked back as Vyner's clawing fingers raked at her face. Almost too bloody fast to evade—his moves were simian, fluid and flexible beyond the limits of a body that looked like it spent most of its time shut indoors in dark rooms.

Pierce was no spring chicken herself, and weeks of medical leave with the use of only one arm hadn't lent itself to building up her fitness. She tried to duck away, but Vyner's next swinging blow still clipped the side of her head, sending her reeling. As she staggered, dizzied, across the uneven ground, her foot came down on a candle. It rolled under her shoe, and she lost her balance and put her hand out to stop herself from falling, pain jarring through her still-healing shoulder.

Mostly desk work, she'd told the doctor who'd approved her return to work. A little bit of walking around. Not the DCI's job to grapple with suspects.

She'd barely straightened up before Vyner slammed into her, gnashing teeth just missing her ear. She shoved him back with her good arm and ducked under the next swipe, scrambling past him at a crouching run. As she reached out to snatch the mirror case up from the grass, a brutal kick to her back sent her sprawling to the ground. She rolled over to see Vyner looming over her, red eyes wild and teeth bared, the knife in his hand.

As he lunged at her with the blade, Pierce opened up the two halves of the mirror and shoved it into his face.

Vyner froze, the knife dropping from suddenly loose fingers. Neutralised, or only temporarily distracted? There was no way to be sure.

"Cuff him!" she bellowed from her position on the ground. "Silver cuffs!" And prayed that Dawson or Taylor had their RCU-issue cuffs with them, because, fuckety fuck, she hadn't yet picked up replacements for the pair she'd lost on the shapeshifter case.

Above her Vyner quivered, and she wondered, tension tightening her chest, if there was any hope she could kick him away before he fell on her...

And then Dawson and Taylor were there, wrestling his hands behind his back and hauling him away. As Taylor closed the first silver cuff around his wrist, Vyner let out a howl—not a human sound of rage or pain, but an ululating shriek that clawed along her nerves like fingernails. His head snapped back, and Pierce could see blood pouring from his nose and weeping from the corners of his eyes.

"Get that salt container over there," she ordered Taylor as she struggled up. "Make a circle round him." It might not do a damn thing, but when it came to magical threats, you threw everything but the kitchen sink and hoped you weren't making things worse.

Dawson hauled Vyner over to a patch of open grass and shoved him down to the ground; he went with no resistance, knees folding under him as he sat down in a dazed stupor. Taylor had the sense to keep a safe distance away as he poured out a ring of salt around him on the grass. As the circle closed, Vyner's head and shoulders slumped, all the breath and the resistance going out of him.

"Could be a ruse," Dawson warned sharply. "Keep an eye on him."

Deciding things were as much under control as they were likely to get, Pierce took a moment to look around and assess the rest of the scene. Bowers was being attended by a uniformed PC; didn't look like his knife wound was too serious, or at least he was still upright and keeping pressure on it. The handful of others who'd reached them—the whole thing had happened in moments—had faltered, obviously uncertain of what to do next.

She raised her voice to address them. "Get the paramedics down here." Bowers should get that wound checked out, and Vyner might well need attention of some sort, though she doubted the NHS would have much clue what to do with him.

She wasn't sure the RCU were any wiser on that front. How could they know if Vyner was back to himself? He sat huddled in the salt circle for several long minutes, making no effort to escape, and then at last he took a shuddering breath and straightened up. His face was wan, cheeks hollow, and the corners of his eyes and nose were smeared with drying blood—but his eyes were no longer deep red, just bloodshot human brown. He stared forward blankly and incuriously, either unseeing or just not taking anything in.

Dawson folded his arms. "Can you tell us your name?" he asked brusquely.

Vyner took another deep breath and lifted his head towards the voice, though his gaze still seemed unfocused. It took him a moment to dredge up the answer. "Martin Vyner."

"Today's date?"

That took him a bit longer. "The... sixteenth of December? Still?" Pierce surreptitiously checked her own watch to make sure he was correct. Two months off with no daily duties bar the odd hospital check-up had played havoc with her sense of time.

Dawson didn't give him any confirmation of the answer, still watching intently. "You know who I am?" he asked.

Vyner squinted blearily at Dawson. "You're... Inspector Dawson?" He was beginning to sound and look a little more alert. "You called me in to raise a spirit for the Ritual

Crime Unit. But something wasn't right, I felt—I should have..." He shook his head, squinting as if pained, and then looked around, for the first time seeming to register his circumstances and surroundings. "Did I hurt anyone? I don't really remember what happened..."

To Pierce's eyes he still seemed to be in a state of half-numbed shock, but Dawson pressed on regardless, barking questions in quick succession like a hail of conversational bullets. "How did the spirit you raised get out of the circle? Was it too strong; what? How did it take you over?"

Pierce hesitated on the verge of calling a halt to the questioning, but Vyner shook his head and spoke up fairly quickly. "Didn't raise a spirit," he said, squinting. "Not from the skull. This was..." Another headshake, but this one seemed more like a frustrated attempt to clear his thoughts. "Outside," he said.

"Explain," Dawson demanded, and she gritted her teeth. Words needed to be had about using this kind of aggressive interrogation style on a vulnerable witness, but she was loath to interrupt things just when it seemed he might be getting at something significant.

"There was no spirit in the skull to raise," Vyner said. "Felt like I wasn't getting anything, but then I got something, but it wasn't..." He squeezed his eyes shut, seemingly trying to brute force himself into a more articulate state. "The skull was contained by the circle," he managed, laying each word down with careful emphasis. "This spirit wasn't *in* the skull, it was... across the whole site. Distributed. Circle wasn't big enough."

"What does that mean?" Dawson asked.

Vyner shook his head again, biting his lip, and made a fraction of a shrug before he remembered or was halted by his handcuffs. "Don't know. Just... no lingering spirit in the bones. Not killed recently. The bones aren't victims, they're... material. Part of the ritual to do something else. Whatever I raised was separate from the skull. From outside it. I don't know. I don't know."

He was starting to sound frantic even through his tired tone, and Pierce stepped in before Dawson could press him any further. "All right, let the man rest," she said. "Doesn't look like we're going to get any more excitement here. Break the circle—carefully," she instructed Taylor. "If nothing happens, take him out of the handcuffs. Whatever that thing was, we're just going to have to hope it's gone." Because if it turned out their makeshift measures hadn't managed to remove it from Vyner permanently, she was buggered if she knew what to try next.

They uncuffed the shaken necromancer without further incident, and the paramedics arrived to take care of him and Bowers. When everything seemed to be under relative control, Pierce took her chance to pull Dawson aside.

"This was an unnecessary risk," she said. "You heard Vyner—those skulls weren't recent murder victims. There was no time urgency. We could have investigated the site more slowly and safely before leaping straight to performing new rituals without knowing what we were dealing with."

"Would we know as much about what we're dealing with if we hadn't?" he countered. "I *did* hear Vyner, and I saw him too. Whatever took him over didn't do it by chance.

Someone left it here to attack anyone who interfered with the site. I'd say that's even more reason for urgency than plain old murder."

He turned to move away, apparently considering the matter closed; she couldn't chase after him without drawing their infighting to the attention of the local police. Who had more than enough reason to badmouth them already. Pierce gritted her teeth, feeling a headache coming on. Dawson was going to be trouble, all right.

She grimaced around at the debris of Vyner's ritual, now a second crime scene to be documented. She had a feeling this case wasn't going to be plain sailing, either.

THE REST OF Pierce's first day back was swallowed up by paperwork and catching up on details of the cases that she'd missed. At least her subordinates had been around to curate the contents of her paper in-tray; one look at the number of emails waiting for her, and she was tempted to just do a mass delete and wait for anyone whose message mattered to resend.

Which of course was not an acceptable tactic when it came to police business, so she spent most of the afternoon sorting emails into folders according to how urgently they needed to be dealt with, rather than actually dealing with any of them.

On the other hand, the inbox archaeology did unearth a half forgotten contact from an old case, a university lecturer in occult studies who'd written a book on demonology. Pierce managed to catch her on the phone and arranged to drop by to ask her opinion on the Bingley skulls first thing tomorrow. No guarantee it would turn up anything, but at least it would get her out of this chair for a while.

Even with half the day spent doing paperwork, she was knackered by the time she made it home. The rest of her good intentions for a fresh new start on her return to work went up in a blaze of takeaway pizza, toffee ice-cream, and two glasses of wine she probably shouldn't have had after the painkillers for her shoulder. She could start being healthy and virtuous tomorrow.

She'd survived her first day back. That was something, she supposed.

She just wished she could believe it would be plain sailing from here.

CHAPTER EIGHTEEN

PIERCE LEFT THE house in good time for her meeting at the university, but the rigmarole involved in sorting out a visitor's parking permit forced her to jog across the campus to the School of Occult Studies to make it in time. It was a grubby yellow brick building tucked away around the back of the site behind some trees. There was a card lock on the main door, but a young lad with a scruffy beard held it open to let her in.

Human nature: there was no plan so flawless that someone wouldn't take a shortcut somewhere for convenience. While it might seem at first glance that whoever had planted the skulls in that field hadn't left a single clue, there was almost certainly *something* they'd felt safe to cut a corner on. The trick was to keep tugging at every thread in the hope one would unravel.

Maybe this Doctor Moss could help with that.

Deciding the building's creaky old lift wasn't likely to be any faster than her creaky old joints, Pierce took the stairs up to the upper level. The first closed office door she came to bore the name plate DOCTOR A.C. MOSS, OCCULT STUDIES, and she rapped with her fist, hoping her adventures in car parking hadn't cut things too late. She couldn't just leave confidential crime scene photos on the woman's desk with a Post-it.

"Come in!" called a deep, resonant female voice, the kind that would sound at home ordering teenagers around a netball pitch or shepherding a group of recalcitrant Brownies.

It belonged, Pierce discovered as she let herself in, to a tiny woman not far south of seventy, with a head of grey-white curls and round glasses on a neon green neck strap. Her impeccably tailored navy suit jacket and skirt made Pierce feel like even more of a scruffy bugger than usual. Police work didn't lend itself well to being overly precious about clothes, and neither did one-armed ironing.

"Doctor Moss?" she said. "Claire Pierce. We spoke on the phone yesterday."

The woman waved the formality away with a veiny hand. "Annie, please. Can't stand ceremony. Which is why I work for a university, obviously," she added, with a dry lift of her eyebrows. She cocked her head. "You said there was something I might be able to help your department with...?"

"Well, it's a long shot," Pierce said, "but given your field of expertise, we were wondering if you might be able to make anything of this." She brought out the folder she'd put together with a few photos of one of the skulls and Constable Taylor's meticulously measured crime scene sketch—the *first* one, drawn before Vyner's attempt at necromancy had complicated things. "We have reason to believe that it may be some sort of attempted summoning." Maybe not just attempted, if Vyner's possession hadn't been a self-induced cock-up.

Moss readjusted her glasses and studied the pictures intently, long enough for Pierce to start to get twitchy in the silence. She jumped when it was broken by a loud chime from a phone on the desktop. Doctor Moss set the folder down.

"My apologies, Chief Inspector, but I'm supposed to be meeting one of my PhD students for coffee," she said. Nonetheless, she spared another moment to peer at the site diagram as she stood. "This arrangement." She tapped the drawing with the base of her phone. "I'm not sure, but it does ring a bell. I'll have to check my books... Would it be all right if I consult with a few colleagues?"

It was always a risk involving outside academics, but the esoteric subjects RCU work encountered rarely left them with much choice. This could be their only chance of getting any information.

"Yes, but please could I ask you not to share the photographs or the fact that this concerns an active police investigation?" she said. The last thing they needed was for details to get out—not just because of the risk of compromising the investigation, but the chance of idiot copycats buggering about with rituals that they didn't understand. There was always someone out there with just enough knowledge to be dangerous and not enough sense to know they were out of their depth.

Pierce didn't think this case was one of those, though. No, this one had the scent of somebody who understood *exactly* what they were doing.

That might be even worse news.

Her phone rang as she was on the way back to her car, and she hurried away from the drifting students to take the call in relative privacy among the trees. An unfamiliar mobile number. "DCI Pierce."

"Er, Guv, it's Constable Taylor." The accent would have identified him even without the introduction. "We just received a call about the necromancer who helped us yesterday."

About, not *from*. "Has he relapsed?"

"Er, not exactly, Guv," he said, awkwardly. "Local police found him dead. Looks like a suicide."

PIERCE GROUND HER teeth as she drove to the scene of the death, going back over all the decisions it was too bloody late to change now. Should've gone with her instincts and countermanded Dawson's bad idea of trying necromancy, instead of worrying about departmental politics. Should've called a halt to the interrogation of Vyner earlier. Should've done more to see he was looked after in his vulnerable state of mind post-possession.

It was always easy to pick the best option in hindsight. But all the same, one ugly truth remained: they'd called him in to consult on a case, and now he was dead. This was the RCU's fuck up.

It was tempting to lay it all on Dawson's head, but the

fact was the buck still stopped with her. She was the one in charge, and she could have overruled him. *Should* have overruled him. Probably would have, if she hadn't been hesitant to rock the boat on her first day back on the job.

She had to get her head back in the game.

Pierce pulled up on the end of the row of police vehicles clogging up the residential street. The address Taylor had given her was an unassuming, narrow terraced house, not much different from the streets of student housing she'd been driving through on her way to meet Doctor Moss. There was barely a front garden, only a scrap of grass beside the steps that led up to the weathered front door. A small square window at ground level revealed the presence of a basement, though concealing blinds blocked any view inside.

Nothing about this place hinted that it might have been the domain of a man who called himself a necromancer— which only made it more likely that Vyner had been for real. Fakes always operated with more flash.

But even if he'd had some true experience in the field, he'd clearly been quite shaken by yesterday's events. They never should have left him on his own.

And it appeared that he had lived alone. The front door opened directly onto the living room, which had a functional fireplace and alcoves full of bookshelves. The shoe rack inside the door held only men's shoes, all the same size at a casual glance. There might be a girlfriend— or boyfriend—but probably not a live-in one, and there was nothing in the slightly cluttered but relatively tidy living room to suggest the presence of children. Thank God.

"Where's the body?" she asked a convenient uniform.

"Bathroom. Photographer's up there now."

Meaning she, as an extraneous RCU officer, would only be in the way. Vyner might have been called in on their case, but suicides weren't their department unless there was a magical component to the death.

Even so, as she stepped through into the dining room beyond, she saw Dawson loitering by the staircase up to the first floor, with a restlessness that suggested he was either itching to take action or wishing for a cigarette. Probably both.

"Pierce." He didn't sound particularly pleased to see her. "They didn't need to call you in on this. I can handle things here."

"I prefer to be kept informed." She pressed her lips together. "And clearly we should all have been paying this more attention. Why didn't anybody take note of Vyner's emotional state before they let him go off home alone?"

Dawson's doughy face remained unmoved. "The man was a professional necromancer. We had no reason to think that he was going to top himself," he said.

"There's no such thing as a professional necromancer. I've been doing this job thirty years and it's still a rare day when we come across something I've seen before. He wasn't prepared."

"And we can't be prepared for every consultant's emotional issues," he said stubbornly. "There's no predicting who's going to turn out to be unstable."

"*Nonetheless*," Pierce said pointedly, "it's our job to minimise any potential risks—"

She was interrupted by the footsteps of a young constable, descending the stairs with unusual haste. He looked around in search of his own superiors, but Dawson stepped up in their place. "What's going on?"

Pierce doubted the PC had any clue who they were or why they were here, but he was still young and impressionable enough to assume any authoritative figure in a suit was probably important. More fool him.

"Pathologist's just had a look at the body, sir," he said. "He reckons the wounds are inconsistent with a suicide—looks like this bloke was murdered."

UNFORTUNATELY, IT SEEMED the switch from suicide to a homicide investigation also bumped the RCU's status from vaguely unwanted observers to turf invaders who had no business sniffing round an ordinary murder.

"Look, if it turns out a wizard did it, then we'll call you," said the local DI in charge, who'd miraculously turned up from wherever he'd buggered off to when his officers were dealing with what looked like suicide. "But it doesn't take bloody magic to slit a bloke's wrists and chuck him in the bathtub. Believe it or not, those of us without fancy specialisms do actually know how to investigate a murder."

"This man was an RCU consultant," Pierce reiterated, with a firm patience that was getting her exactly nowhere. "He was involved in a supernatural incident yesterday. It's very likely his death is connected to our case."

"Then our investigation will get to that in due time," he said, with the kind of calculatedly obnoxious reasonability that could be deployed on members of the public without giving them grounds for a complaint. "We'll have some people interview your people—take some statements, yes? But let's not go getting things arse-backwards. We process the evidence here. Look into the nearest and dearest. *Procedure*," he emphasized, and shook his head. "The problem with your lot is they always want to start with the most complicated explanation first. One funny-looking shape in the blood splatter and suddenly you've got magical sigils coming out your arse."

It was clear she wasn't going to win them any concessions here. Dawson's backup probably wouldn't have helped—would almost certainly have made things worse, if his performance yesterday had been any indication—but it still vaguely irked her that he'd apparently wandered off while she was arguing their case. Looked like his burning itch to take charge took a convenient hike when it came to the more tedious, thankless tasks.

She drew a breath, aware that unleashing a temper that wasn't even wholly this idiot's fault could only compromise their standing further. No need to trade wilful lack of cooperation for outright hostility.

"Fine," she said, and hoped she'd succeeded in keeping at least some of the terseness out of her tone. "We'll leave this one in your hands. Just keep us updated." Not that they bloody would without repeated nudges to 'remind' them. She looked around again for Dawson, but didn't spot him. "Let me just see where my colleague's got to." At least it would give her a chance to get a quick look around the property before they left.

Of course, the trouble with using her favourite 'just within the rules' ruses on her fellow police was that they knew and used them too. "Well, he's not gone upstairs to look at the body, so there's no need for you to head up there, is there?" the man said, folding his arms with a smug smile.

Pierce didn't give him the satisfaction of a response, just moved back through into the dining room and glanced through the adjoining door. It led into the house's tiny kitchen, and from the window she could see a neglected back garden: bigger than the pitiful scrap of greenery out front, but still not requiring more than a cursory glance.

No sign of Dawson. He hadn't gone out the front, because she'd have seen him leave. Had he managed to sneak upstairs after all? She might be pleased at that show of initiative if she'd been at all confident he would actually share any information that he found.

Then her eyes fell on the door beneath the stairs, which her brain had automatically filed under 'cupboard.' It was standing ajar, and now Pierce remembered the basement window outside; she pulled it open to reveal a flight of wooden steps that ran parallel to the main staircase above. Rather than call down to Dawson, she descended the stairs after him.

The basement room below was relatively large, but made claustrophobic by the lack of any natural light. The one small window was covered by a blackout blind, and the ceiling was too low for hanging lights, several small recessed bulbs doing the job instead. They managed to brightly spotlight patches on the floor and yet still leave the corners thick with shadow.

Dawson was crouched by the remains of a ritual circle on the floor, drawn in neat chalked lines across the concrete. Stubs of candles sat in silver holders at points around it, as if they'd been allowed to burn down. One had been knocked over, spilling pooled wax across the floor; it could have been a fire hazard if there had been anything down here other than the bare concrete to burn.

The chalk circle was made up of multiple concentric rings, each filled with a different set of symbols. Pierce was no expert on ritual geometry, but she'd visited enough scenes in her time to get a vague feel for the common themes. This design gave the impression of being cobbled together from multiple different sources: the symbols inside the protective rings mixed various runic alphabets with Greek letters, and even nonsense words in pseudo-Latin.

As she studied the Latin letters, her mind nagged insistently that something was wrong with the picture. It still took several moments of staring at the chalked inscription before she twigged: the letters were the right way up on the *far* side of the circle, upside-down nearest her.

The words had been written by someone on the *inside* of the circle.

"Vyner was inside the circle," she said. "Not trying to summon something. Trying to protect himself." From a danger that they'd left him exposed to.

"Or this ritual could have been his killer's work," Dawson countered. "This is a murder, not a suicide. There was no reason to suspect anybody would come after him. We did this by the book."

"And maybe that's the problem." Pierce held his gaze. "RCU work requires more than just following the letter of the rules. The rules haven't caught up to what we do." It was pretty hard to codify a set of police procedures for a job that rarely meant facing the same thing twice.

"Can't predict everything," Dawson said, unrepentant. "I know your last big case went tits up, but there's no taking the risks out of the job. Can't take this kind of shit too personally."

She might have said something undiplomatic at that point, but a creak of the floorboards up above reminded her that they'd already technically been kicked off the crime scene. Having a loud argument wasn't likely to encourage the locals to tolerate them lingering. Instead, she jerked her head towards the stairs. "Ask them if they're willing to let our people in to process the secondary scene down here," she said. "If not, make sure they agree to send us copies of their photos."

Bugger all chance of cooperation on the first and little of timely compliance on the second, but it bought her a few moments to linger. As Dawson headed up the stairs, no doubt taking the non-sequitur as a concession he'd won the argument, Pierce drew out her camera phone and snapped a few shots of the ritual circle. Nothing that they'd be able to use as evidence in court, but the odds of getting anybody convicted for drawing on a floor in chalk were stone cold zero in any case, regardless of what the pattern might be meant to do. At least she'd have her own photo record of the design to research and maybe pass on to Doctor Moss.

She'd be a fool to rely on the local police helping her do her job—and, she was becoming increasingly sure, it might not be too wise to bet on Dawson, either.

CHAPTER NINETEEN

PIERCE HAD BARELY got back in her car to drive away when she had to pull over to take a call from Deepan. Apparently they'd had a break-in at a gallery in Halifax that matched the MO of a string of artefact thefts over the past few months: ritual mask snatched from the wall without any attention paid to the more valuable pieces on display. She left Dawson in charge of following up on Vyner's movements—not without some misgivings—and went to join Deepan at the scene.

The Hemsfield Gallery of Ritual Antiques was a grand name for a poky little shop tucked in between a Chinese takeaway and an empty unit. At least the takeaway's opening hours narrowed the window for the theft; it didn't close until eleven, which made it unlikely their thieves would have risked striking much before midnight.

The break-in had been discovered when the owner arrived for work that morning, though the local police had been and gone before anyone had thought to put a courtesy call in to Ritual. Technically the local forces kept them apprised of any crime that might potentially have a magical component so the RCU could maintain a database; in practice, the notifications vanished into the endless drift of Post-it notes and print-outs to be dealt with 'when we get a minute.' Deepan must have been on the ball to link these seemingly trivial thefts together.

Not that any theft was ever trivial to the victim, of course. Pierce affixed the appropriate polite but not too cheerful smile and let herself into the shop, accompanied by the faint tinkle of the bell above the door. Deepan had his notebook out to interview a woman who must be the owner, twig thin and somewhere in her upper forties with stringy ash blonde hair and a multi-coloured blouse. She was flitting about checking and straightening things in a fit of nervous energy, though as the reports had said, there was little sign of disarray beyond what the forensics team had left behind them. She jumped at the sound of Pierce's arrival.

"This is my boss, DCI Pierce," Deepan introduced her before the woman could mistake her for a customer. "Guv, this is the gallery owner, Ms Hemsfield."

"Oh, Sarah, please," the woman said by sheer social reflex. She twisted the end of her wrapped scarf in her hands, obviously at a loss for further etiquette. It would be convenient if nervousness facing the police really was an indicator of having something to hide, but in Pierce's experience, the innocent were apt to be just as twitchy as the guilty: they were less used to being questioned.

"Don't mind me," Pierce said, holding up a hand. "I'm just here to observe." She nodded for Deepan to continue as she stepped back to take a glance around the shop. It veered more towards the 'antique' side of its name than the 'gallery' part, the small interior made claustrophobically closer by being crammed with all manner of objects. It had the inescapably musty scent of aging tat, not aided by the shelf of mouldering taxidermied animals that peered down at them with sightless glass eyes.

Pierce scanned the contents of the room with the eye of both a copper and someone who'd seen a few ritual artefacts in her time. That glass display case of jewellery was easily smashed: some gold and silver pieces in there that would have been easy to carry away. The bloody great candle holder in the corner looked like it was solid silver too—probably worth having despite the bulk. And that shelf of old leather-bound books in the corner, always an insatiable market for anything that looked like a halfway authentic occult text.

Deepan's instincts were right on the money. Regardless of whether this theft was linked to the earlier series, this hadn't just been an opportunistic smash and grab: this burglar had been targeting something specific.

"So you told the officers who were here earlier that the only thing missing was a wooden mask?" Deepan asked the owner.

"Yes... so far as I can see, yes." Hemsfield looked faintly befuddled. "I don't quite know why anyone would take it over the other pieces in the shop—it wasn't the most impressive looking thing, and quite uncertain provenance as well. Possibly seventeenth century, but with no documented history, the value's really a matter of what anyone's willing to pay." She gestured to a wall display of several hanging masks, next to a conspicuously empty hook. "There'd be much more of a market for something like these African masks, for example."

"Do you have a photo of the mask that was stolen?" Pierce put in.

"Oh! Yes, yes, it's on the website," she said abruptly. "I should have thought... I should take that down in case someone tries to make an offer." She fluttered for a moment. "Um, would you like me to—I can bring it up on the computer now, if you like. In fact, I can print you a copy, if the printer's got ink in it."

"That would be very helpful, yes," Pierce said. And at least it gave the gallery owner something to do that made her feel like she was being somewhat useful. Pierce could sympathise with the frustration of being seemingly unable to do anything beyond waiting for something else to happen; it came up more than often enough in her job.

And it might come up here, given the lack of any obvious clues as to the perpetrators. She doubted they'd be so lucky as to have the local police come up with usable fingerprints, let alone a helpful match.

"Did you notice anyone hanging around the shop recently?" Deepan asked as the owner led the way up the narrow STAFF ONLY staircase at the rear. "Anyone behaving oddly?"

"No, no, not that I noticed—not that I *would*," she added, wringing her scarf apologetically as they reached the top. "Lots of people come in just to look, and of course it's a small shop, it makes people awkward when there's nobody in there but them and me... People quite often come in and go back out again. I wouldn't notice."

The private room at the top of the stairs was, if anything, even more stuffed than the shop below; boxes of bubble-wrapped antiquities were crammed in beside office supplies. Hemsfield leaned under the table to switch the computer on at the plug.

"Sorry, it's terribly slow, this old thing," she said, offering an awkward smile as it started up. "I don't really use it that much—my niece does most of the website stuff for me." She moved the mouse in a circle and peered at the screen. "Oh, is it installing updates again? Sorry... Always seem to get millions of the things every time I switch it on. I really don't know what it's doing half the time."

Pierce looked around at the cramped environs of the upper room. "Was anything taken from up here?" she asked, though she wasn't sure how anyone would tell.

"No, no, I don't think so," Hemsfield said. "I had a quick rummage around when I first came in—probably shouldn't have, I know, fingerprints, but you don't think, do you? I didn't see anything else missing aside from the mask downstairs." She turned back to the computer screen. "Ah, here we go. Now, let me just get the internet..."

Pierce shared a small, rueful smile with Deepan, who was perceptibly twitching with the itch to leap in and take over. Poor lad had ended up with more than his fair share of report-writing when he'd first joined the RCU, thanks to his inability to stand around and watch while her former sergeant made a hash of his painstaking two-fingered typing. It had stood him well when he'd taken the sergeant's role himself—the first one she'd had who'd been promoted from within. The RCU didn't generally have much luck with retaining people long enough for them to advance through the ranks.

She wondered if Dawson was planning to change that by gunning for her job. Under Superintendent Palmer she would have been sure that her boss had her back, but with Snow in charge now, there was no such reassurance. A big break in this theft case could give her some much-needed leverage, if the investigation had been stalled while she was gone.

She grimaced as the shop owner brought up her photo of the mask, a small low-res snapshot of a wooden leaf mask that looked little different from a ton of other Green Man depictions you could pick up cheap in your average New Age shop.

Of course, *getting* a break in the case might be easier said than done.

The gallery owner seemed to have little more help to offer, so Pierce grabbed lunch with Deepan at a nearby sandwich shop. His disgustingly healthy veggie option inspired her to go for the virtuously low calorie end of the menu herself, which she was already sure she would regret in a few hours' time. She tried not to eye the rack of chocolate bars by the till.

"I don't know how you stay awake living on rabbit food," she said, stirring her tea.

"It *keeps* me awake, Guv," he insisted. "My energy levels always crash when I'm eating all that heavy sugary crap."

"Ah, but the solution to that is to eat *more* heavy sugary

crap," she said, filching another sachet of sugar from the tray to add to her tea. Baby steps.

It was a relief to sit down and unwind after being on the go since early morning, but as usual her mind soon steered back to the job. "So how have things been with Dawson while I've been away?" she asked. This was the first chance she'd had to talk to Deepan without other ears listening in, and while he wasn't the type to badmouth a colleague, she trusted him to shoot straight with her. "Any trouble?" She blotted the bottom of the dripping teacup on her serviette.

He shook his head, absently twisting and folding the paper wrapper of his drink straw. "Nothing major. Teething troubles—well, obviously he outranks me, even if I'm the one with the RCU experience, so... bit awkward. You know." He waved it away with a dismissive shrug.

"Left you in the lurch a bit there, didn't I, son?" she said, twisting her mouth in an unhappy grimace. Unavoidable—she could hardly have come back to work with a duff arm, and the first couple of weeks after the surgery she'd been no bloody use to anybody—but still, far from ideal. It made her grimly aware of just how easily her entire unit could be put out of action at a stroke.

She supposed she ought to be grateful for Dawson, a second in command to hand the leadership off to in the event she was injured again, but she still had grave doubts about how much he could be trusted.

"Wasn't exactly your fault, Guv," Deepan said, shaking his head with a faint snort. "I got off lightly compared to the rest of you." There was a silence, and she knew they were both thinking about Tim. An inexperienced young constable, murdered on her watch; no matter how hard they worked towards it, sometimes it felt like there was no justice.

And the thought of the disastrous outcome of that case was a stark reminder that there might be forces within the police actively working against it. Pierce leaned forward over the table. "So what's your opinion of Dawson? Personally."

Deepan pressed his lips together, contemplating the question rather than brushing it off with polite pleasantries. "Headstrong," he said ultimately. "He likes things done his way. Bit of a steamroller, too: he'll take advice from people who know what they're talking about, but he doesn't much like listening to caution. Prefers to be taking action, even if it's risky." He sat back in his chair and shrugged. "Decent enough at the job though, and he doesn't seem to be playing favourites or trying too hard to climb the ladder. Could've got a lot worse."

"Mm." Probably true, even if it was faint praise. "What about the new superintendent?"

He shook his head. "Haven't really met him, apart from when he first came in and gave his big intro speech. You're lucky you missed it—all very 'standards,' 'targets,' 'media image,' and all that guff. But then that's pretty much what they all talk like, at that level."

"So what exactly happened with Palmer?" she asked. "Did he announce he was going?"

"I'm not really sure, to be honest—I was out of the office a lot at the time," Deepan said with an apologetic shrug.

"This was back when we had the Oxford RCU guys in: we didn't get the new personnel until Snow arrived. I did have to take a few things to Superintendent Palmer, since I was kind of *de facto* in charge, but he was pretty harassed—he basically just let me go off and do whatever. Didn't want to hear the details."

"Not like him," Pierce noted, keeping a neutral tone of voice. Not like him—because she was pretty sure it hadn't *been* him, but the imperfect impersonator who had worn his skin. Yet there was no way to prove it; all she had to back her assertion was gut instinct, the disappearance of Palmer's customary silver watch—the touch of which would have broken the enchantment on any shapeshifting skin—and the later disappearance of Palmer himself. It barely even qualified as circumstantial evidence.

And Deepan certainly hadn't known the man well enough to be able to corroborate her suspicions. He gave a faint shrug. "Like I said, he was stressed. He was looking pretty ill—I wasn't surprised when they told us he'd taken time off for ill health."

She straightened up. "So he didn't announce his retirement right away?"

"Well, nah, but we could see it was on the cards," he said. "It was obvious he wasn't going to be coming back."

"So who was in charge in the interim?" There clearly hadn't been any official handover.

Deepan gave a wry smile. "It was a bit of a pig's ear, to tell you the truth, Guv," he said. "Nobody knew!" She got the impression, from the way that the words tumbled out, he'd been sitting on the built-up frustration of that era for some time. "I mean, there's me, technically sort of in charge of the RCU, except obviously I'm only a sergeant, and then there's Matheson from Oxford RCU, who outranks me but doesn't know what he's doing... then you've got the rest of the station's operations, which is *probably* Bob Shannon's job to run when the super's not there, except you know what Bob's like with additional responsibilities."

"Wouldn't touch it with a barge pole," she said. Oh, yes, she knew Bob of old. The turnover in the rest of the station was dramatically less rapid than that of her unit— even where it could probably use a good stir to shake things up.

"Wouldn't even pick up the barge pole, in case you made him officer in charge of barge poles," he said wryly. "So the RCU hasn't got anybody who can take charge, the regular police have got Bob who doesn't want to, nobody's quite sure what the super's instructions are because he's buggered off without telling anybody, and meanwhile we've got all these internal investigations bigwigs in ordering everybody about."

"Oh, yes?" Pierce tipped her eyebrows at him over her tea cup as she raised it for another sip, trying to act casual though she was down to the sugary dregs. "So what happened with that, anyway? Were they investigating Palmer?"

"I'm not sure," he said, glancing over his shoulder, as if someone might be listening in who gave a damn about police internal politics. But the sandwich shop was deserted except for the two of them, even the girl serving behind the counter disappeared into the back with only the slosh and clatter of half-hearted washing up to betray her presence. "No one really knew who they *were*, to tell you the truth," he admitted. "Palmer just told us they were investigating this whole business with the shapeshifter case and we should give them our full cooperation."

Now it was her turn to take a wholly unnecessary glance around, paranoia making her spine prickle. "You think it was that Counter Terror Action Team?" she asked. Not a real organisation, she was almost sure, but the name given by the group that had interfered with her investigation every step of the way. She'd been trying to put the skinbinder murdering people for shapeshifting skins behind bars; they'd been trying to secure his services for their own ends, and never mind the trail of bodies that he left behind him.

"I don't know, Guv," Deepan said, shaking his head apologetically. "It wasn't any of the ones who tried to take those case notes off us before, but... we never saw any ID. Not that anyone asked—I mean, you keep your head down in that kind of witch hunt." He frowned minutely. "Superintendent Palmer wouldn't have let them just waltz in, though, surely? Not if they were the ones who cocked everything up in the first place."

"He might not have had a choice." For more reason than Deepan could guess. Pierce sighed heavily and set her tea down. "So, whoever it was, it's all been swept under the rug, and we're never going to find out who it was in the police or the government fucking us about. Sally injured, Tim killed, one of the officers from the Firearms Unit killed—"

"And you injured, Guv," Deepan reminded her.

"That, too." Though her shoulder wound was almost trivial at the end of that list. "And yet no one's going to be brought to justice for any of it." Pierce grimaced as she pushed her cup away. "Still, at least we caught the bloody skinbinder." One small victory wrested from the jaws of total shambles. "Don't suppose there's been any word about a trial?" she said, without much expectation.

Deepan's face twisted awkwardly as she began to stand. "Did you not get notified?" he said. "There's not going to be a trial—the bloke's dead."

She dropped back down into her seat. "What? Suicide?" Arrogant little sod hadn't seemed the type—too sure his unique gift for skinbinding would win him a reprieve, and too uncomfortably close to being right about it. And he ought to have been in high enough security accommodations to make any major self-harm impossible.

But Deepan was shaking his head in any case. "Transportation accident," he said. "Lorry driver went through a set of red lights and smashed into the side of the police vehicle while he was being transferred. Both the lorry driver and the prisoner were dead on arrival."

Pierce let out a small, bitter snort. "Oh, yeah? Pretty convenient." She didn't need to be a DCI to recognise a coincidence that neat wasn't likely to be much of one at all.

Someone high enough placed in the police to know transfer times, even arrange them, removing a liability from the playing field?

Or merely making them *think* that he'd been removed, when he wasn't really dead at all?

Pierce pressed her lips together as she cleared the remains of her meal with a clatter. These trails were weeks, months old. She'd been out of action too long to have much hope of catching up to anyone behind all this. There was nowhere to start.

But Pierce had spent thirty years of her life working for the RCU. Nowhere to start was practically routine.

CHAPTER TWENTY

PIERCE LEFT DEEPAN to liaise with the local police and see about getting them CCTV footage from the surrounding streets, and drove back to the station. No sign of her DI in evidence. "Dawson call in?" she asked Freeman.

The young DC shook her head, and Pierce tried not to grimace. It could be that Dawson was just caught up in the drudgery of routine police work and didn't have anything to report, but she didn't fully trust him out of her sight. If he *had* found some kind of lead, what were the odds he'd actually notify her instead of going off half-cocked to chase it down? She was all in favour of her team showing initiative—Lord knew the RCU was too small and too busy to keep officers tied to her apron strings—but it would help to be sure she could trust their judgement before turning them loose.

Time to get to know her new pair of constables. She drew their attention with a clap. "All right, these artefact thefts," she said. "What do we know?" Always easier to get up to speed from a verbal briefing than reading dry reports, and it would give her some chance to take their measure as investigators.

Freeman was the first to speak up, sitting up smartly while Taylor was still sporting the stunned rabbit look that seemed to be his default response to snap tests of his abilities. "There have been four incidents that we're treating as connected," she said. "Five now, if we're including last night's theft from the Hemsfield Gallery."

"It seems to be the same MO, but let's stick with the earlier cases for now," Pierce said.

Freeman nodded earnestly. "Erm... all of the break-ins occurred at night. Two museums, an antique shop and a private collection, at locations scattered across Yorkshire. The thefts look like they're professional—alarms and internal CCTV disabled, no witnesses or useful trace evidence left at any of the scenes. Targeted, too—in each case, the thieves could easily have got away with far more than they took."

"So what exactly have they taken so far?" Pierce asked. She'd skimmed this file yesterday, but the details of the items taken had been secondary in her attention to clues about the thieves and their operation.

By this time Taylor had riffled through his notebook and found the appropriate spot. "In the first museum heist they took a ceremonial dagger."

"They opened up a glass case full of them, but only took the one," Freeman added. "Quite plain, leather scabbard, nothing fancy in the design. There were others in the same case that would have been worth thousands."

"But this one would be easier to fence," Taylor countered.

"Possibly," Pierce allowed, though she doubted that had been the motivation. "What else?"

He consulted his notes again. "The second museum theft was a wooden cup. Goblet, is that what you call it? Wine-glass-shaped thing." He sketched it vaguely in the air, looking faintly worried, as if he might be marked down for failing to get the right word. "Chalice?" he hazarded.

"Cup'll do." Pierce waved the detail away. Facts mattered, not the terminology.

"Carved, but not very valuable," he went on with greater confidence. "They also took a wooden box from an antique shop in Leeds." He held his hands out to illustrate an object about the dimensions of a tissue box. "With little subdivided sections inside. The owner thought it might have been an old magician's herb and powder store, but there was nothing in it, just an empty box."

"And what was taken from the private collection?"

"A bag of rune stones," Freeman put in. "Only twelve stones, though, not a complete set. The owner used to buy them up cheap at auctions—antique sets of stones with some runes missing." Not much use to anyone for casting runes, then; Pierce was dubious towards most alleged forms of divination in the first place, but you certainly couldn't get an effective reading with only half the runes available.

"Maybe the thieves have the other part of the set?" Taylor suggested.

"It's possible," Pierce allowed. "Or they're looking for it."

"Why this set, though?" Freeman bit her lip thoughtfully. "Why not grab one of the others instead? Why not steal a complete one, even? We know they're capable of pulling off the thefts."

"Obviously they're after these specific items for a reason," Pierce said. "So what links them together?"

A moment of contemplation, then Taylor shook his head. "Nothing, Guv," he said. "It could be components for a ritual—the dagger, the goblet cup thing—but I don't see how a box and a few useless rune stones fit into that."

"It's not just about the magic," Freeman said, sitting forward. "We've got to think of it as a crime. What's the motivation if it's not about money?"

"Jealousy, revenge, obsession," Taylor reeled off, and shook his head. "Maybe we're looking for a rational connection when there isn't one? They could be stealing things because the ghost of Elvis told them to. Or using some kind of ritual to divine what they ought to steal next."

"Ownership," Freeman suggested, with a self-deprecating shrug. "They think these objects are theirs by right. Maybe the thieves used to own these items, or have some reason to think they ought to."

"But we don't know the provenance of most of the items," Taylor objected. "We don't have any evidence they were ever linked together."

"*We* don't," she said, cocking an eyebrow. "Maybe the thieves do."

Pierce sat forward. "Maybe we're thinking too recent," she said. "The item stolen last night was a seventeenth-century carved mask. This is not necessarily about who owned these things ten years ago, or even fifty—maybe the thieves are trying to unite a collection from much longer ago." She stood up from her chair. "Find me everything you can about the history of these artefacts before they ended up in collections."

IT WAS A frustrating afternoon of effort without much result. The only thing their research into the history of the artefacts managed to dig up was that the dagger and carved box were both estimated to be of a similar age to the mask, supporting the idea that all five pieces probably had a common origin. But exactly what that might be proved impossible to track; the history of the dagger dead-ended with the man who'd sold it to the museum in the 1930s, and none of the others had even that much of a paper trail, picked up in house clearances and auction lots with no details attached. They weren't visibly valuable enough for anyone to have bothered keeping records.

Dawson's search for more detail on Vyner's actions had come up similarly blank. He'd been checked out at the hospital but found to have nothing more obvious than a headache and some bruises, gone straight home afterwards, and no doubt his body would still have been lying there undiscovered if the constable sent to get a statement from him hadn't been concerned he'd done a runner.

Deepan had secured them some CCTV footage from the cameras in the region of the Hemsfield Gallery, but none of them were positioned to show the building or the street in front of it directly, which left the needle-in-haystack task of watching the whole lot in hopes of spotting anything of interest.

"Any joy?" Pierce asked towards the end of the afternoon, walking round to rest her hands on the back of his chair. Deepan sat back and rubbed his face with a groaning yawn.

"None of the cameras we've got show anything unusual at the time of the theft," he said, shaking his head. "I'm going back through the days before now, see if there's any sign of anyone casing the place."

"Need a fresh set of eyes?" she offered. Watching security footage for any length of time was hypnotically dull, but you had to stay alert for little details, especially when there was a chance some form of magic might be involved.

Deepan waved the offer away with a tired smile. "No, I've got all my recurring guest stars memorised by now," he said. "Curly-haired woman with pushchair. Bloke walking overweight pug. So far the pug is my most likely suspect."

"Yeah, they're shifty little buggers—always heavy breathing." She clapped her hands on the back of his chair. "Don't stay up all night on this, all right? It's a pretty long shot."

He just leaned his head back to smile wryly up at her. "You should take your own advice, Guv," he said. "I doubt we're going to see any breakthroughs tonight. You might as well get out of here on time for once."

He had a point: more hours staring at her computer screen weren't likely to produce much but a headache. On the other hand, sitting around at home making a half-hearted effort at being domestic didn't seem very appealing either. Pierce pulled out her phone and flicked through the address book until she found Sally Keane's name. She'd been putting this visit off for far too long.

SALLY OPENED THE door herself when Pierce knocked at the small terraced house, a warm smile already in place. "Hiya, Guv!" she said brightly, stepping back to let her in.

She looked a world better than the last time Pierce had seen her, not long out of hospital; though she hadn't put back all the weight that she'd lost, it now looked like healthy slimming instead of alarming gauntness. The tracheostomy tube was now gone, and in the chill December weather, it wasn't immediately obvious that her high-collared shirt was hiding the horrific scars from the shapeshifter's claws.

"You're looking good," Pierce told her, the words sincere but still ringing awkward. With Sally no longer in quite such a bad way, this visit fell in an uncertain etiquette limbo between social call and checking up on a subordinate. Assuming Sally was still her subordinate. If there had been any discussion of her returning to work, Pierce hadn't been notified.

"So are you," Sally said, as she stepped in and closed the door behind her.

"And you lie well, too," Pierce noted. She followed Sally

through into the front room, exchanging a brief nod of greeting with her husband Mike where he sat on the sofa watching TV. There was a Christmas tree in the corner, and a few googly eyed reindeer and snowmen standing amid the row of cards on the mantelpiece. It had been years since Pierce had bothered with decorations herself; they always lingered for months if she did.

"So are you back at work now?" Sally asked, bustling into the kitchen to get them all drinks, while Pierce perched on one of the armchairs next to the dining table. The room was on the cosy side of cramped, shelves of books and DVDs in the corner, framed photographs clustered on the window ledges and TV table. It had a lived-in feel that Pierce's own home had never really acquired despite the fact she'd probably been there longer.

"Went back on Tuesday," she said, and shook her head slightly. "It's all new faces—did you know that even Palmer's gone?"

She wondered if Sally, out of everyone, might be willing to believe her theory that their old superintendent had been replaced before he left. Sally was the one who'd seen the full extent of the skinbinder's handiwork in the raid, moments before the shapeshifter in panther form had slashed her throat; she was the one who'd seen that he had human skins prepared among his collection of shapeshifting pelts.

But with Mike here in the room with them and the lightness in Sally's tone as she raised her voice over the boiling kettle, it was difficult to imagine broaching the topic. "Yes, Deepan told me," she said from the kitchen.

"He and Anita came round with the kids a couple of weeks back—they're lovely girls. So well behaved." There was the clink of mugs being set down on the counter. "Mike and I have been talking about starting a family, actually."

"Oh, right?" She politely returned Mike's nod and smile, feeling at once both very old and very much out of her depth in this sort of conversation. Pierce couldn't say she'd ever had any desire to have kids—she wasn't overly fond of other people's, and had spent too many years in the police to believe everyone really *did* find it 'different when they're your own'—but she'd always vaguely imagined she'd get round to doing the marriage thing at some point.

Apparently a bit too vaguely, since past other halves had been and gone without it ever coming up, and in fact, it had been a while since any had come and gone at all. The last one had been Paul of the regrettable taste in cardigans, and that had probably been longer ago than it seemed if she stopped to work it out.

For Christ's sake. This was why she didn't do social visits: too much maudlin contemplation and self-pity, when it wasn't other people's pity. She shook the thoughts off and accepted the mug of tea from Sally with a grateful smile. "Cheers."

"We've got biscuits as well if you like," Sally offered. "Or you're welcome to stay for tea—Mike was just going to make a curry."

Rude to invite herself round for a meal at such short notice, but she did want this chance to talk to Sally, and since depressing self-reflection seemed to be the other option for her evening: "Curry would be great, if it's not too much trouble."

Mike soon headed into the kitchen to start the meal, probably as eager for an excuse to duck out of being the third wheel as she was to talk to Sally alone. But Pierce was still conscious of his presence in the next room, inhibiting how much she could safely spill about RCU work, let alone the murkier waters of conspiracy around it.

All the same, the conversation inevitably turned towards the devastating events of last October.

"So terrible about Tim," Sally said, gazing distantly over the top of her mug of tea as she held it in both hands. "Poor kid. I wish I'd been able to make it to the funeral."

Pierce made a soft noise of understanding. She'd been there herself, though she probably shouldn't have been; too soon after the operation to be struggling into formal clothes and sitting through the service at the crematorium half dazed from pain and the pills that were supposed to kill it.

It had been a secular service, thankfully—she could take or leave other people's religion, most of the time, but she wasn't sure she'd have sat well through platitudes about God's plan as they gathered to cremate the remains of a lad in his twenties who'd been skinned for no better reason than he made a convenient figure to impersonate.

She wasn't sure if Sally had even been told the full circumstances of Tim's death; if not, Pierce didn't have the stomach to enlighten her right now.

"Just a baby," she said instead, and shook her head. "They're all babies. You should see the two new constables they've given me—so fresh and shiny they still squeak when they move. And they've landed me with a DI who's convinced he knows better than the people with RCU experience. I'm just lucky I've still got Deepan."

Sally sighed and lowered her now empty mug. "Guv," she said after a long pause. "I'm not going to be coming back."

Pierce tilted her eyebrows her way. "No?"

She'd suspected as much from the beginning, but it was still a blow. If she'd had both Deepan and Sally to call on, she wouldn't have felt quite so outnumbered by inexperienced unknowns.

"I've been talking it over with Mike," Sally said, with an apologetic twist of a smile. "I love RCU work, it's fascinating—but it's just too much of a risk. I was lucky to survive this time, and it could easily have been me in Tim's position. And if we do end up having kids..."

Pierce nodded with a sigh of her own, knowing anything she could say to reassure her would be lying.

"I've been thinking of transferring to something safer," Sally said. "Maybe part time. What I'd love to do, actually, is get into the forensics side of things—Magical Analysis. But that probably means going back to do another degree, and even if I can get some sort of credit for my time with the RCU, doing it part time..."

"That's going to take a while," she said, nodding. And there was no guarantee, even if Sally got the necessary qualifications, that she would end up getting a job in the RCU's research department. The demand was always there for more trained staff, but the budget wasn't, and unlike the detective branch, Magical Analysis didn't have the same alarmingly high turnover.

Pierce pressed her lips together, not quite ready to concede defeat even though she knew it was on the cards. "So your mind's made up?" she said.

"'Fraid so, Guv," Sally said with a wry smile.

Pierce sat back with a sigh, peering into her mug at the last mouthful of tea that was probably too cold to finish now. "Fair enough," she said. "So you're all finished up with the department? Did they send someone round to take a statement about the raid on the farm? Deepan said there was some kind of official investigation, but I haven't heard anything about what came of it."

Sally nodded, her frown taking on a few deeper wrinkles. "Yeah... it was while I was still in hospital, actually. You were probably in hospital after your op yourself, come to think of it. God, aren't we a pair?" She grinned, but it soon faded back into a frown. "Internal investigation, was it? Seemed more like Special Branch, from what I could tell. Made it very clear that"—she gave a reflexive glance towards the kitchen where her husband was cooking the meal, but went on without obvious pause—"the nature of the skinbinder's activities was to stay under wraps."

Pierce grimaced. She couldn't help but wonder, from the slightly tense set of Sally's face, exactly what kind of threats had accompanied the injunction. Threats enough to be responsible for her reconsidering returning to the RCU at all?

Maybe—but if so, that only made her stated reasons for quitting all the more true. Working for the RCU was dangerous. Getting involved in any off-books quest to find out the truth about who was responsible for Palmer's disappearance and all the shenanigans surrounding their last case could only make it more so.

Pierce had already put Sally in the path of a shapeshifter's claws. The least she could do was avoid dragging her in to face even worse trouble.

THEY CALLED AN end to the grim shop talk, and spent the meal chatting about more pleasant things. Pierce left shortly after they'd eaten, not wanting to outstay her welcome. It had grown dark outside, and she stopped under a streetlight to delve in her handbag for her car keys.

Whereupon she promptly discovered a set of folded printouts that she'd shoved in there hours earlier. "Bollocks!" The photos that she'd taken of the ritual circle in Vyner's basement. She'd gone to the effort of transferring them from her phone to the computer and printing them off so she'd have hard copies she could pass on to Doctor Moss at the university. Then she'd clean forgotten about it in the stultifying haze of fruitless research in which she'd spent most of the afternoon.

Odds were Doctor Moss had already left the office by now. She could run the pictures over in the morning... But that would mean getting into work late again, and with Dawson's penchant for wandering off without permission she'd rather be there first thing just in case anything new had come up overnight. She might as well take them over now, even if she could only shove them under the door of the locked office with a note.

Mind made up, she drove back over to the university campus. The place was still occupied by wandering packs of students, but while the academic buildings were still lit they seemed largely deserted, and by the time she'd crossed the campus to the out-of-the-way corner that housed the School of Occult Studies, she'd lost most of the company.

The glass doors onto the building's outer porch swung open to let her in, but inside was a more solid fire door, this one requiring a card key. There was no sign of anyone around to let her in this time. Pierce reached for the door handle to test it, more out of habit than any actual hope that she'd get in. If there were no security staff on duty, she might have just wasted a trip.

Yet the handle turned and the door started to move. She glanced at the lock and saw the light was green, despite the fact there was no card in the slot. Her gaze fell on a small device like a USB flash drive plugged into a port at the base of the lock. She was pretty sure that hadn't been there this morning.

She was pretty sure it shouldn't be there at all. Someone unauthorised was in the building... and she had a dark feeling she knew which office they were here to visit.

CHAPTER
TWENTY-ONE

PIERCE RAN THROUGH her options as she stepped into the building. She had no police radio, and backup was too far away to get here at a useful speed. Campus security were closer, but if there was anything here that she couldn't handle herself, she doubted they could help.

So far all she had was evidence of a potential break-in. If the intruder was still in the building—and the fact they'd left that device behind in the lock pointed to yes—seconds might count. She should assess the situation first before she called for backup.

And thus also handily avoid looking a complete tit if this was just some idiot student showing off their hacking skills without thinking of the consequences.

It could be that. It could just be a bog standard break-in, thieves after whatever could be lifted from an out-of-the-way corner of the campus. But her instincts were ticking like a car indicator, and she took the stairs at speed, unwilling to be trapped inside the slow, noisy lift. She'd be a sitting duck if anyone was waiting outside of the doors.

The lights were on, but the building felt empty; that subtle quality to the silence that rang differently from a space that only seemed quiet because your brain was tuning out the background noise. Pierce was hyper-aware of the sound of her feet on the stairs, the faint jangle of car keys in her pocket before she closed her fist around them to stifle the sound. She reached the fire door at the top and peered out through the narrow pane of safety glass. The hallway looked clear at first glance.

She eased the door open and then closed it again behind her, guiding it to rather than risking a betraying slam. The corridor beyond was carpeted: easier to move with stealth, but that applied to others just as much as her. She glanced into each doorway as she passed, alert for shadows.

A row of lecture theatres, all apparently unoccupied. Beyond them were staff offices, these with solid wooden doors that had no windows to peek through. Her stomach tensed as she approached Doctor Moss's door. She didn't try knocking this time, but grasped the handle to test it with slow care.

It turned. Abandoning stealth, Pierce threw the door open and took in the room in a rapid glance.

The office that she'd been in just this morning, but now thrown into wild disarray. Books and papers tossed about, too thoroughly for casual vandalism. The wheeled chair shoved back into a far corner—and Doctor Moss slumped in it, a bloody cut visible on her forehead.

Crouched before her was a black-clad figure in a hoodie, caught in the act of marking out a ritual circle on the floor, candles scattered on the carpet. At the sound of Pierce's intrusion, he spun around, and she saw that his mouth and nose were covered by a scarf so she could see no more than a strip around his eyes.

"Police!" she barked, but the man didn't falter, hurling the object in his gloved right hand towards her face. She flinched and threw her arm up to defend her eyes before she registered that it was just a pen. He snatched something else up from the floor—a lighter, she realised as he flicked it on—and swept it across the wicks of the candles lying at his feet.

They went up as if they were soaked in petrol.

Probably were, she realised, or some equivalent, her nose picking up on the chemical scent too late to be useful. A hastily faked magic circle, candles soaked with accelerant... the ingredients for arson disguised as a ritual gone wrong.

That plan might be out of the window with Pierce's arrival, but it seemed that the would-be assassin was willing to leave collateral damage. He grabbed the table lamp from the edge of the desk and smashed out at her with the weighed base. She blocked the blow with her elbow and grabbed his arm to try and wrestle it away, cursing as the move pulled on her weak shoulder.

The assassin let go of the lamp and cracked her in the jaw with the elbow of his other arm, sending her staggering backwards. He slammed her back against the bookshelves on the opposite wall and forced his way out past her through the door. Pierce made a lunge for him, but her fingers only snagged the back of his hood, yanking it down before he twisted out of her grip.

The momentary glimpse it bought her told her next to nothing: white male with short brown hair, his face still mostly hidden by the wrapped scarf as she glimpsed it in profile. He ran on out into the corridor.

Pierce pushed away from the bookshelves and gave chase, but it only took half a dozen paces to know she wouldn't catch up. Turning back to the office door, she could already see the smoke beginning to form a haze in the air. The fire alarms had caught on as well, electronic wails breaking out.

And Moss was still inside. *Shit*. Pierce almost ran back in before her eyes fell on a fire extinguisher in the corridor. She darted across to grab that instead. Foam, thank fuck, not just water; she yanked it off the wall and charged back to Moss's office.

The fire was already spreading at an alarming rate, spilling across the half-drawn lines of the fake ritual circle. Through the smoke of stinking carpet fumes, she could see Doctor Moss weakly stirring in her chair, obviously dazed even without the choking smoke.

Pierce tore the plastic tag from the extinguisher and aimed the hose, wincing as the shift to supporting the thing by its handles put all the weight on her bad arm. She struggled to hold it steady as it spewed foam over the twisted mess of half-melted candles and burning carpet.

"Can you move?" she shouted to Doctor Moss. There might have been some coughed words in response, but the fact she couldn't make them out didn't bode well for the answer.

The fire was shrinking, but Pierce wasn't sure there was enough foam in the extinguisher's tank to fully smother it. Regulation said at this point it was the fire brigade's job, and not to put herself in danger trying to assist.

Maybe so, but regulation expected fire and police to be responding to the same 999 call, not her on-scene with them minutes away. Making split second decisions in the field wasn't always about what was smartest or safest—it was about the choice you knew you'd have to live with.

Still spraying the hose back and forth over the fire, Pierce skirted closer than she should around the edge of it, feeling the heat bake her skin and coughing in the smoke. She tried to call out to Doctor Moss again, but the words became a wheeze.

Moss was struggling to get up, but she needed help, and Pierce couldn't assist her and keep aiming the hose. The extinguisher felt like it must be near empty, so she let the hose drop and hauled the lecturer from her chair, unable to take the time to be gentle. The older woman seemed dazed, but she was still awake, and managed to grab hold of Pierce in turn.

Pierce swung back to face the remains of the smothered fire, and saw that it wasn't out yet. "Shit!" She raised the extinguisher for one last burst of foam, blasting the flames back towards the desk side of the room as best she could. Then she let it fall to the floor and charged across the office, pulling Moss with her. Her feet almost skidded on the foam-slick carpet, but she made it across and shoved Moss out into the corridor.

"We need to get to the stairs!" she barked, turning to slam the office door behind them. Maybe that last blast of foam had killed the fire, maybe it hadn't; either way they'd be fools to stick around here and find out. Doctor Moss needed medical attention, and Pierce was feeling faintly light-headed herself as she led the lecturer at a staggering dash towards the stairway. Fumes or just the adrenaline rush?

"My books..." Doctor Moss said feebly, turning partway back towards the office. Not just lack of priorities, Pierce knew—some of those occult works were doubtless irreplaceable.

Still less valuable than human lives.

"The fire brigade's coming," she offered as a sop. Prophetic: as they pushed through the door into the stairway, she heard the sound of sirens in the distance. They descended the staircase, Doctor Moss leaning on her with a dizzy groan. She looked pale, the wound on her forehead starkly drawn.

As they pushed out through the fire exit, fresh alarms joining the cacophony, Pierce drew in a great gulping breath of air. The cold evening hit like a slap, ice water thrown on skin that still felt scorched. It took a moment to adjust her eyes to the darkness dotted with artificial lights.

A small crowd of students had gathered to gawk at the smoking window, teenage appetite for spectacle overriding common sense. "Police! Back up, back up," she yelled at them. "Get away from the burning building!" She didn't think it would go up, hoped that she'd smothered the blaze well enough that it wouldn't even burn out the office, but only idiots would take that sort of thing for granted.

She helped Doctor Moss to sit down on the grass and looked around for anyone who looked like campus security or a paramedic. As she started to straighten up, Moss tugged on her trouser leg—not in immediate medical distress, she realised after a heart-dropping moment, but trying to communicate something. Pierce crouched down to speak to her. "Don't try to talk," she said.

But Moss sucked in a gasping breath, persisting stubbornly though her voice was a croak. "The ritual. I was researching..."

"I know." Doubtless the photos and any notes Moss had made had been the first things to be disposed of, but that wasn't a major concern right now.

Moss shook her head, insistent. "The ritual," she repeated. "More skulls. More sites. Part of a greater d-design..." She broke down coughing, and Pierce patted her back uncertainly, not confident that thumping would help rather than harm.

"Okay," she said. "All right. Don't try to talk now." The details could wait until a time when Moss didn't look like she was on the verge of keeling over. As Pierce straightened up, she could see blue flashing lights. "All right. Help's coming."

The immediate crisis seemed to be over, but a grim feeling still gripped her stomach like a clenching fist. First Vyner killed, now this. Whatever they'd stumbled over in that field, it was big. Big enough for whoever was behind it to keep tabs on the police investigation, and deal professionally with anyone who knew too much.

And if Moss was right that the site that they'd found was only one part of a greater ritual at work, then this could well be something far nastier than they'd guessed.

* * *

AFTER A QUICK check-over by the paramedics, Doctor Moss was taken to the nearest hospital, while Pierce stayed behind at the site to coordinate with the local emergency services. The fire brigade went up, and came back down, rather anticlimactically: it seemed she'd more or less done the job of containing the fire, and hopefully at least some of the rare texts in Doctor Moss's office would be recoverable.

If Pierce hadn't decided to drop by with the photos from Vyner's house this evening, they wouldn't have been so lucky. It seemed that Doctor Moss had been the only one still working after hours, and she doubted very much that anyone would have noticed anything amiss until the building was ablaze.

The device that had been used to override the lock had vanished with the man who'd used it; she should have thought to take it as evidence before she'd entered the building. The local police would dot the 'i's and cross the 't's when it came to processing the office for trace evidence and checking campus CCTV, but she already suspected they'd find nothing. The hooded assassin had been too professional to leave any obvious trail.

Once she'd given her statement of events to anyone who needed to know, there was little else useful that Pierce could do here. Exhausted, aching and chilled, she trudged back to her car and called in to the RCU to report the incident.

The northern RCU team was too small to be worth

further subdividing with round-the-clock shifts; in the absence of urgent time-sensitive cases, they worked a theoretical—if often extended—eight hours and then left it to dispatch to determine whether anything was urgent enough to recall them to duty. Aside from the semi-regular bollockings about the amount of overtime her officers inevitably drew, it worked about as well as any other system for covering half the country's ritual crime cases with only a handful of staff.

So with Deepan unlikely to have stayed more than an hour or so, she was expecting the office to be empty when she called in, and it threw her off-balance to be put through to Dawson. "What are you doing working this late?" She didn't recall authorising anything that should have taken him this long.

"Just dropped back in to write up a report," he said. "Got word back from the Vyner post-mortem. Definitely murder dressed up as a suicide."

As a confirmation of earlier assumptions, it didn't really need him to rush back into work to deal with, but she could charitably assume that despite the continued brusque tone, Vyner's death was eating away at Dawson more than he cared to show.

Or he could be making another attempt to do an end run around her authority and pursue the case however he pleased.

Or he could be flat out lying to her, to cover some less legitimate reason to be at the office on his own. Suspicions prickled, but she was too damn tired to sort conspiracy theories from reasonable doubt. She let it pass.

"I've got an attempted homicide here that may be the same attacker," she said instead. "Doctor Anne C. Moss, lecturer in occult studies—I gave her some photos of the ritual skull arrangement to research. Came back this evening, and caught the perpetrator in the act of setting the scene to have her killed in a seemingly accidental fire. White male, brown hair, average height, probably under forty..." She shook her head, aware it was so generic it could hardly be termed a description. "Had his face covered by a hood and scarf, so I didn't see much of him. I doubt the CCTV got a good picture, either."

"Get a witness statement from Moss?" he asked.

"No opportunity," she said. "She was taken to the hospital—smoke inhalation and a blow to the head; hopefully nothing worse." Doctor Moss wasn't a young woman, but hell, neither was Pierce, and she'd bounced back from a battering or two. Even if her current bounce felt more like a feeble totter right now. "I've asked the local uniforms to keep an eye on her," she said. "I doubt the killer will make another attempt in the glare of the spotlight, but if he does, then hopefully we'll nab him."

From Dawson's noncommittal grunt, he didn't believe that outcome was any more likely than she did.

"So it's the same thing," he said. "We bring in an expert, they send someone after them."

Pierce gritted her teeth, biting down on an unwise urge to snap at him. Asking an outside academic to take a look at some pictures was hardly the same as recklessly ordering an attempt at necromancy on top of an unidentified ritual, and he had to know it. She could deal with officers who made mistakes—Lord knew Ritual Crime ran on a haphazard process of trial and error even at the best of times—but ones who were too bloody stubborn to admit when they'd done something wrong were a much bigger problem.

"It's not the same," she said. "Vyner was much more directly involved—more so than he should have been. He should never have been allowed to attempt necromancy before we had any background on the intended purpose of the ritual." She sighed. "But yes, it's looking like these people are willing to go after anyone even peripherally involved in the investigation." Had they simply followed Pierce to the university office—worrying enough—or had something Moss's research dug up got them spooked?

She grimaced, aware she was going to have to concede further ground to Dawson's conviction his bull-headed way was the right way. "And yes, it does look like this case is more urgent than it first seemed," she admitted. "Moss managed to tell me that she thinks there are more sites like this out there. What we've found so far may be only the tip of the iceberg."

As she hung up the phone and sagged for a moment, mustering the energy to drive herself home, she couldn't help but grimly contemplate just how slim their chances were of finding the rest before things went to hell.

CHAPTER
TWENTY-TWO

PIERCE ARRIVED BACK at work the next day with a gritty-eyed feeling of too little rest that even coffee wouldn't shift. At least she'd beaten Dawson into work today, however; the only one in the office when she arrived was Constable Freeman.

"Morning, Guv!" she called out from behind her computer, bright eyed and enthusiastic enough to make Pierce feel even more ancient. She hoped the greeting she managed past her sip of coffee didn't come out too much of a grumble.

"I'll be over in Magical Analysis," she said. "Let me know if anything important comes in." Preferably before Dawson had any chance to get his sweaty mitts on it, but she probably shouldn't say that sort of thing in front of impressionable young constables.

"Will do, Guv," Freeman chirped, then bowed her head again to her computer. Pierce wondered if she was actually as absorbed as she looked, or just out to impress the new boss. With their overstretched resources, much of the RCU's work came down to remote consultation, advising police departments around the country whether X bit of random graffiti looked like a legitimate occult ritual and how to handle artefacts seized at the scene of a crime. Pierce supposed even that might be fascinating to an RCU rookie used to far more mundane police matters, but after decades on the job, the shine of advising officers who didn't know their ritual arse from their occult elbow had well and truly worn off.

Of course, that was why the good Lord had made constables, that DCIs might be free to get on with more interesting cases, at least when not buried under mountains of paperwork. Pierce had more than enough of that to be going on with, but hopefully Magical Analysis would have something on the skulls by now to spare her.

She popped her head into Cliff's lab, still faintly whiffy after her first smoke-related incident this week. "Cliff! Got my skulls?" she asked him, once he'd untangled his headphones and pulled them from his ears.

"These fine fellows?" He indicated a table across the lab, where one of the skulls had been set up with ribbon-wrapped scroll and surrounding ring of stones in careful reproduction of the crime scene. On the next bench sat a second, but this one disassembled into parts, the stones lined up and the scroll untied and unfurled.

She couldn't spot the third skull anywhere. "One of them gone walkabouts?" she asked.

"Jenny has the third one," he said. "I do believe she was planning on attempting some divination with it first thing this morning, actually. She's probably down in the ritual lab if you want to see what she's made of it—I'm afraid we haven't had much luck up here."

"No?" Pierce wandered over to look at the unfurled parchment scroll. As she'd suspected, inked on it in careful brushstrokes was what looked like a spell, a nine-layer pyramid of runes surrounded by an intricate design. The unfamiliar alphabet made its purpose impenetrable.

Cliff moved over to join her, running a latex-gloved finger along the line of rune stones. "You'll note that there are no common characters between this rune set and the set on the scroll," he said. "Documents believe that *this*"—he indicated the scroll—"is some form of phonetic alphabet—see, you have several repeating characters, here, here, here, nineteen separate unique symbols in total—whereas *these* are most likely ideograms. Alchemical symbols, spirit names—planets, if they haven't got the message about Pluto yet..." He spread his hands with an apologetic grimace of a smile. "Without the necessary text to decode them, we are, alas, completely in the dark."

"And the runic alphabet?" she asked, without much hope.

"Also unfamiliar. Possibly a cypher of some sort, but with no knowledge of the underlying language..." He shrugged.

"Bit harder than doing the daily Codeword puzzle." With a message in a language where they knew the rules of grammar and patterns of letters, they might get somewhere decoding it; with an unknown spell, the words could be literally anything. They didn't even know how to read the pyramid—left to right, right to left, upwards, outwards from the middle? Unless they could match it to a source text, the spell was a dead end.

"What about the rest of it?" she said, gesturing towards the skull set up to match the original burial. "What does this arrangement say to you?"

Cliff pulled an awkward smile. "Mostly, I'm afraid, it says that more context is needed. Skulls, blood... they're used for any number of ritual purposes. Something powerful, certainly. My instinct says a summoning, breaching the barrier with the spirit world. But I can't give you any more than that without more details to go on."

"Mm." She nodded grimly, aware that she probably couldn't have asked for much more, but still frustrated by the lack of information.

"Oh!" Cliff brightened beside her. "But I have managed to do some more tests with our friend the singing watch lantern from Tuesday."

"Contained experiments, I hope," Pierce said with a wince, remembering the smoke.

"Nothing so extreme as our first adventure, worry ye not," he said. "Now that I have some idea of the strength of the reaction, I can calibrate my tests accordingly. I've been measuring the increase in the warning signal since yesterday morning."

She turned to look at him. "It's increasing?" That was never a good sign.

"Yes, and rapidly," Cliff said. "Now, based on my measurements, and what I've been able to research in the literature about watch lanterns—and do please bear in mind that this is not an exact science—I believe that the warning signal indicates the approach of an event in roughly four days' time. Probably some point on the twenty-second of December, though potentially it could fall as much as a day to either side."

"An event," she echoed.

"'Something wicked this way comes,'" he said. "As to what, I'm afraid our metal friend is ill-equipped to tell us."

"The twenty-second of December," Pierce repeated. She pulled her notebook and pencil stub from her pocket to scribble that date down. "So, we can expect something unspecified, but probably bad, to happen on... this coming Monday?"

"That's about the size of it, yes," he said.

"Marvellous." Typical—the one time they actually had advance warning of something going down, and they didn't even know what they had advance warning *of*. "And do we know which direction to start looking in?" she asked. "You said watch lanterns could indicate that."

"Ah." His cheeks dimpled in a wry smile. "That would be the wrinkle that we fell afoul of on yesterday's test. The smoke should, in theory, have issued forth from one of the lantern's mouths to indicate the direction of the threat."

"It didn't do that," she noted.

"No," he said. "Because, you see, the danger is coming from all sides."

* * *

ON THAT CHEERFUL note, Pierce left him to it, taking the stairs down to the station's basement.

While the Enchanted Artefacts department merited their own lab space upstairs—though recent events might see that reconsidered—the rest of the RCU's researchers had to make do with shared use of the ritual lab down in the basement. A small concrete box of a room not much different from the station's holding cells, it had protective circles permanently marked out on the floor and ceiling to contain any magic worked down there. In theory.

Also in common with the cells—whoever had designed this station hadn't stretched themselves or their budget far when it came to specialist facilities—the lab door had a sliding hatch for observation. Pierce checked through that rather than risk bursting in on a ritual in progress, and saw Jenny rooting through the storage cabinets at the far side of the room.

She knocked. "Is my head going to fall off if I come through this door?" she asked, raising her voice.

"If it does, it won't be my fault," Jenny called back, and waved at her through the observation window. "Hiya," she said, as Pierce opened the door. "Just doing some tests on those skulls you sent us the other day."

"Yeah, Cliff said." She closed the door behind her, and regarded the skull currently standing on the central lab table in a sealed plastic bag. It looked much the same as the two she'd seen upstairs—adult, human, daubed with geometric patterns in what looked like blood... her expertise stopped there. Maybe with facial reconstruction they could figure out more, but good bloody luck getting any results back before the new year. If the superintendent would even authorise it for what might just be grave-robbery rather than murder.

Magical Analysis might be less certain and less useful in court, but when it worked, it was a hell of a lot faster than waiting for results back on traditional forensics. If only because Pierce had the staff here under her nose to prod into handling her priority cases first.

"Right," she said, peering into the skull's eye-sockets. "What can poor Yorick tell us, then?"

"Well, that remains to be seen," Jenny said, staggering back to the table with a large wooden board about a metre square. As she set it down on the table, Pierce could see it was an elaborately painted thing like something out of a Victorian fairground, with rings of letters, numbers and symbols around a faint dip in the middle where it seemed some kind of centrepiece could be set. Jenny straightened it on the table and took a brief huff of relief.

"Obviously the skull's been used as part of a ritual," she continued. "That complicates things. There are divinations I could do if he was just an ordinary skull, but whether they'll still work..." She made an ambivalent noise and spread her hands in a pantomime shrug.

"So what are you going to try?" Pierce asked.

Jenny went back to the cupboard and returned with a round wooden disk about the size of a serving platter, with an arrowhead pointer extending from one side. She slotted it into place on the baseboard, then rotated it round with a touch so that the arrowhead was aligned with the top of the painted design.

"Well, beginning with the 'Keep It Simple, Stupid' principle, I'm just going to do a basic divination for point of origin," she said. "Now, that *might* just point straight back at the field that you took them from, which is admittedly not that much use to us. Or it might point back to the resting place of the skull prior to being used in the ritual."

"That would be good," Pierce noted.

"*Or* it might go back even further than that, and point at the site of this individual's death." She waved a hand at the skull.

"Which would also be good." It might not lead them directly to the criminals, but with the bones still unidentified, any little snippet of information would be useful.

"Or it might point at our evidence room at the station," she added. "Or it might—and this is the most likely outcome—do absolutely nothing."

"You're always such a ray of sunshine," Pierce said.

"We aim to please," Jenny said. She drew a compass from her pocket and made steadily more minute adjustments to the position of the boards until she was satisfied, then took the skull from its plastic wrapping and placed it on the central rotating plate.

"So how does this divination work?" Pierce asked her, standing back to watch the preparations.

"Poorly," Jenny said, and grinned at her own bad joke before reaching out to tap the wooden board that held the skull. "This gadget here is a specialised form of dial planchette, a bit of a variation on the theme of a Ouija board—it can be used for contacting spirits, but we're going to use this one for divination. You can buy little ones in the shops, which the instructions generally tell you to start spinning by hand, because, surprise, they don't actually work. In theory, this one will move under its own power."

"In theory," Pierce echoed.

"*If* all goes well." Jenny moved back to the cupboards to root through more of the storage boxes. "Now, we haven't had a *great* deal of success with it," she cautioned over her shoulder. "Pet theory is that, because this is quite a weighty thing, it probably takes a fair bit of magical juice to get any form of movement out of it. Now, since we're generally discouraged from performing human sacrifices ourselves—"

"We get snitty memos about it from Human Resources," said Pierce.

"It's health and safety gone mad," Jenny said, shaking her head. "Anyway, the point being that since there's a limit to how much we're actually empowered to do ritual-wise, it's hard to test whether it's just generally useless, or it requires a bit of the old blood and bone to get it going." She gestured to the skull. "However, since this thing is obviously a powerful ritual artefact in itself..."

"It should be enough to power the ritual on its own," Pierce assumed.

"That's the hope," Jenny said. "If there's a powerful enough magical pull on the thing, then it's like rolling down a hill: it already *wants* to move, just needs a little bit of a nudge to get it going." She gave a shrug. "But as I say, this may do nothing at all."

"Well, let's see." Pierce stood back and watched as Jenny completed the rest of the preparations. Various small items were placed at points upon the painted baseboard: what looked like iron filings, a crystal, a small brass incense burner, a sprig of some kind of herb Pierce lacked the knowledge to identify. Finally, Jenny tore a strip of paper off the edge of a notebook page and wrote what looked like a few words in Latin on it with a cartridge pen, before tearing it into tiny pieces and dropping them into the oil atop the burner.

"All right," she said, looking back at Pierce. "Here goes nothing." She struck a match and lit the candle under the incense burner. Once the flame had caught she danced back out of the way, and they both watched intently as the cloying scent of the incense spread through the small room.

After choking on smoke two days in a row, Pierce's throat tickled warningly at the first hint of it on the air, but this time it was a false alarm, no sign of any greater blaze about to erupt. The tiny flame was a bright spot in the dimness of the room, drawing her gaze and blinding it to the sight of anything else. It took a moment to register the slight twitch of the rotating platform, longer to be sure that it was more than just a trick of her tired eyes.

"Is that movement?" she asked in a low voice, the thickening atmosphere somehow demanding a funeral hush. There was a thunderstorm tension in the air that made her spine tingle and sweat pool on her back despite the coolness of the concrete room.

"Maybe," Jenny murmured back, just as quietly. Pierce barely blinked as she watched the swing of the arrow, slow and subtle enough that it was easy to believe it was no more than an optical illusion. A tiny fraction to the right, a tiny fraction more... had it stopped? No, it was swinging back the other way, at first equally slow but then gaining in speed. The incense smell in the room was growing stronger, or else her senses had become so acutely focused that it seemed more overpowering.

The spin of the pointer was definitely speeding up now, the skull on its turntable visibly beginning to turn away from them—but then it reversed direction again, still increasing in speed. It was spinning like a record player, getting faster, turning further... another sharp reverse, and she heard the wood creak with the strain. The iron filings on the board fluttered in the wind of the increasing rotation.

The thing was going round almost once a second now; surely the divination ritual didn't call for this kind of pace? She shifted closer to Jenny. "Is this supposed to happen?"

"I don't know..." she said, biting her lip. "It could be—" The rotating board made another sharp reverse, and Pierce could swear she saw a wisp of woodsmoke rising from the friction. "Shit. No!"

The skull was rattling in position, beginning to shift around the turntable. If it was an electrical device Pierce would have yanked the plug by now, but interrupting a ritual wasn't quite so straightforward. "How do we stop this thing?" She had to raise her voice over the increasing noise of the thing going round.

"We don't, it's self-perpetuating!" Jenny said. "Maybe I can—" She darted forward to snuff the candle out with her fingers.

The second she made contact, there was an explosive crack, and the overhead lights went out. Pierce cursed as a flying fragment of who-knew-what stung her cheek, dozens more pinging off the walls and clattering to the floor.

Then there was silence and total darkness.

"Fuck," said Jenny dazedly, from somewhere down on the floor.

"Are you hurt?" Pierce said, groping for the heavy door and throwing it open. Light flooded into the room from the corridor outside; at least they hadn't blown the power for the entire station.

"Apart from the bruise on my bum? No, I don't think so." All the same, Jenny gave a pained groan as she hauled herself back to her feet with the aid of the table. Taking in the state of the room, Pierce saw that it was littered with fragments of splintered wood—and bone shards.

"Did our evidence just explode?" she said, nudging one of the larger pieces of bone she could see with her shoe to move it closer to the light. She'd seen a few dismembered skeletons in her time, but what was left of the skull now looked like it had been blasted apart from the inside.

Jenny flattened her wavy hair back into place with a sheepish grin. "Erm. Well, we appear to have had what is known in technical circles as a Goldilocks incident. Our earlier attempts with the divination board didn't have enough power to work. This one..."

"A little bit too much?" Pierce said.

"Just a tad." She smiled wryly. "Still, on the bright side, I can definitely confirm that there is magic in those skulls. Quite a high potential for it."

"Mm." Pierce surveyed the remains of this one, scattered all over the concrete floor. The magic circle hadn't been a whole lot of use in keeping *that* in; it might have spared her from being struck by the raw force of any magical blast, but when it came to flying projectiles, it was just as much use as any other line drawn on the floor. There were bits of skull and splinters just about everywhere, including, more than likely, in her clothes and hair.

Not quite the result they'd been hoping for—and not exactly respectful and dignified treatment of human remains in their care, either. She sighed. "So, what does your divination expertise allow you to read from *this* arrangement?" she said.

Jenny pursed her lips and wrinkled her nose as she studied the debris that littered the room for a moment. "I predict a very high chance of us getting another snitty health and safety memo," she said.

"Marvellous," said Pierce.

So much for that idea.

CHAPTER TWENTY-THREE

WITH DIVINATION APPARENTLY a no-go, they were stuck with more conventional methods of identifying the skulls. Pierce popped her head into the RCU office. "Freeman. Any more progress on the history of those stolen artefacts?"

"Looks like that's a dead end, Guv," she said, shaking her head. "But Sergeant Mistry says there might be something in the CCTV footage," she added. "He's just gone next door to speak to somebody from Arcane Documents."

"Excellent." Something resembling progress at last. "In the meantime, I want you to try and find some kind of a source for these skulls we pulled out of the field on Tuesday," she said. "Check into deaths—not necessarily recent—and grave robberies in the general Bingley area. I'll give you my case notes."

She flipped through her notebook until she found the right page, puzzling briefly over the date that she'd scrawled in the corner until she remembered her earlier meeting with Cliff. Something wicked this way coming on the twenty-second of December. Another bloody thing that they had no clue where to start with. Oh, well. For now, as the superintendent had said, best to focus on the cases that were actually cases.

She handed the notebook over. "All right, that's what we've got so far, assuming you can read my handwriting. Ask Dawson if you need more to go on. Wherever he's got off to." Had he even showed up to work yet?

"He's taken Eddie out to a call—suspected illegal artefacts," Freeman told her helpfully.

It took a moment for Pierce to link 'Eddie' with Constable Taylor in her mind. She really needed to get to know her new people better.

Case in point: Dawson had taken Taylor with him to the Bingley crime scene, too—just the luck of the draw when it came to who was closest at the time, or was he favouring one of their new constables over the other? She should probably run the question by Deepan, see if he'd noticed a pattern.

Christ, taking time off work was a pain in the arse. Any health benefits from the rest were more than outweighed by the amount of stress and extra work it took to get back up to speed on her return.

"All right," she said to Freeman. "Get on with that research, and I'll see what Deepan's got for us on those thefts."

"Will do, Guv." Freeman scrutinised the notepaper with what was either commendable attention to duty or an indictment of Pierce's terrible handwriting. Pierce left her to it and headed down the hall back to Analysis.

The Documents room was a large space made smaller by the many rows of shelves, an incongruous mix of forensic lab with the impression of one of those second-hand bookshops that had given up on finding room and just started piling books willy-nilly. Well-thumbed modern mass market reference books rubbed shoulders with battered hardbacks from past decades and old leather-bound tomes. More carefully stored in the room at the rear were those even older, rarer texts that required careful handling.

It was a collection to rival most specialised libraries of the occult. Unfortunately, they only had two busy document techs to curate it, so they were reliant on memory, luck, and an ancient card index that had yet to be more than partly digitised to find anything useful.

Deepan was leaning against one of the lab tables studying a computer print-out as she entered, while the sound of papery rummaging drifted from the shelves at the rear.

"Morning, Guv," he said, straightening up as she entered. "Anything new on the skull case?"

"All the wrong kind of bombshells," Pierce said. "Have I mentioned that self-destructing evidence is my least favourite kind?" She rubbed her cheek where the flying shard of bone had struck her face.

"A few times, yeah," he said. He waved the print-out at her. "Well, the good news is I might have found something on the Hemsfield Gallery theft."

She took the paper from him and saw that it was a screenshot cropped from grainy grey CCTV footage, showing the passenger side of a grubby white Transit van at an angle to the camera.

"This is footage from the car dealership across the road from the gallery," he explained. "This van went back and forth multiple times in the days before the thefts; it parked in the dealership for a while, but the driver never got out. I spoke to the salesman who was on duty at the time—he remembers the van, but he said he figured the bloke was just taking a phone call. Couldn't get a good description out of him, and the camera angle's all wrong to get a proper look at the driver."

Could be suspicious, could be nothing. "Did you run the plates?" she asked.

"I did. They're fake. But..."—he tapped a finger on the front window of the van—"see this here, on the dashboard?"

She squinted at the indistinct image. "Am I going to need to break out the old lady glasses?" she asked.

"No, because here's one I blew up earlier." He brought out another print-out, this one a marginally clearer expansion of the section of dashboard glimpsed through the front window. There was something lying on it, a book or a leaflet or similar; the text was distorted beyond readability, but there was some kind of symbol on the front, like a crossed question mark in a circle with three radiating lines.

"Can you get the image enhanced any further?" she asked.

"I asked. They told me off for watching too much bad TV." He gave a wry smile. "This is, apparently, as good as it gets. But I thought that symbol rang a bell—the museum that had the goblet stolen described a similar maker's mark on the base, though they didn't have a picture. Figured I'd bring it down here, see what Documents made of it."

"And we have come up with the goods!" a triumphant female voice rang out from behind the shelves. Pierce nodded in greeting as Fatima Shakoor hurried out to join them, a plump, moon-faced woman with a bright, cheeky grin. "Ta-dah!" She brandished what turned out not to be an ancient occult document, but a cheaply printed brochure that looked like something found in the 'local interest' section of a library.

"Took me a moment to find it, because I was looking in the wrong section, but here you go." She flattened the brochure out on the table before them. "The Society of the Crooked Hook—one of your average dinky little occult societies where everybody meets up every Tuesday to play dress up and do some dancing around trees." She waved a vague hand back towards the shelves. "We've got flyers for millions of them. And by millions I mean about fifty."

"Anything to make this one stand out?" Pierce asked, scrutinising the leaflet. Sure enough, there was a picture of the symbol in question on the front, though it looked like a crude photocopy of something drawn in marker pen. She opened the folded pages to see a poorly reproduced photograph of a group of people clustered around a standing stone.

"Your guess is as good as mine," Fatima said with a shrug. She gestured to the leaflet. "That's the only paperwork we have on them."

Pierce turned the leaflet over, looking to see if it gave an address. It did, complete with a little hand drawn map. "Then I guess there's nothing to do but pay them a visit for ourselves," she said. "Right. Off we go to sunny Huddersfield, then."

THE HEADQUARTERS OF the Society of the Crooked Hook turned out to be a room above a shop with a homemade poster in the window promising Tarot readings. Not a likely looking centre of criminal enterprise, but it took all sorts.

Nobody answered the buzzer to help with their enquiries, but the manager of the shop below kindly furnished them with a telephone number for 'Ron.' Pierce waited for him to arrive while Deepan went off to canvass the staff of the surrounding buildings for any evidence of the white van.

Ron, when he eventually arrived, turned out to be one Ronald Halford, a nervous, earnest little man somewhere in his late forties, wearing a suit that strained around his burgeoning beer belly and a tie covered in cartoon snowmen.

He didn't look like a criminal, or at least not the kind who climbed through museum and gallery windows in the dead of night. She'd learned early enough in her career that timid, mousy little men could still get up to all manner of vile activities, not least because nobody ever suspected they would have the nerve.

But her instincts said that Ron was not their man. He almost fell over himself apologising for the fifteen minutes it had taken him to arrive, over-explaining in the slightly frantic way she most associated with those who had too much of a guilt complex to get around to committing any of the crimes they feared being accused of. It could all be a spectacular act, of course, but without greater reason to suspect him, Occam's razor ruled the day.

Halford let her in to the society's base, which looked like any other shabby private clubhouse for a group with more ambitions than resources. The main room had a mismatched collection of furniture, probably assembled from whatever the members and their friends and relatives happened to have cluttering up their garages. The occult paraphernalia scattered about mostly seemed like cheap junk to her eyes: fancy candles, arrangements of crystals, lots of dangling beads and wind chimes and generically 'ethnic' art.

A pinboard in the corner held a copy of the society's latest newsletter, seemingly more concerned with badgering members to make their contribution towards the Christmas meal and hawking somebody's self-published book than any real occult activities. A few curling newspaper clippings, some group photos, and a slew of takeaway menus and flyers from nearby businesses took up the rest of the space.

There was a small cloth-draped altar at the rear of the room, but frankly, the centrepiece appeared to be the tea-making facilities in the corner. Ron fluttered around them uncertainly. "Um, can I get you anything to drink, er, detective? We've got tea, coffee... There are biscuits." He brandished a packet of custard creams hopefully, like a pacifying sacrifice to ward off any harm.

Pierce had already seen at a glance that there would be little need to hang around, but she let him go ahead anyway. It would give him something to do keep him calm, and at least she'd get a custard cream out of it.

"None of the society's members are in any trouble," she said. There was always an unspoken 'yet' appended to such statements, but most people chose to be reassured by them anyway. "We're just looking for some information in connection with one of our cases. Some paperwork with your group's symbol was spotted inside of a van that we're trying to trace. Can you think of any reason for that?"

"Oh. Oh, dear." He peered at her over his teacup with worried, pale eyes. "Well, um, I really don't think that can be any of our members. Let's see, um, Jonathan drives a Volvo, and Lisa doesn't drive at all—her hip, you see. Her husband usually drops her off, but he doesn't drive a van, it's an—oh, I'm not sure, is it a Peugeot or a Vauxhall? I can never remember which one's which. But anyway, it's quite a small car. And Alice... I think Alice still has her Mini, though she was talking about trading it in. Um..."

Pierce was fairly sure he'd have reeled off the full driving histories of the society's roster of members if she'd let him. "So none of your members drive any sort of van," she summarised.

"No. No, I don't think so. Not one that I've seen—and I *would* have seen, I'm fairly sure. We all know each other quite well. Most of the society have been members for, oh, it must be over a decade now. More than that, I suppose, now I come to think of it." He shook his head. "It still feels like the 'nineties were only a couple of years ago. Do you find that? It's as if my sense of time stopped at the year two thousand."

Pierce nodded and smiled along to what could be nervous rambling or just the man's normal mode of speech. Either way, he was clearly going to need regular chivvying along, or they'd be here all afternoon. "No new members joined, recently then?" she said, taking a risk on dunking a custard cream; few things compromised your aura of authority quite like having to fish half a biscuit out of your tea with a spoon, but she managed to pull it off without disaster. "Say in the last six months or so?"

Ron shook his head ruefully. "No, sadly not. The kids, well, they're not interested, are they? They've got all their iPhones and whatnot—they're used to everything happening with a touch of a button. You tell them magic takes effort, you need licenses and training and it's all got to be exactly right, and they don't want to know. They just want, 'point, bang, fireballs,' and it's a bit more complicated than that."

"Thankfully," Pierce said dryly. About the only defence they had against magical anarchy was the fact that ninety-nine percent of people who went in for ritual magic gave it up as a fiddly pain in the arse long before they managed to achieve anything measurable. Unfortunately, that did mean that the criminals they were left with were the ones with some patience and perseverance and attention to detail—all traits you preferred not to be facing in someone you were trying to apprehend.

She sat forward. "So, if, as seems likely, the van driver isn't a member of your society, how do you think he might have come to have papers with your symbol on in the front of his vehicle?"

She didn't pitch it as an accusation, but Ron still looked flustered. "Well, um, we do have a newsletter that Alice prints off: all our members get it, of course, and there are free copies in the library and at Crystal Village—that's the, er, local shop that sells supplies for the craft."

Pierce nodded; another lead they could check out, though she already doubted that either shop or newsletter would be of much interest to anyone with genuine occult knowledge. Assuming the thieves had any, of course: their motive in picking the particular set of artefacts they were trying to assemble was still hazy, but the lack of monetary value or recent paper trail argued against either financial or sentimental reasons.

"And of course, it's not strictly our symbol in particular," Ron added, almost as an afterthought.

"Oh?" Pierce raised her eyebrows at him over her mug.

"Er, no, it's the mark of Francis Maundrell. He was a warlock who could talk to tree spirits—unjustly hanged for putting a curse on the local farmers here in 1675, or so my grandfather told me. He was the one who founded the society. Er, my granddad, that is, not Francis Maundrell, although we do try to continue in the spirit that we imagine his works—"

"1675?" she said. And a collection of stolen artefacts believed to be circa seventeenth century...

Maybe this visit hadn't been a complete waste of time after all.

CHAPTER
TWENTY-FOUR

PIERCE GOT A list of the society's members to follow up on, but she doubted it would amount to anything. Deepan's canvassing of the local shopkeepers had proven similarly unenlightening; nobody had anything of note to say about the occult society—most were wholly unaware it existed—and none of them recalled seeing a white Ford Transit van hanging around. Not that they were likely to remember if there had been one: criminals made their choice of nondescript vehicles for a reason.

"Looks like this Francis Maundrell character is our best lead right now," she said as Deepan drove them back to the station. "We'll see if Documents can dig up anything more about him now we've got a name. If we can tie the stolen artefacts together, we may be able to anticipate the thieves' next target, or what it is they're trying to accomplish."

Deepan nodded, then frowned a little as he made the turn towards the station. Pierce looked ahead to see what had captured his attention. "Oh, what have we got here?"

she said. "New police vehicles?" Their car park appeared to have been colonised by a rather conspicuous green Volkswagen bus.

"It's probably the druids back again, Guv," Deepan said. "They've been bugging us for weeks—it's coming up to the winter solstice, and they don't have access to the stone circle they used to use for their rites because some company bought up the land."

"That's not our department, surely," Pierce said as they paused at the car park entrance. A pair of young women dressed in white robes were climbing down from the bus in front of them, carrying placards. Bloody marvellous. "Tell them to get in touch with the heritage people if they're worried about it being built on."

"We did," he said. "According to them, it *should* be a protected site, but it's mysteriously not listed."

"Well, even if that's true, it's still not a job for the RCU," she said. Someone might well be greasing the wheels to have paperwork go missing and dodgy deals pushed through, but that kind of thing had been going on since time immemorial, no magic involved. "We don't handle shady deals unless they're pacts with demons."

"We've told them all this," he said, nodding along. "But they're adamant that it's a conspiracy, and that someone's up to something nefarious on the site."

"And do they have evidence of this?" Pierce asked, narrowing her eyes as more robed figures stepped down from the van, these ones carrying a looped banner between them. They were never going to get into the bloody car park at this rate.

Deepan gave her a sidelong look. "Well, the Archdruid got bad vibes, apparently."

"Oh, did he now?" She pursed her lips, then waved a hand at Deepan. "Honk your horn. We'll be here all day otherwise."

He gave a discreet beep of the horn. A few of the druids in their path looked briefly mutinous, obviously considering whether to block their entrance, but they hadn't had the time to get organised yet, and they scattered out of the way as the car began inching forward.

"Don't run anyone over. We can't afford a lawsuit," Pierce said.

They avoided any druid-splattering incidents, but getting into the building was a gauntlet of its own. A small squad of robed druids bore down on them as they got out of the car, led by a long-haired, thickly bearded man who would have been at home in an aging prog rock band. She was guessing he was the big boss, from the subtle clues of his long red cloak, wooden medallion, and the tall staff he was leaning on.

Lord, even when these people did have some form of magical ability to their name, she had a bugger of a time taking them seriously.

"Sergeant Mistry," the Archdruid called out as he approached them. He had a magnificent theatrical baritone, commanding attention. "I wonder if we might have further words about the progress on the invasion of our sacred site."

"You've spoken to these folks before?" Pierce asked Deepan.

"Many times," he said, with a barely noticeable sigh.

She clapped him on the shoulder. "Then I think you're best placed to liaise with them again," she said. "See what they've got to say, and then just make sure they're out of our car park before the superintendent leaves." Even on their short acquaintance, Snow didn't strike her as the type to have much tolerance for a group of attention-attracting protestors hanging around his car park. Not that many police higher-ups would.

"Thanks, Guv," Deepan said with a weary smile, as she slunk away and left him to the wolves. The druids, unfamiliar with her face after all her weeks off, ignored her to focus on the officer they knew, and she made it to the front door unmolested. When she glanced back, Deepan was in the midst of a huddle of white robes, trying to politely state his position while they all talked at him at once.

She offered a brief wave that he probably didn't see, and headed back into the building. Rank did have its privileges, and right now the main one was getting back to her desk so she could sit down and have a sandwich while she went through her emails.

Even these modest lunch plans, however, were interrupted by an excited hail from Constable Freeman as she walked in. "Guv, I think I might have found something on those grave robberies you asked me to look for," she said.

"Oh?" Pierce went over with sandwich in hand to join her at her computer.

Freeman had, by some act of computer wizardry a bit beyond Pierce's ken, put together a map of the area around Bingley complete with little markers in various colours. She swept the mouse pointer over the display to indicate the lone black marker in the midst of brighter colours. "This is the site where the skulls were found," she said. "I've been going through reports of graveyard disturbances and grave desecrations—not much of note recently, so I expanded it to the last six months. There are a lot from around Hallowe'en—"

"Always are," Pierce said. "More often idiots arsing about than anyone who knows what they're doing." Lord save them from the yearly flood of wannabes who thought that doing vaguely mystical things on a significant date was a better way to develop magical talents than years of study.

Freeman nodded in acknowledgement. "I tried to filter out some of the noise: all of these incidents marked in blue are Hallowe'en or Hallowe'en adjacent, and if you hide those it's a bit less busy, but there's still quite a lot of data to dig through—I didn't know grave-robbery was such a popular crime!"

"Welcome to the wonderful world of the RCU," Pierce said, taking a bite out of her sandwich. "It's glamour all the way down. You and Taylor are going to get pretty used to squelching around graveyards in all kinds of weather."

She remembered that duty all too well from her own days as a DC and DS. They were always getting called to bloody graveyards—it only took a group of idiot teenagers playing dares or a vandalised gravestone to start a panic about Satanic cults raising the dead. Never mind that she'd never heard of any successful incident of zombie-raising in her long career, and was deeply sceptical of the few historical accounts.

"Is there any way to sort the false alarms and grave desecrations from actual instances of remains being removed from the scene?" she asked.

"Yeah, I was looking into that," Freeman said, nodding. "And then in one of the crime scene photos I noticed this gravestone—the date." She brought the photo up on the screen, and Pierce looked on in vague incomprehension at a picture of the headstone beside an opened grave. A relatively modern stone, in memory of one 'Henry James Heath, died 22nd Dec 2003, beloved father and grandfather.'

Then the date rang a bell. The twenty-second of December, D-day for Cliff's prophecy of some kind of upcoming supernatural crisis; not related to the skull case, but she'd thoughtlessly scribbled it on the page of notes she'd given to young Freeman. She grimaced. Her own damn fault for being hasty and unclear. "That's not—"

"And it's not the only one," Freeman pushed on, switching the screen back to her map. "So far I've managed to find *four* cases of graves being dug up in the last few months where the date of death was the twenty-second of December— different years, but all relatively recent graves where you'd expect to find a fairly intact skeleton. Two of them were in cemeteries near the ritual site in Bingley, while the *other* two"—she scrolled her map—"were up near Silsden." She turned and grinned triumphantly at Pierce.

Pierce studied the indicated set of markers on the map. One grave featuring that date would be a small coincidence; four, two of them in exactly their area of focus, started to sound an awful lot less like one. Maybe Cliff's big supernatural event and their large-scale ritual weren't so disconnected after all.

And that meant they now had a second area of focus. She clapped Freeman on the shoulder. "Good work," she said. "Keep chasing other cemeteries in the area, see if you can find any more disturbed graves with that date. I'll get on the horn to Silsden and see what we can do about getting a search organised. Our outside expert tells me that there's a big chance the Bingley site isn't the only one, and you may have just got us a jumpstart on finding a second."

Freeman beamed at her, and Pierce smiled back, feeling a surge of rising optimism. At last, after days of dead ends, they had somewhere concrete to start. There had to be something in Silsden—maybe another ritual crime scene, or maybe the home base of the perpetrators, but either way, if they could track it down, they'd be one step closer to the root of this mess.

THE SERIES OF phone calls that followed gave her optimism more of a battering. While the local police would have no doubt been fast on the ball if she'd asked them to search for a missing child or a fresh body, they were than less impressed by the prospect of pulling officers from their current duties to hunt for a few stolen skulls. Without a clear picture of what exactly the ritual was intended to do, all she could fall back on were empty warnings that it was probably both big and dangerous.

"What kind of search force are they lending us?" Freeman asked when Pierce hung up.

"Apparently, we can have two PCs, three community support officers, and someone with a dog," Pierce said.

"To cover the whole area?" she said incredulously.

Pierce twisted her mouth wryly. "We get what we get," she said. Hard enough getting the local teams to play nice with the RCU at the best of times, and Dawson's rough handling of the Bingley scene hadn't done them any favours on that front. With the number of senior officers in the region already slashed thanks to recent budget cuts, Bowers being out of action from his injuries meant stretching thin coverage even further, and she didn't doubt the news of the RCU's involvement had done the rounds.

"We'll make do," she said. "I'll go and rescue Deepan from the hippie druid invasion in the car park—you get in touch with Dawson, tell him we'll be out for the afternoon and he's holding the fort." She wasn't entirely happy with the thought of leaving the department in his hands, but he'd been running it for weeks already, and frankly she'd rather have him behind her back than be butting heads with him at another crime scene. "And see if he can send Taylor back to us," she added as an afterthought. "We're going to need all the help that we can get."

WITH SUCH A limited search force on offer, Pierce's role was less one of oversight, more one of mucking in beside the rest. They needed every pair of eyes that could be spared, but all the same she was reluctant to involve the local public in the search. For a start, the news of potential ritual magic in the area would be bound to leak out to the press—and more importantly, she didn't trust folks with no police training to obey her strict instructions not to touch anything.

She wasn't sure she trusted the community support officers that far, either. They might have the basic training needed to do their duties, but it wasn't the same as having experienced police under her command—and even those could be mighty shirty about taking the word of outside specialists that they needed to go beyond standard procedure. She supposed the one advantage of the inadequate search force was that she outranked everyone here by a mile.

"All right," Pierce said, assessing her assembled forces. They were gathered outside the gates of the cemetery where the two grave robberies had occurred. It would no doubt be a pleasantly shady spot in the summer, but in the depths of winter the overhanging trees were bare and gaunt, the pavement at the base of the wall thick with a mush of rotted leaves.

"We'll partner up," she decided. "RCU officers should be teamed with a local. Taylor, Freeman, you go with Constables Winters and Jackson." Possibly risking some chain of command friction, putting her two least experienced officers with uniform constables equal in rank, but she'd rather they have proper backup than leave them wrangling PCSOs when they were this new in the job. She'd just have to trust they'd have the confidence not to let the locals ignore or override them when it counted.

She nodded at the trio of community support officers.

"You'll be with me and Sergeant Mistry," she told the nearest two. "And you with Constable Collins." Their dog handler, a tall, ruddy-faced woman who seemed to be the most enthusiastic of the lot about being seconded to the RCU for the day. "And Magnus," Pierce added, eyeing the German Shepherd lying watching their feet with soulful canine patience. "Make sure the dog doesn't get too close if we do find disturbed earth."

"He's well trained," Collins assured her, giving the dog a supportive stroke that caused his tail to thump. Maybe so, but Pierce would still have preferred it if all the search teams could have at least one RCU officer along for guidance. Not practical, though: with the shortest day approaching, they'd be lucky if the light lasted till four o'clock, and they had to spread their search coverage as wide as it would go.

She checked her watch. Not as much time as she would have liked to give a proper briefing on the dangers of touching the wrong thing, so she'd have to make the lecture short and sweet.

"All right," she said. "We're looking for a site with multiple shallowly buried human skulls, most likely three in a triangular arrangement some metres apart. They may have been buried recently, or as much as several months ago. Concentrate on unused fields, waste ground, abandoned or seldom used properties—places where the ritual-workers would have reason to think their work would go undisturbed. *Do not* be the one to disturb it," she added emphatically. "If you find anything that looks suspicious, call it in on the radio and await instructions."

She couldn't tell if it was going in; anyone who'd spent any time working for the police force soon learned to perfect the art of looking politely attentive while superiors talked bollocks. The only one she could be sure was definitely paying attention was the dog.

But time was a-wasting, and labouring a point never won more supporters. Pierce clapped her hands. "All right, we're short on time and we don't have a clear radius for how far from the cemetery our location might be, so move out, split up, and keep checking in on the radio to let the others know what ground you're covering." She flagged the first community support officer whose name she could remember. "Archer, you're with me." He trotted along after her with an affable smile, a sturdy young blond lad who once upon a time would have been considered too short to be a policeman.

They started along a steep lane that was hemmed in by the graveyard wall and a high hedge on the other side; there was no pavement, and the white line that divided it to take two lanes of traffic looked a tad too optimistic in her view. Still, it didn't look like the matter got tested much: right now, everything was pretty quiet.

Except for her companion. "So is this ritual really dangerous?" Archer asked her eagerly as they walked. "I always wanted to work for the RCU; my granddad was in the police, and he was there at that big cult bust in 1963 where they found all those coffins in the grounds of Greywood School. He said all the lids were moving when they dug them up, and there were skeleton fingers trying to get out. Is that even possible, like, animating skeletons?

Do you think that's what these cultists are trying to do? I mean, if you think it's cultists, but I guess it must be, mustn't it, if they're doing all these big rituals and that."

Chatty was a good trait in a community support officer, she supposed. A warm and friendly face for interacting with the public. But Lord, she had a feeling that, however few hours of light they might have, it was going to be a very long afternoon.

CHAPTER
TWENTY-FIVE

IT DIDN'T TAKE long for a chill, overcast day to become a cold and wet one. Pierce pulled the hood of her coat up against the worsening weather, which was rapidly becoming an impedance. They should have had more time before they lost the afternoon's light, but the clouds turned the day dim, street lighting not yet kicking in to compensate.

Archer trotted on ahead of her, high visibility jacket doing its job in the rainy gloom. The young PCSO had lost some of his chatty enthusiasm as the wet, windy afternoon wore on, but to give him his due, he was still game to make an effort, peering under hedgerows and over farm gates. Pierce, by contrast, was feeling very much her fifty-four years, and the gut instinct of years of experience was proving more of a demotivator than a help right now. It didn't *feel* like this was getting them anywhere.

"What's down this way?" she asked Archer, looking down another narrow hedge-lined lane to her left. He pushed his peaked cap further back on his head as he squinted through the rain.

"Er, it's all just farmers' fields, I think, pretty much all the way," he said. "Don't really have that much call to come out here, to be honest."

With miles and miles of fields to cover, there was little point continuing the needle-in-a-haystack hunt; the longer the rain kept on, the harder it would be to spot the signs of digging anyway. Pierce glanced up at the sky: the charcoal edges of the clouds foretold that it would soon be chucking it down.

She reached for her radio. "Romeo Charlie One to all teams. Weather's getting worse. Anyone got anything to report?"

Quick negatives from each of the RCU officers; a longer pause before she got a response from Collins on the dog team. "*Might have something here, Romeo Charlie One,*" she said. "*Got some signs of digging under the trees, and Magnus has picked up some kind of scent.*"

The fresh kick of hopeful adrenaline took some of the chill out of the rain. "All right, all teams join Romeo Charlie Five at their location," Pierce ordered. "Romeo Charlie Five, investigate, but don't disturb the scene. Look for other burial sites in proximity."

If this turned out to be nothing, they would pack it in for the day—but maybe their luck had turned at last.

FIFTEEN MINUTES DOWN the road, and it was clear they'd be calling the search off whatever the outcome. The heavens had finished rehearsing and decided to open for real, and the rain hammered down as they hurried along the narrow rural lanes. A few cars swished by them, the traffic increasing as the day slipped into the build-up towards rush hour, and she was grateful for Archer's hi-vis jacket as they pressed back into the hedges.

The radio burst into life again as they were passing the walls of the graveyard. "*Romeo Charlie Five to Romeo Charlie One, looks like a secondary burial site here,*" Collins reported. "*I think this is the place.*"

Pierce felt the swell of anticipation rising in her gut. This time, with a complete scene in a relatively isolated place, they might have their chance to study it *in situ*. The rain was going to make it a bastard to gather any evidence tonight, but most of what they were interested in was underground in any case, and might well have been buried for days or weeks already. They'd just have to do their best to preserve what they could.

"Received, Romeo Charlie Five. Look for a third in a similar radius and get that site cordoned off, and await the arrival of the other teams." Anticipation felt a lot like agitation, her mind ticking off all the myriad ways things could go wrong before they arrived. Who would be closest to the spot where they'd parked the cars—Taylor's team? "Romeo Charlie Four, get back to the vehicles," she ordered. "Bring them round to the location. We're going to need tarps to protect the scene."

The sky had already darkened to the point where it was hard to see; it would be pitch black before they were done, maybe even before they arrived. Pierce hastened her pace. Maybe it was just the weather, or the itch for useful action after too long achieving too little, but her heart was hammering in her chest. Gut instinct howled that this was all about to go tits up.

Archer took the lead as they finished backtracking their previous route and moved on towards the crime scene, but something in her hasty pace must have been contagious: he led the way at a jog that was almost a run. Shorter legged and older, Pierce still kept up without complaint; she'd feel stupid when she reached the crime scene out of breath and aching, but for now the fear of what might happen before they arrived still ruled the day.

Collins spoke on the radio again. "*Romeo Charlie Five to Romeo Charlie One, think we might've found the third location. Davenport's trying to get a—*" A burst of frantic barking interrupted her words, only silenced when the transmission cut out. Pierce's stomach dropped.

"Romeo Charlie Five, report!" she ordered. Pregnant silence on the airwaves until Collins' voice returned a moment later.

"*Sorry, Guv. Magnus is—*" More barks. "*Magnus! Magnus! Quiet! Stay!*" The barking eased, but even over the radio Pierce could still hear the German Shepherd's grumbling whine. "*Magnus is going nuts. This isn't his usual behaviour.*"

"All right, pull back, pull back," Pierce ordered. "Get the dog off of the scene." She puffed for breath, chest beginning to burn as she ran on. The journey was starting to take on the consistency of a nightmare, racing down dark rainy avenues that all looked the same. "All teams, report," she demanded. "Is anybody *there* yet?"

"*Romeo Charlie Two here—we're still five minutes away, Guv.*" No closer than Pierce and Archer themselves.

"*Romeo Charlie Three here—we're almost there now,*" Freeman told her. "*We're just coming up on the hill.*"

"Romeo Charlie Four? Where are you with those cars?" Pierce asked.

Taylor sounded breathless. "*I can see them now, Guv,*" he said. "*We'll be on our way in a couple of moments.*"

All of them converging on a point, but she feared that it was going to be too slow. "Romeo Charlie Five, what's your situation now?" No response. Her heart thudded even harder than the exertion demanded. "Collins, whatever you're doing, *report!*"

A long stretch of seconds, and still no answer. Fuck, fuck, fuck...

"*Guv—uh, Romeo Charlie Three here—Guv, we're almost there now!*" Freeman repeated over the radio.

Almost wasn't cutting it now. Pierce tried the PCSO. "Davenport, are you with Collins? Can you hear the dog from where you are?"

No response from Davenport either. Shitfuck. She tried to push her battered body into one more burst of speed, straining for breath to speak into the radio. "Everybody, however fast you're moving, move *faster*. And Taylor, get those cars here! We're going to need the ritual kit from the boot." If what had happened to Vyner was happening again, they were in trouble. "Collins, Davenport, Romeo Charlie Five, respond!"

But they didn't, and some grim part of her had already stopped believing that they would. Something was happening in those woods, and even only minutes out was still too far away.

"*I can hear the dog!*" Freeman reported. "*He's somewhere in the trees. I can't see anybody on the road.*"

Pierce's gut clenched at the thought of sending young, untested coppers into the unknown, but that was the job. "All right, Romeo Charlie Three, go in after the dog. And be careful! It may be aggressive." Under outside influence or just plain scared, an out-of-control German Shepherd was nothing to mess with.

And it might not be the biggest danger right now. "Find Collins and Davenport, but stay wary," she puffed into the radio. "We could be dealing with a case of spirit possession, or other, unknown threats. Everybody stick with your search partner, *do not* separate, and check in with me with regular reports."

They didn't even know yet that the threat was magical in nature—they could be dealing with that old favourite, lurking criminals with blunt instruments. Or radio interference.

Wouldn't it be nice if, just for once, loss of contact was plain old radio interference?

They should be so bloody lucky. Pierce ran on, feet pounding the rain-drenched tarmac; she was already feeling every bit of her age and weight, and they still weren't there yet.

Blurted updates on the radio, a steady stream of info that still felt inadequate. Freeman and Winters entering the woods. Taylor just arrived back at the cars. Deepan on the approach.

Still not a peep from Davenport or Collins.

Even PCSO Archer was starting to wheeze a little from their prolonged run as the road curved round another corner and he pointed ahead through the rain. "That's the woods!"

Pierce could just about make out the dim shadowed lines of the trees on the right-hand side of the road. "Got your torch?" She pulled hers out as Archer nodded and fumbled for it under the edge of his jacket. As she clicked it on, the beam lit up the high visibility fabric dazzlingly, but did little to penetrate through the surrounding rain. Water ran around their feet as they hurried up the hill.

"Romeo Charlie Three, what's your position?" she asked the radio. "We're approaching the woods now."

"Still searching the woods, Guv," Freeman responded. *"The dog's running loose, I think; we're chasing him all round the houses. No sign of PC Collins or PCSO Davenport."*

"Have you found the ritual scene yet?"

"I can't tell! It's too dark in here. We haven't crossed any police tape." Which could mean they hadn't found the place, or that the others hadn't had time to cordon it off.

"Coming to join you now," she shouted into the radio. "Romeo Charlie Two, what's your position?"

"Just coming up on the other side of the woods right now, Guv!" She squinted, but she couldn't see the light of any other torches nearby. Between the trees, the rain, the sharply curving roads and sloping hills, visibility around here was a nightmare. Searching the woods in this would be a bastard.

But they had people missing, and they couldn't afford to wait. "Right, let's move in," she said to Archer.

A low stone wall separated the woodland from the road. Pierce didn't waste time hunting around for the proper access, but instead headed straight for a point where the capstones along the top of the wall had tumbled, leaving a lower barrier. She scrambled over, a hand from Archer steadying her before he followed her lead.

On the other side, the ground sloped sharply down away from them, the undergrowth thick even in the winter. Wet mud and leaf mould made the footing treacherous, and bare branches jabbed at her hands as she grabbed at them for support.

In the distance, further downhill, she could hear the dog barking. She spoke into the radio again. "This is Romeo Charlie One—we're coming down from the road. Romeo Charlie Three, what's your position?"

"*We're about... halfway down the slope, I think,*" Freeman said. "*Dog's somewhere quite nearby, but I don't have a visual.*"

"Coming to join you."

As she descended the slope, she could hear the radio chatter of the other teams checking in, but she relegated it to the back of the line for her attention. They had to stay alert now; danger could come from any side.

"Spread out a bit, but don't move out of line of sight," she ordered Archer. "Check the ground for signs of digging, or any recent disturbance." Or bodies, but she didn't need to tell him that. "You check that side, I'll check this side."

They made their way downhill. The sparse trees provided little shelter from the rain, only channelled it to run off in larger quantities. Pierce envied Archer his uniform gear, better designed for the weather than the suit and shoes she'd picked out for a day that wasn't supposed to involve hiking in the woods. The hood of her coat had become plastered to her head, just as miserably cold and damp as if she'd gone without it. Among the trees it felt closer to midnight than early evening.

She shone the torch over the uneven ground, strewn with rocks and fallen leaves and the odd scrap of litter. Impossible to pick out any clear signs of disturbance; there was no smooth dirt here to disturb. Impossible to listen out for creeping danger either, while the rain drummed down, the trees rustled, and Magnus the police dog kept barking—somewhere closer now, but still difficult to pin down.

"I see lights!" Archer blurted, and she turned to see the glimmer of a torch beam off through the trees to her left. She thumbed her radio.

"Romeo Charlie Three, is that your team that I'm seeing?"

The torch flashed briefly off and on again. "*It's us, Guv*," Freeman confirmed over the radio, and Pierce could faintly hear the duplication of her voice from further away.

They made their way towards each other, but Pierce didn't see a second torch beam emerge from the trees. "Where's PC Winters?" she asked, as her own torch picked out Freeman's squinting face.

Freeman turned to gesture. "He's just—" She faltered.

"Fuck. He was with me a second ago." She raised her voice to shout. "Winters?"

Pierce went for the more direct route of the radio. "Winters, check in," she commanded. Silence.

"He was right *here!*" Freeman repeated with frantic dismay. She shone her torch round in an arc, illuminating nothing but the sparse winter trees.

"All right, *stay close,*" Pierce ordered her and Archer, keeping a tight rein on her own rising sense of things spinning out of control. "Back to where you saw him last. He can't have gone far."

Not physically, anyway—but it only took a moment to send a victim off to somewhere nobody could follow. Where the *hell* were her missing officers?

They started on down the slope in tense silence, broken by updates from the other teams over the radio. "*Romeo Charlie Two here at the edge of the woods now,*" Deepan reported. "*How do we proceed?*"

"Stay on the road," Pierce decided. There weren't enough of them here to effectively cover the whole of the wooded region in the dark, and sending the teams in two by two was just putting more of them in danger. "Keep watch for anyone trying to exit the woods and wait for the others to join you. We don't know what we're dealing with here, and we're missing Winters as well as Collins and Davenport now."

Call for further backup? But there might be little to be had, with the local force already depleted of as many officers as they could spare for the search, and outside assistance would take its time arriving. And besides, all the officers with relevant training were already here—the only other RCU member she had to call upon was Dawson, and he had less experience than either her or Deepan.

"Guv—dog!" Archer said abruptly. She followed the line of his torch with her own, and saw the German Shepard crouched in a gap between the trees, ears flattened back and hackles bristling even in the rain. He was emitting a low growl that became a flurry of frantic barks as the torches lit him up. Pierce held completely still; the quiet, placid police dog that had sat calmly by their feet earlier in the afternoon was now very visibly a threat.

"All right, easy," Freeman said soothingly, raising a hand towards the dog from a safe distance. "Magnus?" The dog's ears twitched a little at the sound of his name, but he remained warily crouched and growling. "Good boy, Magnus," she persisted. "It's all right. It's all right."

"Careful," Pierce said in a low voice, barely above a whisper. She'd seen a dog attack or two in her early years in uniform, and it hadn't been pretty. Police dogs were trained to detain, not to savage, but in a charged situation like this all bets were off.

"I can see something on the ground," Freeman murmured back, just as quiet. "Just behind that tree on the left side. Is that somebody...?" Pierce's stomach jolted as a dark shadow in a hollow resolved itself into what might well be somebody's leg. Archer shifted nervously beside her, and she wanted to snap at him to be still, but she was afraid that he'd jump at the sound and set the dog off.

Freeman kept inching closer to the gap in the trees that Magnus was guarding, murmuring a stream of placating words as she tried to slip past. "Yeah, you're a good boy, aren't you? Good boy. You remember us—you met us earlier. We're doing our job, just like you're doing yours, yeah?"

As she eased past the tree, keeping as far back as possible, a branch snagged on the back of her jacket and bent backwards before pulling free, shaking the tree and sending a cascade of water droplets pouring down. Magnus lunged towards her, barking furiously. Freeman flinched back against the tree, and the dog retreated, running further off into the trees and barking again.

"He's pretty freaked out, Guv," Freeman said, still pressed back against the tree as she looked their way.

"Him and me both," said Archer, looking pale in the torchlight.

"All right, let's check that body," Pierce said—a pessimistic slip of the tongue, but correcting herself would only draw more attention to the fact. "And keep an eye on that dog!" She doubted any of them would be up to the task of corralling a petrified German Shepherd; she wasn't sure even Collins would be able to calm Magnus right now.

Definitely not, in fact, because as Freeman moved forward to shine her torch into the hollow between the trees, Pierce saw that it was the dog handler who lay slumped on the muddy ground, face a mask of blood as it lay turned away from them.

She cursed and grabbed her radio. "This is Romeo Charlie One—we need medical support!" she said as Freeman knelt down to try for a pulse. "We have police casualties here." Pierce expected to see a grim headshake, but instead Freeman's eyes widened as she looked up.

"She's still alive, Guv!"

Archer hurried forward to join her, prompting a flurry of new barking from Magnus, but the dog didn't try to approach them, running in circles and whining. As Pierce relayed the information into the radio, she glimpsed a figure in a police uniform through the trees ahead of them. She stepped forward, squinting past the rain. "Winters, is that you?" she called. "Why didn't you respond?"

He was just standing there under the trees, unmoving as the rain poured down on him. Shock? Injury? Pierce moved towards him. She shone her torch on his face, but the peak of his cap cast a shadow over his features.

Cap, not helmet. PC Winters had been wearing a police helmet—it was the community support officers who were in caps. Not Freeman's missing partner, then, but Davenport, the PCSO who'd been on patrol with Collins. She took another step forward... and registered dark stains on the reflective surface of his hi-vis jacket that she didn't think were rain.

And then he lunged out of the darkness towards her, swinging a tree branch as thick as his arm straight towards her head.

CHAPTER TWENTY-SIX

Pierce yelped and jumped back from the assault, taking the hit on her forearm with almost enough force to jar the torch out of her hand. Davenport swung at her again before she'd had the time to catch her breath, only the tangled branches above her robbing the blow of its force. She scrambled backwards up the slope, feet tripping and slipping on the sodden leaf-carpeted ground.

She shone the torch into Davenport's face—and saw that the man she vaguely remembered from a few hours ago was gone. His face was a ruin, eyes rotted away in their sockets to ooze blood and decay down his cheeks, skin waxy pale and blistered as if by some dreadful disease. If he hadn't been moving, it would have been quite clear that he was dead.

And she didn't think that he was moving under his own power. Possessed, as Vyner had been—but while the necromancer had apparently been protected enough to escape the worst of the effect, here the parasitic spirit had full reign. Whatever was controlling Davenport's moves now was nothing the human body had ever been designed to host, and his body and mind were rejecting the invasion like a failed transplant. Given time, the thing would be neutralised just by physically falling apart.

But they couldn't afford to give it time.

Pierce cursed and leapt out of the way as the possessed Davenport lunged at her with his club, hitting the tree beside her hard enough to break branches. She fumbled for her radio, the buttons slick with rain. "PCSO Davenport is under magical influence!" she shouted, dodging away from him. "Detain with silver cuffs!"

Much easier said than bloody done, but that was all she had time for before he was coming at her again. She grabbed the end of his branch club, trying to wrestle it off of him before he could try for a second swing, but the strength that ripped it from her hands was more than human. She turned and sprinted away through the trees, heading downhill away from the others less by choice than because it was the path of least resistance.

The running that she'd done already was exacting its toll; she'd barely had the chance to catch her breath back, and it was burning in her chest as she scrambled between the trees. Bursts of chatter on the radio, but she couldn't spare the attention to listen, dodging obstacles by the narrow beam of the torch in her jolting grip, trying to track Davenport's pursuit by the sound of splintering trees.

The possession might be causing his body to degrade, but it didn't slow him down. He had no bloody *eyes* left, yet he still kept after her, crashing heedlessly through obstacles in his path. There was no time for Pierce to look around and formulate a plan or pause to yank her silver cuffs out from under her coat.

Her foot hit something more solid than a loose branch and she tripped, sprawling across the warm bulk of a human body. She grabbed her radio. "I've got Winters—" she started to report, but Davenport was on her before she could say more. She threw herself to one side as he smashed out with the club, wincing when it cracked down on Winters' chest instead, wincing more when it brought no reaction. Winters was dead, or at least in a bad way.

And Pierce was in danger of joining him. As Davenport lunged again, she kicked out at him and scrambled away, finally managing to yank her coat open and grab for the cuffs. Before she'd fumbled them out a sweep of Davenport's club cracked the side of her knee, sending her staggering and cursing. She crashed into a tree and water poured down on her head, the torch knocked from her hand to bounce off down the hillside. "Fuck!" She could see it was still switched on, lighting up the rain, but before she could chase after it, Davenport was there.

The first blow of his club struck her in the stomach, knocking her breath away; she barely caught the second with her arm. As she jerked away from the third swipe, it crunched against the tree behind her, the branch breaking in two with a splintering crack. Davenport gave an indistinct roar and let the club fall, grabbing for her throat instead.

The strangling hands that closed around her windpipe were cold as the dead. As Pierce clawed at his hands to try to wrench them away, the wet skin under her nails slid and ripped, as if it was no more than loose wrapping around decaying flesh. She couldn't even gag; the crushing fingers stayed remorselessly tight even as the skin encasing them sloughed away.

She yanked her silver cuffs the rest of the way from their pouch, hooking her fingers through one of the loops. No time to try to deploy the things properly; she used them like a set of knuckle dusters, punching Davenport in the jaw. He growled like he was gargling his own decomposing flesh, but the grip around her throat didn't slacken.

Pierce was losing air, a deeper darkness than the night beginning to bloom around the edges of her vision. She pressed the edge of the cuffs against Davenport's hand, and the skin sizzled like pork crackling at the touch of the silver.

But it wasn't enough. Even as his body burned, he still kept up the pressure. Her rushing blood was pounding in her ears, and she could feel her struggles weakening, fading...

A furious explosion of barking, and Magnus burst out of the trees, the light from her dropped torch painting the dog in hellhound shadows. Davenport didn't react, heedless of the sound or perhaps already deaf to it as his body decayed. Something about his scent was clearly driving the dog wild, and it growled and barked madly before rushing forward in a frantic lunge. Jaws closed on Davenport's leg, but his dead face showed no sign of pain as he loosed his grip with one hand to backhand the dog away.

Pierce wrenched away from him the moment that he let her go, scraping her back on the tree behind her as she lurched sideways. She fell to her knees in the mud and wheezed, grabbing at a tree for balance as she tried to force enough breath back into her body to get moving again. Her vision was a chaos of light and shadow, torches through the trees and driving rain. Magnus was still barking, and she could hear people shouting somewhere nearby in the woods as well as over the radio.

Focus. Davenport. She staggered upright, trying to resolve the blur. He was still close, he had to be—shit! She stepped back from his swinging fist and grabbed at his arm, trying to force it away before he could go for the throat again. Even though she could feel his flesh slip like well-cooked meat off the bone, he was still impossibly strong, and she was using her weak arm because in the other hand she still had the—

—Fucking *handcuffs*, for fuck's sake. She shook the cuffs open and snapped the first loop around the wrist in her grip, turning her head with a hiss as the rotting skin began to smoke. Still panting, breathless, she lunged around behind him, succeeding in wrenching his arm behind his back because he lacked either the wit or the pain centres to turn with her. Instead he twisted round the other way to meet her, snatching at her clumsily with his free hand, and she grabbed at it to close the second cuff.

Even with his arms pinned back Davenport was still too strong for her, throwing himself backwards to smash her aside with a blow of his shoulder. He tossed his head back, trying to headbutt, trying to bite, the movement carrying them both skidding and staggering down the slope. A police torch shone on the two of them in a blinding burst of light. Freeman, Archer, someone else? Couldn't tell.

"Mirror, need a mirror!" she gasped, thinking of Vyner. His might have been enchanted, it might be useless, but still—"Try to reflect his eyes!" Of course he didn't bloody *have* eyes left, not physically at least—but something was steering him, and symbol was as powerful as fact in ritual magic.

Her own compact mirror was still in her bag in the car, no bloody use to man or beast right now. Would Freeman have one? Probably not, for the same reason: you didn't carry crap around while you were on the job.

As Davenport swung round again, Pierce darted back from him. He was clumsier now at least, both from the cuffs and his rapid decay, but no less determined to do violence to anyone who came near.

"We found Winters, Guv," Freeman tried to report to her. "He's—" She had to leap out of the way as Davenport charged at her full tilt. In the momentary flash of torchlight Pierce could see that his skin had turned an ugly greenish black, beginning to split. His body was decaying faster than a corpse in any natural conditions, but it wasn't slowing him down nearly as much as it should.

She glimpsed a flash of hi-vis yellow at the corner of her eye. Archer. "Stay back!" she said. He wasn't trained for this kind of confrontation—not that any of them bloody were, but he was just a PCSO.

But he dodged around the hand that she'd held up to warm him off. "No, I've got..." He fumbled something out of his pocket, running towards Davenport but jerking back as the butting head and gnashing teeth snapped his way.

As Davenport turned away from her, Freeman darted forward, grabbing hold of the silver cuffs that chained his hands. "I've got him!" she said—over-optimistically. He bucked and fought in her grip, and she had to bend backwards to escape a crack to the chin.

"Watch it!" Pierce yelled, not sure who she was warning. Archer ran forward again and shoved whatever he held in Davenport's face. For a moment the trio were a struggling tableau in the rain, and then Davenport went limp in Freeman's arms.

Entirely, horribly limp, dissolving from an upright if decaying figure into a lifeless, putrefying heap of flesh. Freeman stepped back with a yelp as the corpse slithered out of her arms, pouring from the tattered uniform like so much slurry.

And it was now, unquestionably, a corpse. Pierce finally found some breath from somewhere and sagged against a tree. "Mirror?" she asked Archer.

Not exactly: he turned to show her the dark screen of his switched-off smartphone. "Guess it was reflective enough," he said.

She nodded wearily. "Good thinking, that man."

He grinned briefly in triumph, but the expression slipped from his face as he looked down at the half-liquefied corpse and seemed to register for the first time that it had been not just a person but one wearing a uniform that matched his.

"Oh, God, is that *Terry*?" he moaned, and twisted away, managing to stagger only a few steps before he was noisily sick in the undergrowth.

Pierce looked away, her own stomach lurching in sympathetic nausea. No point chiding him for fucking up her crime scene; he wasn't trained for anything like this, and her crime scene was already pretty fucked. She could hear the dog still barking somewhere further off in the woods, and in the distance sirens spoke of backup arriving.

Too late for Davenport for sure, and probably for Winters too. Collins hadn't exactly been in promising shape either. It was raining, the crime scene had been trampled, and she still wasn't even certain where Davenport and Collins had found the three skulls. Or where *she* was, for that matter; she'd lost all sense of orientation with respect to the road. She reached for her radio.

The cleanup for this was going to be miserable as hell. But it was all that there was left for them to do.

IN THE DARK and the rain it felt deceptively like the middle of the night, and it was only after she'd trudged back out to join the group gathering on the road that she checked her watch and found that it was barely half past five.

The one sliver of good news was PC Collins, returned to consciousness and apparently mostly concerned for the fate of her missing dog as she was led off to the ambulance in a semi-dazed state. "Let me go and get him," she was repeating to anyone who came near. "He'll come when I call him. Let me look for him." Pierce hoped for her sake the dog would prove to have calmed now the possessing spirit was gone, and wouldn't be too traumatised to rehabilitate.

The spirit's other victims were sadly beyond help. Davenport had more than likely been doomed from the moment that he was taken over, and PC Winters had been dead by the time the paramedics got to him. COD would have to wait for the pathologist's pronouncement, but in the meantime, Pierce could only hope that he was already gone by the time she'd tripped over his body and had to run on without stopping.

Either way, she knew that this one was going to haunt her.

She spotted Freeman re-emerge from the woods a short distance away, looking distinctly wearier than the perky young officer she'd started the afternoon as. She'd been in the thick of the action, and Pierce knew too well how that could prove a big shock to the system. Freeman would have done her time as a uniform constable—in Manchester, to boot, not just a sleepy village beat—so she'd undoubtedly seen some unpleasant scenes before, but the RCU had its own unique standards for investigations going pear-shaped, and all the standardised tests in the world couldn't necessarily predict which officers would be able to hack it.

So far, however, Freeman seemed to be holding up well. She gave Pierce a tired nod as she approached. "We've found the last of the skulls, Guv," she said, pushing her hair back to flatten the stray frizz that had worked its way loose from her bun. "From what we can tell, looks like Davenport unearthed one of them, possibly touched it or interfered with the scene in some way."

"And that's our vector of possession." A theory they could run with, at least, though it opened as many questions as it closed. Why had he done it? Just straightforward failure to listen to her advice? Even as a PCSO he should have had the training to know better. Maybe he'd been trying to make sure of his find, eager to prove himself or fearful of making a stupid mistake.

Or maybe the enchantments on the site had acted as some kind of lure, making him act more foolishly than he usually would. Maybe it had even been an accident, fresh dug mud sliding away in the rain, the dog starting to dig...

They could try to reconstruct the scene, but with the limited evidence already trampled and rain-soaked and the only surviving witnesses a head-injured woman and a dog, it was likely most questions would go unanswered. She sighed.

The sound of tyres on the wet tarmac drew her attention. A car approaching down the lane, without blue flashing lights. One of the local uniforms went to intercept—they'd suddenly managed to produce a whole army of them from somewhere, and Pierce knew it was bitter hindsight to resent not having had them available for the search, but it still pissed her off all the same.

She expected the officer to send the car off to seek another route, but instead he waved it on and it rolled up to park nearby. Her headache intensified at the sight of DI Dawson getting out.

"Dawson," she said, voice neutral, though her mood was anything but. "What are you doing here? I didn't call you in." There was nothing for another senior RCU officer to do here that couldn't be done just as well by the local police force.

"Superintendent sent me to relieve you," he said. "He wants to see you back at the station before he leaves."

She bristled at the micromanagement. Whose idea had that been—Snow's or Dawson's? Either way, she wasn't used to being brusquely ordered home from a scene before she was done with it; Palmer had always given her more rein.

But Palmer was gone, more than likely dead, and the prospect of finding the truth behind his disappearance seemed as remote as every other dead-end case that she was working right now. The urge to duke it out with Dawson in a pointless fight deflated. The order had been given, and even if it was at his instigation it wasn't his to countermand.

Besides, if she was honest, she was too bloody tired to turn down an excuse to get off of her feet.

"All right," she acknowledged with a nod. "Sergeant Mistry will fill you in." And hopefully restrain him from antagonising the already unhappy locals, though she couldn't ask for miracles. She turned to Freeman, still hovering nearby. "Freeman, you can drive me back." Her shoulder could use the break, and so could Freeman, no doubt. "It'll give you a chance to get cleaned up." The slackening rain was no substitute for a proper shower when they'd both been up close and personal with a decomposing corpse.

The interior of the car made a merciful escape from the worst of the elements, though it also made her freshly aware of just how soaked she'd become—and not just with rain. Now that they were inside the enclosed space of the car the nauseating scent of death had returned with a vengeance.

The drive passed in brooding silence until they left the rural roads behind and joined the rush hour traffic. Freeman looked sidelong at her as they paused at the end of a line of cars tailing back from a junction. "Guv, was there something more we could have done?" she asked, biting her lip.

Pierce grimaced, and then sighed. "There's always something more we could have done," she said. "Doesn't mean it would have made much sense to do it at the time."

You could second-guess your decisions for ever in their aftermath, but in the end, the only way to sleep at night was to trust yourself enough to believe you'd done what you could with the info you'd had at the time.

Freeman made a vague noise, somewhere between acknowledging and dubious. All to the good; just because Pierce had a few hard-earned platitudes to offer didn't mean she had much truck with officers who accepted them too readily. A little second-guessing and self-doubt didn't hurt, as long as it didn't cross the line into complete self-flagellation.

They arrived back at the station to find the group of druids still occupying the car park despite the puddles suggesting they'd suffered some of the same heavy rain. A larger camper van had pulled up beside the VW bus, and they'd even set up tents, apparently planning on spending the night. At least the continuing drizzle seemed to be keeping them from protesting too visibly, the only evidence a drooping banner strung between the vans that insisted they should *Save Our Nation's Sacred Sites From Government Depredation!*

"Oh, it's the bloody government's fault now, is it?" she muttered to herself as they passed it. Probably lucky for the protestors they were tucked up safe inside their vans: she didn't have the patience to deal with time-wasters right now.

"Hmm?" Freeman glanced back at her.

"Nothing useful or informative," Pierce said, shaking her head. She ran a hand back over her hair; it hardly seemed worth putting her hood back up when she was this drenched already. "You should get yourself cleaned up and head home," she advised. "Paperwork can wait until we've got full details from the scene." She drew a fortifying breath as they reached the door. "Meanwhile, I'll go and see what's got his nibs's knickers in a knot."

Whoops, so much for thoughts of setting a good example for the newbies. Freeman just flashed her a momentary grin, though. Smart girl. Right attitude. She'd go far.

Assuming she didn't end up dying an ugly early death, like so many other young officers who'd had the misfortune to get mixed up in RCU work. Didn't seem fair sometimes that Pierce was the one who kept on trucking while the youngsters fell like dominos around her, but that was the way it went sometimes: you had to be lucky for long enough to learn the art of survival. Not everyone could be that lucky.

Pierce sighed, and went to face the music.

PART THREE

CHAPTER TWENTY-SEVEN

THE BOLLOCKING ABOUT the operation from Superintendent Snow went about as well as she could have expected, which was to say not very.

"This operation was entirely mishandled from the start," he said, peering at her sternly through his narrow glasses. He didn't pace the way Palmer had when he was agitated, but stayed planted behind his desk where he could give her a supercilious look like a disapproving headmaster. "Rushed, shoddily put together—the local forces had no idea what they were getting into!"

"Neither did we, sir," Pierce said wearily.

"All the more reason there should have been planning, consultation—why wasn't this operation cleared with me?"

"Sir, it was just an exploratory search operation, initially," she said. "We were following up on some disturbed graves. There was no way to be certain that the ritual scene was even in the area, or to think that it might pose a danger to police personnel. The first scene in Bingley was excavated with no harm to the forensics team."

"Yes, until your unit came along and purposely called forth a supernatural effect that resulted in multiple injuries!" he snapped.

Which had been Dawson's bloody stupid idea, but as DCI in charge she couldn't pass blame down the command chain, no matter how richly it was deserved.

"That was... a miscalculation," she agreed. She wasn't going to say it had been hers. "But nothing like that was attempted at the Silsden site. We're still working to ascertain how PCSO Davenport came to be possessed." Or at least they had been before he'd had her unceremoniously yanked away from the scene.

"And you used PCSOs for this!" Snow threw up his hands. "The media's already been up in arms about them taking on too many police duties in place of regular constables. When it emerges that they were deployed in an operation that ended in multiple deaths..."

That wouldn't have been Pierce's first concern when it came to the tragic deaths of two young men, whatever their roles. She pressed her lips together. The only self-defence that she had here was not to budge an inch. "I contacted the officer in charge of the local police," she said. "They supplied me with the personnel that they felt would be adequate for the search."

Bollocks, of course: at best they'd provided as many as their overstretched force could spare, at worst as few as they could get away with, but what was the point of stating as much on the record? The locals couldn't be blamed for not wasting more personnel on a needle in the haystack search, and it was their people who'd suffered for it. Just a miserable fuck-up of a situation that couldn't be laid at anybody's door—but of course, the people who dissected such things after the fact never wanted to hear that as an answer.

"Well, don't think that's going to stop them blaming us for this!" Snow said. "There's already been a history of complaints from other departments about the RCU using their personnel for tasks they haven't trained for. This is only going to add fuel to that fire."

Nobody was trained for the kind of unpredictable situations that Ritual Crime cases dealt with, but if he thought it was a bad idea to keep relying on outside personnel, she wasn't going to disagree. If Davenport had been one of hers, could he have avoided whatever mistake had led to him becoming possessed?

"Sir, I know it's not an ideal situation to rely so heavily on outside forces," she said. "But without more dedicated RCU personnel—"

He pressed his lips into a thin tight line. "This is hardly the time to campaign for a greater departmental budget," he said. It seemed like the *exact* time to her, in all frankness, but for some inexplicable reason the political entities that played with their livelihoods seemed to view extra funding as an incentive for success rather than a remedy for shortfalls. The Catch-22 of target-setting: earn your cash injection by first proving that you could do without it.

"Sir... this was not a situation that could have been foreseen," she said tiredly. "It's a terrible tragedy. People have died. But everybody involved was doing the best they could with the information and resources that they had available."

Snow sat forward in his chair to hold her gaze. "Then *do better*," he said. "This is not the first police operation that's ended with casualties on your watch, and I can't allow your unit to just keep staggering from one disaster to the next without the slightest thing to show for it. I expect to see some results on your cases very soon, or we will have to think very seriously about a change of leadership."

Pierce didn't trust herself to make any remark in response, so instead she just turned on her heel to go.

"And one more thing," he added, before she could leave. "I understand that there's a group in the car park who are refusing to leave until they get the RCU's attention. Why haven't they been dealt with?"

"They're just your average neighbourhood cranks," she said. "Protesting things that don't have anything to do with the police. They'll probably have given up by morning."

The way things were going right now, it was tempting to do the same.

PIERCE SLEPT POORLY that night; in spite of all words to the contrary, she couldn't help but keep turning over thoughts of all the things she might have done to ensure matters turned out differently. Joined up with the dog team herself, for a start; chosen to reduce the number of search teams rather than let anyone go out without an RCU officer to accompany them. Maybe if she'd been there she could have made a difference.

Or maybe she'd have been caught unawares like Collins and poor Winters, just another name on the casualty list. The worst part was the fact that there was no way to know, only endless second thoughts to chase around.

She woke in the morning feeling every one of her years, not to mention all the war wounds from the last few days. Too much running, and definitely too many scuffles with people who were younger and stronger. DCI wasn't supposed to be this much of a front-line job, but in the RCU it came with all the management responsibilities and not nearly enough junior officers to delegate the scut work to.

If she'd had more people, then maybe yesterday...

But there she was, going back down that same futile path again. Ugly as yesterday had been, she had to put it out of her mind and focus on the next job.

The half-arsed make-up patch job to cover the bruises blossoming on her neck and her jaw—never one of her greatest skills, but necessary if she was going to be interacting with the public—made her later than she'd planned to be. And that wasn't the only problem. When she arrived at the station, she saw that the druids hadn't given up as hoped, but had set themselves up a proper encampment, placards and banners everywhere.

They weren't the worst of it. Pierce grimaced as she spotted a news van parked on the corner, a woman with a vaguely familiar hairdo doing a piece to camera in front of the station's main doors. She could see several other cameras taking shots of the protestors, and no doubt some of the milling crowd were journalists.

The sad thing was that them being here to cover the protest was probably the *best* case scenario.

She parked her own car across the road from the station car park, in defiance of the stern edicts of several circulated memos. With luck, and her lack of a uniform, she might be able to slip around the side unnoticed. Most people still defaulted to expecting to see men when they were looking for high-ranking police.

Unfortunately, luck wasn't with her, while a journalist who'd covered RCU business before apparently was. "DCI Pierce!" a brash voice called out as she attempted to nonchalantly slip past, and then the pack descended.

"DCI Pierce! DCI Pierce!" A microphone was thrust into her face. "Can you comment on the RCU's involvement in the deaths of two police officers in Silsden last night?"

"DCI Pierce! Is it true that last night's deaths are connected to the skulls that were excavated in Bingley?"

"Does the RCU accept any responsibility for the suicide of the necromancer Martin Vyner?"

She hated this shit when it came in press conference form, and the ambush version was even worse. "I can't comment on the details of any ongoing investigations," she said, holding up a hand as she strode past. And they shouldn't *have* those details to be quizzing her about. How had the press connected the dots so fast? A leak from any one of the crime scenes was perfectly plausible, but multiple spills at once started to seem like enemy action.

Was someone deliberately feeding information to the press? That was all they bloody needed.

The journalists chased her across the car park, the cameras swinging to follow. "Will there be an internal investigation?" someone demanded.

"Does the RCU routinely employ necromancers?"

"DCI Pierce! DCI Pierce!"

Apparently the words 'can't comment' didn't translate well, since they didn't stop baying questions until the doors were closed behind her. Then, giving up on her, they rapidly turned their attentions back to the group of druid protestors, who were doing their best to get their signs into every photo, aided and abetted by the cameramen. Pierce sensed news stories tenuously stitching the unrelated protest into a tale of widespread unhappiness with the RCU in her near future.

And a headache. She rubbed her temples. The headache was here already.

"How long have the hyenas been out there?" she asked Jill, on desk duty again.

"Since first thing," she said with a grimace. "The Superintendent's livid."

"*Quelle surprise.* Oh, well, don't tell him that I'm here, would you?" Snow would probably want to speak with her soon enough regardless, but with any luck there would be a lead or a new case that got her out of the office before he had a chance. She didn't fancy starting the day with a louder, faster remix of last night's bollocking.

Jill tapped the side of her nose confidentially. "I was regrettably distracted when you came in," she said.

"Very regrettable," Pierce said. "You should be careful with that. Anybody could sneak up the stairs while you weren't paying attention." She proceeded to do just that.

The rest of her team had beaten her to the office, all looking tired but present and correct. She stuck her head in for long enough to confirm that nothing more of significance had happened at the woods after she'd left, then moved along to Magical Analysis.

"New skulls. Anything?" she asked Jenny, leaning in through the doorway of her office.

Jenny shook her head. "Preliminaries suggest they're the same as the others, and after the last one exploded..."

"Kid gloves?" she presumed.

"And a blast shield." She shrugged. "You might have better luck going through regular forensics, I'm afraid—looks like mixing any magic with the existing enchantments is too chancy, so there's really not much more that we can do."

Pierce pressed her lips together unhappily. "I'm not sure we have that kind of time," she said. "According to Cliff, the clock is ticking: D-Day in three days."

Jenny gave her an apologetic grimace. "I'm studying the bone fragments from yesterday," she offered. "*Carefully*. So far nothing's gone boom, but it hasn't got us anywhere either." She shook her head. "If you need results fast, I don't think they're going to be coming from us."

A check-in with Cliff revealed much the same prognosis. Excavation of the Silsden site had revealed a set of three skulls seemingly identical to those dug up at Bingley, right down to the dimensions of the triangular pattern in which they were arranged.

"If they're that carefully arranged, the sites can't have been chosen at random," she said. "What links a farmer's field in Bingley with a patch of trees in Silsden?"

Cliff shrugged at her. "The Leeds and Liverpool canal?" he offered, somewhat facetiously.

"I doubt we're looking for a canal boat operator." All the same, she found herself turning the idea over in her mind, pondering the idea of water as a boundary, the fact that running water was supposed to contain magic... She discarded the idea still half-formed. *Constructing* links was easy. Finding one that genuinely meant something was different. The trouble with having only two points to connect was that you could draw a line between them almost any way you pleased and get a pattern that seemed to fit.

All the same, she had to try. Pierce stuck her head into the Arcane Documents office. "Bingley. Silsden. What connects them? Cliff's already done the canal joke."

Their second document tech, Kevin, stared at her blankly from over the pages of the book she'd roused him out of. "Er... will this be on the test?"

She flapped a hand, dismissing the longshot question. "Probably not your department, but if you get a minute, see if you can find anything connecting the map references of our two skull locations."

He nodded, continuing the polite fiction that any of them ever had a spare minute that wasn't already accounted for by a dozen active cases. He almost resumed his reading, and then his head jerked back up. "Oh! Fatima had a thing for you," he remembered. He moved to fetch a book from the table across the office and squinted at the Post-it note stuck to it. "Francis Maundrell...?"

It took Pierce a moment to switch mental gears. "Oh, yes. Seventeenth-century warlock, artefact thefts. This is one of Deepan's cases." She took the proffered book, an elderly hardback with a tattered cover titled *Mystical Traditions of the Moorlands*. "Cheers, Kev," she said, flicking through to the marked pages even as she moved away. He gave a vague mumble in response, already preoccupied with his own reading.

She drifted back along the hallway slowly, skim-reading as she went. Blah, blah, blah, born 1638, reputation as a warlock, chapel on the family estate alleged to have been used for sacrificial rites, burned down by a mob 1672... Traces of the ruins still possible to find. She straightened up, glancing first at the black and white photo showing a few overgrown partial walls, and then at the publication date in the front of the book.

Ruins of the chapel at Maundrell's ancestral home had still been possible to find as of around forty years ago. Assuming they hadn't been bulldozed and turned into a supermarket by now... Pierce raised her head as she reached the RCU office. "Deepan! Might just have a lead for you on your theft case," she said.

SHE AND DEEPAN headed out to the site of the former Maundrell family estate with DC Taylor in tow. "There may not be much left for us to find," Pierce cautioned as they drove, having read through the pages more thoroughly. "The ruins were in a poor state when the author of this book visited them in the early 'seventies, and they don't seem to have been considered particularly important outside of the beardy weirdy sect."

"'Beardy weirdy,' Guv?" Taylor echoed with careful pronunciation, as if it was a technical term he might be expected to define later.

"The likes of our druid friends we left back in the station car park," she clarified. At least she'd been forewarned of the press presence this time, and sent Deepan to fetch the car and bring it round. She wasn't convinced that young Constable Taylor would manage to make his way through a media gauntlet without freezing up like a rabbit in the headlights.

Deepan gave her a small, wry smile in the rear-view mirror. "I think we call them 'alternative worshippers' these days, Guv," he said.

"We call them a number of things, depending on how much of a pain in the backside they're being," she said. "But in fairness to them, they're generally harmless. Like to wander around sites of alleged ritual significance and prance around soaking up the vibes in the hope they'll become magical without having to do anything." She'd rarely known a group like that with enough discipline to actually work any large scale rituals. "They're the only ones likely to have ever heard of the Maundrell name, let alone come looking for the ruins."

"Aside from our thieves," Deepan said.

"Hopefully." The thieves seemed to know more about

Francis Maundrell's life than this book did—no mention in here of any of the artefacts that had been stolen—so it was likely they were at least aware that the chapel had existed. Her experience said that they would probably want to see it, touch it, stand where Maundrell had stood, even if there was nothing to be found.

So, not so different from the beardy weirdies, after all, really. Everything a matter of degree.

The satnav program on Taylor's phone chimed in with the instruction to take a right. "I hope that thing knows where it's going, because we're out in the back of beyond here," she said, peering out of the car's side window. "What was the name of the people that owned the land?"

She heard Taylor riffle papers in the passenger seat. "Er... Rural Treat Cottages, Guv. There's a farm and two separate sets of holiday cottages. We couldn't get anybody on the phone."

"Might not be anyone in residence at this time of year." There would probably be caretakers, but they'd be concerned with potential squatters in the properties, not visitors to burned-out ruins elsewhere on the land. "We'll see if we can find anybody at the farmhouse."

Their knocking received no response, but the woman in the village shop was happy to chat. "Oh, they'll be in Florida, this time of year, most likely. Barbara's sister lives out there, and they've got a place. All right for some. Not that I'd like it out there—can't stand the heat." She tucked her shawl tighter about herself. "Of course, I can't take the cold these days, either. It's a bugger getting old. Is there a problem?"

"Nothing serious," Deepan said with a reassuring smile. "We just received information that there might be trespassers. Would you know anything about ruins on the property?"

"Oh, the old chapel?" she said. "Well, that's what we used to call it when I was a girl—not much of it left, of course, even then. The ruins are down past that wooded bit on the other side of the hill, though you'd probably have to poke about a bit to find them. It's all overgrown these days. Used to be the thing for teenagers to spend the night there as a dare, but I suppose they've got better ways to amuse themselves these days. Is it ghost hunters you're after?"

"We're not sure at this point," Deepan said, somehow keeping his place in the rapid flood of words. "It may be nothing."

"Ah, well, you'd best go on over and have a look, then," she said. "Barb and Jimmy don't mind people wandering the place, but they don't want anybody setting up residence. Had some campers set up in their field once— left the place littered with beer cans and all kinds of rubbish, can you believe it? You'd be amazed how many people just don't seem to grasp that a country field still belongs to someone."

They managed to extricate themselves from her over-friendly grip and followed the vague directions to the ruins.

"All right, they've got to be somewhere around here," Pierce said as they passed what she presumed to be 'that wooded bit.' "Let's spread out and search." She swallowed her first instinct to tell the others to stay in sight: couldn't let yesterday's events make her too jittery.

The wooded bit in question didn't so much come to a defined end as gradually peter away into more widely dispersed trees and bushes. The rise and fall of the land made it hard to survey the area without actually walking it, especially when they weren't sure how much of a ruin they were looking for. After the first few minutes, Pierce was wishing that she hadn't left the book back in the car: even an outdated photograph would have given them some aid in getting their bearings.

It was Taylor who spotted the ruins first, calling out from somewhere behind the rise off to her left. "Guv, Sarge, I think I see—oh, shit," he said abruptly. "We've got a runner!"

A figure in jeans and a combat jacket burst out from the trees ahead of them, taking off across the hills at a fast sprint.

CHAPTER TWENTY-EIGHT

PIERCE BROKE INTO a run at Taylor's shout, but she was still feeling the effects of the past few days' battering, and Deepan was further away across the hillside. By the time she'd puffed up to the top of the steep slope, DC Taylor was well ahead of both of them, in pursuit of a suspect who was fast outdistancing him.

"Deepan! He's coming round the hill!" she shouted down to him as he raced up behind her, but even as he altered course, the running man did the same, turning towards another clump of trees a short distance ahead. She glimpsed the white paint of a vehicle through the sparse branches.

"Fuck, that's the van—don't let him get to it!" she shouted to Taylor. The DC found a burst of speed from somewhere, lanky limbs windmilling, but the suspect was already well ahead, shoving through the trees to reach the van.

Taylor closed the distance as the man scrambled in and started up the vehicle, but it coughed to life and drove off before he could catch up, bumping away across the hilly ground. Pierce tried to get a look at the number plate, but the trees and the vehicle's erratic bouncing made it impossible.

Taylor chased another dozen paces before it sank in that he was just wasting his time. He stumbled to a halt. "Sorry, Guv, not going to catch him now," he panted, shaking his head as she jogged up to him. "Couldn't get the registration either—it's covered up by mud."

"Bollocks," Pierce said wearily, as the van hurtled away down the hill to rejoin the road. Probably just more fake plates in any case. They couldn't get back to the car in time to make a chase of it, and there was little point in calling for support from local units: they'd take a while to get out to anywhere this rural, and by then the van could have been ditched or lost among any number like it. She doubted they'd have much luck finding cameras along the route, either.

"All right," she said, gathering her own breath. "Let him go. Let's just hope he left something behind." Their suspect might have got away, but he hadn't had the chance to do his housekeeping before he left.

She descended the slope towards the ruins of the old chapel. It required foreknowledge to recognise what she was looking at: there really wasn't much more left than the crumbled corner of a wall and some fallen rubble, half swallowed up by ivy and brambles.

But then she spotted the camo fabric behind the last standing wall, and realised they'd hit paydirt after all. "There's a tent!" She reached for her crime scene gloves.

The tent was small, but could still have taken two, and might have done so: one rumpled sleeping bag lay stretched out, apparently used, while another had been chucked in a corner, still rolled up inside the drawstring cover. She inventoried the rest of the tent's contents. A basic camping stove and several days' worth of food and drinks cans—all energy drinks, no sign of alcohol. A discarded T-shirt and some balled up socks.

And a suitcase, laid flat on the ground. Pierce lifted the lid, and saw that the inside was packed with white fabric: not just clothing, but something bigger, like a sheet.

Who brought bedding along on a camping trip? She carefully drew the topmost layer of cloth away. Nestled beneath she saw a wooden cup; as she tugged more of the fabric aside, a dagger in a leather sheath was revealed, and then the wooden mask from the Hemsfield Gallery. Pierce started to smile.

"Gentlemen!" she said expansively. "It seems that this has not *entirely* been a cock-up."

IT WAS A result at last, but not quite the decisive one Pierce might have hoped. They'd recovered what looked the full set of stolen artefacts, but the fact was that the value of the pieces in question was relatively negligible: their main concern was preventing the thieves from striking anywhere else. They could only hope the hastily abandoned site would yield some further clue that would help them trace whoever had been camped there.

She left Deepan and Taylor to await the arrival of

forensics and headed back to the station on her own. She could report this to the superintendent as a win, but she doubted it would be enough of one for him. Snow struck her as a man who didn't much like being left with inconvenient loose ends.

Like, for instance, those bloody druids. Their tents were still taking up one end of the station car park, and she could swear the group had even gained in number, probably bolstered by the excitement of getting some media attention for their cause. At least the journalists had given up and gone by now, though it was too much to hope the lack of police statement would stop them from running with what they already had.

And what they had was far more than they should. She'd like to know who'd spilled the beans, but the last thing they needed was to worsen their relations with the local police still further by throwing accusations around. Maybe someone was trying to drop the RCU in it for getting their officers hurt and killed—unprofessional as hell, but she couldn't exactly blame them for being angry. She and her team had fucked up at both of the skull scenes, and the fact she couldn't really see how it could have been avoided at Silsden didn't make for that much consolation.

Done was done. Couldn't plug a leak that had already done its leaking—best to just let it go, and hope like hell it didn't prove to be ongoing. This case was enough of a disaster already without having every detail splashed across the newspapers.

Deciding reporting their partial success to Snow could wait until he called her in to speak to him, she headed back up to the RCU office. Freeman looked up from her computer as she came in. "Find anything at the chapel site, Guv?" she asked.

"We recovered the artefacts, but the thieves got away," Pierce said.

"Oh, well, that's... sort of good?" Freeman offered uncertainly.

"'Sort of good' about sums it up," she said, dropping into her seat with a sigh. She logged back in and squinted warily at the horror that was her inbox. Only a few things flagged 'urgent,' at least, none of which looked like they really were. "Any trouble with the media?" she asked. They might have disappeared from the doorstep, but that probably only meant they'd moved on to trying their luck with the phones.

"We had a bunch of calls this morning, but Inspector Dawson talked to them in the end," Freeman said.

Oh, God, that didn't bode well. Pierce could feel the headache settling over her temples. "Dawson talked to them? What did he say?"

Freeman's forehead wrinkled with concern, as if she thought it should have been her job to corral her idiot superior. "Er... just reassurances, mostly," she said. "The RCU is on the case, we expect to have results very soon."

Yes, definitely a tension headache. "Oh, well, that's just bloody wonderful," she said, rubbing the back of her neck. "You tell the media 'soon,' they take it as licence to ring you up every fifteen minutes and demand to know why you haven't solved the case yet." She glanced around. "Where's Dawson now?"

Freeman still had that slightly cringing look, as if she thought any unwanted news she had to report might reflect back on her. "He went to meet an informant. Someone called saying they wanted to speak to us about the skull case, but it had to be in person."

"And he went, without speaking to me?" She might have to downgrade her opinion of the man to something stronger than 'bull-headed idiot.'

Freeman grimaced apologetically. "I asked if I should inform you, but he said it wasn't necessary."

Then perhaps she should have disregarded that... but Pierce bit back any urge to say as much. Giving that kind of order could lead nowhere good, no matter how much she might personally dislike Dawson's presence in her chain of command. Let Freeman learn to judge for herself when she should or shouldn't listen to a superior being a prat.

"Let me guess, he didn't take any backup with him either." She didn't wait for the predictable answer to that. "How long ago did he leave?"

"The meet was set up for one o'clock, but he left early so he could keep a lookout for the bloke arriving."

Pierce checked her watch. Still time to catch up to him, maybe, if it was somewhere close. "Did he say where he went?"

"Yeah, I made a note." Freeman rolled her chair across to snag a Post-it from where it was stuck to the side of the cabinet.

"Good." At least someone round here was doing their job. Pierce stood up from her chair, any hopes of a brief break forgotten. "All right, let's go."

The informant had asked to meet Dawson round the back of an industrial estate: somewhere with enough traffic that cars wouldn't draw attention, but with secluded corners where they could talk unobserved. A logical enough call, but it still made Pierce twitchy; maybe it was just the fact her last meeting in a similar location had ended in attempted murder, but she didn't have a good feeling about this.

She tried to call Dawson on his mobile as Freeman drove, but it was switched off. She doubted if he'd have his radio on him: a burst of police chatter could easily spook a source wary of being seen talking to them.

Which meant that he was incommunicado: perhaps a necessary evil, but still exactly why he shouldn't have gone without backup. There was no guarantee that their mystery informant was truly planning on helping the police; at best, it might just be a time-waster or a wannabe journalist fishing for hints, but at worst he could easily end up with a knife between the ribs. Pierce didn't know if Dawson was just a macho idiot who thought he could handle anything, or ambitious enough to be trying to crack the case without sharing the credit. Either way, the lone wolf tactics were pissing her off.

"Which way now, Guv?" Freeman asked as they approached a roundabout.

"Left, down here."

They passed parked cars and industrial units that hummed with the sound of working machinery, but there was no foot traffic on the roads out here. They took several twists and turns through the estate before Freeman slowed. "That's Dawson's car," she said, indicating a discreet silver Mondeo parked in front of the metal fence to their left. There was no one inside. Beyond the fence were the tree-covered grounds of a disused factory that might have made a potential meeting point, but the gates were padlocked shut.

Pierce glanced off to the right, where the road continued a short way before turning off to the left and vanishing behind the buildings. The informant could have insisted they walk a distance away from the car, but Dawson would have to have been foolishly cocky to agree. Possible, but... She looked again at the row of industrial units in front of them. The leftmost didn't quite butt up against the high brick wall that surrounded the factory grounds: instead, there was a narrow strip of grass and bushes running in between them.

She reached for the seat belt release. "I'm going to check around the back," she murmured to Freeman. "Turn the car around. Cut the engine, but be ready to leave fast if we have to run." Excessive precautions were only paranoid if it turned out that you didn't need them.

Pierce left the car and headed around the side of the building, the wet grass muffling her footsteps as she left the tarmac. She stuck close to the side wall of the industrial unit, edging down to the end to peer around. There was Dawson, speaking with a man in a grey hoodie a short distance away under the trees. The informant kept shifting from foot to foot and looking around nervously, so Pierce withdrew around the corner to listen rather than watch. She could barely hear the hushed whisper of the man in the hoodie, but Dawson wasn't trying quite so hard to keep his voice down.

"Where is this site?" she heard him press.

"I can't tell you," the informant said. "If they realise—"

"Well, you've got to give me something to bloody go on, man! How many people involved in this operation?"

"A lot. I mean, this is... large-scale shit." The man gave a nervous laugh that sounded more sick than amused. "Huge. They call themselves Red Key, but that's just the group I'm working for. I don't know who they really are. They've got people high up—they've got people in the *police*, man. I'm risking my life even talking to you. I don't know that you haven't talked to them."

His voice sounded closer, as if he was on the verge of considering making an exit. No way for Pierce to withdraw without being spotted, so she stayed where she was, ready to detain him if necessary. Not that there was much 'if' about it. The scale of operation he was talking about sounded a lot like the people she'd tangled with back in October's shapeshifter case, a fake company called Solomon Solutions who'd vanished into the mist after the raid where she'd arrested the skinbinder. If this was them resurfacing again, she needed to know about it.

"Then make it worth our while," Dawson said forcefully. "You say they're going to come after you—d'you think they care if you're betraying them a lot or just a little? You're in deep shit already. You want to crawl out? Tell us everything."

"Oh, no. No," the man said. "There are things I know that anybody could have told you, but the high clearance stuff... No way. They'd trace it straight back to me—there's only like five guys that it could be and they're already suspicious." As he backed away from Dawson, Pierce could see the back of his hood around the corner; a pace or two more and he'd see her. She edged further back along the side of the building.

The roof above her head creaked, and she froze, thinking that she'd bumped against a drainpipe. Then the faint noise came again, and she realised it was something moving up there on top of the roof.

Something too heavy to be a bird or a squirrel. The roof creaked, and Pierce stepped back, trying to see, but the narrow strip between the building and the brick wall didn't give her enough room to get the viewing angle.

A sudden burst of frantic beeping from a car horn broke the hush of the scene. Pierce spun to look, thinking it was a car alarm, but then she saw Freeman waving frantically, gesturing at the roof. As Pierce turned back, the informant spotted her and let out a shocked yell. "You fucker!" he shouted at Dawson as he scrambled away from both of them. "Who the fuck did you bring?"

"I didn't—" Dawson's words were cut off as Pierce moving out from around the building. "What the hell are you doing here?" he demanded, face red with indignation.

"Forget that; move!" she ordered them both, twisting to try and look up at the roof. "There's someone—"

A dark shape sprang down lightly from the edge of the roof, too sinuously graceful to be human, too big for any native animal.

A shapeshifter.

Pierce barely had a chance to register the sleek feline shape before the beast had bounded up again, leaping towards the informant. She cursed and grabbed for the equipment on her belt; silver would break the enchantment on a shapeshifting pelt, but getting cuffs on a live, moving panther was a joke. She had malodorant spray, a stink bomb in a can that should give a shifter's sensitive nose pause.

A pause that ought to involve Firearms being there to take the thing down with silver bullets. Without that backup, they were pretty fucked. All they could do was run.

Before she'd even pulled the spray can out of the belt pouch, the shifter had trapped the informant. He had nowhere to flee, hemmed in by the brick walls and the trees, and she could only watch, too far away, too slow to act, as the panther sank its teeth into his thigh. Blood droplets flew in a spray as it shook him like a rag.

"Fuck!" Dawson had his own can of the malodorant out, but he might as well have spritzed the thing with water. The stinking cloud didn't even have time to start to spread before the shapeshifter twisted and sprang away, dragging the screaming man along by his leg like a careless child bumping a doll along the ground. Pierce cast around for some kind of ranged weapon, but there was nothing, not even a rock.

The panther shifter reached the foot of a tree by the wall and briefly let go of its human prey, but only for long enough to take another, better grip before it scrambled with him up the trunk. The tree bent under the combined weight with an ominous crack, but before the branches could break, the panther heaved its victim up over the top of the wall and let him fall down with a crunch of bones and an agonized cry. The tree whiplashed away from the wall and then back again, and the panther leapt after him, cresting the wall in an inelegant scramble.

"Shit!" Dawson ran forward, Pierce following on his heels, but they could already hear the big cat crashing away through the trees on the other side.

"What's past here?" she shouted, but he didn't answer, instead making a grab for the branches of the tree to try and haul himself up after. The branch splintered and cracked as he put his weight on it, and he hastily let go before it snapped. He whirled to look up at the wall, but it was clear at a glance it was too high to climb.

Pierce was already running back towards the road. "Come on!" she shouted to him. "Freeman's in the car!" She barrelled back to the vehicle, which sat waiting as she'd ordered, the nearest back door already cracked open. She hauled it the rest of the way and leaned her body in, not bothering to climb in properly.

"What happened?" Freeman asked, looking back at her with wide eyes. "There was something up on the roof—some kind of a big animal—"

"Call backup!" Pierce told her. "Ask for Firearms Support—tell them to bring Tasers, silver bullets if they've got them. We've got a shapeshifter in panther form on the loose, and it's abducted our source!"

CHAPTER TWENTY-NINE

PIERCE GOT ONE of the nearby businesses to provide them with bolt cutters so they could break the padlock onto the factory grounds. They found the informant's body dumped a short distance away, on a patch of brick-strewn waste ground between the trees. His chest had been ripped open: a faster death than waiting to bleed out from the leg wound, but not a kind one.

When Firearms Support arrived they searched the region thoroughly, but to no one's great surprise the shapeshifter was long gone by then. More than likely he'd stripped out of the pelt, stashed it in a car, and driven off with nobody the wiser.

Another operation gone completely to shit. This morning's minor victory in retrieving the artefacts already seemed both small and far away.

"You should have taken backup to the meet," she told Dawson. "If we'd had more people on scene from the start, we could have watched for attempts on his life."

"Would we have been prepared for shapeshifters?" he countered. "The RCU shouldn't be reliant on outside Firearms units. We need to have our own silver bullets."

"Take it up with the government." Personally, she'd rather not have to deal with the responsibility of carrying a gun; she'd had to briefly handle one in the clusterfuck of their last shapeshifter case, and she'd been at least as worried about hurting somebody as she had the shapeshifters trying to kill her. She certainly didn't want an impulsive maverick like Dawson in a position to literally call the shots.

A dedicated Firearms Officer of the RCU's own, though... But that was a pipe dream, and way down a wishlist that started with a desperate need for more manpower of any variety. She could have had her whole team on safeguarding the informant, and it still wouldn't have given them a hope of watching every angle well enough to stop the shapeshifter's attack.

Which didn't excuse Dawson's idiocy. "Shapeshifter or not, you shouldn't have been out here alone without even a radio check-in," she said. "If we hadn't come out here after you, that could be your guts decorating the woods alongside our informant. The shifter would have had all the time in the world to conceal the crime, and we wouldn't have even been sure till tomorrow that you were missing." She should not have to be talking to a forty-something DI like the parent of a recalcitrant teenager.

"If you'd been here when I arrived, the bloke would have done a runner, and we wouldn't have got anything out of him at all," he said.

"It didn't sound like you were getting very much," she said.

"Got enough to prove he was involved," Dawson said, with a dispassionate glance down at the corpse. "He told me he was working for a group called Red Key. He confirmed he helped them plant the skulls—and he said that was only the start."

"The start of what?" she asked.

"A much bigger ritual. They're trying to summon some kind of major demon. The skull sites are like bait—little spirits trapped in cages, drawing the big one closer. Those things that attacked our people are just worms on hooks, there to lure the big fish to the surface."

If those were the worms... "How big a fish are we talking, exactly?" she said, feeling the hairs rising on the back of her neck. Read a dozen texts on demonology and you could find an equal number of quibbling definitions of demons versus spirits versus djinn and ghosts and fuck-knew-what-else, but if there was one thing they agreed on, it was that anything grouped under the banner of 'major demon' was apocalyptic levels of bad news.

Maybe literally.

"Our man didn't know the details, or he didn't want to risk his neck by sharing them," Dawson said. "But it was bad enough to make him risk coming to us even though he thought they'd kill him for it."

Pierce grimaced as she looked down at the savaged body between them. "Wasn't wrong, was he? Poor bastard."

They didn't even have a name to put to the dead face: the man had no ID on him, and while they could take prints and dental X-rays, she already had a hunch it wouldn't get them far. An outfit this professional, using shapeshifters to silence awkward witnesses? She had a bad feeling she'd tangled with these people before, and they didn't leave any loose ends behind. She stretched her injured shoulder out, feeling the ache.

Last time, she'd won a minor victory but lost the war: only the skinbinder Sebastian taken into custody, and by Deepan's account, he hadn't stayed there long. This time, with the prospect of a demon summoning, they might be playing for even higher stakes.

And if Cliff was right about Monday being the deadline, they only had three days to stop it happening.

MOST OF THE rest of the day was spent on the futile hunt for the shapeshifter and dealing with the fallout from the incident. Pierce received *another* bollocking from Snow over the shambolic proceedings, which made it impossible to discuss any concerns about Dawson's reckless behaviour without seeming as if she was shifting the blame.

At least she had their partial success in the artefact thefts to pull out of her hat, but as predicted, it didn't do much to sway him with the perpetrators still on the loose. They needed an arrest, something concrete he could put down on his crime statistics, and then maybe he'd finally back off.

Or maybe he wouldn't. The involvement of the panther shapeshifter had only brought her paranoia back. If the group she'd tangled with were still operating in the area, then maybe it wasn't so crazy to think that they hadn't just packed up and left the RCU after their operative took Palmer's place. Snow *might* just be the innocent successor filling dead man's shoes, but he could also be their inside man. And what about DI Dawson? Just a bull-headed cowboy operator who was used to getting his way, or was he actively working against her?

There were no answers, only the headache of continued uncertainty. It went nicely with the matching headaches of her unsolved cases and the bloody druids still hanging around. She treated herself to red wine and ice-cream that night, and studiously ignored the footage running on the news of herself evading questions and the anchors quoting Dawson's false assurances over haunting photos of Terry Davenport and Alan Winters looking all of bloody twelve years old.

Even with the wine, she didn't sleep too well.

Pierce returned to work the next day to more media presence, ongoing druid occupation, and, more promisingly, a message from Doctor Moss to say she was out of the hospital. Pierce arranged to meet the lecturer at her house, and snagged Dawson to take with her, both to keep him out of trouble and because he was the only one who'd actually heard what their informant had said about the ritual.

Moss was the same woman that she'd met with just days ago, but now somehow she looked her age. Even in home surroundings she was just as well turned out, blouse and skirt and suit jacket and hosiery *et al*, but in place of her previous energetic presence she seemed almost dwarfed by the armchair that she sat in. She looked pale, blue veins visible through the skin, and she still had a wound dressing taped to her forehead.

But though her movements seemed faintly shaky as she stirred sugar into her tea—served from a dedicated sugar bowl, into delicate china cups with matching saucers—the lecturer's voice was as strong as ever.

"First I should thank you, Chief Inspector, for your help the other night," she said. "I'm told that thanks to your actions the fire damage was minor, and mostly confined to the—frankly, dreadful—carpet. I shudder to think what would have been lost if the books in there had been allowed to burn."

Her own life, for a start, which would have weighed on Pierce more than academic knowledge, no matter how irreplaceable. "I can only apologise for having put your life in danger in the first place," she said. "If we'd had any idea that there would be an element of risk involved, we would never have brought you in on the case."

"Nonsense," Moss said briskly, breaking a wafer biscuit in half to consume it in delicate bites. "People don't try to murder you over things that aren't important." Pierce's police experience argued it was often otherwise, but she let the overall point stand. "If it matters that much, you need an expert, and I flatter myself enough to be fairly assured I'm as much of one as you can hope to find."

"So can you tell us what the ritual's all about?" Dawson said, sitting forward. He looked distinctly out of place perched on one of Moss's Queen Anne chairs, like a bulldog pressed into taking part in a child's tea party.

Moss smiled smoothly, unfazed by the bluntness. "I can't give you particulars," she said. "I *can* tell you that the site you documented will be the first of three."

"Definitely three?" Pierce exchanged a glance with Dawson. They'd found two, and suffered for it both times. The idea that there was a third out there, as yet undiscovered...

Moss nodded over her cup. "Potentially nine, but yes, given the scale of the operations involved, I think most likely three. Magical patterns create amplification. 'As I was going to Saint Ives, I met a man with seven wives, and every wife had seven sacks...' There will be three sets of three skulls, and you can expect the arrangement to mimic the placement of the skulls."

"So we're looking at an equilateral triangle," Pierce said. That should narrow their search down at least, to two locations either side of the line formed by the first two. But given that they'd been lethally overstretched covering only one, the prospect of that search was far from simple.

"Yes, almost certainly," Moss said.

"We spoke to someone involved in setting up the sites," Dawson said. Leaving out the fact said informant had died a gory death moments later, but Pierce couldn't really blame him for that omission. "He said that the skulls were a lure. Holding low level spirits as bait."

"Oh." Moss's eyes widened behind her glasses. "Ohhh... Yes, that would make a lot of sense. Demonic chum. Oh, that's *clever*," she said, almost admiringly. "The big demons are... deep, you see? Very far from this world, on whatever plane you postulate they actually exist. The ocean analogy works well enough: the really big beasties, the leviathans, you don't find them hanging around a few inches under the surface. It takes a *massive* amount of power to raise a major demon, but if you can lure it close to the barrier between worlds of its own accord..."

"Less massive?" Dawson guessed.

Her gaze snapped back to sharpness from the reverie she'd drifted into. "Less, in the sense that it's easier to pick up a bus than an aircraft carrier," she said. "It's still going to take an awful lot of work."

"Sacrifices?" Pierce presumed. Beyond a certain level of trivial enchantments, there wasn't much that could power magic besides pain and death.

"Human, fresh, and many," Moss told her in clipped tones. She set her cup and saucer down and stood up from her chair. "Let me consult my books for a while and get back to you," she said. "I might be able to tell you more about what kind of summoning we're dealing with. But I'm warning you now—whatever this is, it's vital that it's stopped before it happens. This *won't* be the kind of genie you can put back in the bottle."

"LOOK, WE NEED to work together on this one," Pierce said, as she and Dawson drove back to the station. "I can't have you running off half-cocked and doing your own thing on a case as big as this." Preferably not on any case, but time to pick her battles. "We have to coordinate. I know you've been used to running the department on your own for the last couple of months, but now that I'm back, you need to clear what you're doing with me."

"Red tape's going to get people killed," Dawson said. "This thing is big and it's dangerous, and we don't have time to fart around crossing every 't' on the paperwork."

"What we *don't* have time to do is bugger about, acting at cross purposes," Pierce said sharply. "From now on, everything related to this case, you clear with me. And at the very least, take backup, even if you have to borrow some uniforms to do it. These Red Key people have proved that they're not hesitant to kill."

"And they have at least one shapeshifter on their team," Dawson said, sliding the subject away from his own behaviour. He took his gaze off the road momentarily to glance sideways at her. "Any relation to your last case?"

"We caught the skinbinder," she said neutrally. "I'm told he was killed in an accident during prisoner transfer." She wasn't sure she believed that—but she also wasn't sure she wanted Dawson to know of her suspicions.

"Convenient accident," he noted, nonetheless.

"Maybe," she said, committing to nothing. "Nobody told me a damn thing about it until I was back on duty, so your info is as good as mine."

"What about pelts?" he asked. "Were they all impounded?" He glanced over at her once again. "I tried to get the details of your last case. Might as well have been trying to get into the Queen's knickers."

"Not my choice to classify it," she said. "The Counter Terror Action Team seized all our evidence." They'd had their sticky paws all over her case the second they knew that human-form shapeshifting skins were involved. Before *Pierce* had known, and her people had suffered for it. "Whether they got all the shapeshifter's creations..." She shook her head. "Hard to say."

And she doubted that the so-called Counter Terror Action Team would be responding to any queries any time soon. She wouldn't be surprised if they'd already melted back into the melange of vaguely defined, highly classified counter-terror operations and reformed as something else, renamed and unaccountable.

She wouldn't trust a damn thing that they tried to sell her anyway. They'd proven more than once that they were willing to be ruthless in pursuit of what they wanted, and what they'd wanted was the secret of the skinbinder's ability to make functional human skins. It was entirely possible that they still had him alive and in their custody... and that if there was something in it for them, the panther shapeshifter from yesterday could have been on their payroll.

"Panther skins are hard to source," Dawson noted. "The shifter that attacked your team had his pelt destroyed, yes?"

"Shot with a silver bullet. Should have been." So far as she knew, it was impossible to restore the enchantment on a shapeshifting pelt once it had been breached by something silver.

Of course, as far as she'd known a couple of months ago, it was impossible to create a working shapeshifting pelt from human skin.

"We should look into animal smuggling, any big cat sightings in the area," Dawson said.

"Mm." He was right, but she couldn't be optimistic about their odds of finding anything.

They reached the police station. The journalists had gone off to pursue some other angle, thank God— probably ghoulishly haunting the crime scene at Silsden, or trying to prod the bereaved relatives into taking a pop at the police—but the car park was still awash with milling druids. Dawson forged a way through them with a few pointed horn honks and just enough of a nudge over minimum speed to imply that he might not actually stop if they didn't move. They took the hint.

As soon as he and Pierce got out of the car, however, the druid protestors closed in around them. They'd learned her name from the journalists yesterday, and weren't shy about throwing it around.

"DCI Pierce! Why isn't the RCU doing anything about the wholesale desecration of sacred sites?"

"The Earth is crying blood!"

"How much is the government paying you to look the other way?"

"Why have you been ignoring our calls? DCI Pierce!"

Several of the group had taken up the rather unimaginative chant of, "We demand action now!" It all blended together into the vague blur of mob noise. Pierce focused her gaze on the doors of the station and marched through, avoiding making eye contact with anyone. Stopping to reason and offer platitudes was always a mistake, because it never got you anywhere and only caused the group to close in further as they spotted the first hint of an opening.

She shouldered her way through the demonstrators, peripherally noting that their numbers seemed to have swelled still further—probably glory hunters who'd spotted a glimpse of the protest on TV and rushed down to try and get in front of the cameras themselves. She passed one bloke who was wearing a baseball cap with his robes, not very druid-like...

"Look out!" Dawson's roar of warning came only a fraction of a second before his shoulder slammed her aside—and just before the druid with the pulled-down baseball cap slashed out at her with the knife he'd had concealed in his sleeve.

CHAPTER THIRTY

THANKS TO DAWSON'S shove, the knife blade missed Pierce's turning cheek by inches, but the force sent her staggering into bodies in the crowd who hadn't yet had the time to react.

Or else they were part of the attack. The grabbing hands might have been meant to restrain or to help, but either way they hindered her efforts to find her feet. As the knifeman came at her again, there was no way to retreat: she kicked out at him, a glancing blow off the shin that barely made him stumble. But it delayed him for long enough for Dawson to grab his arm, wrestling to get the weapon off of him. Pierce shoved away from the people holding her as they started to scatter and yell, recognising the scuffle in their midst if not yet its deadly nature.

Her attacker twisted away from the DI's grip, driving his free elbow into Dawson's stomach. As Dawson doubled over, the man threw his head back, cracking him in the middle of the face. Dawson staggered sideways, and the man tore free from his hold, whirling around with the knife held up.

Pierce launched herself after him, grabbing at his back to try and pull him away from Dawson. She caught a fistful of his druid robe, but found that it was just a makeshift costume, the fabric so thin and frayed that it tore apart in her grip as she pulled. The attacker wrenched away from her, staggering as the fabric gave way. He fell against a woman in the surrounding crowd, who screamed and shoved him off, only to go sprawling sideways herself as she tried to pull away with him still standing on her robes.

All around the struggle was a press of panicked bodies, people trying to get away through a ring of others pushing forward to see what was happening. Pierce straightened up to try and see the knifeman through the scrum, and got clonked on the back of the head by a protest sign. She doubled forward, cursing, her eyes watering with pain.

Something struck her arm; she spun around to face the threat, but there was no one, just a random flailing limb from the crowd. She spotted Dawson through the throng of people, still clutching his bleeding nose. "Dawson! Get—"

He opened his mouth to shout something back at her, but it was his widened eyes that warned her before he had the chance. Pierce whirled around, stepping away even as she did, and raising her arms in self-defence before she saw the flash of the knife coming towards her.

She blocked her attacker's forearm with a strike of her own, grabbing his wrist and trying to force him away. But she didn't have the angle to stand firm, and he pressed forward, bringing the knife down towards her neck. She tried to retreat, but a barrier of moving bodies blocked her way, shoving back against her and forcing her forward.

Desperate, she stamped down on her attacker's foot. He flinched and jerked back, buying her a split second of time. She struck out at his chest with the heel of her free hand, but her weakened shoulder muscles let her down; there wasn't enough force behind the blow to drive him back. Despite her grip on his wrist he was winning the battle, the knife blade getting closer and closer to her face.

And then something whooshed past her head to crack against the side of his, a sweeping blow from something she thought was a police baton. Her attacker went reeling, the knife falling from his fingers to bounce off across the car park. As he staggered sideways, the baton's wielder thrust it between him and Pierce like a restraining bar, yanking it tight across the knifeman's chest to hold him immobilised.

Pierce registered after the first blink that what she'd assumed was a baton was actually a carved wooden staff, and then that the man wielding it was the tall, bearded figure of the red-caped Archdruid. She caught her breath and straightened up. "Thanks," she said. The druid leader gave her a dignified nod, still holding her attacker prisoner with an ease that suggested a surprising amount of muscle hidden under the robe.

"Get cuffs on him," she ordered Dawson as he came storming through the crowd to join them, jerking her head at the prisoner. Pierce stepped back to stand guard over the fallen knife and tried to calm her panting breaths before she raised her voice. "Everybody back away!" she ordered the jostling crowd. "This is officially a crime scene, and we don't want your feet trampling evidence. Your witness statements will be required, so no one is to leave the car park without police permission."

Impossible to stop the group collaborating with each other, but this was about as open and shut as any crime could get; the real interest was in whether they could give any information on the knifeman's identity or movements before the attack.

Pierce tried to see through the crowd to the station doors, wondering if anybody inside had noticed the attempted murder in their own car park, but her words had done little to calm the general panic. Dawson, bloody-nosed from the headbutt, arrested the knifeman with a certain degree of vindictive satisfaction, and once he was cuffed the Archdruid relinquished the man to their control. He then thumped the base of his staff on the concrete and raised his sonorous voice to ring above the hubbub.

"Brothers, sisters! Calm yourselves, please. The danger is past."

Pierce was slightly gratified that his call didn't *immediately* halt the chaos where hers had failed, but it did still seem to calm things down after a moment, the shoving and screaming gradually petering out into the faintly embarrassed shuffling of a mob coming back to its senses.

"Back away from the crime scene, please," she ordered them again, and this time they obliged her by shuffling back. Through the widening gaps she spotted a group of uniformed officers coming to join the fray at last, and she raised her voice to address them over the crowd. "Had a little bit of an incident!" she said. "This man needs to go into the cells, and we're going to need statements taken from everyone else here."

"My people had no part in this attack," the Archdruid told her.

"Well, we're still going to need their statements, all the same." The knifeman had been dressed as one of their number, however makeshift the disguise: someone must have noticed when and where he'd joined them, and others in the group could have been involved in some capacity.

The big question was what could have motivated the attack. The druids' beef with the RCU was hardly big enough to resort to attempted murder—there was always a chance of fanatics on the fringes, of course, but more than likely her would-be killer was a cuckoo in their nest. But planted by who? This seemed overly crude for the group who'd deployed the panther shifter and gone after Vyner and Doctor Moss—unless it was deliberate refuge in ineptitude, a professional assassination set up to look like a senseless, amateurish stabbing just as Vyner's death had been meant to appear a suicide and Moss's a tragic accident.

On the other hand, with the wide swathe of cases the RCU handled, the motive could have been just about anything. They were always a magnet for the kind of nutters who thought the Prime Minister was putting a hex on their cat through the television.

"Anything you'd like to say for yourself, my lad?" she asked the man in cuffs, still being restrained by Dawson though he'd yet to make much of a real effort to bolt away. Average-looking bloke: white, somewhere in his twenties, with a square jaw and beaky nose and what looked like short, curly brown hair under the baseball cap. Nothing about him struck her as immediately familiar, though he could have had a brush with her department in the weeks she was off work.

He said nothing in response to her words, glaring sullenly. Well, there'd be time enough to try and prise a story out of him, and the crowded car park was hardly the place to start an interrogation in any case.

"Take him down to the cells," she told the first young PC to reach them. "And get someone out here to photograph the knife before it's taken into evidence." She nodded down at the blade lying by her feet. "We've got CCTV of this, I assume?" They definitely weren't going to be lacking for proof of such a brazen attack, but still best to be thorough. "Better get someone to photograph Dawson's face, too," she added as an afterthought. She turned to the DI, and saw that he was still rubbing his nose, though the nosebleed seemed to have stopped. "Is that broken?" she asked him.

"Don't think so," he said, drawing his hand away with a grimace. "Not going to be winning any beauty contests tomorrow, though."

"Get it checked out, anyway. And thank you, by the way." That had been a well-timed warning; a second or two later, and she could have had her throat slit.

Dawson gave a vague nod in acknowledgement and strode off into the station without further words.

Pierce stayed around briefly to direct the police officers who flooded out onto the scene, before heading back into the station building herself. Superintendent Snow would want some sort of report on this, but he could wait: she wanted to be in on the questioning of the prisoner rather than leave the job solely in Dawson's hands. She made her way down to the custody suite.

"Morning, Arthur." She nodded a greeting to the sergeant on duty, a rotund soul who'd been part of the station scenery before she'd arrived and probably would be after she was gone. "Got our new boy settled?"

"Just about." He smiled. "Heard this one delivered himself straight to our front door? Didn't know you could get them takeaway."

"Well, this one tried to make me a shish kebab, so best to keep an eye on him." He'd seemed to be targeting her, but he could just as easily have it out for the police in general. "Don't suppose he was kind enough to furnish us with a name?" she asked. She presumed he wouldn't have brought a wallet with genuine ID to an attempted stabbing right outside a police station, though a surprising number of criminals could be—and were—that stupid.

Arthur gave her an arch look over his glasses. "Would you believe that it's John Brown?" he said.

"Not Smith?" she said, matching his tone. "Better be careful, I think we've got a bright one here."

"Your DI said you wanted him in for questioning right away," he said.

She hadn't given Dawson that order, but fair enough; it was a reasonable assumption, and she supposed she could be magnanimous considering he'd just saved her from getting stabbed and been nutted in the face for his trouble. "Are we waiting for a solicitor?" she asked.

"Didn't want one," Arthur said with a shrug. "And after we went to the trouble of offering all nicely, too."

"Cocky." Or more likely, just not planning on saying a single thing. Oh, well, they already had him bang to rights, so anything else they could squeeze out was bonus information. And assuming he was a fanatic or a nutter as he seemed rather than a professional killer, the odds were good they'd be able to provoke him into saying something.

To give Dawson his due, he was definitely good at being provocative.

Pierce saw her DI coming along the hallway from the cells and moved to intercept him before he reached the interview room. He lowered the ice pack he was holding to his nose. "Going to do the interview now, while he's still full of adrenaline." he said.

And more apt to react without thinking. Pierce nodded. "All right. I want to be in there with you," she said, moving towards the door.

He frowned at her. "That wise? You're the one he was after."

"We can handle an aggressive prisoner."

"Maybe, but there's no guarantee he's going to talk as easily with you in there with us."

She sucked her lips back over her teeth, reluctantly aware that he was right. "All right," she said, letting her breath out in a sigh. "You go in, see what you can get out of him—if that gets us nowhere, then I'll try my luck."

She doubted their prisoner was going to be cooperative either way. "Let me just call Deepan down to sit in with you." If she couldn't sit in on the interview herself, she could at least make sure there was a voice of moderation in there as her representative.

On that, however, she was doomed to disappointment, since it seemed Deepan and Freeman were out dealing with a potential animal sacrifice down in Barnsley. The only one she had left available was DC Taylor, who she doubted would do anything to keep Dawson reined in. She was already second-guessing her agreement to step out and let the DI handle things, but it would probably cause friction to go back on it now. "All right, get down here," she told Taylor.

The prisoner was brought through to the interview room; Dawson stepped in front of Pierce protectively as he approached, which she supposed was reasonable under the circumstances but still raised her hackles. But the prisoner showed no visible reaction to her presence: no hint of getting aggressive, nor even any sort of negative emotional response to the fact that she was still standing after he'd failed to stab her earlier.

As if there hadn't been any real hate or resentment driving the crime, and he wasn't particularly bothered to have failed. Her instincts prickled. Something didn't add up here, but they had too few pieces of the puzzle yet to see what didn't fit.

She turned as Taylor arrived to join them. "Right. Prisoner's gone in," she said, jerking her head at the interview room door. "Identity and motive unknown—

all we know is that he was among the group of druids and decided that he felt like stabbing a copper. You and Dawson see if you can get more out of him."

"Yes, Guv." Taylor nodded sombrely. He moved to follow Dawson through into the interview room, but stopped short as his gaze fell on the prisoner inside. He turned back towards her, his eyes widening. "Guv, that's the bloke!" he said.

She frowned in confusion. "What bloke?" she said.

"The bloke I was chasing at the chapel ruins yesterday! The one who got away in the white van."

"That's one of our artefact thieves?" Pierce peered through the doorway at their prisoner again. Still a nameless, nondescript white bloke—but now one who came with a context to his seemingly meaningless crime. She started to smile. "Right, then. Let's find out what this gentleman can tell us," she said.

CHAPTER THIRTY-ONE

GIVEN THAT, IF anything, their artefact thief should have more of a grudge against DC Taylor than her personally, Pierce opted to join his interview after all, though she stood at the back and let Dawson do the talking. She was still convinced that something about this attack didn't add up: it didn't fit with what they knew of the artefact thieves and their tactics. Had the knife attack been a fumbled attempt to take her hostage and ask for the artefacts returned? Her attacker had to have known that it couldn't end well.

Or maybe just he'd been too obsessed to see that much. Something about this 'John Brown' was triggering her alarm bells: he was too calm—not just overconfident, but serenely self-assured in a way that she associated with fanatics and cultists.

And people who were sure that they knew something that she didn't.

"We know you were at the ruins of Francis Maundrell's family estate yesterday," Dawson said. "We know that you were in possession of stolen artefacts from multiple different thefts, and driving a vehicle matching the description of one spotted at the latest scene." A bit tenuous considering that description was 'white van,' but when it came to convincing a suspect that the case against them was airtight, every little helped. "We also know you just attempted to stab a senior police officer in broad daylight, on CCTV, in front of a whole crowd of witnesses." He sat forward in his chair, staring the man down. "Maybe it's time to start thinking about how you can earn yourself a little bit of goodwill."

Brown met his eyes with an affable smile. "Maundrell was a genius, a philosopher of magic," he said. "It's wrong for his works to be chained, locked away in storerooms instead of being used for the grand purpose they were made for."

"But it's fine to stab a police officer. Okay," Dawson said flatly.

Brown gave a casual shrug. "No one was stabbed," he said pleasantly.

"So you're only looking at *attempted* murder," he said. "That's not going to help you much. You know what will? If you can tell us about your accomplices. We know you weren't working alone on those thefts. How many others? Give me names."

Brown only smiled.

"No?" Dawson said, cocking his head. "All right. Then how about you tell me what you were planning to do with all those artefacts you stole. Having yourselves a little ritual recreation? Playing at being mighty wizards?"

That brought the first flicker of an annoyed frown. "We

stole nothing. Maundrell's works were liberated from the hands of heretics."

"Who's 'we'?" Dawson pounced, but if it had been an unintentional slip, it didn't seem to bother Brown that he'd confirmed it.

He just smiled enigmatically. "We who recognise the value in his work."

"And what value is that?" Dawson sat back, folding his arms. Pierce could tell he was getting steadily more short-tempered; he could do with a cooler head to join him in his questioning, and she wished again that Deepan had been around. Taylor was just sitting there, obediently watching the prisoner but deferring entirely to Dawson's line of questioning. Still, she held back for now, reluctant to butt in just yet. Let Dawson play this interview his way, at least at first.

Brown leaned forward in his seat, but he seemed simply earnest, not about to attack. "Maundrell's work holds the key to all higher understanding," he said. "He touched other worlds. Spoke with gods. And yet the ignorants murdered him before he could complete his life's work. Before he could bestow the gift of eternal life on his followers, as he promised."

Dawson raised an eyebrow. "Ah, the old immortality chestnut," he said. "Just on the verge of discovering eternal life, was he? Aren't they all."

Brown's eyebrows lowered petulantly. "Francis Maundrell was a true visionary. He left the instructions for the final ritual, entrusted to those he knew would stay most faithful to his way."

"So that's what you were trying to achieve," Dawson said, folding his arms. "Collect all the pieces and then win a prize? Must've been a real blow to your plans to have the police come and seize them from your hidey hole. That why you decided to come to the station today? Thought you'd have yourself a pop at a police officer in revenge?"

There was a continued tone of adversarial mocking to the words that Pierce wasn't sure was the best approach, but it was his interrogation. Probably wasn't much in it either way, with Brown so unlikely to cooperate. He simply smiled again, poise returned now that Dawson was attacking his plans rather than his messianic figure.

"Or did you think you were going to get them back?" Dawson said, leaning forward again and planting his crossed elbows on the table. "Had some grand vision of busting into the police station, taking us all down with your little pig-sticker and getting your property back, did you?"

Brown only grinned wider, turning his face away as if holding Dawson's gaze too long would only cause him to break into giggles.

Wrong reaction.

Instincts tingling, Pierce stood away from the wall. "Carry on here," she told her two officers as they turned to look back at her. "DCI Pierce, leaving the interview room," she added for the benefit of the tape.

She jogged back to Arthur's station, urged on by faint alarm bells sounding at the back of her mind. Something was afoot here, she just didn't know what yet. "Anything happening on your CCTV?" she asked him.

"Well, the drunk bloke in the end cell seems to be trying out some disco moves," he said. "Otherwise all quiet." He regarded her over his glasses. "Something wrong?"

"Maybe…" She just didn't like Brown's attitude; the aura of a man who knew a secret. "But probably not down here," she concluded. "Keep an eye on our interviewee, in case he gets aggressive." Or Dawson did, she thought, but didn't say. He surely couldn't be *that* much of a cowboy in this day and age, but still, better safe than sorry considering Brown had cracked him in the face earlier. She wasn't sure Taylor had the backbone to stand up to his tank of a superior if he got out of line.

And she also wasn't sure that Dawson was her biggest concern right now.

She headed for the stairs, her mind whirring furiously. All right. Brown was a prisoner. Already searched. Didn't have anything on him that could be a risk. Could he have planted something: a bomb, literal or magical? Maybe on one of the cultists, whether with or without their knowledge, if he was running with the assumption that they'd be brought into the station with him.

But no: Brown's goal was to retrieve the stolen artefacts. He wouldn't want to risk them being damaged by some kind of explosion, magical or otherwise. Getting arrested didn't help his goal; stabbing her wouldn't have helped it—so maybe he'd been the distraction all along. He had at least one accomplice; clever thieves, good at getting into places unseen…

Pierce reached the top of the stairs and kept on going up the next flight, onto the first floor that was the RCU's home territory. Past the main office, still empty—Deepan and Freeman not yet back from their case. Past the first few offices in Magical Analysis, where the researchers had their heads down, oblivious to much that went on outside of their doors. On towards the end lab: Enchanted Artefacts.

She pushed the door open, and it bumped something on the floor. Some*one*. Shit. The unconscious—she hoped just unconscious—form of Nancy Willis, one of Cliff's lab assistants. Pierce half bent down to check her pulse before her instincts yelped at her to check the room for danger *first*.

Not fast enough. As she started to look up, she caught a blur of movement surging through the lab towards her, and barely had the chance to duck away. An elbow, maybe a fist, collided with her arm as she threw it up to shield herself. She couldn't see the attack coming at her: there was only a vaguely human-sized distortion in the air, like a shadow glimpsed through murky, rippling water.

"Hey!" she shouted, lunging at the moving blur. Her hand closed on something like a fistful of slippery silk, and beneath that the solid warmth of human flesh. A person, dressed in some kind of a magical stealth suit—not quite invisible, but close to it. Even as Pierce grabbed for a better grip the thief twisted away, the material slipping through her fingers.

She saw the blur dart for the door, and threw herself in front of it. The intruder might be near-invisible, but this was no ghost: there was a solid human body underneath the suit, and if they wanted out, they'd have to go through her.

"This is a restricted area!" she barked. "Remove your concealment and come quietly." Words for the sake of getting them down on the record; no surprise when in place of a response the rippling blur dashed off towards the shelves at the far side of the room. Pierce didn't let herself be lured into chasing: there was only one way out of the lab, and she was blocking it right now.

It only took one blink for her to lose all certainty: had the intruder moved behind the row of shelves, or just disappeared by going still? Was that patch of darkness a distortion in the air, or just the odd-shaped shadows cast by objects on the shelves?

Wary eyes still on the rows of shelving, Pierce crouched down to take the fallen Nancy's pulse. A strong beat beneath her fingers; her heart unclenched a fraction. Unconsciousness was bad news regardless of the cause, but it still beat the hell out of a corpse.

Straightening up again, Pierce reached for her phone, wishing she'd brought her radio in with her from the car. She couldn't risk waiting around for someone to pick up; instead, eyes flicking between the screen and the shelves, she found Dawson's number and sent him a terse text. INTRUDER IN RCU.

She just hoped he bloody checked it—and still in interview, he might well not. Shit. Who else could she try? She wasn't sure if Jenny had been in her office; Pierce hadn't paid attention, hadn't checked who else was on the floor. Had anybody out there heard her shout?

A sound in the far corner, something clanging off the metal supports of the shelf units. Pierce whipped towards it. Was that a shadow behind the shelves? Or—She turned back at a flash of movement at the corner of her eye, but by the time she focused there was nothing there. She blinked her eyes, feeling them start to blur and water from staring too intently at what might be empty air.

A door slammed somewhere else inside the building. Nerves on edge, she instinctively turned to look out through the pane of glass in the lab door. As she did, she caught the reflection of a blurry shape behind her that hadn't been there the last time she looked.

Pierce whirled back round, and couldn't see a thing. She held her breath for long moments. No sound. No movement. She turned her head in tiny fractions, until she could see into the small window pane again.

And saw the reflected shape that was looming right behind her. She swung around and struck out blindly, feeling like a child practising made-up karate—until her hand clipped someone's shoulder in what looked like open space.

The empty air before her exploded with ripples, the intruder's shape revealed by distortion where the enchanted silk was too slow to restore the camouflage after its wearer moved. Pierce grabbed for where the head should be, trying to unmask the thief, but she missed her aim and the silk cloth poured away through her fingers.

"Give it up!" she shouted, intimidation tactic more than any sense of having the advantage. She might be blocking the door, but if the thief had some drug or magic that could drop her like Nancy, she could be downed without seeing it coming.

Then she heard moving feet and voices out in the hallway. "In here!" she shouted. "We've got an intruder!" Her attacker danced away, running back towards the shelves.

Pierce heard the door open behind her, barely sparing the time to register whoever came through as more than a black and white blur. "Help her, but stay by the door," she snapped. "There's someone in here using magic to stay concealed." Where were infrared sights when you needed them?

She'd lost the intruder already, in the brief moment that she'd looked away. Drawing the handcuffs from her belt, Pierce moved warily into the room, scanning the corners of the lab for any sign of ripples. All too aware the first warning she got might be the blow that took her down.

Her eyes fell on a wheeled trolley at the side, loaded with Cliff's ritual kit. Odds and sods of candles, chalk, mirrors, markers, string... and a big canister of sea salt. She ran forward around the lab tables to grab for it—

And smashed into an invisible body in her path.

The thief squirmed away from her as she fought to get a better grip. She struck out blindly and missed, cracking her hand against the trolley. A shove sent her stumbling into it, jarring her hip in a rattle of wheels and falling objects.

She moved to snatch the canister of salt from the debris, the attacker's next strike just clipping her chin as she turned away. She grabbed the cloaked arm while she still knew where it was and yanked the lid off of the salt, tossing the contents over the cloaked figure.

Flour might have clung better—but salt had its own power. Where the salt flakes struck the silk cloth of the thief's disguise, some small number clung, but most immediately poured away towards the ground. As they tumbled down the slick cloth they left bleached streaks behind, revealing the thief's shape like a transparent sculpture that had been splashed with white paint.

A much easier target. As the intruder turned to run towards the door, Pierce pulled the trolley out from the wall and shoved it at the running figure, prompting a very human *oof* of pain as the thief collided with it and tripped, sprawling across the tiled floor. Pierce lunged after the fallen form and this time got a solid enough grip to grab the hood of the costume and yank it back. The very pissed off face of a bearded man in his early thirties was revealed.

"Nice try, son," she said, holding him down with a knee and reaching for his arm to snap her cuffs around his wrist. "But you're not going anywhere."

She recited the words of the caution on automatic, and then looked up, out of breath, to see a group of uniformed officers had crowded through the door. A pair of them were tending to the fallen Nancy, while the others looked a bit lost.

"We need this guy searched and stripped out of the magical camouflage gear," she said. "It's possible he's got some of our artefacts on him, and he might have a few more of his own as well." Pierce stood up, keeping a hold on the silver cuffs to encourage her prisoner to stand with her, and gave him a tight smile that he returned as a scowl. "Then stick him down in the cells with his mate from out the front," she said. "Station invasion's over."

CHAPTER THIRTY-TWO

THEIR NEW PRISONER seemed fairly disinclined to talk, switching between sullen silence and explosions of cursing as the uniforms took him downstairs to be processed. But once she returned to his partner in the interview room with news that he'd been apprehended, 'John Brown' folded like a paper swan. Yes, they'd stolen the artefacts, yes, he could give them names and details on his unfortunate partner, yes, he'd confess just about anything if it got him off the charge of attempting to murder a police officer. Pierce left the interview with the feeling of a job well done. At bloody last.

She checked in on young Nancy, and was relieved to find she'd already regained consciousness, responding well to the first-aider's tests.

"I didn't really see what happened," she told Pierce. "The door opened and there was no one there, and there was just this *smell*—like, you know when somebody's been smoking some kind of weird funky herbal cigarettes, and then they

357

breathe it out right in your face? Like that. And then just: zonk." She mimed falling over with a sweep of her forearm. "I really do feel fine, by the way," she insisted to the bulky officer still hovering nearby with the first aid kit.

"Yeah, well, see a proper doctor anyway," Pierce told her. "No offence, Baz," she added to the first-aider.

"None taken. They didn't train me for all this mystic shit," he said.

"Me neither, but somehow I get paid to deal with it anyway." She nodded at them both and headed out the door. Plenty more work still to do before the artefact theft case could be laid to bed, but the hard part was over, and now they were just left to clear up the details.

Like the gaggle of druids she'd had herded in for questioning, who it seemed were probably innocent of any wrongdoing after all. Pierce grimaced. She had a feeling the superintendent wouldn't be too happy to hear that they'd hauled a whole group of protestors in off the street to help them with their inquiries. She just hoped the uniforms she'd had to delegate that task to had kept a light, polite touch and treated them as witnesses rather than suspects.

Pierce collared the uniform sergeant in charge of the questioning, Higson. "Our knifeman's confessed," she said. "Looks like this lot are all in the clear, so we just need witness statements from them. Where's their boss?"

"Beardy fella with the big stick?" Higson nodded his head towards the door on the corner. "In there, having a chat and a cup of tea with Constables Lewis and Markham, all very civilised, like. Didn't think the man in the fancy office would be too happy with us if we ruffled too many feathers dealing with this lot."

A shrewd assessment. "You'll go far, mate," Pierce told him.

"Rather not, if it's all the same to you, Guv," he said with a smile. "Seems like the higher you go up the ladder the more paperwork falls on your head. I get enough of that where I am as it is."

"If only we all had your sense." She girded herself to go and make nice to the Archdruid, hoping he didn't decide to kick up a fuss about his people's treatment; it would be all too easy to spin that kind of story to a media already thirsty for blood.

"DCI Pierce." He greeted her with a pleasant smile as she entered. The outfit somehow looked even more incongruous seated in one of their cheap plastic chairs, but the voice still gave him a presence that stopped him from seeming completely ridiculous.

"All done here?" Pierce asked the two PCs, who seemed only too happy to get up and scuttle out to leave her to it. She took over one of the vacated chairs and drew it closer to the table. "Firstly, I'd like to apologise for keeping you and your people here so long," she said. "We appreciate your cooperation, Mr—" Mr what? The PCs hadn't left her any convenient notes to skim from. "I'm sorry, sir, I never did catch your name," she was forced to admit.

"Archdruid Alastair Greywolf," he said, in measured tones.

Pierce very respectfully didn't snigger, but she couldn't help but raise a sceptical eyebrow nonetheless. "Is that what it says on your driving licence?" she had to ask.

"It does," he said, but then smiled. "Not my birth certificate," he conceded.

Praise the Lord, a glimpse of a sense of humour. Maybe there was a chance he could be reasoned with yet. "Well, thank you for your assistance earlier, Mr Greywolf," she said, letting the matter of names go. "That could have been a very nasty incident, and we appreciate your help in containing the attacker."

He inclined his head regally. "Surely what any good citizen would try to do," he said.

"Well, generally we prefer good citizens to stay back out of harm's way. Which is why, I'm afraid, I really do have to ask you if you can move your people away from the station building. As today's incident has demonstrated, we do regrettably deal with some dangerous people from time to time, and having crowds around the station is only risking the safety of my people and yours." She didn't overtly state that the crowd had allowed her attacker to get close, but he was a bright boy, he must have realised it. Maybe his sense of good citizenship would extend to getting the hell out of their car park.

"Then I in turn must make my apologies," Greywolf said solemnly. "These are not my preferred methods, I assure you, Chief Inspector—but my people's concerns really must be heard."

"And they will be," she said, refusing to concede control of the situation. "However, you have to appreciate that the RCU deals with many dozens if not hundreds of cases across the whole of the north, and we have to prioritise those incidents that pose the most urgent danger to people's lives and welfare." She would have been delighted to *have* enough officers to let one of them waste time chasing up trivial land use disputes with no proof of a crime, but this was the real world.

"This *is* urgent," the Archdruid said forcefully, locking eyes with her. His were a rare shade of brilliant blue that were difficult to meet directly, and Pierce didn't doubt that he was used to getting his way by sheer weight of personality. "The stone circle my people venerate is a site of great ritual potential. I believe that the farmer who used to grant us access was pressured into selling against his will, and now he fails to answer any of our communications. The site has been completely sealed off, and we believe the new owners are making preparations for a ritual."

Pierce resisted the urge to sigh and rub her temples. All right. He *sounded* relatively sane, and while she doubted there was much substance to the allegations, perhaps some evidence that they were taking steps to investigate would be enough to get him and his druids off their backs.

"All right," she said. "If you really can show visible indications that there may be illegal magic going on at the stone circle, I will try to detail an officer to go and check that out just as soon as we have somebody available. Now, in return, can I please ask that you be willing to move your encampment away from the police station to avoid any further incidents like today's?"

"Of course," he said, inclining his head with an affable smile.

She just wished she was optimistic enough to believe it would be that easy.

* * *

AGREEMENT OR NOT, there was no way the druids' issue was going to make its way onto her priority list any time soon. They might have all but resolved the artefact thefts, but right now they still needed all hands on deck to deal with the matter of the skulls. As soon as Deepan and Freeman returned to the station she gathered her team together for a briefing.

"All right," she said, surveying her forces, limited though they were. "From this point on, the skull case is officially the RCU's top priority. Here's what we know so far." She indicated the photos from the ritual scenes in Bingley and Silsden, pinned to a board behind her; high-tech was all very well, but in her experience you usually spent more time trying to get the computer and projector to agree to talk to each other than you actually saved by using the fancy equipment.

"These two sites are apparently spirit traps or cages," she continued. "They were keeping disembodied spirits—or minor demons, possibly, it's a matter of terminology—of some form penned up inside." She swept her gaze across the team. "Now, as we've learned, those things are bloody dangerous in themselves. It could be that this is intentional, and the traps are primed to unleash the things on anyone who interferes. Or it could just be an ugly side effect. That doesn't really matter for our purposes." It might when it came to figuring out the appropriate criminal charges, but Pierce would worry about that when they had some suspects in hand.

She pointed at their map of the region, made up of several sheets of printed A4 pinned together. The Bingley and Silsden sites were marked, with intersecting circles drawn around them so that the whole thing looked like a lopsided Venn diagram.

"Now, we've consulted with an expert in ritual demonology, and she believes that there will be a third site, echoing the triangular arrangement of the skulls at the two we've already discovered. That gives us two potential locations for the third." She squinted at the map. "Somewhere around... Oakworth? And somewhere just south of Ilkley, on the moor." At this scale, any triangle they marked out was going to be inexact.

"That's not very much to go on, Guv," Taylor said dubiously. They all remembered just how well a vague, directionless search had gone in Silsden, and now they had two sites to cover simultaneously.

"No, it's not," Pierce said. "And there's worse. Our intelligence suggests that whatever this ritual is supposed to accomplish is due to go down on the twenty-second of December—that is, for those of us who haven't spent enough time looking at the calendar lately, the day after tomorrow. That means we only have a very limited time to act on this information and locate the site before it all goes pear-shaped."

Freeman looked like she was on the verge of raising a hand to be called on with her question before she remembered that she wasn't in school any more. "Do we know what the ritual is intended to accomplish, Guv?" she asked.

"According to DI Dawson's informant"—still an unidentified corpse, poor bugger, despite their best efforts with prints and dental records—"the spirits imprisoned by the skull traps are effectively bait for something even bigger and nastier," she said. "We believe that the group behind this ritual are trying to summon a far more dangerous entity—what's generally referred to in the literature as a major demon. The lesser spirits in the traps are to draw its attention, luring it closer to the barrier between this world and the Other Side—whichever theory you subscribe to about what kind of 'other side' we're dealing with."

Pierce wasn't sure if that one was a question for the ritual theorists or the philosophers. Certainly, none of the sources that claimed to have had a glimpse of said beyond sounded remotely convincing, and if the ones who'd died horribly trying had actually managed, nobody would ever know.

As far as she was concerned, it didn't really matter *what* demons were or where they came from; it wasn't her job to make sense of it all, just to police those bits of it that caused trouble in her territory.

"Have we spoiled their plans by destroying two of the skull traps?" Freeman asked, sitting forward.

"It would be nice to think so." Which was why Pierce didn't trust that thought. "But we have to proceed from the assumption that whatever they're trying to lure is already close enough for them to perform the final summoning—whatever form that takes. Our expert's going to come back to us with more research on that, but it's safe to assume it will involve large scale sacrifice. And probably large scale slaughter if it succeeds."

She had a bad feeling she might be underselling it even with that. Major demons in the literature were the kind of thing that wiped whole towns off the map, if not entire countries.

"Do we have any clue who might be behind the rituals?" Deepan asked, face uncommonly sombre. Pierce hesitated, thinking of the shapeshifter and her suspicions. But then her gaze slid past him to DI Dawson where he stood in the doorway, one hand rubbing the bridge of his bruised nose. He might have come through for her earlier, but she still wasn't entirely certain how far they could trust him.

"Not at present," she said crisply. It was true enough. "Our informant claimed that they're calling themselves Red Key, but I doubt that pursuing that will get us any paper trail. What we *do* know is that they're highly organised, and they must have a fair number of people in their employ. The skulls were set in place with great precision and presumably some degree of ritual, without drawing the attention of the public. That suggests a group of people working together with a high degree of professionalism. They've sent killers after two of our consulting specialists, and they have at least one shapeshifter on their team, panther form."

She saw Deepan press his lips together. He hadn't been with her in the barn when Sally had got her throat slashed by the last panther shifter they'd tangled with, but he'd seen the aftermath.

"These people are dangerous," Pierce said, meeting the eyes of her two newest young rookies in particular. "Extremely so. We have to assume that they *can* accomplish what they've set out to do. We have to be aware of the possibility they may be keeping tabs on our investigation." She drew in a deep breath. "And, somehow, we have to get ahead of them."

She turned back to gesture at the map behind her. "We can't afford to gamble on picking the right site and risk wasting our time," she said. "It'll stretch us thinner, but we have to try to tackle both at once." She indicated the northernmost of the two sites, near Ilkley. "Dawson, you're in charge of the search on the moor. See if you can borrow additional warm bodies from across the county line in North Yorkshire."

After Silsden, the regular police should at least be taking the situation seriously, even if they were less than happy about cooperating. She just had to hope that Dawson could keep enough of a lid on his obnoxiousness to avoid riling them any further, because she really couldn't spare the resources to keep an eye on him.

She turned back to face the others. "Sergeant Mistry and Constable Taylor will be handling the second search in the Oakworth region." With his lesser rank, Deepan might face more obstruction from the locals, but hopefully a greater degree of RCU presence would balance that out; Pierce didn't want to commit herself to either location before they knew which was the real one. "Freeman and I will be following up other leads from here." Assuming they could find any.

She surveyed her team, locking eyes with each of them in turn. "From now until D-Day," she said, "consider this case the only one that matters."

The clock was ticking.

CHAPTER THIRTY-THREE

AFTER DEALING WITH their two new prisoners and reporting in to Snow, there were only so many hours of afternoon left to get anything done. They were coming up for the shortest day of the year, and the two area searches barely had a chance to get started before the winter dark dropped like a blackout curtain. After what had happened in Silsden, Pierce reluctantly vetoed any idea of continuing into the night, and ordered the two groups to resume at dawn. She could only pray that the lost hours wouldn't come back to bite them.

She wasn't certain that finding the third skull site would get them any closer to dealing with the main demon-summoning in any case. What they really needed was more information back from Doctor Moss—but that was a process she had no power to accelerate. Pierce had the itchy feeling of sitting at a traffic light when she was in a hurry, knowing that things needed to be done but unable to take any action until things outside her control had lined up. She spent far too long pacing the office when there was no reason for her to still be there, too restless to settle to the actual work that *was* available for her to do.

When she finally left, the druids' vans and tents were still set up in the car park, but the druids themselves and their placards and banners were nowhere in sight. Pierce pressed her lips together. The Archdruid had appeared to accept her request for them to clear off, but he hadn't given any promise of how soon they would do it. She'd already struggled to get Snow off her back after the incident with John Brown in the car park.

Apparently a glutton for castigation, she kept flicking the news on all night, looking for fresh evidence that details were leaking, even hoping that somehow the media had learned something she didn't know yet. But right now the vultures were still picking the corpse of their juicy story from Silsden. Police officers dead, the potential for an inquiry... this was all going to crash down on Pierce's head eventually, but if some kind of major demon ate Yorkshire next week, they'd all have bigger problems.

She was too wired to sleep easily—taking the job home with her in her head, the big thing they warned you against, though when the job involved a looming threat to who knew how many lives, it was advice that was impossible to heed. She couldn't risk taking any pills that might leave her groggy and hungover in the morning, so she only dropped off in the early hours, spending her dreams running through endless corridors in search of a vital meeting she was supposed to be leading.

She snapped awake to the sound of the alarm after what

felt like no time, and spent several minutes contemplating the possibility of just staying in bed before she remembered why she couldn't. Right. Back to the grindstone.

To her displeasure, the camper vans had *still* yet to disappear from their car park when she arrived back at work. She went over and knocked on the window of one until a ruffled head in a druid's hooded robe poked out.

"Where's your leader?" Pierce said. "I thought we'd agreed that you lot would be leaving our car park."

"The Archdruid says we stay until you come through on your promise to investigate," the young woman told her, jaw set stubbornly.

Bloody marvellous. "Well, at least stay in your vans and don't interrupt police business, please," she said. "We could have had a nasty incident yesterday."

She headed back into the office. Most of her team were already out, gone off to direct search efforts beginning at first light, but Freeman was there and waiting for her despite the early start. Almost too efficient, that girl; hopefully she'd ease off a little when she wasn't trying to make a good impression on the new boss, or else she'd burn out. There might be an urgent case underway, but when it was done the next one in line would probably be just as urgent.

"Any word from Deepan or... DI Dawson?" she asked. Bugger, it was awkward being on first name terms with one of her team and none of the others. Usually it was the other way around, one unfamiliar officer easing in to the team rather than having all but one replaced at a stroke. She'd have to get used to calling the newbies by their first names. Well, the constables at least. Dawson didn't really strike her as a 'Graham.'

"No, Guv, but, er, Superintendent Snow wanted to see you. He said it was about the druids?"

"Fabulous." Pierce drained the rest of her coffee too fast and set the mug down with a wince. "Right. Off to face the lion in his den. Thank you..."—for a moment that she hoped didn't stretch too long, she fished for the name—"Gemma." From the bright smile, she'd either remembered it right, or she had a very polite one here.

Small victories, she sensed, would have to be the theme of the day. She'd be pretty bloody lucky to get any big ones.

For a start, Snow was predictably unhappy about just about everything.

"You assured me yesterday, Chief Inspector," he said, glaring over his spectacles, "that the protestors occupying the car park of our station would be *gone*."

"As their leader assured me." Buck-passing; probably not a good tack. Pierce hurried on. "I've given him our word that his allegations *will* be investigated, and he's promised that his people will be moving out of the car park accordingly."

The superintendent pressed his lips together. "*Accordingly* is not good enough—I want them gone today, this morning. Send someone with them to address their concerns, and get them *out*."

They really didn't have the time or resources to spend on that, but she sensed that the superintendent wasn't listening to her protests. Was he actively working to sabotage her efforts, or was he just a PR-focused pain in the arse stuffed shirt? It was well-nigh impossible to tell the difference.

Either way, unfortunately, she still had to obey his commands.

"Right, Freeman," she said as she returned to the RCU office. "His nibs is insisting we have to get the protestors out of here today. I want you to go with them to this sacred site of theirs—take a look around, listen to them, take some notes... but then get back here as soon as you can. Tell them we're investigating, assuming that there's anything to investigate—in fact, tell them that even if there isn't, or we'll have them up our arses all bloody week—and we'll follow up as soon as we can. Which will be, if they insist on being told, sometime next week."

After Monday, either the worst crisis would be over, it would have proved less urgent after all, or both she and the superintendent and possibly the druids as well would all have bigger problems on their minds.

"On it, Guv." Freeman jumped up from her seat.

"And keep your radio on you, and your phone," Pierce advised. "We might need to call you in if anything comes up at either of the sites."

No messages had come in to that effect, but she checked in with both searches all the same. "It's a pretty vaguely defined search area," Deepan warned. "We've got a fair bit of help from uniform branch, but it's still a lot of ground for our team to cover. Inspector Wade wanted to draft some of the locals in to help with the search, but I said no."

"Too dangerous," she agreed. "They listening to you out there?" Getting the RCU's authority recognised was always a challenge, and despite being one of its most experienced officers, Deepan didn't have the rank to throw around with local forces.

"So far. Everybody's heard about Silsden: they're paying attention, but they're all on edge."

And a twitchy copper could be as dangerous as a careless one. "All right, keep them in line. If anybody finds anything, tell them to just stay the hell away from it. Right now, it's less important to deal with the skulls than it is to find the damn things." If they could pin down the third corner of their ritual triangle, it might help them locate the site of the main summoning. "Let me know the moment there's any chance your team have found something."

"Will do, Guv."

He hung up, and Pierce had a similar if more brusque conversation with Dawson. She was already regretting not heading one of the two searches; all very well to say she'd coordinate from their home base, but she needed something to bloody coordinate first.

The clock had now ticked over into what most of the rest of the country called business hours, so she phoned Doctor Moss. "Have you managed to find any new details on the ritual?" she asked.

"I might be able to narrow it down for you, but I need more information—is it possible I can see the skulls that you have in your possession?"

"We've got them here at the station," Pierce told her. "Take a taxi if you need to—we can reimburse you." Out of her own pocket, if it was necessary, since there might be whines about expensing that. But the agitation in her gut outweighed the pragmatic concerns; they only had one day to go, and her instincts were buzzing at her to take action.

If only she had something to actually *do*. She strode down to the Enchanted Artefacts office, as much for the walk as anything else. Cliff was back on duty today. "How's Nancy?" she asked him.

"She seems well." He pressed his lips together, shaking his head. "Nasty business. That's the first time we've had a break-in at the actual station, and I wasn't here," he said. "Obviously, I should just never take days off."

"That's my strategy," Pierce said wryly. She'd planned to take this weekend off, easing back into her return to work, but the approaching deadline had put paid to that. "Listen, we've got a demonology expert coming in to take a look at the ritual paraphernalia from the first two skull sites. Can you line up what we've got?"

"Oh, that should be fascinating," he said, brightening as he moved to sort through his shelved boxes. "I did want to consult with somebody better informed about the spell runes on the scrolls."

"Documents have had no luck with identifying the language?" she asked.

"Alas not. But it seems that despite being identical in all other aspects, each skull has its own unique set of symbols."

"Parts of a greater whole?"

"Indeed," he said.

It seemed to take forever for Doctor Moss to arrive at the station to join them. Pierce had to resist the urge to physically hustle the woman through the building to get to the Artefacts office faster. Cliff had obligingly laid out each of the six skulls and their accoutrements, including the broken fragments of the one that Jenny had accidentally exploded with her attempt at divination.

Once furnished with her own set of evidence gloves, Doctor Moss started picking them up and turning them over, examining the markings on the underside and in the cavities that she couldn't have seen on a photograph. Her mouth was flattened into a thin, troubled line.

"Yes, that's consistent... see here, the radial lines around the neck?" She showed Pierce the underside of one of the skulls. "They're like... magical circuitry, if you will. Probably long vanished into the soil by the time that you got there, but there would have been connecting lines of blood poured when the ritual was first laid out, linking the skull to the rune stones. Plugging it in to the larger ritual circuit. Powerful stuff."

She moved on to peer at the set of six scrolls retrieved from the mouths of the skulls, now all opened out with their ribbons laid beside them. "Do you know the positions in which these were all found?" she asked.

Cliff pointed to them each in turn. "Bingley one, two, three, Silsden one, two, three... I have the site maps over here." He waved at the diagrams. Doctor Moss rearranged the scrolls into two triangles to match their original layout, and stood over them for a moment, mouthing to herself as she sounded out the runes.

"Well, the incantation is definitely incomplete," she said, "but based on this I believe it's intended to summon a major demon for the purposes of striking some form of bargain—sacrifices in exchange for mystical knowledge is the usual formula, though the summoners could be seeking some other form of exchange." She pulled her lips back in a grimace and shook her head. "However, it's hard to say from this whether they'll be able to keep it safely contained and return it to the plane from which it came. They do seem to have a relatively good grasp of the principles—but of course, the history of the art is littered with people who seemed to know what they were doing right up till the moment it went wrong."

"The question is, do *we* know what they're doing?" Pierce asked. "Based on this, are you able to tell us what we can do to stop the ritual from taking place?"

"You can't," Doctor Moss said flatly, holding her gaze. "You simply don't have the required knowledge." She inclined her head. "However, I imagine *I* probably could, if I was able to visit the site of the final summoning ritual."

Pierce's police instincts rebelled at the idea of bringing an untrained member of the public deeper into this murderous mess, but the fact was that they didn't have much choice. "Can you pinpoint that final location for me?" she asked.

Moss glanced back at Cliff's marked-out map of the sites. "Not unless you can bring me the scrolls from the third set of skulls," she said, shaking her head. "It may be at the centre of the triangle defined by the three skull sites, or it may be projected outwards in a line from one of them, or from that centre point... I can consult my books with the information we have now and possibly give you an educated guess, but if I had the complete inscription, I could be more sure."

"An educated guess is better than what we've got right now," Pierce said. They barely even had the information to make an ill-educated one. She drew in a deep breath and straightened up. "All right, realistically, what are our likely outcomes here?" she asked.

Doctor Moss met her eyes with a composed frown. "Well, the best case scenario would naturally be to avert the summoning entirely, or for the summoners to fail so completely that nothing happens at all."

"I don't think we can safely count on that." These people definitely had a good idea what they were doing. They might or might not achieve exactly what they'd aimed for, but Pierce was willing to bet it would end with more than a sad puff of smoke and a bad smell.

"Mm." Doctor Moss nodded in agreement. "The second best scenario, then, is that we fail to prevent the ritual, and it goes exactly as the summoners planned. Whoever and whatever they planned to sacrifice—and it will be a large-scale sacrifice, believe me—will suffer and die... but the major demon will remain contained, and be dispatched back to the plane that it was drawn from without wreaking any further havoc."

Cliff looked up from his work station beside them. "'Large-scale sacrifice' is a term you rarely want to hear in your best case scenarios," he noted.

Pierce smiled tightly, without humour. "I'm guessing the worst case scenario involves further havoc."

"Yes." Doctor Moss peered at her seriously, eyes pale behind her glasses. "If the summoned demon does break loose from its containment... well, all we can realistically hope is that it will burn itself out like a wildfire, eventually running short of the tremendous reserves of energy required to stay manifest in this world."

"How eventual is eventually?" Pierce asked.

"The simple, most accurate answer would be, 'not soon enough.'"

Pierce didn't know what kind of damage a major demon could do in burning itself out. She had a strong feeling she didn't want to know. Nothing like understanding the full pressure on you to increase the chance you'd choke.

As always, the only approach was one step at a time. Locate the ritual. Stop the ritual. Worry about the might-have-beens when it was too late to lock up over the fear of making a mistake. "All right," she said. "Thank you, Doctor. If I can ask you to get back to your books and gather together whatever you may need to stop this ritual? Our information says that this is going to happen tomorrow, so we may well have less than a day to act."

Doctor Moss paused. "Oh," she said. "Oh, dear. I think there may have been a bit of a misunderstanding. You see, the date of the twenty-second of December is not meaningful in itself—it's simply the fact that the winter solstice often fell that day in past years. This year, however, I'm afraid the moment of solstice occurs on the twenty-*first*—the ritual will be at eleven o'clock tonight."

Pierce closed her eyes. "Wonderful," she said.

CHAPTER THIRTY-FOUR

PIERCE CHECKED IN with the two searches again. Still no results. She studied the map of the region pinned up in the office, looking for inspiration. Too many potential sites, too much ground to cover... She could tell the local forces to keep an eye out, but she had no concrete information to give them, and as many officers as could be spared were already committed to helping her teams around Oakworth and Ilkley.

With Freeman out of the office on useless busy-work, the RCU couldn't respond to any other cases. Pierce was pointlessly cooling her heels, currently stymied on the demon summoning but unable to commit to anything else while she was waiting for news to come in. She paced, checked her messages, ate an early lunch that sat uncomfortably in her stomach; time was ticking away both too quickly and too slowly. Knowing it was futile pushing but unable to prevent it, she phoned Doctor Moss to see if she'd made any progress yet.

"I'm just about to head back to my office at the university," Doctor Moss told her. "I'm told I should be able to get back in there now, and there are materials there that might be of some use, if they've survived."

"I'll join you there," Pierce said. Probably nothing more useful she could do at the university than here, but at least keeping moving gave her the illusion of accomplishing something. And while she didn't have a background in demonology, she'd picked up enough snippets over the years that she might be of some limited help in flicking through the books to narrow down what they were looking for. Time was of the essence.

She resisted the urge to annoy her team by checking in on their progress again, and headed out to the car park. The druid vans were still there. She went and rapped on the window of the VW bus again. "Thought we gave you lot instructions to clear out? Your chief said you'd be gone."

She wasn't sure if the tousled head that popped up was the same druid that she'd spoken to before or a different one. They were all much of a muchness: young, drippy student types interspersed with aging ones with too much hair who could have been rock band roadies.

"We're leaving, but there are important rituals of consecration we need to perform first," the woman told her. "And Damon and Kelly have gone to buy us lunch."

"Fine," she said. "But get a move on. The superintendent's not going to be happy if you're still here by the afternoon." He probably wasn't happy that they were still here now, but that didn't have to be her problem for a while.

Pierce drove back to the university. The place was relatively quiet on a Sunday morning this close to Christmas, most of the students presumably gone home for the holidays by now. The Occult Studies building showed little sign of the events of earlier in the week, aside from the churned up tracks left in the mud outside by the emergency vehicles. Doctor Moss's office still stunk of burned carpet, but the fire damage didn't seem to be too extensive.

"Anything lost?" Pierce asked, standing in the doorway to watch as Moss flicked through a stack of books on the back shelf. The lecturer had exchanged her smart clothes of earlier for sensible boots and trousers and a sleeveless khaki jacket with many pockets, the sort of thing somebody might wear on a fishing trip.

"Nothing irreplaceable," she said. "Though the exposure to the smoke won't have done the books in here much good." She nodded at the closed cabinet at the rear of the room. "Fortunately, we keep most of the truly nasty grimoires locked away from curious students as a matter of course, so they should have escaped the worst of the harm." She let the cover of the book she was perusing fall closed, and laid her hand on top of the stack. "I think I have everything I need here," she said. "Let me just get a few things from down in the labs."

"You perform rituals here?" Pierce said, raising her eyebrows as they left the room. That sounded like a recipe for disaster if ever she'd heard one.

Moss gave her a wry smile. "Not summonings, no. Nor do we teach the students the specifics of how to perform them, even theoretically. But we do teach the basic principles of ritual geometry, so that when they're inevitably foolish enough to try it anyway, there's at least a better chance they'll have made a good protective seal around the area."

She led the way through to a lift, pressing the button for the basement level. "Now, most of what we keep down here is for undergraduate students to practise with," she said, "so obviously it's of limited usefulness against this magnitude of threat. However, we do keep a few other supplies on hand in case of greater magical disaster."

"That happen often?" Pierce asked her.

"Well, we did have one young idiot almost burn his face off trying to raise some kind of fire spirit," Doctor Moss said. "We were just lucky he did it down here in the lab where there are protections worked into the floor, or he could have set the whole campus ablaze. That was back in the 'eighties, though," she added. "Can't say our newer batches of students are any wiser, but the safety rules are certainly stricter."

"None of your former students spring to mind as a possible candidate for this demon-raising, then?" Pierce asked her.

"Few of my former students spring to mind as great candidates for anything that required that much effort, frankly," she said. "And the ones that *were* hardworking were also correspondingly sensible." She shook her head. "I find it hard to believe that any of them could be involved in something as malevolent as this... but then again, it's hard to imagine why anyone would be, isn't it?"

Pierce could think of any number of possible reasons, with simple callous self-interest right up there at the top of the list. It came to something, she supposed, when your job gave you a darker outlook on humanity than a lecturer in demonology.

The lift reached the bottom level, opening onto a dim basement corridor with several adjoining doors. As the lift closed behind them and it began to rattle its way back up, Pierce thought she heard a thump somewhere above them, like one of the building's heavy fire doors falling closed.

"Anyone else in the building today?" she asked, instincts going on the alert.

"One of my PhD students, possibly?" Doctor Moss said, raising her voice before Pierce could caution her not to. "Yasmin, is that you?"

No response. Just silence, and then another not-quite sound: maybe the soft click of heels on tiles or coins in someone's pocket, maybe just pipes down here in the basement making noises. Pierce drew a breath around the solid weight of tension in her chest and turned back towards Doctor Moss. "Right," she said.

And then the lights went out.

"Shit!" She spun back, grabbing for the police torch that she wasn't carrying. Double shit. Penlight—she fumbled for her keys and the feeble little keyfob torch that still beat groping in the dark. Even as she yanked them out, cursing the betraying jingle, there was the small flare of a cigarette lighter in the dark beside her.

"Is that the fuse?" Moss said, looking up at the ceiling.

"If it was, it didn't blow by chance." Pierce moved in front of her, protective in the face of a threat that could be coming from any direction. She glanced towards the lift: a risky choice of an escape route—and a useless one. The dull glow of the floor indicator had gone out. Fuck. "Where are the stairs?" she asked urgently.

"This way." Moss waved vaguely off to their left, taking a step in that direction.

Pierce grabbed her wrist to halt her. "Stay by me." She flicked the narrow beam of the penlight around the walls. Closed lift doors. Closed and card-locked lab room on the opposite side. No one along the corridor behind or ahead.

She still didn't relax.

"All right," she said slowly, taking a few steps ahead of Moss towards the stairs. "Let's just get out of this basement and check the building's clear." She fumbled her phone out of her pocket. The bright glow of the screen was a relief, the lack of reception far less so. Police radio likely wouldn't be much better down here in the concrete basement even if she hadn't left it in the car. The same protections needed to keep rituals contained left the two of them cut off from any kind of help.

Pierce paced along the corridor, Doctor Moss close behind; both of them had fallen silent, but she could hear the older woman's breathing in the hush. Not too panicked yet, Pierce didn't think, but if they had to run, could she do it?

And down here, where the hell would they run *to*?

She took another few steps, passing the door to the lab on the corner. The tiny red light on the card lock was still on, at least—maybe it was just the overhead lights and the lift that were out.

That didn't exactly make her feel much better. A targeted power outage boded even less well than a total blackout. Pierce flicked the tiny torch at the window in the lab door. Couldn't see much beyond the reflected light, but it looked shadowy and empty.

"This is where the ritual supplies are kept," Doctor Moss said. "Should we—?"

It wasn't a sound so much as a moving shadow that made Pierce whirl about, throwing an arm in front of Moss's chest to shove her back. A dark shape, bursting forward from the shadows on the corner; she hardly had the time to register it at all before the bulk of it slammed into her, animal-smelling and coarse-furred.

"Shapeshifter!" Her attempted shout came out as a pained groan, still loud in the near silence of the basement. The shifter moved with barely a whisper of sound: was it the panther that had killed their informant? She couldn't see, the faint beam of the penlight lost in the thing's rough fur as she tried to shove it off of her.

She might as well have been trying to shove a sofa full of people, for all her strength could move it; the thing was solid muscle, and her only saving grace was that it couldn't snap or slash at her while it held her crushed to the wall. As it twisted around to rectify that, Pierce squirmed away, scrabbling to pull her silver cuffs out; she'd never get them on the thing, but the touch of the metal would hurt it and hopefully drive it back.

"Run!" she yelled to Doctor Moss. She had to be the shifter's main target. But instead, the lecturer let out a cry and thrust her cigarette lighter into the creature's face. Transformed human or not, it couldn't fight animal instinct to flinch away from flame. Pierce glimpsed snarling teeth and golden feline eyes in a dark face.

"Run!" she shouted again as she scrambled towards Moss.

But the lecturer was fumbling with the door behind her; Pierce heard the clunk as the card lock popped open. "In here!" Moss said.

Her sense of tactics rebelled. "We'll be trapped!" They might be able to barricade the thing out, but for how long? And without any prospect of help on the way...

Moss ignored her, darting inside and holding the door open. The panther was regrouping, muscles bunching up to spring... "Shit!" Pierce dived for the doorway. She barely squeezed through the gap, half crushed by the door's weight before it sealed with a click after she'd gone through.

Sudden stillness. With the panther momentarily shut out, Pierce sagged and gasped for breath. Her heart was pounding. She turned the penlight on the window in the door, but it was set at human height, too high to show the beast prowling outside.

She turned to Moss. "Is there another way out of the room?"

The lecturer shook her head, looking pale but composed. "We should get the supplies while we're shut in here," she said, moving towards the store cupboard at the side.

Pierce could applaud her aplomb, but it wasn't going to help them much if the shifter broke through the door—or just plain opened it. The previous would-be assassin had managed to hack the locks, and this one had to have got into the building somehow. Their best chance of survival was if the shifter had to revert to human in order to operate the door. One brief window of vulnerability... She shone the torch around the lab, searching for a weapon.

There wasn't much to find. The lab was designed for ritual work, kept clear of any moving parts and dangerous distractions. The floor was bare concrete, set with a great protective circle in the form of a thin inlaid ring of metal that ran around the whole room. There were individual lab benches inside the ring, bolted to the floor and surrounded by their own smaller etched circles. There were no chairs or lab stools, and no other furniture besides the cupboards in the corners. Safety posters warned to MAKE SURE CIRCLES REMAIN UNOBSTRUCTED AT ALL TIMES.

The heavy fire door muffled any sound from outside. Was that a rustle? Pierce shone the light back on the door. Nothing but shadows.

Was the panther still outside, or had it gone?

She moved across the lab to Doctor Moss. "Do you have ritual knives in here? Silver?" Taking a knife to a tooth and claw fight with a creature much stronger and faster was about as wise as wielding one against a tank, but a lucky stab or slice could still break through the pelt and ruin the enchantment. She could hold her own against an ordinary man weighed down by a heavy animal pelt.

Moss shook her head. "PhD students have their own personal blades. We've got silver powder—"

"I'll take it." Probably wouldn't be enough to break the enchantment, but maybe it would burn for long enough to act as a distraction. She still had her malodorant spray to confound the thing's nose, but it wouldn't help them much if they were penned up in this room and the shifter was sufficiently determined.

A heavy clunk from the door. Pierce spun round, and saw that the light on the card lock had just turned from red to green. "Shit! It's coming in!" She flapped her hand urgently at Moss. "Silver powder, now!" She raised the penlight to aim at the door as it opened.

The weak beam was barely enough to cross the length of the room to the door; by its diffuse light, all she could see was the figure's outline. Human, walking upright, but distorted into monstrous by the pelt strapped to his back—and then distorting more as bones bent and muscles shifted in ways no body should move naturally. A fluid transition from man into beast, bright feline eyes emerging from the shadows as the shifter dropped onto all fours.

And bunched up, ready to spring.

"Silver!" Pierce demanded desperately. A canister was thrust into her hand, and she fumbled to yank the lid off, forced to take the torch beam off the panther for a second. She flicked it back again and the big cat was running at her, half the distance crossed in an instant. Pierce raised her hand to hurl the silver powder, praying it would make the creature flinch and cower back—

But then Doctor Moss grabbed her by the wrist. "Not yet!" she said urgently, yanking her arm back and causing Pierce to shake silver powder over her own shirt. There was no time left to react as the shifter crouched to leap; it snarled and surged forward...

And collided hard with the empty space in front of them, as if it had hit a transparent wall. It rebounded off of nothing and crumpled to the ground with a painful sounding thwack of flesh on concrete.

Not animal flesh, either: as Pierce trained the torch on their fallen assailant, she saw that she was now looking at a shaven-headed, tattooed man with the panther pelt strapped to his back like an outsized fur wrap.

He looked as if he was unconscious, but she didn't trust that enough to try to remove the pelt. Instead she tugged his arms together and locked his wrists into her silver cuffs: at least he couldn't transform with those on. Then she checked his pulse. Alive, but there was no sign of him stirring. She retreated to a wary distance and glanced at Doctor Moss. "What just happened?"

Moss had a hand pressed to her chest, breathing raggedly despite her earlier seeming calm. "The circle," she said. Pierce shone her torch down, and saw that the invisible wall that had stopped the shifter was none other than the boundary of the circle in the lab floor.

"It's... comprehensively warded," Moss explained. "Poured iron on the surface. Runes. Copper pipes under the floor filled with running water. Everything the architects could think of to prevent an active enchantment escaping from the circle." She closed her eyes and breathed out shakily. "Of course, it's only been tested on intangibles before, so I couldn't be *sure* it would stop a shapeshifter..."

"But probably better odds than silver powder," Pierce said, looking down at the canister of the stuff. If she'd thrown it, more than likely she'd have scattered some across the boundary of the circle itself, breaking the line and rendering it useless. "Big gamble," she said, pushing her hair back.

Moss smiled at her tightly. "Yes. Let's just hope we haven't blown all our luck on the warm-up act."

"Shit." Abruptly Pierce remembered that the shifter was far from the biggest problem on their slate today. In fact, he was only the distraction. She checked her watch. "We've got to get somebody here to take him into custody." There was no time to question him; he'd need a medical check, and she didn't know how long he might take to regain consciousness. She doubted he'd cooperate when he did.

"All right, get what you need from here, quickly," she told Moss. "I'm going to head for the stairs and see if I can get a signal on my phone. If he looks like he's starting to wake up, get out of the room and yell." She didn't like leaving Moss alone with the shifter, even with him cuffed and apparently neutralised, but time was growing more pressing with every passing moment.

She jogged to the foot of the staircase, drawing her phone and dialling Freeman's number as soon as she'd climbed enough steps to start getting a signal. Forget the druids and their land sale issues—protecting Doctor Moss was a higher priority now.

The call connected—but only to a recorded voice telling her that the mobile phone she'd dialled was switched off. She frowned, the heartbeat that had begun to slow quickening again. She'd told Freeman not to be out of contact. Did she have the right number? This was the first time that she'd tried to use it.

No time to waste on double-checking now; she needed police backup ASAP. With a grimace, Pierce called into the station, hoping they could spare her some semi-experienced uniforms who could see their prisoner back to a reinforced cell at RCU headquarters.

Might just be a phone problem with Freeman—but still, with the way things had been going so far today, a prickle of unease crept down her spine.

Things were already bad. But they could always get worse.

CHAPTER THIRTY-FIVE

IT TOOK LONGER than Pierce liked for the uniforms to arrive, listen to her instructions for securing the crime scene, and then escort the still-unconscious prisoner off for a medical examination to determine whether he was fit to be sent on to the cells. At least Doctor Moss had the time to gather the materials she would need to prevent the summoning, though forensics raised a stink about them taking anything away from the basement lab.

"Emergency," Pierce said curtly. "Lives in danger take priority over integrity of the crime scene."

The officious little man who'd tried to stop her curled his lip dubiously as he eyed the stack of papers and ritual materials that Moss had gathered. "Good luck selling that one to a jury," he said, shaking his head.

"I'll consider it good luck if we get this one in front of a jury at all." The last shapeshifter that they'd taken into custody had touched off a suicide rune on the roof of his mouth and died a messy death; with a chance to examine this one while he was still unconscious, they might be able to prevent a repeat, but after what had happened with the skinbinder during his prisoner transfer, Pierce wasn't sure even that would be enough to keep the man alive.

Assuming that the skinbinder was dead. Other people could make panther pelts, of course—it didn't require the same unique gift as working with human skins. And even if this pelt should prove to be one of Sebastian's, he could have made it sometime before his supposed death. Pierce hadn't had the chance to inventory the pelts seized in their raid on his illegal skin shop; the Counter Terror Action Team had taken over her crime scene and laid claim to everything.

This panther pelt might well have wandered out of their possession, or been in the hands of Sebastian's allies. If she could tie this summoning to one or both of those groups, she would have reason to reopen the skinbinder case, and start digging into what had really happened back in October.

Of course, that could well all be moot, if they couldn't find a way to stop the demon summoning tonight. She turned to Moss as they left the building. "I'm going to take you back to the station with me," she said. "Whoever's behind this is clearly concerned that you might be some risk to their completing the ritual, and there may be further attempts on your life."

Moss nodded, pale-faced but collected as she got into the car. Pierce had seen for herself she had pretty strong nerves for an academic—perhaps not a surprise, given her chosen specialty—but she'd been through a lot in the past week, and if her prediction was true they were going to have to ask more from her before the day was out. No one else had the expertise required to stop the ritual.

Pierce had never liked having all her eggs in one basket. It made her nervous.

She tried to contact Freeman on the radio when they got back the car. No response. Another phone call got the same 'mobile switched off' message.

"Something wrong?" Doctor Moss asked her, as she grimly started the engine.

"Possibly." Freeman could potentially have ignored her instructions, deciding it was necessary to go incommunicado to avoid being spotted as police—but even that would mean she'd found something more than the simple land use dispute that they'd been expecting. Not good news.

Pierce had to make a conscious effort to keep to the speed limit as she drove back to the RCU. The adrenaline rush of the shapeshifter's attack hadn't really drained away, only transmuted into edgy, twitchy nervousness. Every flicker of movement at the corner of her vision drew her eye, alert for an assault that could come from any direction.

Even when they arrived back at the station, she didn't relax. As she pulled into the car park, her eyes fell on the druids' Volkswagen bus, apparently just on the verge of departing as a few of the group's members packed bags and placards inside.

"Wait here," she said to Moss. She got out of the car and jogged over to join the group of druids. "Who's in charge here?" she asked.

With Greywolf gone, the question seemed to spark general confusion, but eventually a woman in her forties with John Lennon glasses and waist-length ash blonde hair stepped down from the bus with a slight sneer.

"Right, who are you?" Pierce asked her.

"Cynthia," she said, somewhat sullenly. Might not be her real name, and it wasn't a very useful one, but it wasn't her identity Pierce cared about.

"I sent one of my police officers off with your Archdruid this morning. She hasn't come back, and she's not answering calls. Where is she?" she demanded.

Cynthia shrugged. "Maybe she's got her phone turned off," she said. "It's not my job to keep track of your coppers."

"Well, it's my job to make sure nothing happens to them while they're under my command, and the fact is she was last seen following your leader to this sacred site of yours. How do I get in contact with Mr Greywolf?"

"*Archdruid* Greywolf," the woman corrected her, eyes narrowed in a scowl, but she pulled out a mobile phone from her robes and scrolled through the contacts. "We're not doing anything wrong," she said petulantly, as she put it to her ear.

"Then I'm sure this little misunderstanding will be cleared up very quickly," Pierce said. Returning the public's rudeness was never a good idea, but sometimes you could be just as sharp with pointedly applied politeness.

She tried not to betray the air of confidence and control by visibly jiggling on the spot. She could feel the tension gathering with every moment: call it gut instinct, some subconscious awareness of a magical build-up, or just plain pessimism, but she sensed disaster on the verge of breaking like a thunderstorm.

Cynthia lowered the phone after a moment, for the first time showing a hint of concern rather than just obstructive indifference. "Phone's switched off." She turned to the other half-dozen druids from the bus, clustered around the door to listen in. "Who went with the Archdruid this morning?"

"I think Rachel was driving," a young lad with a straggly beard ventured.

Cynthia tried another number on her phone; Pierce barely had to wait for the shift in her expression to guess the result. "She says they're waiting at the camp site for the Archdruid to meet them—he went off with the copper earlier, and he was supposed to have come back, but he hasn't showed up yet," she said. "They haven't been able to get him on the phone either." She turned back, suddenly more cooperative now it seemed that they might need some police assistance after all. "I don't know why he's not answering," she said.

Pierce wished she had some assistance to offer; right now, all she had was a bad feeling in her gut. "This stone circle of yours," she said grimly. "Where is it?" Deepan might have mentioned it earlier, but she'd dismissed the detail at the time.

An oversight that might be coming back to haunt her, if there was something to the druids' fears after all.

"Bradup, north-east of Keighley," Cynthia said. "It's on Rombalds Moor, just off of Ilkley Road."

Ilkley Road. The moors. Her stomach dropped. "*Shit*." She hurried back to her car, where Doctor Moss looked up from the passenger seat with concern. "Map," Pierce said immediately, extending a hand. "Have you got the map with the possible locations for our third skull site?"

Seeing her urgency, Moss didn't query it, but rifled through the sheaf of papers in her hand. "Here."

Pierce took the map and turned it round, focusing on the region that she'd studied all morning. Bradup wasn't even marked at this scale, but there was Keighley, Rombalds Moor... "Bradup stone circle," she said, hovering a finger over the map. "Somewhere... here?" She twisted round to see that Cynthia had followed her, and showed her the map.

"Round about," she said, with a worried nod.

"Right here." Pierce spread the map across the steering wheel for Moss to see, and tapped the location—right in the middle, between Bingley, Silsden, and the northmost of the two projected sites up near Ilkley. At the heart of the triangle. She turned to look at Doctor Moss. "I think we've found the site of our demon summoning."

PIERCE CALLED HER suspicions in to the rest of her team, but they were scattered far and wide, and the local uniforms were already spread too thin to assist without more reason than her say-so.

"I'm heading to the druids' stone circle with Doctor Moss now," she told Dawson over the phone. "She believes the ritual is due to go down at eleven tonight, at the winter solstice. If we can't stop it by then, all bets are off. Get in touch with Deepan down in Oakworth—if we're right, then the third point of the triangle is on the moor where you are and we can pull him and Taylor away, but let's not go counting our chickens yet."

This could still be a coincidence, unlikely as it was, or they could be wrong about the triangular shape of the overall ritual design. "I'll organise backup if I find anything in Bradup," she said. "If it all goes tits up and you don't hear from me again, consider yourself in charge of the case."

Another decision she just had to hope wouldn't bite her in the backside later on. Deepan didn't have the rank or the experience to organise the kind of large-scale operation they were going to need if this thing went south; Dawson she wasn't sure would have the temperament. If he went charging in to tackle Red Key's people without adequate preparation...

Well, she was just going to have to do her damnedest to make sure nothing took her out of the action before that happened.

She returned to the car, where Doctor Moss still sat waiting for her patiently. "Do you have everything you need to stop the ritual?" she asked, leaning in.

"Insofar as I'm confident I can stop it at all, yes," she said.

Pierce nodded. "All right. Then we're going to follow the druids up to their stone circle, and see what's to be seen."

* * *

WITH THE DRUIDS driving ahead of them in their VW bus, it was impossible to approach the scene inconspicuously. On the other hand, that could work to their advantage. Whoever was there wasn't likely to be too surprised to see more druids show up on their doorstep, and at least the bus would take the attention off the unmarked car that followed in its wake.

Or perhaps it wouldn't. The approach to the circle was a straight road surrounded by open fields, their only concealment in the rise and fall of the land. As they crested a hill, Pierce could see what looked incongruously like a construction site ahead, a large section of the fields to the right of the road closed off by tall hoardings with no obvious business name on display. A small Portakabin and a temporary barrier across the access road leading round to the side gave off the air of a makeshift guard post.

Was this the place?

The sight of Freeman's car parked on the verge seemed to confirm it. Pierce signalled for the druid bus ahead of them to stop and pulled in behind it.

"We need to get a look at what's behind those boards," she said to Moss. "And find out what the hell happened to Constable Freeman." The idea of bringing a university lecturer into an unknown situation didn't fill her with happiness, but she needed Moss's expertise to be certain what they were dealing with.

She got out of the car, moving round the side of the bus in an attempt to stay somewhat out of sight of anyone in the Portakabin. She jerked her chin at it as Cynthia stepped down from the bus. "Have you spoken to the people in there?"

"Yeah, they're dicks," she said. "Little boys playing soldiers. Wouldn't let us see anybody in charge—just told us to sod off and wouldn't answer any questions."

"They're used to you coming by, then?" Her conscience twinged at the thought of involving even more members of the public in this business, but they were up against the wall. "Can you drive your bus up and distract them while we take a look at what they're doing inside of the fence?" she asked. "Do a protest demo or something."

"We can do that," piped up one of the young druids clustered inside the bus.

Cynthia frowned more suspiciously before she gave a grudging nod of assent. "Only because you need to see for yourself what these bastards are doing," she said. "The Archdruid warned you himself, but you bloody coppers never trust anything that you can't photograph and write down in a book."

In this situation Pierce was glad of the cynicism. Reflexive distrust of the police was a pain in the arse most of the time, but if it meant the druids were more likely to cut and run than blindly follow instructions into trouble, she was all for it.

"Don't put yourselves in any danger," she said. "If they get shirty, just get back in your vehicle and leave."

"Not without the Archdruid," Cynthia said stubbornly.

"If he's here, and being held against his will or otherwise incapacitated, we'll make sure that he's taken care of," she said. "But it won't help anything if the rest of you are put in harm's way trying to rescue him. He and Freeman may not even be here anymore, for all we know."

Or he could be beyond rescue already. Pierce wouldn't let herself assume it unless she saw a body, but these people played for keeps. The possibility the Archdruid could have died due to her dismissal of his issues would weigh no less on her for the fact that he'd been so pompous and hard to take seriously—never mind that she might also have doomed the promising young officer that she'd sent with him.

Right now, those were just fears and speculation. Focus on the situation as it was. And to do that, she needed more intelligence. "All right. Distract whoever's keeping guard in that place," she said. She beckoned Doctor Moss out of the car to join her. "We need to find some way to get a look into the site."

Easier said than done: the whole point of erecting hoardings was to keep the gawkers out, and somehow she doubted this lot would be sloppier about it than the average construction crew. As the druids moved in on the Portakabin with an eagerness that suggested they were only too happy to stage a genuine protest, she led Moss round the back side of the cars, hoping it would be enough to help them to stay unnoticed.

She peered into Freeman's car as they passed: nothing left on the seats, so unless it was stuffed in the glove compartment, she'd taken her radio with her as Pierce had ordered. Pierce fought the futile urge to try it or the mobile again; the odds of getting through hadn't got any bigger, and trying might only alert the very people she was trying to evade.

They headed further down the road towards the blocked off site. She could hear people moving on the other side of the hoardings, indistinct voices and sounds of unknown objects being shifted. She cautioned Doctor Moss to silence with a raised hand; Moss nodded, her lips pressed together in a bloodless line.

Pierce eyed the wooden hoardings. Could she climb them? Not without a run-up and a heavy thump that was sure to draw attention even if she managed it first try. She turned to study the rest of the scene. There were dry stone walls running around the edges of the surrounding fields; much lower than the wooden hoardings, but consequently easier to climb, and if she took advantage of the rise and fall of the land...

She found the highest vantage point that she could, and scrambled up on top of the wall, wishing that she had a younger, taller constable on hand. With a supporting hand from Doctor Moss she managed to balance precariously on top of the stones, but even straining up she couldn't see over the top of the hoardings. Instead she raised her phone up high and blindly aimed the camera over the barrier, hoping the video recording would pick up more than sky and ill-placed fingers.

After taking a few seconds of footage she dropped back down, and she and Moss craned over the small screen. At first it showed just sky and the top of the boards, but then the angle shifted, and she hastily thumbed the button to pause the video. Even on the small screen, it was obvious they were looking at an extensive setup, numerous figures in dark clothes, regions of the ground marked out with spray paint and rope lines.

"Is that the circle?" she asked Moss, making out a

central region surrounded by an embankment. It was no Stonehenge, just a ring of low flat stones that barely rose above the ground. "Will it work for the summoning? Looks like a few stones are missing."

Moss gave a grim nod. "It's not the condition of the circle that matters, it's the potential of the site," she said. "The location will have ritual significance, and the ground here has been used for rites of all kinds for thousands of years. All of that will add power to the summoning, make it easier to breach the barrier between this world and the plane from which they're hoping to pull the demon through."

"Can you tell how close they are to completion?" Maybe they could still hope that the summoning was doomed to failure.

Moss pushed her glasses further up on her nose and squinted at the small screen, but she quickly shook her head. "Not at this scale. I would need to see their preparations up close."

Pierce restarted the video, hoping the shaky footage might show them something more, perhaps a glimpse of Freeman or Archdruid Greywolf.

A dark shape prowled through the corner of the image and she jabbed pause again as her stomach lurched. "Shit." It was unclear what the thing was, but it was moving on four legs and of a similar size to the people around it. "Looks like they've got another shapeshifter." This setup was looking an awful lot like the research facility where they'd busted the skinbinder in October.

That time, he'd been their only live prisoner. Maybe they could do better this time around.

"Is that the evidence you need?" Moss asked, turning to look at her.

"Good enough," she said grimly. The ritual nature of what was going on around the stones could be argued as up for debate, but the presence of a shapeshifter, more than likely unlicensed, was good enough to justify the RCU going in. Time to call the cavalry. She quit the video and thumbed through her contacts to find Dawson, raising the phone to her ear.

And looked up into the face of a man clad in black army surplus gear, a Taser in his hand pointed at her. He was flanked by two other large, muscular men in the same clothes, both of them also armed with Tasers.

"Put the phone down, please," he said.

Manners or not, it wasn't a request.

CHAPTER THIRTY-SIX

PIERCE LOWERED HER phone, but only to draw her warrant card, taking a chance that an outfit as professional as this wouldn't attack her on a public road without real provocation.

"Police," she said, showing the card, though she kept her fingers over the RCU badge. She nodded at the Taser. "That seems to be a prohibited weapon you have there. Care to tell me where you got it?"

"Come with us," the man said, ignoring the question. "Now, please." He motioned her and Doctor Moss around the far side of the closed off site, away from the druids and the Portakabin.

"You have no authority to order us anywhere," she said, without moving. Getting it on the record, playing for time and a chance for their situation to be spotted, rather than any hope he would back down. This lot were clearly professionals—they wouldn't panic at the first hint of passive resistance, and fighting or running would only make things worse. She was unarmed, lacking even the uniform standards of a police baton and stab vest, and she had a vulnerable member of the public with her. She couldn't afford to antagonise their captors.

It didn't seem that she was going to get far with the delaying tactics, either. "Now," the man repeated, with a motion of his head. With three Tasers on her, and the likelihood of being overpowered by three strapping lads even if they didn't use them, Pierce didn't push her luck. She nodded for Moss to follow, hoping the demonology lecturer was old enough and wise enough not to try anything stupid either.

The road failed to oblige her with any passing traffic. She wasn't sure their situation would draw enough attention to raise alarm anyway—actual guns might cause a panic, but at a glance the Tasers would have passed for power tools, and it wasn't obvious that she was police. Their best bet now was to hope that Dawson, in his impatience, would move in as fast as possible.

So, primary objective: keep herself and Moss and any other innocents involved alive until that backup arrived. Secondary: try to find some way of disrupting the ritual before it was too late. At least they still had time in the bag, with the main event not due to occur until an hour before midnight. A magical ritual this size wasn't easy to reschedule.

As they were led through a side gate into the enclosed region of the fields, she could see that the preparations were well underway already, teams of people measuring, marking, and digging. The surface turf had been stripped away, and circular ditches had been dug around the stone circle's original embankment, more figures in military surplus filling one with rock salt poured out from big sacks. Wooden stakes carved with runes had been pounded into the ground around the circle, long taut lines of exposed copper wire strung between them.

But even that great set of rings around the stone circle was only one small part of the ritual. The stone circle lay at one corner of an enormous triangle, marked out on the barren ground with what looked like lines of ashes; at the two other corners were more circles of equal size. Inside one knelt a figure that she was sure must be the warlock masterminding the ritual: he was shrouded in blood red robes, talismans hung round his neck, and on the ground before him lay several open tomes.

The third corner of the triangle held a deep pit; as they were led past, Pierce looked down and saw that the bottom was piled with chopped wood, like a pyre. Somehow she doubted it was intended for an innocent bonfire.

Across the field she spotted another shapeshifter, or perhaps the one glimpsed on the video: a burly bear-like figure, prowling the perimeter. The field was crawling with black-clad pseudo-military types, all of them armed with Tasers; she doubted that the lack of any actual firearms was due to difficulty getting hold of them. Live hostages they could feed to the sacrificial pyre were probably more use to them than bodies, and she doubted they would want to risk the chance of a stray bullet damaging the protections around the circles. Snap a copper wire, kick a furrow in the line of salt, and suddenly what had been a powerful magical barrier was no more than a line drawn in the dirt.

Red Key were clearly taking their preparation seriously—but no matter how much effort they put into the defences, they couldn't know their designs would keep the demon contained. A ritual as big as this couldn't have been refined and repeated before it was set down in the occult texts: it might well even be a hypothetical projection, never put into action before tonight. Just because they followed every step outlined in their books didn't mean that the ritual would work.

Pierce looked up at the sky, hoping for rain or snow to disrupt the proceedings, but despite the chill and the clouds there was no sign of salvation.

Her escort didn't give her or Doctor Moss time to gawk, hustling them uphill past the stone circle and through a farm gate into the next field. A knot of penned sheep stood huddled there, packed shoulder to shoulder and bleating in agitation. *Lambs to the slaughter*, she thought—all too literally. The fire pit inside the circle would need sacrifices to feed it, and she doubted that the sheep were all the summoners had in mind.

There was probably a reason they were keeping her and Doctor Moss alive, and she doubted very much that it was altruism.

Past the pens were several JCBs parked on the churned-up earth, and a large metal shipping container, padlocked and watched over by one of the guards. Pierce already had an idea of where this was going before their escort prodded them towards it.

"Drop your phone on the ground," the guard who'd spoken before ordered her. "Got a watch, got any police equipment, got any other electronics? That goes too." He jerked his head at Doctor Moss. "You, drop your bag and do the same."

Pierce could see that though Moss's jaw was trembling, it was set, and she feared the lecturer would cause herself trouble by refusing. Wary of giving any verbal caution against it that might put thoughts in the guards' heads, Pierce tried to forestall any conflict by obeying instructions herself. She winced as her phone hit the ground, hoping that the springy grass would shield it from the impact. She doubted she was going to get a chance to snatch it back, but if she did, she needed the thing working.

She stripped off her watch, and, more reluctantly, the malodorant spray from her belt. Her silver cuffs were still on the panther shifter they'd arrested at the university. Her penlight probably counted as electronic equipment, but it was on her keys; she might get away with keeping it, or at least be able to claim that she'd overlooked it. Might as well try her luck.

For all the good the tiny rebellion might do her.

Beside her Doctor Moss grimaced unhappily, but after a moment she lifted her bag from her shoulder and moved to set it down at her feet. The guard raised his Taser warningly. "Don't bend down. Just drop it."

She held his gaze, pressing her lips together. "There are materials in here that could potentially interact to cause a magical effect," she said. "While I don't countenance what you're doing here, I don't think it will help anybody if I introduce unpredictable effects to the equation." She stooped deliberately slowly to set the bag on the grass, and this time the man let her do it without incident.

Once they'd finished divesting themselves of items of interest, he gestured for them to step away, and then had one of his associates give them a further pat-down, as efficient and impersonal as any the police themselves could have delivered. Pierce was tense until he'd finished searching Moss and stepped away, apparently finding nothing of concern besides her cigarette lighter.

Then the lead guard banged on the doors of the metal shipping container, an echoing *clang* that must have been deafening to anyone inside. "Get back from the doors!" he ordered, and aimed the weapon through them as the man beside him hauled them open. Pierce wasn't sure what a Taser would do if the electrodes struck the metal walls of the storage unit, but she hoped no one inside was eager to test it and find out.

There was no rush from out of the darkness, and another jerk of the guard's chin motioned her and Moss inside. "Get in. Down the back," he ordered. They obeyed. This was a tight operation, no obvious carelessness or blind spots in their captors' procedures that they could easily exploit to get away. Meekly biding her time didn't sit well with Pierce, but trying something half-baked would almost certainly just fail and make things worse. These people might be willing to keep them alive for now, but that didn't mean they'd stick to that plan if it became more trouble than it was worth.

And she and Moss clearly weren't the group's only

captives; as she shuffled into the dark interior of the shipping container, she was conscious of dim shadows and rustling noises further down, an unknown number of people at the back.

The guards threw the doors closed behind them with an echoing clang, and the gloom abruptly gave way to pitch black; the only way to tell which way was out were the thin lines of light that framed the doors. The inside of the shipping container was distinctly chilly, but the air felt still and stale. Pierce avoided any mental speculation on how close it was to airtight and how many hours of air it held. Nothing they could do about it either way inside, and panicking would only burn through the air supply faster

"DCI Pierce, Ritual Crime Unit," she said aloud, once the ringing echoes of the slamming doors had died away. "Who else is here? Identify yourselves."

"Guv?"

Pierce felt a stab of relief as she recognised Freeman's voice, sounding even younger than her twenty-something years without visuals to back it up. "That you, DC Freeman?" she asked. No first names now—emphasize rank, make it clear they were police, try to act in control for the benefit of any panicking members of the public. "Who else is in here with you?"

"I'm here, Chief Inspector." She recognised the sonorous voice of Archdruid Greywolf. "We came alone. No one else was captured with us."

"All right," Pierce said. "Everybody stay calm. People know where we are, and they'll send someone out after us if we don't manage to check in. All we need to do is sit tight and await rescue." She left out the more difficult question of exactly when they could expect that to occur. "First of all, is anybody hurt?"

"We're both fine, Guv," Freeman said. She sounded slightly rueful. "We weren't expecting trouble. Went round to ask if we could take a look at the site and got herded in here by men with Tasers and a shapeshifter—lioness. They're definitely doing something big at the stone circle here."

Pierce had forgotten how much the situation had developed in the brief time since she'd parted from her officer. "We're pretty sure this is the central site for our demon-summoning," she said. "I've got Doctor Moss here, from the university—she believes she should be able to counteract the summoning ritual if given the opportunity." Pierce turned to look her way, though she could make out little more than a patch of deeper shadow in the darkness. "Are you going to need the bag that they confiscated back, or can you do it without the equipment?" she asked.

"I still have a few things," Moss said, a faint crinkling noise audible as she checked through her pockets. "Fortunately that young yahoo who patted me down was apparently only concerned with weapons and electronics. Between that and the ritual materials that this group have lying around, I could probably do something to disrupt or delay their plans if I get access to the warlock's circle."

Pierce grimaced. Even if they could somehow escape this prison, that was going to be tricky.

Greywolf spoke up from the rear of the shipping container. "I saw enough to know these people are intent on corrupting the sacred ground," he said. "They're obviously planning to perform sacrifices at the circle: I assume we'll be among them."

"They'll need to shed blood, and vast quantities of it," Doctor Moss said, a touch of the habitual lecturer in her voice despite the grimness of the situation. "No doubt all of that livestock out there is lined up ready for the chop, but they'll need to offer human lives too—the more the better, from their point of view." She paused. "I'm afraid, Archdruid, that they more than likely plan to sacrifice as many of your group as they can lay their hands on. As worshippers with a prior connection to the site, their lives can only increase the potency of the ritual."

Not to mention that it would be all too easy for the perpetrators to spin the resulting carnage as the actions of a suicide cult. Pierce set her jaw, thinking of how easily they could have lured the druids in tonight with promise of a compromise and access to the land for the solstice. With any luck the police involvement had disrupted that plan, but anyone descending on the site unprepared could still be nabbed.

Her stomach twisted at the thought of the group of druids she'd asked to act as a distraction outside. She could only hope Cynthia and co. had been alert and sensible enough to do a runner as soon as she and Doctor Moss were picked up by the guards.

"Your people brought us here," she told the Archdruid. "Cynthia was helping us by setting up a diversionary protest outside the barriers. I asked them to leave if they encountered any danger, so hopefully they will have all made their escape by now."

"Unlikely," he said. "Cynthia won't leave the sacred ground unless compelled to do so. I've warned my people that this company who took our land is intend on corrupting the purity of the circle with evil magics. We're prepared to do battle for the sanctity of the site."

Pierce couldn't help the unhappy noise that slipped out through her lips. "I'd rather nobody was doing battle, if we can avoid it," she said. "This ought to be a matter for the police."

Assuming that they were able to hit the site with enough force to overcome its defenders. After seeing the setup outside, Pierce had to admit she had her doubts. There must have been at least two dozen guards, most of them armed with Tasers, and at least two shapeshifters—the bear she'd spotted and the lioness that Freeman had seen. Plus if she was right that this Red Key crew were connected to the group who had funded the skinbinder, they might have even greater resources still to call on. She could only hope that Dawson would pull out all the stops, and not charge in with limited backup and cause a bloodbath.

"Our people will handle this," she insisted. They would. They had to. It was their job.

"I hope they do," the Archdruid said. "But, forgive me for this, Chief Inspector—right now you don't seem to be any more in control of the situation than we are."

She didn't like the fact that he was right.

CHAPTER THIRTY-SEVEN

PIERCE PACED THE full length of the shipping container, confirming without much surprise that it had no weak points they'd be able to exploit without tools that they didn't have. With a sigh, she returned to the others and sat back against the metal wall.

"Well, there's not a lot that any of us can do from in here, so we might as well conserve our energy," she said. "Freeman. They leave you anything of use, or did they confiscate everything you had with you?"

"Er... still got a biro, Guv," Freeman said after a moment; if she was leading with that, Pierce didn't hold out much hope for the rest of the list. "They took my silver cuffs and incapacitant spray—not surprising, with the shapeshifters—and the phone and radio. Still got my belt and shoelaces, hair-tie and so on—and my keys. I had them in my pocket."

Keys were a potential weapon in a self-defence situation, but Pierce wouldn't want to bring them to a fight where the opponents had Tasers. Let alone where they had teeth and claws. "What about you, Mr Greywolf?" she asked.

"They took my staff, but they did leave me my amulet of office," he said. "Both were carved from fallen wood from the same oak, and my followers all carry acorn charms from that same tree. If it's true they're still close by, I should be able to draw on their support to work some form of magic, but I fear these metal walls are blocking my energies. I tried to call on my staff earlier and couldn't raise its power."

That sounded like a suspiciously convenient excuse to Pierce, but she heard a rustle beside her as Doctor Moss searched for something in her pockets. "I might be able to provide you with the elements of a basic circle to amplify your power," she said. "I have a few things here that those idiots didn't bother confiscating... Chief Inspector, do you still have that penlight you had earlier?"

"I do." She'd been planning to conserve its power unless it became essential, but she drew the set of keys from her pocket now and clicked the keyfob torch on. "What do you need?"

"Just a little light ought to do for now." Moss pulled various items out from the many pockets of her sleeveless jacket and squinted at them, putting some back, keeping a few others. "I have chalk... no candles, alas, and no flame—probably not wise to light one in this enclosed space in any case... Ah, birch twigs, they may be of some use, and I have a few powders; it'll be a bit of a bodge, but since we're not trying to contain anything, only boost existing magics, it's probably worth a punt."

That wasn't the sort of terminology Pierce was hugely comfortable hearing bandied about when it came to magical rituals—she was usually the one in charge of clearing up after such famous last words—but right now, they didn't have much choice. Between the options of sitting and waiting for uncertain rescue or trying a long shot, she'd take the shot.

"All right," she said. "See what you can do."

IT MIGHT BE Pierce's job to deal with the aftermath of ritual magic, but aside from looking over the shoulders of the team from Magical Analysis as they performed basic divinations, she was rarely there for the preparations beforehand. Generally by choice.

The truth was, contrary to the general public's and certainly the media's impressions of magic, ninety-nine percent of it was really bloody boring. Half the reason that it was still an obscure and poorly understood art even in the internet age was that achieving any measurable result took a huge amount of setup and finicky preparation. Everybody wanted to do magic; few people wanted it enough to spend six months practising drawing the basic circles before they got started on the simplest of rituals.

One break or wobble in a ritual circle, one shoddy stroke drawing a rune, one candle flame that flickered out at the just the wrong moment, and everything would fail. Usually, that just meant nothing would happen at all. Sometimes, it meant just enough would happen to go spectacularly wrong.

Pierce's job probably gave her an overinflated sense of just how often things ended with the messy disaster option, but all the same, watching Moss and Greywolf set up their ritual was both incredibly dull and painfully tense. The darkness and the still air inside the shipping container made it all the more oppressive as she stood by to hold the torch on them while they worked.

Greywolf had taken up a cross-legged sitting position on the floor, his druidic robes hiked up rather inelegantly to reveal an ordinary pair of faded jeans and brown leather walking boots. Rather than adopt some meditative pose he simply watched and waited patiently as Doctor Moss drew her chalk design on the floor around him.

The pattern was an unusual one to Pierce's eyes. Ritual geometry had a million and one possible variations, but the basic intent was usually the same: keep what was outside out and what was inside in. The most basic kind of protective design was a simple circle, convenient for defence because there were no corners or sides of different lengths to provide an obvious angle of attack. Magic circles could be jazzed up in any number of ways, but generally they were built out of layers of concentric rings, the more the better.

This design was different, the intent not to contain, but to amplify. Not a solid closed shape, then, but looping lines that spiralled outwards, crossing over each other and fragmenting the design into chambers that steadily increased in size towards the outer edge. It built up into something like an intricate spiderweb, with runes chalked or assembled from carefully placed birch twigs at the points where segments intersected.

Pierce could see Freeman was watching avidly, clearly itching to ask questions, but she had the sense not to interrupt and ruin Moss's concentration. Pierce herself was far less curious; Freeman would learn with time that the details of specific rituals were rarely all that useful to know. You couldn't learn them all, so it was better to ignore the specifics and look for the wider patterns. Outward spirals and expanding shapes for amplification; that was enough information to be going on with.

Assuming, of course, that this makeshift ritual even worked.

At last, Moss set her chalk down and walked around the design several times, studying it intently before she straightened up and rubbed her neck. "All right," she said. "If this is going to achieve anything, this is as close as I can get to achieving it. Archdruid, if you would?"

Greywolf nodded solemnly and sat up straighter in the centre, heavy eyebrows descending in concentration as he clasped the wooden medallion between his hands. He closed his eyes, murmuring low words into his beard, and Pierce fought the urge to cough and shuffle in the thick silence. She couldn't tell if what felt like a building pressure in the atmosphere was just her own growing tension or some form of magic gathering.

Just as she was considering whether to switch the penlight off to conserve its batteries, she heard a subtle cracking noise behind her. She spun about to shine the penlight in the direction of the doors, alert for any sign that their guards were about to enter—or worse, pump some kind of gas in through the cracks to knock them out before they had a chance.

Instead, she saw that the line of light under the doors was gradually disappearing, as if something was encroaching along the ground, covering the gap. The shadow of something large approaching the doors?

No—she realised that she could hear a continued crackling, a stressed metal groaning, as if someone was trying to prise the container's doors open. Pierce stepped forward to shine the penlight's weak beam more closely into the shadowed corners, and jerked back with a hiss as she saw pale, worm-like tendrils squirming in through the gaps, crawling across the floor and up the walls like...

Roots. The tendrils were roots, she realised, spreading across the metal walls like a scene watched in time-lapse photography; forcing their way in through the gaps around the doors like questing fingers probing for weaknesses.

They found one in the join between the shipping unit's doors, held together only by the padlock on the outside. The container creaked and strained as the ever-growing mass of roots began to force the doors outwards, warping and buckling the metal with a succession of sharp cracks.

Pierce glanced back at the others, and saw Greywolf still sitting cross-legged at the centre of the ritual spiral, his face tense with concentration. Was this his doing?

Even if it wasn't, it was something that they might be able to take advantage of. Inching as close as she could to the doors without stepping on the web of roots, Pierce adjusted her grip on the set of keys in her hand, letting the penlight fall to dangle from the ring and instead threading a pair of keys between her fingers like spikes. A feeble weapon against Tasers—she'd been thinking as much earlier—but perhaps with the advantage of surprise...

She turned to jerk her head at Freeman, gesturing for her to come up closer to the doors, and Freeman began to move along the length of the container to join her, careful to skirt around the edges of the chalked design on the floor.

Pierce had only just turned her gaze back when the overstressed padlock finally gave way with an audible snap. With a metallic screech like a car accident, the roots ripped the doors open, blinding light flooding into the container. She lunged forward, half blinded and almost tripping over the crawling carpet of roots.

She was a sitting duck—but the guard outside the doors was gone. As Pierce blinked teary eyes, scanning the area, she saw that plants all over the field had exploded with the same wild growth. The tufts of springy grass around them had grown up to waist high, mounds of weeds erupting between them like Mesozoic megaflora. Roots snaked everywhere along the ground, a squirming, tangling mesh.

The barriers around the sheep pen had been heaved up by the growth, setting the animals free to fight their way through the grass in bewildered bleating panic. The guard who should have been watching the prisoners had run down to close the field gate before they could escape into the lower field and trample over the ritual. He was struggling to move it, the gate already half buried by a thickening grass mound.

The field below had been stripped down to bare earth for the ritual, but the burrowing roots were spreading down the hill. Pierce heard frantic shouts from the Red Key forces below as they scrambled to defend their preparations for the ritual. Just how far had the Archdruid's enchantment spread?

She turned back to see the shipping container behind her was now almost completely covered by layers of roots, the roof buckling ominously as they cinched in tighter. "Get out of there!" she barked. Freeman was already on her heels; Doctor Moss hurried to join them, offering a hand to the Archdruid. He snapped out of his trance and stood up just as the roof creaked and began to bow inwards with a groan of over-stressed metal.

"Come on!" Pierce yelled. She stepped back in to grab Doctor Moss's hand and haul her out past the mound of roots. The metal container was crumpling like cardboard, Greywolf forced to duck down as he scrambled out just before the whole roof caved.

The sound of a vehicle's engine coughed to life behind her, and Pierce whirled to see that the guard at the gate had abandoned his efforts and run to one of the parked JCBs, revving as if he hoped he could tear free from the high grass that held it mired. Maybe he still planned to try to block off the gate; maybe he was thinking of nothing but a chance to make his escape.

Either way, his luck had just run out. The crawling roots burst through the windscreen like groping fingers, and he ducked beneath the dashboard with a yell. More roots were winding up the scoop at the back of the digger, gradually tilting it backwards despite the thick grass that mired the tyres.

Deciding the guard had bigger problems than chasing them, Pierce turned back to Greywolf. "Is this your doing?" she demanded, forced to shout over the crunching, splintering, shattering din as the plants rapidly consumed the remaining vehicles, spreading up and under the high wooden hoardings around the site. Panicked sheep fought and bleated, tangled in plant snares that grew through their fleece before they could move. It was like some dark simulation of nature reclaiming the world after the end of civilisation, cranked up to high speed.

"It's my spell—but I'm not controlling this!" the Archdruid said. For the first time his mask of calm self-assurance had slipped to show a degree of alarm. "It should have stopped. There shouldn't be this much power!"

"The ritual," Doctor Moss said, looking grim. "Our spell has interacted with the others... this may be very, very bad!" She started to force her way through the tall grass in the direction of the lower field.

Pierce chased after her. "Watch out! There are still guards all over the place."

"My staff," the Archdruid was saying behind her. "If I can get to my staff, I might be able to bring this back under control."

"No," Doctor Moss said soberly, as she reached the line of fencing that separated the two fields, and hauled herself up on top of one of the posts to get a good view. "No, I don't think you will."

Pierce joined her at the fence, setting a foot on the bars of the metal gate to raise herself up above the rising tide of grass and take a look.

Down at the base of the hill everything was anarchy. A chain of wooden hoardings had fallen like dominos across the road, forced outwards by the thrashing, spreading plants. The group of druids had driven their VW bus over them to keep the breach open; they'd been joined by more of their people, and they were tussling with the guards. Pierce saw one of the girls whack a guard with her wooden placard, another one go down shuddering from the shock of a Taser...

There was no way the druids could hope to win this fight; the shapeshifters would cut through them in seconds.

Pierce looked around frantically for the two shifters they'd seen, but something else grabbed her attention first. The innermost ditch around the stone circle had been filled with water, like a moat: the first line of the magical defences. Except that as Pierce looked on now, she could see ribbons of pale steam rising up from the ditch.

The water was boiling away.

"Tell me this isn't what I think it is," she said hoarsely.

"If it's not what you're thinking of, then I'm afraid it's worse," said Doctor Moss. "The ritual has, to quote my dear late husband, 'gone to cock.' We're not waiting for the solstice now—and we're not dealing with a controlled and contained summoning." She drew a deep, shaky breath, staring up at the sky. "The demon's coming through."

CHAPTER
THIRTY-EIGHT

THE WARLOCK ORCHESTRATING the ritual had risen to his feet, shouting words that Pierce couldn't make out over the general din. From the rhythm of his voice it was a ritual chant, but whether he was trying to raise the demon or prevent its early emergence she couldn't tell.

If it was the latter, it wasn't working. There was a rising tension building in the atmosphere: the air felt thick and difficult to inhale, and carried a metallic taste like blood. The world had dimmed as if a cloud had passed over the sun; looking up, Pierce saw that the sky had turned a bruised yellow. Clouds swirled outwards in a spiral from the spot above the stone circle, as if a hole had been punched in the sky and the poison atmosphere of some alien place was pouring through. She thought, as she stared up into the heart of that impossible vortex, that behind the clouds she could see the dim red glow of some celestial light, a foreign sun or moon, or something else they had no words for.

It was mesmerising, difficult to tear her eyes away from.

And it shouldn't be happening.

"Tonight! You said that it would be tonight!" she shouted at Doctor Moss.

"The *ritual* was planned for tonight!" Moss said. "The demon isn't playing by those rules. Our spell has intersected with the summoning, fed it too much energy too fast. It's trying to claw its way through on its own!"

"But what about the sacrifices?" The four of them had been intended to be fuel for the pyre, but the guards running about below were too busy trying to contain the druids or rescue their preparations to notice or care that they'd escaped their prison. The fire pit inside the ritual triangle had yet to even be lit, and the sheep destined for the flames had escaped their shattered pen and fled for the hills through the gaps in the fallen fencing. "How can it be coming through without the sacrifices?"

Doctor Moss looked grim. "It's going to get them," she said. "They don't need to be offered to the fire—any blood shed on this ground will feed the demon now. The circle is incomplete. It's uncontained."

"Well, how the hell do we *contain* it?" Pierce demanded.

But Moss only shook her head, looking overwhelmed; the muddy yellow light of the unnatural sky reflected in her glasses as she gazed up, awestruck. Pierce looked down on the druid protestors battling the guards; they were hopelessly outmatched, and she could already see white-clad bodies fallen and trampled in the fray. She looked back, and saw the shattered shell of the JCB their prison guard had tried to run for; no sign that he'd managed to crawl his way back out.

Moss was right. The demon would receive its sacrifices. They could run, make sure the four of them weren't among that group—but Pierce had the ugly feeling that if this wasn't stopped, then nowhere they ran would be far enough.

She turned back. "Freeman!" Where the hell was she? Pierce had lost her and the Archdruid in the seething mass of spreading foliage. Then she spotted the two climbing down from the cab of one of the shattered vehicles, already half devoured by the plants. The Archdruid had his staff now—had he risked their lives for that? But then she saw Freeman was also clutching some kind of bundle.

"Is that my bag?" Doctor Moss turned back from the fence to take a step towards Freeman. She staggered and almost fell, and Pierce grabbed her to keep her from falling. She realised as she did that the ground was shaking faintly, a subtle tremor that almost passed for wobbly vision.

"Guv! We got the stuff they confiscated—some of it," Freeman called out as she stumbled closer. She shoved the bag into Doctor Moss's extended arms. "I don't know if it's all there... I got my cuffs, and one of the phones." She grabbed it from her pocket and shoved it towards Pierce.

Pierce thumbed the power, but it didn't just lack a signal—the screen was showing nothing but a flickering jumble of distorted colours. She looked up at the boiling clouds, a level of interference far beyond anything the natural world could produce.

They were alone, cut off from any help.

Greywolf staggered to join them, leaning heavily on his oak staff. He wasn't any younger than she was, and he'd spent hours cooped up in a metal box, but there was no time to care about anyone's frailties now. "Can you do anything with that staff?" Pierce demanded.

"Against that?" He gazed up at the maelstrom over the circle. "No. But if I join up with my people I might be able to bring these plants under better control."

Pierce swung back towards Doctor Moss as she took inventory of her gear. "Do you have what you need to end the ritual there?" she asked.

"I don't know," Moss said helplessly, shaking her head.

"Guv, what do we do?" Freeman asked her.

"Buggered if I know," Pierce said. "But we're going to have do something. Come on!" She led the way over the fence at an ungainly scramble.

The stones of the ancient circle shimmered like a heat haze. The wooden fence posts around it had become blackened, burning stumps, the copper wire flash-melted into a mist of droplets. Even as they ran, Pierce saw the sacrificial pyre down in the pit burst into flames—spontaneous combustion or some action of the warlock's, she didn't know. The flames burned yellow-green, leaping high over the boundary of the pit like a portal into hell.

And in the third circle the warlock knelt, arms raised and hands contorted in clawed shapes as he seemed to almost grapple with invisible forces in the air. His hood had been thrown back, and she saw his face, scalp shaved bald and decorated by interlocking tattoos, the waxen skin stretched back against his skull as if under tremendous g-forces. He was still shouting words into the void, swallowed by a screaming rush of wind that Pierce could feel tugging at her clothes and hair as she ran, sucking everything towards the stones.

The spreading plants they fought through had stopped dead at the line of ashes that marked out the ritual triangle, as cleanly as if sliced through with a blade. "What happens if we breach the triangle?" Freeman shouted.

"I don't know!" It was no protective barrier, she was sure: rather, the design was surely intended to feed energy between the three circles, warlock to pyre to demon to warlock. But as to what would happen if they crossed the line of ashes and snapped its power, like cutting a stretched elastic band....

"It makes no difference," Doctor Moss said from behind them. "It's not the ritual here that's keeping the demon contained—only the effort of crossing into our plane. Look at the *clouds*."

The alien sky had already spread far beyond the boundary of the ritual design, casting strange moving shadows over the fields below. The late afternoon light had taken on a shifting hue, painting all the colours wrong, blacks as blues and greens ruddy, giving everything a strange staccato quality like strobe lighting. Pierce knew the guards and druids running about the hillside below were really only a short distance away, but somehow it seemed as if the space around the circle had been compressed, more distance than ought to be possible folded up into the landscape. Sound was distorted, adding a nightmarish quality to the shouts and cries of pain and the distressed bleats of stampeding sheep.

Like a black hole, she thought. Fucking with all the laws of time and space as they drew closer to the event horizon.

"Come on!" she shouted, and it felt like her own words were stretched and torn, as if she was yelling them out of the window of a fast-moving car. She led the charge towards the triangle.

A guard ran forwards to intercept them, half raising his Taser, but his eyes were drawn sideways by the spectacle of the flashing clouds above the circle, and the Archdruid whacked him aside with a blow of his staff. Pierce reached the boundary first, and forced her way through; it felt like shoving into a taut sheet of rubber that resisted her, stretching and stretching like a bungee cord...

And then it snapped. A blast of heat rushed over her like a roaring furnace; rippling, crawling sensations squirmed over her skin like swarming insects. Her ears popped and filled with a feedback screech that sounded almost like distant voices, shrieking cries that scraped her nerves like nails on a blackboard.

"What do we do, Guv?" Freeman shouted, scrambling after her.

"Stop that warlock finishing his ritual!" One way or another.

Younger and fitter, Freeman pulled ahead, sprinting past the flaming sacrifice pit to run on towards the warlock's circle. As Pierce followed, she spotted trouble: the lioness, a rangy sandy-coloured shape, hunched amid the plants at the far side of the triangle.

"Shifter!" she yelled hoarsely, the word eaten by the screaming of the wind. "Freeman! Watch your back!"

The lioness burst forth from among the writhing plants as they too poured forward, no longer held back by the boundary line that Pierce had broken. The shifter bounded across the triangle towards Freeman, taking a direct line between the stone circle and the flaming pit.

Pierce saw the way the big cat's ears were flattened to its skull, the fur of the enchanted pelt bristling; there might be a human mind in there somewhere calling the shots, but it was at war with the animal's instincts—and even human instinct had enough monkey nature left to be howling with panic about the proximity of something *wrong* in that circle.

The shifter was distracted, and that might be the only chance they had.

"Look out!" she yelled at Freeman as the big cat loped after her, looking almost slow in the distortion of the circle, yet covering the distance all too fast. Pierce grabbed for her cuffs, and let out a string of curses as she remembered she didn't have them. All she had in her pockets was her bloody useless phone. She hurled it at the shifter before it could reach Freeman, missing and hitting the ground by its feet in a spray of dirt.

It might have done more good than any ineffectual hit; in a panic, the animal reeled away from the dust of the impact, swinging back towards the stone circle before it caught itself and turned again, now heading towards the flaming pit. Freeman followed Pierce's lead and hurled her silver cuffs after the thing: they struck the lioness's flank, and it jumped at the sting of the silver. Half mad with animal fright, the shifter took a running leap at the fiery pit, trying to clear it to escape. Despite everything, Pierce held her breath, half willing the jump to succeed just out of the horror of the alternative.

But it was an impossible leap. The great cat's front paws scrabbled at the dirt at the far edge of the pit, but found no purchase, clawing soil loose. Pierce turned her head away with an involuntary hiss as the lioness fell amid the flames. The agonised yowl and sickening scent of burning fur and flesh brought stinging tears to her eyes as she gagged.

Across from her, Freeman staggered to a halt, wide-eyed and horrified as she clapped a hand over her mouth. "Christ. That was a *person*," she said.

One who would have gladly condemned them to the same fate, but that was bitter consolation. If they were doing their job, *nobody* should die: not police officers, not innocents, not criminals.

Today wasn't going to be one of those blessed days. Pierce closed the shifter's dying howls off behind the walls of her mind; there'd be time to face those nightmares tomorrow, if they survived.

"Come on! Warlock!" she barked at Freeman. Their target was still working his spell in the other circle, gestures growing steadily more frantic as the fires of the sacrifice pit flared up beside him. The earth tremors were growing stronger, visibly shaking the ground, and the atmosphere had taken on that staticky feeling of the moment just before a lightning strike. The shifter's death had fed the ritual more power, and now the warlock was building towards a crescendo—or losing control.

Either way, the spell had to be stopped.

As they ran towards the warlock's circle, he began to stand—not facing them, but raising his hands towards the stone circle. It looked almost like the funnel of a tornado now, swirling shadows in the centre of the circle that stretched up to meet the clouds above. Staring into the vortex, Pierce saw flickers of alien shapes and impossible colours, glimpsed and gone too fast to leave any clear impression, only unsettling impressions.

"Stop!" she yelled at the warlock. "This is a prohibited ritual! Cease all magical activity and leave the circle!"

From the expression on his face, a rictus that looked like half rapture, half terror, the warlock was far beyond listening. He might not even have heard; the screaming, screeching, howling wind from inside the circle was like a roaring jet engine in her ears. The warlock made a sweeping gesture, spreading his hands as if preparing for some final grand motion.

"I've got him, Guv!" Freeman shouted, reaching the edge of the circle. As he began to howl the final syllables of his spell, she dived forward in a rugby tackle that knocked him staggering backwards outside the bounds of the ring.

There was a mighty flash, and the world tore inside out.

CHAPTER
THIRTY-NINE

PIERCE FELT LIKE all her senses had been wrenched away
and then handed back in the wrong order. She couldn't
even tell if her eyes were open or closed: migraine patterns
of light and darkness flashed in iridescent colours like a
petrol spill. The earth shuddered beneath her feet, and she
felt like she was falling in every direction at once. Was
the rushing in her ears somebody screaming nearby, or the
sound of the blood pounding in her head?

At last her vision halfway cleared, her surroundings
reappearing from the smear of blurry light. The ground
was still shaking, and between that and the wind that
seemed to drag instead of pushing, she stumbled a few
involuntary steps forward. Her foot crossed the line of
the warlock's circle, and she flinched, half expecting a
shock, but there was nothing. The power of the circle was
broken. Freeman lay slumped across the outer edge of it,
the warlock equally unmoving a few feet away. They were
both on their backs, as if they'd been blasted apart by an

explosion when they made contact.

Pierce scrambled towards Freeman, cursing, and bent to take her pulse. The quaking of the ground made it almost impossible, but the young DC stirred weakly at the brush of her fingers, though her eyes looked dazed when she blinked them open.

"Freeman. You all right?" Pierce helped her to sit up.

Freeman touched the back of her head and squinted at her fingers. No sign of any blood, but she seemed pretty out of it. "Where are we?" she asked blankly, and Pierce wasn't sure she recognised who she was talking to.

Concussion, more than likely, but there was nothing she could do right now—and little chance of diagnosing a head injury when the world was so askew that Pierce's senses weren't reporting anything reasonable.

"We're on a case. You hit your head. Just stay there," Pierce said, and hoped that being inside the warlock's circle would afford her some modicum of protection.

If not, well, it wasn't as if anywhere else would be much safer.

The warlock's efforts had stopped when he fell unconscious, but it hadn't brought the summoning to an end. Instead, it seemed to be burgeoning still further out of control: staring into the stone circle was like looking at the halo around an eclipse, painful to look at and leaving her eyes burnt with coloured afterimages that she feared might end up permanent.

She looked back behind her, and saw Doctor Moss struggling across the shaking ground towards her. The plants were pouring over the ritual ground in a wave, the barriers that had kept them out now shaken to pieces. Greywolf had disappeared: Pierce didn't have the time to care where to.

"Can you end this?" she bellowed at Moss. As she looked up at the clouds, they no longer seemed to be clouds at all, but something like a nebula, a hole torn in the sky to reveal ghostly constellations. Night had fallen over the site, naturally or otherwise, but everything was still lit up in shifting hues from the fire pit and that alien sky.

"Perhaps!" Moss said, but she looked doubtful, almost going to one knee as she stumbled away from the spreading roots. "I need to be inside the warlock's circle—and I need it kept clear of these plants!"

That was a tall order. Pierce looked around, and saw the fallen warlock slumped across the ditch that marked the boundary of his circle; she ran forward to grab him by his robes and drag him back in. The ditch, filled with rock salt and who knew what else, might be enough to keep the enchanted plants from encroaching for a while, but the constant quaking of the earth was already causing the loose soil to shift and crumble. It wouldn't take much to compromise the magic barrier.

As Moss staggered over to join them in the circle, Pierce tried to check the pulse of the warlock. She thought she felt a thready beat, but it was hard to tell.

Best to get him restrained in any case: one tiny move from him could ruin everything. She had no cuffs, and didn't have the time to hunt for Freeman's; instead, she yanked out the braided cord that belted the warlock's robes and loosely bound his wrists together with it.

There'd be words about non-standard ways of restraining suspects if they got out of this, but right now that was the least of her troubles.

As Pierce rose back to her feet, she saw the crawling roots had already reached the edge of the circle, probing at the crumbling soil around the outer ditch as if searching for any weaknesses. Every magical protection here was now eroding. There was a stench in the air like sulphur, like decomposing corpses, like the metallic taste of blood bringing bile up in her throat.

Every instinct that she had was screaming at her to run, *run*, get away from the hole in the world. She defied them all and turned her back on the great sucking void, reaching out a hand to help Doctor Moss climb across the ditch around the circle.

"Can you work here?" she said, forced to raise her voice over the unearthly screeching even when they were just feet apart.

"I'll try!" Moss staggered forward, and Pierce did what she could to shelter the other woman in the lee of her body as she dropped her bag on the ground and knelt to dig through it. "I can't promise this will work—but if it doesn't, there's no point in running."

With an unconscious prisoner and Freeman hurt, there was little chance they'd make it past the guards in any case. They had no choice but to make their stand here.

As Moss hastily drew a knife from her bag and began to cut symbols in the dirt, Pierce saw figures approaching the ritual ground out of the dark. She opened her dry mouth to give another shout of warning, but then she recognised the staff in the lead figure's hands: Archdruid Greywolf, and a handful of white-clad followers. They all stared, mesmerised, at the maelstrom in the circle.

From somewhere, Pierce found enough breath in her tight lungs to shout. "Greywolf! Stop the plants!" she bellowed over the shriek of the wind-voices. If he and his druids could keep the encroaching roots back, then Moss might have a chance to stop the ritual.

She thought she saw him nod, but then another tremor shook the soil beneath her feet, and she had no time to focus on anything but staying upright. Moss cursed, raising her hands, afraid to risk touching the ritual designs she was crafting until it stopped.

This was the equivalent of magical bomb disposal. One wrong move could blow everything, and failure now would be catastrophic.

"All right there, Freeman?" Pierce called out as the earth stabilised. The constable was hunched forward, clutching her head in her hands.

"I—" She started to lift her head and open her eyes, but recoiled with a cry of pain. "Too bright... What's happening?" Pierce wasn't sure if it was concussed confusion talking, or just general bewilderment.

Either way, the answer was the same. "Fucked if I know! Just don't look between the stones." Pierce immediately ignored her own good advice, taking a glance over her shoulder into something that her senses couldn't even fully process. In the instant before she squeezed her eyes shut and twisted away, an afterimage like a jagged red crack in the world burned through her eyelids.

She was no expert on barriers between realities, but that sure as fuck looked like a hole being torn in one to her. "I don't think we've got long!" she shouted. And there was nothing at all she could do in the time left: it was all in Doctor Moss's hands from here.

Her and the druids. Greywolf planted the end of his staff in the earth, shouting orders to his followers. Less than half a dozen of them with him—where were the rest? Fled, still scuffling with the guards, injured... dead? Her stomach twinged, knowing that she couldn't run to help them; couldn't leave the circle now the counter-ritual had begun.

Moss was making gestures of her own now, muttering, sweeping her hands back and forth over the ground. Pierce had the growing sense of tension gathering, as if every sweep was collecting thicker air around her hands.

The small band of druids had formed a loose ring around the outside of the circle. Five of them, far too few to link hands around it, but they stretched their open palms towards each other with bowed heads, echoing the Archdruid's low chant. Their voices blended into Moss's, into the storm of noise; no distinguishable words, just the rising, falling cadence of magic being worked.

Pierce saw the squirming roots around them gradually fall still, an effect that flowed outward like concentric ripples in a pond. Then the plants began to shrink back, retreating and shrivelling. They cleared from the edge of the circle, leaving the ring of salt around it chewed but still intact. The trembling of the earth eased amid the spreading wave of stillness.

At the heart of the circle Doctor Moss rose to her feet, presence powerful despite her slight, frail form. She raised her hands and bellowed to the sky, rich lecturer's voice booming out above even the screaming wind. Words in languages Pierce didn't know, in languages that perhaps no one knew, but she could *hear* the power in them, feel every syllable ring through the heavy air like a struck gong.

Every word was like a nail being hammered into the thick, breathless atmosphere. Her hair rose. Her skin rippled. It felt as if the blood was fizzing in her veins, and she burned to scratch all over, rip the unbearable itch out with her fingernails. Pressure was squeezing her head like a vice, and beside her she heard Freeman sob with pain.

Doctor Moss's face was drawn taut with the tension, almost cadaverous in the shifting light of the circle. Pierce couldn't see her eyes behind the reflections that danced in her glasses, but she still kept her head up, shouting to the sky. Pierce could feel the rhythm of the ritual reaching a crescendo, the pressure growing, growing, until she felt like something in her head would surely burst, that any moment now her eyes and ears would start to bleed.

"Begone!" Moss shouted in English, as her words reached their climax. "I banish thee! I banish thee! I banish thee! *Begone!*" Her voice cracked into hoarseness on the final repetition, and she threw her arms up crossed to shield her face as there was a great rushing in the air, as if someone had punctured the Earth's atmosphere.

Pierce was almost thrown off of her feet, and she dropped to the ground, sinking her fingers into the soil as if that would somehow help her to cling on to the earth.

The ground was quaking even more violently than before, and she was sure that something had gone wrong. There was a rolling, drawn-out thunderclap...

And then nothing. Darkness and silence.

Pierce took a moment to wonder if she was dead before she became aware of the sensation of soil between her fingers. She realised that her eyes had fallen closed, and cautiously opened them, one at a time. It was still dark, but she could see a little, by the light of the fire burning in the pit to her left. It had died down to the level of a standard bonfire now, and the blaze burned with a normal orange hue.

She cautiously stood up; the ground had stilled, but she felt the way that she did disembarking from a boat, the world still weaving even after the motion had halted. Moving on stiff, uncooperative limbs, she turned around to face the stone circle.

All she could see now was the ring of ancient stones, dull, inconspicuous lumps in the dim firelight. The great crack in the substance of the world had sealed itself.

Looking up at the sky, she saw that the swirl of alien clouds had also vanished, and now there was just the overcast night sky, occasional stars peeking through the grey clouds. She looked down for her watch, but her wrist was bare. Confiscated. Right. She doubted it would have retained the right time in any case. She wasn't sure the *world* had kept the right time. That rip in the air had chewed time and space up into something out of step with their traditional measures, and it was anybody's guess how much they might have lost.

But it was gone. Pierce drew in a deep breath, brushing the clinging dirt off of her hands. "Everybody all right?" she asked. "Freeman, you okay?"

The pained groan that she got in response concerned her a little, but at least the young DC didn't seem to be much worse off than before, sitting rocking forward slightly as she clutched her head. The light show and rapid shifts in atmospheric pressure would be enough to give anyone a headache, let alone somebody who was already concussed.

"We'll get you medical attention as soon as we can," she promised. God knew when that would be. She wondered if the cars parked outside the site had escaped unscathed, if anyone had phones that might work now. She turned to check on the others. "Doctor Moss? Are you injured?" she asked.

"I seem to be in one piece," Moss said, standing cautiously. "Though I think this outfit has seen better days." She squinted at the site of the failed summoning. "It seems my hunch was right. The partially opened portal was unstable from the start—I only had to snip the ritual threads feeding it power, and it collapsed in on itself."

"Good to hear." Pierce twisted round to look at the small knot of druids. "Mr Greywolf? Are your people all right?"

"Those of us that are here are fine," he said, though he was leaning heavily on his staff for support. "But others have been hurt. We need to see what's become of them all."

"Right," she said, turning about to face what she thought was the direction of the road. The great mass of plants surrounding the ritual triangle had withered and died away, but with only the limited light of the dying fire down in the pit she couldn't see much in the darkness. "Let's see what we can do—"

She was cut off as the bright beam of a torch shone in her eyes, quickly joined by half a dozen others.

"Stay where you are, please, Chief Inspector. All of you," said a calm voice from outside the circle. She squinted past the light to try and make the speaker out, and glimpsed the dark army surplus outfits of the Red Key guards. Beside them slunk the hulking shape of the bear-form shapeshifter that she'd lost track of in the general chaos.

This wasn't over yet.

CHAPTER FORTY

PIERCE WASN'T SURE if she and her fellows in the circle were outnumbered, but they were definitely in no condition to fight. Freeman was probably concussed, Doctor Moss had been through far too much already for an aging academic who'd been in hospital just days ago, and the druids seemed shaken and drained after their ritual. Pierce herself might have just about enough energy left to throw a punch or two, but it would be a wholly futile gesture.

She substituted bravado instead. "Cut your losses, folks," she advised. "Your ritual's a bust, and you've already committed enough crimes tonight. Let's not add anything else to the tally."

The spokesman of the Red Key forces didn't bother trading taunts. "Everyone stand up," he said. "Leave all your ritual equipment on the ground and move away from it. We're going to have to ask you to come with us, please."

Pierce held her ground. "I don't think we're going to be doing that, son," she said, staring past the glare of the torches in an effort to meet the man's gaze. Refusing to go along might just get them all killed, but accompanying the Red Key forces anywhere would more than likely end in the same fate, with less chance of their bodies being found.

"I appreciate your reluctance, but I'm afraid you don't have a choice." The lead guard nodded his head towards the bear-form shapeshifter. "Move, or we'll encourage you to do so."

Pierce tensed. Getting hit with a Taser would be one thing—and not one she looked forward to—but the shapeshifter's crushing jaws and vicious claws were another level of lethal. The bear's ears were back as it swung its lowered head from side to side, snarling, animal instincts probably still twitchy from the magical events in the circle. It wouldn't take much to trigger it to attack.

It might not need any real trigger at all.

"All right," Pierce said, breathing out as she raised her hands. "All right." Playing for time. Bear or no bear, she knew they couldn't afford to just meekly go along with the Red Key team. As soon as they let these people take them away from this site, they were done for. "But we have injured here. You're going to have to give us a chance to help them." She moved towards Freeman, but a jerk of the man's Taser made her freeze.

"Not you," he said, and nodded his head at Doctor Moss instead. "You help her up."

After that ritual, Pierce wasn't sure Doctor Moss even had the strength to support herself, but that was probably the point of the selection. The guards weren't taking any chances. "All right," she said, making a point of stepping away to exchange places with Moss.

As Pierce crossed in front of her, the lecturer twisted slightly to reveal something in her hand—the ritual knife that she'd been using to mark symbols in the dirt. She stumbled as she took a step, and in grabbing Pierce for support, managed to shove the knife into her coat pocket. It was an unexpectedly smooth move, Moss already moving away again as the lead guard barked a warning. "Sorry, sorry," she said, still tottering. "Not very steady on my pins right now, I'm afraid."

Pierce kept her back to the guards, subtly lowering her hands as she stepped away from the rest of the group. Was the knife Moss had given her made of solid silver? She hadn't been able to get a good look in the limited light, and she certainly couldn't pull it out to inspect it now.

If it was, then she might have a paper thin chance of damaging the shifter's pelt before it ripped her head off. If it wasn't, they were fairly fucked... but that was hardly a downgrade on their current situation. She kept shuffling backwards, hoping the guards'—and the bear shifter's—attention was more on Moss as she helped Freeman up.

In her peripheral vision Pierce spotted the sprawled form of the warlock, apparently still unconscious on the ground. There was her chance. As she took another step backwards she deliberately let her foot catch the man's limp, outflung arm, and staggered, her hands flailing for balance.

She dipped into her pocket and drew the knife out as she twisted, looking down at her feet. She half raised her hands in a gesture of apology, hoping no one would see the glint of metal tucked behind one of them.

One last chance. Just one card left to play.

"Move away from the rest of the group, Chief Inspector," the head guard ordered.

"I'm moving. I'm moving." Pierce half turned towards the group of guards. Where was the bear? Not within her line of sight, so it must be creeping closer in the blind spot on her other side.

Behind her was the dull thump of something hitting the dirt—the Archdruid's staff, maybe, or some other distraction, intentional or otherwise. Pierce turned towards the noise—and just kept turning, spinning round to lunge at the bear with the knife in her hand, slashing at the creature's thick brown pelt.

But not fast enough. Even as she struck out, the shifter reared away, slapping out at her with one great heavy paw. She jerked backward by reflex before it could make contact, but the rapid movement caused the knife to fly from her fingers. Before she could scramble to recover it, the head guard moved to stamp his foot down on the blade.

One last gamble—and she'd lost.

"Move away from the knife, Chief Inspector," the head guard said, his tone more steely than before. Pierce took a few slow paces down the hill towards the road. Ahead of her she could see more of the guards moving around, torches flashing as they packed away equipment and herded the surviving druids onto a lorry. She tried to eyeball the distance past all of them and down to the road where they'd left the cars behind; cars that might or might not start, that she wasn't sure she'd kept hold of the keys for.

Too far. Too many obstacles. No way she could realistically hope to escape.

But as she heard the metallic click of a weapon behind her that she knew wasn't just a Taser, Pierce tensed to run anyway. If she couldn't get away, at least she could leave behind a crime scene too messy to clean up.

"That's far enough," the chief guard said. She paused. Drew a slow breath. Could she stall them any longer, or just start moving n—?

An incandescent glare filled the world, and Pierce reflexively cried out, throwing her hands up to shield her face even though she was sure the light was the blaze of a fatal shot as it blew through her brain. They said you never got the chance to hear the one that killed you...

Then sound filtered back in past the first burst of alarm: vehicle engines, a hum that built into the rotor noise of an approaching helicopter, and the distortion of an amplified voice over a loudhailer. "This is the police! You're surrounded! Drop all your weapons and get down on the ground!"

Firearms officers swarmed the site, followed by a wave of uniforms. Pierce saw the dark shape of the bear go hurtling past her, charging over the fallen wreckage of the hoardings to flee for the hills. "Shapeshifter's on the move!" she shouted urgently, but she wasn't sure if anybody heard or paid attention.

A bright light was shone in her face, and she reeled backwards, squinting. "DCI Pierce, RCU!" she said, yanking out her warrant card. "You've got a shapeshifter in bear form, making a break for it across the fields—where's your officer with silver bullets?" Anti-shapeshifter rounds were rare and expensive; she'd be lucky if the local Firearms Support Unit had even one officer with training and ammo to stop the bear.

"Do you need medical attention?" the young officer asked her.

She waved him away. "I'm fine." Starving, busting for a pee, and her bad shoulder was aching, but otherwise still in remarkably close to one piece. She thumbed over her shoulder at the circles. "But DC Freeman took the backlash from interrupting the ritual. Make sure she goes to hospital and gets thoroughly checked."

There was little way of guessing what damage the magical blast might have done, nor of predicting whether anyone who'd been here at ground zero would face after-effects. Ritual Crime was a crapshoot of unanticipated consequences, and the scale of tonight's ritual was a first even for Pierce.

She looked around. To her relief, the Red Key guards weren't fighting to the death; some had followed the shapeshifter's lead and tried to flee, but others had surrendered, allowing themselves to be disarmed and cuffed and led away. Maybe they thought their bosses would get them out of trouble. Considering the level of resources that had gone into this setup, they might even be right.

Or else they were just planning to do their time and keep their mouths shut until they got out. Pierce was painfully aware that there was little adequate that they could be charged with. Possession of the Tasers, unlawful detainment of their prisoners; might be possible to single a few individuals out for assault on the druids. But the summoning itself was too big, too complicated, to fall under the limited ritual laws. If they could prove the intent to sacrifice human lives, that made it a prohibited ritual, but the only one they could actually nail for that was the warlock himself.

Wherever he was now. Pierce turned her gaze towards the remnants of the ritual triangle, lit by the fading glow of the nearly exhausted fire pit. Police were everywhere, cuffing the guards, escorting Greywolf and his druids away. She couldn't see the warlock among the arrested; had the Red Key forces freed him from his ropes, or was he still lying trussed up on the ground, forgotten and unnoticed?

For all she knew, he could have been dead before she'd bound him with the ropes. She hadn't had the time to stop and check.

She just hoped like hell he hadn't died while he was lying there, injured and improperly restrained. It had been the best she could do under the circumstances, but that wouldn't make her feel any better if it turned out they'd lost a prisoner while he was in police custody.

Especially one of such importance to a major case. The guards, even the shifters, could all be hired guns, but the warlock *had* to know more about this. You couldn't find somebody to perform a ritual like this just by advertising in internet chatrooms. He must have been training for this for years.

Even he might not be able to tell her much about his employers—but he sure as hell had to know what the goal of tonight's summoning had been.

And Pierce meant to know too. She jogged towards the knot of uniforms dealing with the handcuffed guards. "Where's the warlock?" she barked at them.

Bewildered faces all round. God, they were all almost offensively bloody young, police and prisoners alike. Up past their bedtimes, the lot of them.

"Red robes, tied up on the ground—have you found him?" she demanded. "He was here, in the circle, possibly unconscious."

The uniform sergeant she'd collared continued to look blank, and now faintly worried as well. "Er, not sure, ma'am. DI Dawson's coordinating," he said, passing the buck further up the stream. He pointed towards the upper field where the sacrifices had been held, and she saw Dawson's bulky figure picking his way through the wreckage of broken fencing and vehicles in the dark.

Pierce hurried up the slope to join him. As she drew closer, she could see from the angle of his head and emphatic hand gestures that he was talking to someone further uphill. She was too far back to hear what he was saying, but as the police helicopter made another sweep over the scene, the searchlight briefly lit up the arguing figures. She caught a glimpse of billowing robes: not druid white, but darker.

The warlock.

Cursing, Pierce broke into a faster run, looking around for someone to call out to for backup. But she'd left them all behind down by the ritual triangle, and there was no one up here within earshot. Without a radio, her only options were to go alone, or run back and hope that nothing happened while her back was turned.

Bloody Dawson, charging in like a bull in a china shop again—he'd probably spotted the warlock outside the police perimeter and just gone after him without a thought for procedure. In the brief glimpse she'd had in the light she'd seen he had a stab vest, but that wouldn't help him much if the warlock had some kind of prepared magic in reserve.

As she drew closer, heart pounding, she saw the warlock throw his hands out in an angry gesture, Dawson raising his own arms as if to grab or shove him—

And then the night exploded with bright flames. Pierce cursed and shielded her eyes, still staggering forward at a half-blinded run though she was certain she'd just seen her DI immolated. "Dawson!" she yelled. As she ran towards the conflagration, she collided with a solid body, and she fought before she registered the fabric of the stab vest. Dawson's body wasn't ablaze; the warlock's was.

"What the hell happened?" she demanded. The fire was already burning itself out, faster than any natural flame could have consumed a human being. The warlock's body had barely had enough time to start collapsing to the ground before it was fully incinerated, crematorium ashes fluttering away from the glowing hot bones before they too crumbled down to nothing.

"I was trying to talk him down," Dawson said, still gripping her arms, though there was nothing left for her to run forward and try to save. The flames had ignited and burned out so fast the fire hadn't even had the time to spread over the grass. "He knew he was caught. Guess he didn't want to be taken in alive."

"Hell of a suicide method," Pierce said, as she stepped away from him. Quick, but it couldn't have been painless.

"Fanatics, these bastards," Dawson said.

Possibly—but as he turned and strode away to summon some uniforms to join them, Pierce couldn't help but wish that she'd been close enough to overhear their conversation. Maybe it had gone down exactly as Dawson said... and maybe it hadn't. How did she know that the warlock had been threatening suicide, and not the one under threat? From the little she'd glimpsed in the dark, there was no way to be certain that it was the warlock and not Dawson who'd sparked the magical blaze.

She watched him barking orders to the uniforms down in the lower field. They'd given him control of her department, but she still didn't really know a thing about the man. Who *was* Graham Dawson? Was he just an honest cop with a bad attitude... or was he playing his own game?

Pierce turned to survey the site of the aborted ritual, drinking in all the details just in case they went up in smoke like the evidence from the skinbinder bust in October. She didn't know who was behind this group calling themselves Red Key, or if it was a part of the same setup. But one thing was for sure.

It wasn't safe to trust anyone right now.

CHAPTER
FORTY-ONE

VISITING HER OFFICERS in hospital was never a happy task, even when the prognosis was good. As Pierce walked the stark, antiseptic corridors, she couldn't help but recall all the time she'd spent there in the last few months. Visiting Sally after the panther shifter had damn near slashed her throat; her own shoulder surgery and long recovery... most vividly, the visit she'd received from Superintendent Palmer—or rather, someone she was all but certain had been a shapeshifter wearing his skin.

The RCU was nasty, dangerous work, and Freeman had just had a demonstration. If even a long-serving officer like Sally could be shaken into leaving, what were the odds that a new young recruit with plenty of time to switch specialisms would want to stick around? The RCU had always been a revolving door, few choosing to stay long with the harsh risks and poor rewards.

But as Pierce poked her head into the ward, Freeman smiled at her brightly from where she was sitting up in the chair next to her hospital bed. With her hair loose around her head rather than pulled back into its customary bun, she looked even younger. A lanky lad of maybe eighteen with his hair in cornrows was casually slouched in the next seat, sitting up straighter as Pierce walked in.

"Morning, Guv," Freeman said cheerfully. She pointed a thumb at the boy beside her. "This is my brother Joey. Joe, this is my boss, DCI Pierce."

Pierce briefly shook hands with him, and he got up and stretched. "All right. I'm going to go and see if they have food in this place," he told his sister.

"Smuggle me back a doughnut," she said. "And call Mum, tell her my head's not going to fall off and she really doesn't need to drive all the way up to see me."

"They give you a scan?" Pierce asked her, once Joey had gone.

"Yeah." She smoothed her hair back, wincing slightly as she touched her head. "Apparently my brains are still intact. I feel fine, Guv," she insisted. "Just a bit dizzy. I should be good to get back to work in a day or two."

"Don't strain yourself," Pierce cautioned. "Might as well leave it till after Christmas at this stage." She'd be working over the holiday herself; too much to do, too much time off already, and frankly she'd already spent enough of her medical leave with her mother and sister to last her all the way to *next* December.

Freeman shook her head determinedly, despite the fact it clearly hurt to do so. "I want to be involved in this one, Guv," she said. "This is my first big case for the RCU—I want to make sure these Red Key people don't slip through our fingers."

"Well, the case'll be waiting for you when you get back," Pierce said. Somehow she suspected they weren't going to resolve this one quickly and easily—and this time, she wasn't conveniently out on medical leave so that others could shuffle it all under the rug. "Look after yourself. We need you back, but we need you on top of your game, not dragging yourself back to work before you're ready."

"You can count on me, Guv," Freeman said.

Pierce left the hospital in a slightly better mood. Perhaps this new RCU team could hold together long enough for her to get to know them after all.

She drove back to the station, at last mercifully cleared of picketing druids. She wasn't sure that would be quite enough of a feather in her cap, though, as she went through to see the superintendent. They'd prevailed yesterday, but it had been a bloody close-run thing.

"DCI Pierce," he said, shuffling papers and looking up at her over his glasses. "How are things going at the ritual site?"

"They're still bagging and tagging and taking photographs," she said. "Doctor Moss helped our folks from Magical Analysis to confirm there's no live magic at the site. Right now it's just a big field full of evidence."

Confused, trampled, and half deconstructed evidence, but at least it hadn't all gone walkabouts in the middle of the night. After the deaths of PCSO Davenport and PC Winters at the Silsden scene, Dawson's demands for backup had been taken seriously, and the place was

crawling with enough uniforms and forensics people
to give even the most connected conspiracy pause for
thought. Their evidence might yet conveniently vanish
down the cracks between storage units later, but at least
they'd get their chance to examine it first.

"The third set of buried skulls has been found and
removed safely as well," she said. "Whatever lesser spirit
was originally caged there was apparently cannibalised
by the big one before the ritual last night. Or at least, it
didn't pop up to rip anyone's face off." That was about as
much as they could ask.

"Yes." Superintendent Snow pressed his lips together in
a frown. She got the impression he wasn't much of a fan
of the ephemeral, hard-to-classify nature of most of the
threats they dealt with in the RCU. Unfortunate for him.
"And Constable, er... Freeman?" he asked.

"She's doing well. Eager to be back at work," Pierce said.

"Good, good." He clasped his hand together and
sat forward. "Frankly, Pierce, you've come out of this
operation better than you deserved to," he said bluntly.
"The whole thing has been a shambles of poor organisation
from start to finish. Seconded officers killed, consultants
and informants murdered, loose ends at every turn—if
it wasn't for the sheer scale of the criminal enterprise
you brought down last night, there would certainly be
questions raised about your suitability to continue in this
role."

Pierce held his gaze, refusing to back down. They'd
cocked up along the way, fair enough, but he needed
to appreciate what he was dealing with. "Sir, this is

Ritual Crime," she said. "We're *never* going to have an opportunity to do things by the book with minimised risks. The book hasn't been written, we don't know what the risks *are*, and people can't be trained in the best way to handle things that no one in the police has seen before. We do the best we can with what we have."

"If the book doesn't exist, then I suggest you write it," Snow said crisply. "You may be dealing with the unknown, but I still expect you to communicate, coordinate, and document your work. I've allowed a little leeway given your time off on leave and the fact that the majority of your unit is new, but there will be no cowboy operations under my watch. Is that understood?"

"Understood," she said.

He graced her with a regal tip of the head. "Then... well done."

"Thank you, sir." She moved to leave.

"Oh, and, Pierce?" he said as she was reaching the door.

"Yes, sir?" She turned back.

"I looked into the matter of my predecessor's retirement, since you were so keen to know the details," he said. "It seems that there's no longer anyone at the address Mr Palmer left with the police force." He cocked his head and regarded her coolly over his glasses. "Did you have any reason to suspect that there might be foul play at work?"

She had *every* reason to suspect foul play... but would admitting as much to Snow win her a powerful ally, or only confirm to the enemies above she knew too much? The organisations she was dealing with were breathtaking in scope, far too powerful for her to defeat by herself—

and far too dangerous to her and her team if she made the wrong move. If she wanted to survive and seek justice for those who hadn't, she couldn't afford to make a mistake.

Pierce looked back at Snow as she grasped the doorhandle, professional calm fixed firmly in place. "No, sir," she said. "Just curious."

He nodded, once. "Well, that's a valuable trait in a police officer," he said. "Just see that it isn't turned to idle ends."

"Yes, sir," she said.

PIERCE HEADED BACK up the stairs to the RCU, bypassing the main office for the moment to head through to Enchanted Artefacts. Both Cliff and his assistant Nancy were at work today, for once the ever-present headphones absent from his ears as the two of them catalogued a mountain of boxes of evidence.

"Ah, Claire," Cliff said, with an affable smile. "I gather we have you to thank for the early Christmas? You've sent us quite a bounty, it appears." Indeed, they were overrun with evidence; so much of it, Pierce suspected rather grimly, that they wouldn't have a hope of getting half of it processed before the new cases piled up to push it down the list.

But hope sprang eternal. "And has last night's bounty yielded any fruit?" she said.

"Early days, yet, early days," he chided, but he did cross the room to lay his hands on a plastic-wrapped bundle, which he unrolled to show a mass of thick black fur. "However, you might recall that just before things went *quite* mad, you arrested a young man in a feline romper suit." He shook out the fur to reveal the dead-eyed stare of the black panther pelt.

"He's in the cells downstairs, but he's not talking." Not that she'd had the chance to try questioning him herself yet; one more task on the never-ending list.

"Ah, but as I always say, why listen to the criminals when you can listen to the evidence instead?" Cliff said. He flipped the pelt over, revealing the maker's rune marked on the inside. "Recognise this?" It was one of the more intricate examples that she'd seen: multiple interlocking strands forming an hourglass design that, glimpsed from another angle, looked rather like a stylised letter S.

She recognised it well, from various seized pelts and the tattoo on the back of the neck of another shapeshifter they'd once arrested.

"Sebastian," she said. The skinbinder who'd stabbed her in the shoulder last October, the one who'd made the human skins; the one she'd been assured was dead after a road traffic accident when he was transferred. She snapped her gaze up to meet Cliff's. "Can you find out how recently this pelt was enchanted?" she asked.

He drew his lips back from his teeth, prevaricating. "Not... with any precision," he admitted.

Pierce laid a hand flat on the lab bench in between them. "Be precise," she said. "Make it as precise as you can."

Because if that pelt had been made after Sebastian's 'death'... then that might just be the first domino that brought the whole lot down.

"I'll see what I can do," Cliff promised her.

Pierce left the lab and strode back to the office. Freeman might be absent, but with the rest of the team all in their chairs the place still looked busy. "Dawson—anything new to report?" she asked.

He looked up from the sheaf of papers in his hand. "Just heard back from the Firearms team that were hunting the bear shifter across the moor," he said. "Got away, but their silver bullet man's prepared to swear he winged it before it did—said the bloke definitely shifted back before they lost him. Odds are that the pelt's too damaged to be used again."

"Good." Not a perfect result, but better than a clean escape, at least. "Deepan. How are things going with the prisoners from last night?"

"Fourteen people brought in. We've shipped them off to different stations, kept them held separately," Deepan said. "So far none of them are talking, but the rumblings I'm getting from the local police are that one or two are sounding a little bit unnerved about the way that things went down last night."

"Excellent," she said. "Tell them to keep the pressure on, and if anybody suddenly decides they've got something to say, we'll send our people over to do an interview." After seeing the sheer scale of the thing that had almost broken through the stone circle last night, she was willing to bet there might be a couple of Red Key guards reconsidering their career choices.

The office phone rang, and DC Taylor rolled his chair across to grab it. "RCU," he said. He listened for a few moments, making brief interjections and scrawling notes down on his battered pocket notebook. "Right. What time was this? Okay. All right. We'll get someone out to you."

Pierce raised her eyebrow as he put the phone down and stood up.

"We've got a new case, Guv," he said. "Haunting at a warehouse in Wakefield. Sounds pretty legit—staff turned up this morning to find the night watchman had his head pulled off, and the CCTV footage they've pulled up from last night is, quote-unquote, 'mental.'"

Pierce clapped her hands together and straightened up.

"All right, people!" she said. "Let's get back to work."

A conspiracy the scale of the one that she suspected might take months, even years to unravel—but in the meantime, there was a job to be done.

ABOUT
THE AUTHOR

E. E. Richardson has been writing books since she was eleven years old, and had her first novel *The Devil's Footsteps* picked up for publication at the age of twenty. Since then she's had seven more young adult horror novels published by Random House and Barrington Stoke. *Ritual Crime Unit* was her first story aimed at adults.

She also has a BSc. in Cybernetics and Virtual Worlds, which hasn't been useful for much but does sound impressive.

FIND US ONLINE!

www.rebellionpublishing.com

/rebellionpub   /rebellionpublishing   /rebellionpublishing

SIGN UP TO OUR NEWSLETTER!

rebellionpublishing.com/newsletter

YOUR REVIEWS MATTER!

Enjoy this book? Got something to say?

Leave a review on Amazon, GoodReads or with your
favourite bookseller and let the world know!